The
Green Man's
Holiday

The Green Man's Holiday
Juliet E. McKenna

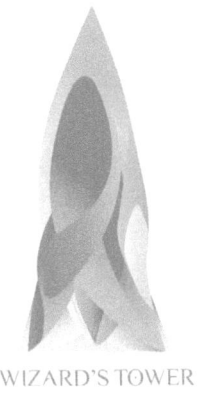

WIZARD'S TOWER

Wizard's Tower Press
Rhydaman, Cymru

The Green Man's Holiday
The Green Man - Book 8

First edition, published in the UK October 2025
by Wizard's Tower Press

Paperback ISBN: 978-1-917950-10-7

Cover illustration and design by Ben Baldwin
Editing by Toby Selwyn
Design by Cheryl Morgan

http://wizardstowerpress.com/
http://www.julietemckenna.com/

Contents

Praise for the Green Man Series   8
Chapter One   15
Chapter Two   28
Chapter Three   41
Chapter Four   56
Chapter Five   69
Chapter Six   82
Chapter Seven   94
Chapter Eight   108
Chapter Nine   120
Chapter Ten   129
Chapter Eleven   140
Chapter Twelve   153
Chapter Thirteen   167
Chapter Fourteen   179
Chapter Fifteen   190
Chapter Sixteen   202
Chapter Seventeen   212
Chapter Eighteen   225
Chapter Nineteen   236
Chapter Twenty   247
Chapter Twenty-One   258
Chapter Twenty-Two   271
Chapter Twenty-Three   283
Acknowledgements   293
About the Author   295

JULIET E. MCKENNA

For my Mum

Praise for the Green Man Series

I'm here to be your good bookfriend and express my own quiet but fervent enthusiasm for this contemporary folkloric fantasy series. You should take the plunge, the water is fine if full of terrifying naiads and nixes. — Imyril on *There's Always Room for One More*

The series of Green Man novels goes from strength to strength, bringing a modern fantastical sensibility to traditional folk tales and things that go bump in the night. — Ben Jeapes on Goodreads

Praise for The Green Man's Heir

Finalist for The Robert Holdstock Award for Best Fantasy Novel, the British Fantasy Awards 2019

"... any way you look at it, the book is a delight from start to finish. [...] It's one of my favorite books so far this year." — Charles de Lint in *Fantasy and Science Fiction*

"I read this last night and thoroughly enjoyed it, more please!" — Garth Nix on Twitter

"I really enjoyed this novel!" — Kate Elliott on Twitter

"Juliet McKenna captures the nuances of life as a stranger in a small town in much the same way as Paul Cornell does in his splendid Lychford series, with the local gossips, the hard-pressed police, the rampaging boggarts and rural legends come to disturbing life. Thoroughly enjoyable; a UK fantasy author branching out (oh god, sorry for the inadvert and terrible pun!) and clearly having a great time doing it. Highly recommended." — Joanne Hall

"So far up my street it could be my house." — K.J. Charles on Goodreads

"*The Green Man's Heir* is a thoroughly engaging, at times almost impossible to put down, tale which, despite besides its titular character, is peopled with an impressive array of interesting and intriguing women." — *The Monday Review*

"After a stumbling start, I found myself unable to put down *The Green Man's Heir*. If you're looking for a book to read on your summer holiday, then this is it." — Charlotte Bond via The British Fantasy Society

The Green Man's Heir is a straightforward fantasy story, with a lively pace and characters who wonderfully come alive. It starts as *Midsomer Murders* set in the Peak District but with added supernatural element and turns out to be the book you won't put down because you enjoy it too much." — *The Middle Shelf*

"I hope this turns into a series. I'd love to read more about Daniel's adventures." — N.W. Moors in *The Antrim Cycle*

"And she has absolutely nailed it. This is a complete and utter joy." — S.J. Higbee in *Brainfluff*

"I'm certainly on board for reading more such novels." — Paul Weimer in *Skiffy and Fanty*

"Brilliant concept, compellingly told" — Virginia Bergin on Twitter

Praise for The Green Man's Foe

Finalist for Best Novel,
the British Science Fiction Awards 2020

"I loved *The Green Man's Heir*, and while I expected to thoroughly enjoy *The Green Man's Foe*, I did not expect it to be even more satisfying than its forerunner. Which was foolish of me, I admit – I should know by now that McKenna is more capable of outdoing her previous tales in a series." – *The Monday Review*

"If you've read the first book then I'm pretty confident you're going to love this one, and if you haven't read the first one then you need to remedy that straight away." – Naomi Scott

"This is one of my outstanding reads of the year." – S.J. Higbee in *Brainfluff*

"*The Green Man's Foe* is a great addition to what is becoming a great series. I was entirely caught up in it for a couple of days. It is a must read if you have enjoyed the first one, and a great reason to start on this series if you have missed it." – *The Middle Shelf*

"*The Green Man's Foe* is a tasty serve of mystery and myth that has done quite enough to cement this series as one I'll be reading and cheerleading for from now on." – Imyril at *There's Always Room for One More.*

"What I loved reading this tale is how genuinely real McKenna makes the story feel." — Matt at *Runalong the Shelves*

Praise for The Green Man's Silence

"These Green Man books provide a wonderful blend of British folklore and ordinary people trying their best to make the world — or at least their corner of it — a better place. The characters are likeable, while the mythical creatures are earthy, dangerous, and full of that Sense of Wonder that makes fantasy such a pleasure to read. Recommended." — Charles de Lint, *Fantasy & Science Fiction*

"Highly recommended for fantasy fans who are looking for well-written fae adventures with a difference." — S J Higbee in *Brainfluff*

"This is undoubtedly one of the best books I've read this year and I thoroughly enjoyed it. I can hardly wait for the next book!" — *The Monday Review*

Praise for The Green Man's Challenge

Finalist for Best Novel,
the British Science Fiction Awards 2022

"I don't usually review every book in a series, but I'm so taken by this one by McKenna that I want to keep touting its virtues so that people will, I hope, buy each one of them." — Charles de Lint in *Fantasy & Science Fiction*

"Wowee! That was one hell of a ride. A fantastic ride, both the main tale and the bonus short story at the end." — Pers at *Goodreads*

"It is also a delight to read a novel written by someone who knows her genre so well and works at finding different ways to exploit its tropes. The threat in *The Green Man's Challenge* is a giant: the hero doesn't have the strength to match the foe, so other ways must be found, ancient knowledge must be discovered again. By doing so, McKenna consciously subverts the expectations of a certain kind of fantasy: no lone hero, no unbelievable physical prowesses, no amazing powers (political or supernatural)." — *The Middle Shelf*

"Ms McKenna has a glorious sense of place" — Jacey Bedford

McKenna has brilliantly utilised the likes of the giant figures cut into chalk hillsides and some of the numerous folk stories around hares to add to her intriguing Brit rural fantasy tale. — S.J. Higbee in *Brainfluff*

Praise for The Green Man's Gift

"If you've enjoyed the previous Green Man books, then you'll enjoy this one without a doubt. If you haven't read them yet... What are you waiting for?" — *The Middle Shelf*

"The Green Man's Gift [...] is another excellent tale in one of the most interesting contemporary fantasy series around." — *Runalong the Shelves*

"As ever, McKenna writes an absorbing, utterly compelling tale." — *The Monday Review*

Highly recommended. You could start here, but I recommend you do yourself a favour and read the whole lot in order. — Jacey Bedford

Praise for The Green Man's Quarry

Winner — Best Novel,
the British Science Fiction Awards 2024

"It's a great place for new readers to test themselves and I suspect many of those who do will rush rightly to read the rest. The Green Man series continues to be one of the most engaging and fascinating series in our current fantasy landscape and is strongly recommended!" — *Runalong the Shelves*

"There's a real sense of peril in this one, with a genuinely scary villain with interesting motivation." — KJ Charles at *Goodreads*

"Juliet McKenna is pushing the bounds of her world and it shows no signs of growing stale." — Ben Jeapes at *Goodreads*

"another story full of adventure and incident in this superb series. Very highly recommended for fans of fantasy in a contemporary setting filled with creatures from British folklore" — *Brainfluff*

"... how rich and complex McKenna's world is. Actions have consequences and unintended ripples that threaten secrets and long established status quo." — *The Middle Shelf*

"Dan Mackmain is a fascinating character in his own right, but he's only half the story: the other half being the depths of British folklore..." — *The Monday Review*

Praise for The Green Man's War

Finalist for The Robert Holdstock Award for Best Fantasy
Novel, the British Fantasy Awards 2025

"Fans of the Green Man Series should roll up and get their
copy now because this is a treat you will not put down. New
readers should come and give this smart, incredibly enter-
taining and richly mythic series a go as for my mind its one
of the best long-running fantasy series out there. The Green
Man is calling, and you really should meet him. This is very
strongly recommended!" – *Runalong the Shelves*

"Every time I revisit this world, I have a huge sense of coming home." – *Brainfluff*

"As usual Ms McKenna keeps up the pace, the interest and
the danger while showing a vast understanding of British
folklore and traditions." – *Jacey Bedford*

Chapter One

Their family ability to turn into swans was supposed to be a secret, but a lot of the women at this wedding were wearing hats decorated with feathers. I noticed that as I looked down the church towards the door at the back. The ancient latch clattered and the iron-bound wood swung open. Everybody stood up. The organ started playing as the guests in the furthest pews turned to get their first look at the bride. I could see over everyone's heads. This was one of those times when being six foot four comes in useful.

I glanced at Conn, waiting with the nice lady vicar by the shallow steps in front of the choir stalls. Those separated the pews from the altar with its backdrop of gilded and painted wooden saints. He seemed calm enough. I always find him hard to read. His brother Seamus looked a lot more nervous. I could understand that. He had to give the best man's speech. All I'd had to do was stand by the door as people arrived. I asked if they were guests of the bride or the groom, reminded them to turn off their phones and gave them an order of service. That had been bad enough.

Simon, Fin's dad, turned the corner at the end of the aisle. He walked slowly and steadily, with Iris's hand tucked under his elbow. They were both smiling, as far as I could tell through Iris's veil anyway. Her cream-coloured wedding dress was sleek and stylish, with long, lacy sleeves.

Fin and Blanche followed, precisely in step. Their violet dresses had been made to the same pattern and they wore matching garlands of silk flowers on their heads. The hairdresser had done something clever so their white-blonde hair looked pretty much the same. Blanche had let her short hair grow after Iris had announced her engagement at Christmas, but she had a long way to go before she could tie back a ponytail like Fin's.

15

Both bridesmaids looked more tense than the bride. Aunts and uncles and cousins from their dad's family didn't know Fin's mum's secret. Fin reckoned that was a big part of why her parents had got divorced, when the girls were kids. Personally, I wondered how much Simon knew, or had guessed. He's not stupid. But it's not an easy question to slip into a conversation. 'By the way, can you really turn into a big white bird or am I imagining things?'

Iris wouldn't have that problem. Conn and his family were swan shifters too. Fifteen of them had come over from Ireland for the wedding. Like Conn, they were dark-haired and brown-eyed. I'd been introduced to most of them in the village pub last night, but apart from Conn's parents and Seamus, I wasn't entirely sure who was who. I'd been distracted, hoping Fin, Blanche and Iris would get through the final preparations at their mum, Helen's, house without someone losing their temper or getting upset. Until this had started, I had no idea weddings caused so much stress.

St Peter's isn't a big church. Simon and Iris reached the steps by the choir stalls. They were only a few feet away. It hadn't been my idea to sit in the front pew. When I was told that was where the ushers would go, I'd been about to say I'd be fine at the back. Then I'd seen Helen's expression and kept quiet. At least I had an excuse to sit at the far end of the polished wooden seat, where sturdy round pillars separated the middle of the church from the side aisles. So I wouldn't block anyone's view. I was definitely the tallest person at this wedding, and I probably had the widest shoulders.

Zan stood between me and Helen, grinning without a care in the world. A sylph can look like whoever they want to, but today Zan would stick to the appearance they had chosen when they first met me, Fin and Blanche. Introduced to everyone as Blanche's boyfriend, he was six inches shorter than me, wiry with tanned skin, a shaven head and bright blue eyes. He had materialised when I arrived at the church with Conn and Seamus. Conn had said he looked like a mod-

el on the cover of some glossy magazine. *GQ*, he suggested
with a grin, or should that be *Green Man's Quarterly*? Like I
say, the groom was perfectly relaxed.

We wore mid-grey suits. I'd said I'd be fine wearing the
suit I already owned. Blanche asked what colour that was.
When I said dark grey, she told me that would make me look
like door staff at the reception. Iris said that didn't matter as
the men in the wedding party were going to be dressed the
same. Fin gave me a look, and I'd kept my mouth shut after
that.

Conn and Seamus had flown into Birmingham – by
plane – where Simon and I had met them, three times in
the last six months. Presumably Blanche came up with some
excuse for her dad, to explain why Zan couldn't join us. No
one mentioned it, and I didn't ask. We had lunch, which gave
Simon and Conn a chance to get to know each other a bit
better. I hadn't needed to say much, which was fine by me.
After lunch, we went to a gentlemen's outfitters, which was
a new experience for me. We weren't having suits made to
measure, just altered for the best fit. Even so, I reckoned the
bill equalled the money I'd spent on every other bit of cloth-
ing I owned. Our ties had been made to match the bridesmaids' frocks by the dressmaker in Norwich, where Fin and
her sisters went on those same weekends.

Next to Zan, Helen was blinking as well as smiling. Her
dress was flowery purple and yellow and she wore one of
those fascinator things instead of a hat. I saw tears on her
eyelashes as Fin and Blanche sorted out Iris's veil. Blanche
took Iris's flowers, and as the service got started, Simon came
to sit in the front pew with us. I saw him give Helen's hand a
reassuring squeeze. They might be divorced, but they stayed
on good terms for their daughters' sakes.

No one said anything when the vicar asked if anyone
knew any reason why Conn and Iris couldn't get lawfully
married. They went on to the bit about taking each other
to be husband and wife. Everyone in church was asked to

promise to support them in their marriage. I'd never seen that on the telly, so I was glad I'd read the order of service yesterday evening, while everyone was practising where they needed to stand through the ceremony.

Then there was a prayer, a reading and a hymn. Now I was glad I was standing at the front. No one could see I wasn't singing. I've never gone to church and my school assemblies weren't religious. Everyone else here seemed to know the tune. Iris had sung in the choir when she was a teenager, and she came to the Sunday morning service if she visited her mum when it was St Peter's turn to have one. Conn went to church in Ireland often enough for the nice lady vicar to approve them having their wedding here. That seemed to matter more than Conn being Catholic. The fact he was Irish wasn't an issue.

Zan wasn't singing either, and not just because he didn't know the words. He'd enjoyed being charming as the guests arrived, but he was losing interest now. He hadn't come to the rehearsal, and I saw his eyes widen as he glanced around and noticed the carving on the pillar above my head. These others were men and women going about their everyday lives when this church had been built, looking like illustrations in a medieval manuscript. One man netted a giant fish, a woman cut corn with a sickle, and someone in a pointed hat played a flute.

Zan's hand moved. I knew what he had seen. Before the sylph could point and say something, I leaned close to warn him off under cover of the music.

'Yes, it's a green man,' I said quietly. 'I haven't seen any sign he's here today. Now, pay attention or Blanche will notice.'

The organ stopped playing. To my relief, Zan turned to watch Conn and Iris move on to the 'for richer, for poorer, in sickness and in health' bit. Seamus took the wedding rings out of his waistcoat pocket and put them on the vicar's prayer book. My mate Aled had made those from Welsh gold.

I realised I was rubbing my right forearm with my other hand. I stopped. I couldn't feel any hint of stinging to warn me something nasty was around. Though it was a few years since a hostile hamadryad had slashed my arm. The intensity of that sensation had faded along with the scars.

I forced myself to concentrate on Iris, Conn and the vicar. I wanted to turn and look at that carving myself, but everyone would notice if I did. The Green Man has been part of my life since I was a kid growing up in Warwickshire. He turns up in my dreams, and occasionally in person, when he needs me to do something for him. Sometimes I catch a glimpse of emerald-green light in the eyes of a leafy, carved face in an old building. That tells me he's nearby. This is because my mum is a dryad, a centuries-old tree spirit. Her blood means I see a whole lot more than most people believe exists. Creatures and people from folk tales and legends. Well, normally more than most people believe is out there. Easily half this congregation could see the supernatural. I hoped nothing turned up to startle the rest.

I'd never seen the Green Man around here. Fin's family home, where Helen still lives, is deep in East Anglia's Fenland. This village, Saw Edge St Peter, is short on trees in general, and there are no oaks at all. Did that mean the Green Man wouldn't be able to warn me if something dreadful was about to happen? It was over a year since we'd last had to stop monsters causing mayhem in the everyday world. I wasn't fool enough to think they wouldn't turn up again.

The vicar declared Iris and Conn were now married, and they knelt down to be blessed. Simon, Helen and Conn's parents went into the vestry with the two of them to sign the registers. The choir sang something pleasant. Fin came to sit beside me. That was nice. I could hold her hand, and Zan was Blanche's responsibility.

Once the paperwork had been dealt with, everyone came back for more prayers. At least I knew the 'Our Father who is in heaven' one. After another hymn I didn't know, the vicar blessed everyone and sent us off with a cheerful smile. Iris and Conn walked down the aisle while the organ played what the order of service said was the 'Prince of Denmark's March'. Fin followed, walking with Seamus. That meant Zan could walk with Blanche. We'd agreed that at the rehearsal. Sylphs can be unpredictable, and this was going to be a long day for Zan to pretend to be human.

I waited for Simon and Helen to go ahead of me. Then I let Conn's mum and dad follow them from the other side of the aisle. They were a bit older than Fin's parents as Conn is ten years or more older than Iris. His dad walked with a stick. That gave me time to sneak a quick look over my shoulder. The green man carved on this pillar is a comical one, sticking out its tongue. There wasn't a hint of green in its eyes. Good.

Out in the churchyard, Fin's cousin Will was organising the wedding pictures. He's a professional photographer and he didn't hang about. For one thing, the weather forecast this morning had included the possibility of unexpected thunderstorms and sudden downpours. For the moment, white clouds were passing quickly overhead, though the breeze had a chilly edge as it tugged at Iris's veil. That nuisance quickly died away. I saw Zan grin and wondered if she had him to thank for that.

Maybe, maybe not. The Fenland has its own sylphs. They're as inquisitive as Zan, and equally capable of masquerading as a human. I wouldn't put it past one or two of them to try to join in the wedding. Only their eyes would give them away to somebody like me. When they blinked, I'd see solid icy blue, without white or pupil. If I was close enough to see it. That had been one good thing about me and Zan meeting people at the church door. I could be sure no one who wasn't supposed to be there had sneaked into the ceremony. The reception would be a different matter.

'Dan!' Helen waved me over to join the family by the church gate.

I had to be in a couple of the big group photos, along with Zan. After that I followed everyone heading over the road to the pub. A marquee had been set up on the long lawn behind The Wheat Sheaf's car park. Helen's house is only a short walk, but it wasn't big enough for the reception and Simon's farm was too far away. Fin also said neutral territory should make sure a couple of relatives on both sides of her family behaved themselves. I didn't ask. My family is me, my dad and my mum. That's how it's always been, and how it always will be, even now a handful of younger dryads are living in my mum's wood.

'That was a lovely service.' Eleanor Beauchene crossed the road beside me. Apparently, meeting her a couple of times when we'd fought some otherworldly menace had been enough for Conn and Iris to invite her today.

'Yes, very nice.' I could still count the weddings I'd been to on both thumbs. Well, ones where I was a guest. Blithehurst House, where I work, is Eleanor's ancestral stately home and the Beauchene family business. She's my boss. These days people can get married there, and I help out with things like getting guests' cars parked where they won't be a nuisance. I don't think that really counts.

People who'd been invited to the reception but not the church ceremony were arriving. I wondered if any of them weren't who Conn and Iris were expecting. Since I couldn't walk around to shake everyone's hand and stare them in the eye, I just had to be ready for trouble. Maybe I should have insisted on wearing my darker-grey suit to look like a bouncer.

Neil Moryinson, The Wheat Sheaf's landlord and long-standing friend of the Wicken family, welcomed everyone into the marquee. Waiting staff offered glasses of champagne. Tables with place settings, flower arrangements, bottles of wine and mineral water had been set up down both sides of the tent. Apart from the top table, where Iris and Conn would sit with their parents, the best man and the bridesmaids, there wasn't a seating plan. Iris, Blanche and Fin had given up on that after a frustrating Saturday afternoon shifting name cards around Helen's kitchen table while I sat and read a book.

People sorted themselves out easily enough. I sat with Eleanor and Zan close to the table with the wedding cake, where Fin had put the bride's bouquet and the bridesmaid's flowers. The sugar flowers cascading down the three white iced tiers were the exact same shade.

Will and his girlfriend, Witta, joined us. He tucked his camera bag underneath the white cloth covering the cake table. Witta's floaty green dress had matching fancy gloves that reached to her elbows. They must have been specially made to hide the webbing between her fingers. A nereid can't hide every trace of her true nature. Helen's sisters, Sylvia and Stella, and Sylvia's daughter, Laurel, came to sit with us. Laurel was holding hands with a man a bit younger than me who I didn't know.

'This is Jack,' Laurel said brightly.

I offered him a handshake. 'Dan Mackmain, Fin's boy-friend.'

'Good to meet you.'

As he accepted, I felt the tension in his arm. So I wasn't the only person feeling out of place at this wedding. But he blinked and I saw his eyes were wholly human. That was okay, as long as the rest of us watched what we said.

'I'm Zan.' The sylph looked at Jack intently. 'Tell us about yourself.'

'Good to see you again,' Will interrupted, standing up to offer Jack his hand. 'So, Laurel, how's life in the sugar trade?'

Laurel brought us up to date with the impact of increasingly frequent floods on East Anglia's sugar beet harvests, followed by what was officially the warmest and driest spring in over a century, even if the last few days had seen torrential rain. Neil and his staff brought plates of buffet food to each table. Good. The wedding had been at one o'clock. I was ready for something to eat. Fin and I were staying at a hotel not far away, and I'd had a good breakfast, but we'd made an early start. Fin had to get to Helen's house, where they were having their hair and make-up done. I'd gone to The Wheat Sheaf, where Neil let me sit in the empty bar with a pot of tea and my book.

It turned out that Jack worked in a lab in Bury St Edmunds, on the science side of the sugar business. Since he was as ordinary as he looked, we stuck to everyday conversation as we ate and drank. Eleanor has a few good stories about the bizarre ideas tourists can have about the history of a place like Blithehurst House.

'Explaining a local squire's role in the nineteenth century can be tricky. People hear "squire" and think it must have something to do with medieval knights. And thanks to Robin Hood, everyone seems to think a county sheriff's job was chasing outlaws.'

Zan opened his mouth, but Will turned to me before the sylph could say anything. 'How's the wetland project getting on?'

'Very well.' I avoided looking at Zan as I explained to Fin's aunts how we had removed the dangerous ruins of an old watermill at Blithehurst. Then we adapted the medieval millpond and the leats that brought water to it from the river to create a habitat for water birds and other wildlife. I didn't explain that a wyrm, a serpent dragon, had trashed the mill while it was trying to kill me and Eleanor. She can see things like that thanks to a dryad ancestor in her family tree.

'You'll have to come and see what you make of it.' Zan's blue eyes shone with mischief as he looked at Will. 'I imagine swans will love it.'

Before anyone could find an answer to that, Jack spoke to the sylph. 'Do you work there as well? At Blithehurst?'

23

'No.' Zan grinned, enjoying seeing the rest of us wondering what he was going to say next. 'I... consult. On climate change, weather patterns, things like that.'

'Oh, you're a meteorologist, like Iris?' Jack glanced at the bride and groom. They were turned away from each other at the moment, talking to their parents on either side. Their hands rested on the table with their fingers interlaced.

'That's how you met Blanche, isn't it?' Will didn't let Zan answer before he carried on talking to Jack. 'You know they're freshwater ecologists, her and Fin? They run their own business.'

'I hear they've been working on rewilding projects,' Witta said to me. 'What have they got on next?'

'We'll be working on something together. A couple who've bought a bankrupt farm in the Mendips want to turn it into mixed woodland and a wildlife refuge. Fin and Blanche will be looking at the drainage and finding the best sites for new ponds, or reinstating old ones if they can find any traces. I'll be assessing the trees already there, to see what needs felling and clearing. Then we'll discuss where to plant new saplings and where we'll leave the land alone to regenerate naturally. Fin and I are going over to Somerset tomorrow for a week's holiday, to get a feel for the area before we start.'

We'd also be looking for any naiads or dryads who lived nearby. Rewilding schemes go a lot better if the local wood and water spirits are cooperating. Piss them off and you might as well pile up your money and set it on fire. I'd already asked Zan to take a quick look, but he hadn't found anyone supernatural there. That didn't mean someone living in a nearby thicket or river wouldn't have strong opinions on what we were doing.

'That doesn't interfere with your day job?' Jack glanced from me to Eleanor.

She smiled. 'He can spare the time, and I'll send my invoice on behalf of the Blithehurst Trust.'

A waiter appeared at my shoulder with a tray of fresh glasses of champagne. The ringing as a knife tapped a wine glass silenced conversations around the marquee.

Simon stood up. 'First of all, thank you, everyone, for coming to share this very special day with us. I'm delighted to welcome Conn's family, who've made the journey to be here.'

He raised his glass briefly to Conn's parents, who smiled back. Simon kept his speech short and sweet. He and Helen were proud of Iris and of everything she had achieved. They were thrilled their daughter had found a husband who loved her as much as they did. He thanked a long list of people involved in everything, including but not limited to the dresses, the flowers and the wedding cake. Then he invited everyone to raise their glasses to the happy couple.

As everyone sipped champagne and echoed the toast, Conn got to his feet. He thanked Simon and Helen and his own parents for everything they had done, not only for their help with the wedding. He talked a bit about how he and Iris had met. It turned out his software business had won the contract to design a new system for the commercial weather forecasting company where she worked.

'I'd been wondering how they got together,' Fin's aunt Sylvia murmured to Stella.

'I wonder when we'll get the full story,' Stella said under her breath.

What she meant was, how had the happy couple discovered they were both shapeshifters? I looked at the other end of the table. I didn't think Jack had heard what Stella had said. If he had, hopefully he wouldn't think anything of it.

'I'd like to thank Finele and Blanche for their help with the preparations for today,' Conn said sincerely. 'And for being such good sisters to Iris and to me, even before we made that official just now.'

I wondered what he meant. Over a year ago, Conn and Iris had split up for several months. Iris and Fin had fallen out over that and ended up not speaking to each other. Blanche had sorted it out somehow. I didn't get involved.

Conn had moved on. 'It's my pleasure to propose the toast to the bridesmaids.' He turned to Blanche and Fin. 'To the ushers.' He nodded towards me and Zan, which meant everyone looked our way. I could have done without that. 'And to my best man, Seamus. Thank you on behalf of myself and my wife.'

Everyone raised their glasses, though no one was entirely sure what to say. Most people settled for 'cheers' or 'thank you'. I think a lot of Conn's family said something in Irish. I was more concerned with grabbing Zan's thigh under the table, so he couldn't stand up.

'We don't have to answer him. Remember what Blanche said.'

The sylph's eyes glittered solid blue with irritation. He leaned back in his chair with a sulky expression and folded his arms. I don't think anyone noticed. Everybody was watching Seamus sort through some cards he'd taken out of a pocket. He looked up and cleared his throat.

'I don't mind saying, a few of us were wondering if our big brother was ever going to give us a day out.'

Sylvia stiffened. Stella looked worried. I don't know why. Seamus's speech was perfectly fine. He told a few stories about what a good role model Conn had been as the eldest, always looking after his brothers and sisters and cousins growing up. He said how glad they were that Conn was putting himself first now, and wished him and Iris a long life and happiness together. He added something in Irish. 'Gob fliuch agus bás in Éirinn.'

His family laughed while everyone else looked politely confused. Seamus raised his glass to drink the last of his champagne. Everyone else made the toast in whatever language they chose.

'And now,' Seamus said with a very relieved smile, 'the bride and groom will cut the cake.'

'Excuse me.' Will got up and fetched his camera bag.

'No speech from the chief bridesmaid?' Stella asked me with a grin. 'Or couldn't they agree if Fin or Blanche was in charge?'

'None of those girls having their say has to be some sort of first. Oh, thank you.' Sylvia held up her glass as a waitress offered her more champagne.

That saved me from having to find an answer. It probably wouldn't be tactful to tell them Fin and her sisters had agreed the interminable speeches at the last family wedding had been excruciating.

'No thanks, I'm fine.' I held my hand over my own glass when the waitress tilted the bottle towards me with a questioning glance. I was watching how much I drank, mostly sticking to mineral water. I needed to be fit to drive later on. Sooner rather than later, with any luck. I wasn't *not* having a good time, but I would be glad when this wedding was over. As long as nothing went wrong.

Chapter Two

Will quickly took several photos of Iris and Conn as they stood poised to cut their cake. People cheered and clapped as the newly-weds sank the long silver knife into the bottom tier for real. Then they stepped back and Neil's wife, Kate, came up to cut the cake into manageable pieces.

Apparently, that was the signal to start mingling. Conn, Seamus and their dad walked over to talk to some relatives on the other side of the marquee. Stella and Sylvia joined Conn's mum and Helen at the top table. Zan headed straight for Blanche. Fin was already surrounded by cousins and old friends who lived around here. Laurel and Witta joined them, laughing and smiling.

'Are you okay?' Eleanor asked quietly.

'Me? I'm fine.' That was mostly true. Eleanor would know if I was fibbing. That's a big plus of dryad blood, along with a few other things that can come in useful. On the other hand, it means I am a crap liar. Uncanny gifts always come with a cost, like the fairy tales say.

I heard clinking crockery and saw Neil's team putting cups and saucers and Thermos jugs on the table by the marquee's entrance, together with milk and sugar.

'Can I get you anything?' I asked Eleanor. 'Tea or coffee?'

'I'm fine, but you go ahead.'

'Okay.' I didn't need telling twice.

I got myself a cup of coffee. This wasn't a day for tea. I saw a couple of groups of male wedding guests heading across the car park towards the pub. Then I heard something I wasn't expecting: Scottish voices. A couple I didn't know were talking to Blanche. He was a tall, amiable-looking bloke with sandy-brown hair. He looked like someone who'd nod hello in a pub, happy to have a chat or to let you drink your pint in peace if that's what you wanted. She was a confident, cheerful redhead, laughing at something Blanche had just said.

I waited, tense, until they walked away to talk to somebody else. I moved fast and intercepted Blanche before she could disappear. 'Who's he? Them? Is he – are they? You know what I mean.'

Zan might be able to tell, but he was nowhere to be seen.

Blanche thought this was hilarious. 'Dave and Wendy Elrick? They've been friends with Iris for years. Honestly, Dan, relax. Not every Scotsman's a cunning man.'

At least she lowered her voice so no one nearby wondered what on earth we were talking about. I wanted to ask if she was absolutely sure about that, but Blanche spoke first.

'Okay? Can I go now? Zan's about to have a game of darts with one of Conn's cousins. I think I should be there.'

I couldn't disagree with that. 'Right.'

I walked out of the marquee with Blanche. She headed for the pub and I went the other way. Circling around to the back of the big tent, I walked across the empty grass towards a wire fence. Houses on both sides of the field showed how the village had spread out from the crossroads where the pub faced St Peter's. Some sort of tavern had been on this site for as long as the church had been over the road. The village green was on the southern side of the crossroads, overlooked by the big house that belonged to the richest local landowner. These days, Neil managed that as bed and breakfast rooms for the pub, by agreement with the last of the Kelley family. That's where Conn and his family were staying.

At the end of the field, a narrow stretch of fen had been left to drain the farmland. The narrow channel joined the ditches dug centuries before to defend an ancient hillfort close to Helen's house. On the other side of the wire fence, spindly birch trees and low tangles of blackthorn edged the fen. Beyond them, tall, feathery sedges stirred, marking the edge of the water. The breeze had got up again, but at least it wasn't raining. The weather had been all over the place for the past month. A couple of days ago, Fin and Blanche had checked that Neil had heaters for the marquee in case today turned really cold. I looked up at the sky and wondered if keeping the rain clouds away was Zan's gift to Iris and Conn.

I drank my coffee and enjoyed not being surrounded by people, just for a bit. Then a cup and saucer rattled behind me. I turned to see Will coming my way with a plate in his other hand.

'Cake? I saw you hadn't had any.'

'Thanks.' I took one of the slices. Dense, rich fruit cake. Very traditional and very good.

Will took a moment to work out how to balance the plate on his coffee cup to pick up his own cake. 'There are times when I think I should take up smoking.'

'Sorry?' That made no sense to me.

'Needing a ciggie is still a cast-iron excuse for stepping outside for a few minutes' peace and quiet.' He heaved a sigh and took a big bite of cake. 'Specifically, to avoid another of Uncle Simon's elderly relatives asking me about Zan. Like where is he from?'

Will's tone told me that wasn't so much a loaded question as one that had been cocked and aimed. 'What are you saying?'

'That he's from Dorset. So they say, "Yes, but where's he *really* from?"' Will grimaced. 'Most of them probably don't mean anything by it, but a couple definitely do.'

'Let's hope Blanche doesn't overhear them, or Zan.' It was a safe bet the sylph spent enough time around humans to know what those questions *really* meant. He'd enjoy tying whoever was asking in verbal knots, as they tried to avoid saying anything outright racist. No one else would find that amusing though.

'When Simon's uncle Colin said, "Well at least her date was a *man*"...' Will shook his head. 'I decided it was time for a bit of fresh air.'

'That sounds fair.' Perhaps I should go and find Zan. After I'd eaten my cake.

'Have the olds been dropping hints to you?' Will asked around another mouthful. 'About you and Fin getting married?'

'Not to me.' My height and build generally stops people asking me personal questions. My mate Aled says when someone irritates me, I look like I'm deciding which of their arms or legs to rip off, to club them with the soggy end. I don't necessarily have a problem with that, if it stops people being nosy.

'How are you two getting on with house-hunting?' Will wanted to know.

'Still looking for the right place.' Trying to sound casual, I hoped he'd take the hint I didn't particularly want to discuss it.

Fin and I had been talking about moving in together for more than a year now. We'd agreed to find somewhere near Blithehurst. Fin can work from anywhere, but my job isn't one I can do from home. We'd seen nice enough houses which we could afford within reasonable driving distance. They were in towns though, or much bigger villages than this one. Neither of us was keen on that. I'd grown up in a little old house out on its own in the countryside. These days, I lived in a cottage in the Blithehurst woods, well away from the manor. I wasn't looking forward to having neighbours.

Human neighbours, that is. We'd both be happy to put a bit of distance between us and the dryads in Blithehurst's woods as well. They seemed to think they could run my life, with or without the Green Man's permission. Frai, the eldest, who'd lived there since the Norman Conquest, said he hadn't called on me for months, so I might as well make myself useful. I'd been up and down the country telling solitary dryads living in remnants of wild wood about each other. They started giving me oak saplings to take from one wood to another, and younger dryads began appearing.

Anyway, finding the right house was nowhere near our biggest problem. Fin and Blanche ran their business from a flat they shared near Bristol. Working together and living in different places would be doable with modern technology, but they had a joint mortgage.

Blanche didn't particularly want to sell up. She had friends in the area, and she'd have to move away to find a place she could afford on her own. She'd be downsizing while Fin and I would be trading up, buying somewhere as a couple. Blanche had said she'd consider getting a roommate, but that wouldn't be straightforward as long as she and Zan were a couple. We'd put off trying to find a solution while everyone had been focused on the wedding. Now, though...

Will finished his cake and tucked the plate under his saucer. 'Can I ask you something?'

I shrugged. 'If you like.'

'When you were born—' He stopped to drink his coffee.

I waited. After a long pause, Will started talking fast.

'The thing is, Iris and Conn, you and Fin, let's say you want to start a family. That won't be a problem. Even Blanche – she wouldn't have to tell anyone outside the family about Zan. Unmarried mothers are no big deal. She's got a national health number, national insurance, doctor's notes since she was a kid. But Witta hasn't got any of that, and if two people aren't married, only the mother can register a birth. I was wondering how your parents managed. Do you know if the hospital and the registry office checked that your mum was who she said she was, when you were born?'

'No clue.' I hadn't expected him to ask anything like this. 'Sorry. Besides, as far as anyone knew, my parents were married. My dad sorted the paperwork for me.'

I'd seen their marriage certificate, though I had no idea how Dad had got hold of that, thirty-five years ago. He's completely human, so he has no problem deceiving people when he has a really good reason.

'Paperwork. Right,' Will said unhappily. 'That must have made things easier. Everything's on computers now.'

'The wise women might be able to help,' I said cautiously.

Some ordinary people still have dealings with the supernatural. If you're stretching 'ordinary' as far as it can go without snapping. A few hundred years ago, these wise women would have been called witches. Nowadays, a good many of them work in jobs where they'll see early signs of something uncanny about to hit the mundane. Hospitals, local government, civilian administration for the police, things like that. They shut trouble down hard and fast.

'They'd want something major in return for a favour like that.' Will sounded dubious.

I didn't blame him. The wise women would drive a hard bargain. They had centuries of experience making deals with arcane powers passed down by their foremothers. They'd also learned from the mistakes of people killed by a monster spotting a loophole in an agreement.

'I can ask my dad,' I offered.

'Thanks.' Will managed an unconvincing smile.

I had no idea how a hospital would check any answers Witta might give them. She could hardly tell them her mother was a river spirit, a naiad, and her father was a merman living somewhere out in the North Sea. A naiad can masquerade as a human, as successfully as my dryad mum. With mermen, though, or tritons as they prefer to be called, what you see is what you get. What you get is downright scary, twice the size of an average human, and green-skinned with thick, scaly tails. Will wouldn't be making wedding plans including his in-laws any time soon.

Since I couldn't think what else to say to him, I found my phone and checked the time. Still plenty of time before the bride and groom had to leave for their hotel near Heathrow, to catch a morning flight to Croatia for a fortnight. Bugger.

'We'd better get back. Here, let me take that.' Will stacked my coffee cup and his own on top of the cake plate.

'Thanks.' We walked around to the front of the marquee.
I looked for Fin as we went inside. She was talking to Seamus
and one of his cousins or brothers. I tried to look friendly
as I approached. That could change if needs be. I could see
Fin's fixed smile wasn't reaching her eyes.

'Daniel!' Declan or Dermot or whatever he was called
grinned and slapped me on the shoulder. 'Don't you agree
there should be dancing at a wedding?'

He didn't wait for me to answer. 'There's no piano in that
pub, if you can believe it, but there's one in the big house.
How about we get some lads together, go over and move
some furniture? The lounge room's a fair size. We can keep
this party going after Conn and Iris have gone on their way.'

I saw Seamus wasn't any keener on this plan than Fin, but
he didn't know how to shut it down. I also saw both Irishmen
had ditched their ties and unbuttoned their collars. The silver chains meant they were swan shifters. That made things
easier.

'You'd better ask the hob who lives there.'

'The what now?' Dermot or Declan blinked.

'There's a hob living in that house. A brownie, a pixie.
Something like a boggart, but nicer. I don't know what you
call them in Ireland.' I took off my own tie and undid my
shirt's top button. That felt better. 'She's lived there for dec-
ades. Centuries, probably.'

Fin and I had met the ancient earth spirit who lived in the
old Kelley house. She found bed and breakfast visitors en-
tertaining, and liked to watch them unseen. That guaranteed
we'd never stay there.

'Are you joking me?' Declan or Dermot narrowed his eyes
with a half-smile.

'No.' I knew he would hear I was telling the truth.

Seamus nodded, looking relieved. 'Iris said we might
catch a glimpse, but she hasn't shown herself so far.'

I rolled up my tie and stuck it in a pocket. 'I don't think she'll like the idea of you moving furniture about. You don't want to get on her wrong side, trust me.'

'Have you ever had dealings with a hob? Do you know the trouble they can cause when they're annoyed?' Fin shook her head. 'Milk curdles in the fridge. Bottles and jars shatter in cupboards.'

'The sink backs up and the loos won't flush,' I added. 'That's just to begin with.'

'Your phones won't charge and you won't get a signal,' Fin went on. 'They keep right up to date with modern technology.'

Dryads and naiads can cause the same sort of havoc, and so can sylphs. I wondered where Zan had got to. I didn't want him hearing this conversation. He'd love the idea of dancing until dawn, and Blanche had suggested an evening do at the wedding. Iris and Fin had outvoted her.

Declan or Dermot's smile faded. 'Best not upset the auld girl.'

'Never mind.' Seamus clapped him on the shoulder. 'Conn said we'll have a ceilidh when they visit after their honeymoon.'

'He did, didn't he?' Declan or Dermot's face brightened. 'You should come over too,' he urged me and Fin. 'You'll be very welcome.'

'I'm sure.' Now her smile was a lot more friendly. 'We'll check our diaries.'

Seamus could take a hint. 'Come on, Donal. Let's see where Aoife's got to.'

As he steered his cousin away, I saw Neil's staff clearing the tables. Kate and Blanche were giving flower arrangements to the older female guests to take home. Zan was talking to Conn and two of his sisters. I could see the sylph was being charming. Conn looked amused. Iris was sitting down not far away, laughing and chatting to Eleanor. The chances of getting through this day without major drama were looking good.

The tables by the marquee entrance weren't being cleared just yet. 'I'm getting another coffee. Is there anything you want?' I asked Fin.

'I want,' she said tightly, 'to get out of this dress and out of these shoes, and to not have the same conversation for the twentieth time with people I see once every eighteen months.'

I put my arm around her shoulders. She leaned against me for about thirty seconds, closing her eyes. Then she took a deep breath and stood up straight again. 'What's the time?'

I took out my phone and showed her the screen.

Fin nodded. 'Let's see if Iris is ready to get changed.'

As we walked over, I caught the end of what Eleanor was saying.

'She can see them, no question, but thankfully she's still a toddler. Of course, they're delighted.'

She was talking about the dryads at Blithehurst. Since Eleanor's the only one of her generation who can see the things that might go bump in the night, Frai and Asca had been thrilled when her little niece had noticed them hanging around a family picnic. The dryads had also decided that the little girl needed company. They didn't give a toss about me and Fin getting married, but their hints about us having a baby were as subtle as a two-by-four to the back of the head. They were going to be disappointed. Fin was on the pill. That was another good reason for me to move out of the cottage in the woods before I said something we'd live to regret.

Iris looked up as Fin and I came over. 'Shall we?'

Fin looked relieved. 'If you're ready.'

'Oh yes. It's been a lovely day, but I'm about done.' Iris leaned over to give Eleanor a quick hug. 'We'll see you when we get back.'

As I watched them go and collect Blanche, I sat on the chair Iris had left.

'I heard from the museum people before I left this morning,' Eleanor said quietly. 'They hope everything should be sorted out by the end of next month.'

'That's good news.'

It really was. We'd both been sworn to secrecy about the stash of apparently Saxon gold which had turned up in Blithehurst's woods. Fin was the only other person who knew about it. The county archaeologists were worried about treasure hunters prowling the estate with metal detectors and stealing whatever they found. Eleanor and I knew any thieves wouldn't find more gold, but they'd get a whole lot more than they expected once they met the dryads and the black shuck who lives in those woods. We didn't need that sort of trouble.

As the landowners, the Beauchene family's share of the hoard's value would make a useful contribution to the business's financial reserves in these increasingly tough times. The manor house's visitor numbers, and what people spend in the cafes, the gift shop and the garden centre, prove the cost of living crisis is nowhere near over. Eleanor would never say so, but I knew she'd be glad to add the cottage in the woods to Blithehurst's holiday lets as well.

Since I was the one who had found the bracelets, coins and neck chains, officially anyway, I hoped my share of the windfall would solve the issues with the Bristol flat. Eventually. Getting the funding together so the treasure would go to a museum had taken much longer than any of us had expected. But that could wait until we were back from our holidays.

Iris, Fin and Blanche must have had everything ready and waiting in one of the upstairs rooms in the pub. They reappeared faster than I expected. Fin and Blanche were still in their bridesmaids' dresses. Iris had got changed into a blue trouser suit. Behind them, Zan and Will were getting other guests out of the pub. When everyone was in the marquee, Conn and Iris thanked everyone for coming one last time, and Iris threw her bouquet over her shoulder. One of Simon's nieces caught it. Fin and Blanche both stayed well clear of it coming their way.

We trooped out to the car park, where a car waited for the newly-weds. As they were driven away, the guests broke into groups, talking about what to do next.

Eleanor got her car keys out of the fancy handbag that matched her plum-coloured dress. 'I'll say my goodbyes to Helen and Simon, then I'll hit the road.'

'Tell me you're taking tomorrow off.' I didn't think Eleanor would, though, not with the tourist season at Blithehurst in full swing.

As she answered me with a smile and walked away, Fin came over to join me. Blanche followed, hand in hand with Zan.

'I told you everything would be fine.' Blanche grinned at me before looking at Fin. 'Stella and Sylvia are going to the house to open a bottle of wine with Mum. Seamus and Aoife will get their mum and dad settled over the road, then a bunch of us are meeting up in the bar. Are you going to stay on for a bit?'

Fin shook her head. 'I'm knackered. I want to go to our hotel and get a good night's sleep before we head off tomorrow.'

For a moment Blanche looked as if she was going to try to change Fin's mind. Then she nodded. 'Fair enough. Enjoy your holiday.'

'You too.' Fin hugged her.

'See you in a week.' Blanche and Zan walked away.

Fin grabbed my hand. 'Let's tell Mum and Dad we're off.'

We did that, and said goodbye to a whole lot of relatives on our way to Fin's car. Several aunts said they hoped to see us again soon. I ignored the smiles that clearly expected we'd be the next family wedding. Fin pretended she didn't notice, and we eventually got to the Toyota. I had made sure to park it where no one could block us in.

'I love my family dearly, but I don't want to see any of them for at least a month.' Fin kicked off her shoes as she fastened her seat belt. She leaned back and closed her eyes.

'We've got a week to ourselves before we have to talk to anyone about anything.' I checked for traffic in every direction as I pulled out of The Wheat Sheaf's entrance.

There's a shortage of routes through the Fens, and as far as I'm concerned, an over-supply of big lorries going too fast between farms and factories. Some HGV driver not paying attention could turn the little Toyota into a roller skate. But Fin hadn't needed to convince me to use her car this weekend and for our holiday. When my share of the money for the Saxon hoard came through, I was thinking about upgrading my old Land Rover to something a few years old and with low mileage. Maybe I'd look at an EV if I was going to have a daily drive to work. I could keep the Landy for use on the Blithehurst estate without having to tax or insure it.

I took the road towards King's Lynn and our hotel. We passed the sign that said we were leaving Saw Edge St Peter.

'Do you want a church wedding?' The words were out before my brain caught up with my mouth.

'God no,' Fin answered instantly.

She didn't say anything else, still leaning back with her eyes closed. I concentrated on the road.

About a mile further on, Fin sounded amused. 'Was that a proposal?'

I slowed down for a curve. The Fens are short on hedges and the deep ditches beside the roads can swallow a car. That hadn't been what I'd been thinking, but since she mentioned it...

'It could be,' I said cautiously. 'If you'd like.'

'I'll think about it.' Fin settled in her seat and closed her eyes again.

We reached the next village. Traffic lights ahead turned amber. I braked and shifted down the gears.

'Yes,' Fin said as we halted.

'Yes, you'd like what I said to be a proposal, and you'll think about it?' I shoved the gearstick into neutral and pulled on the handbrake. People having a perfectly ordinary Saturday afternoon crossed the road in front of the car. 'Or yes, you'd like us to get married?'

'Either. Both. Yes, let's be engaged.' Fin reached towards me. 'But we'll keep it to ourselves for now?'

'Fine by me.' I quickly took her hand and kissed her fingers before the lights changed.

Red. Red and amber. I hit the clutch and shifted into first gear. Green. I released the handbrake and accelerated towards our hotel.

Chapter Three

When I woke up, Fin was propped on her elbow beside me. She was tickling my nose with one of the downy feathers that cling to her ribs. The Irish swan shifters had done a deal generations ago with some cunning men which tied their ability to change shape to the silver necklaces they wore. Fin's family were old-school. They keep their soft feathers next to their skin whenever they can.

I gently blew the feather away. It floated off to rejoin the others. 'I wonder how much Conn will tell Iris now they're married. Especially if they have kids.'

Fin didn't need me to explain what I meant. We were both curious about those necklaces. 'That doesn't mean she'll share what he tells her with us.'

'True.' I rolled onto my side and kissed her. 'What time is it?'

'Just after nine-thirty.' Fin ran her hand down my chest to my belly. 'The hotel serves Sunday breakfast until eleven.'

Her hand moved lower. I smiled as she encouraged my erection. She slid her knee over my thigh. I kissed the hollow above her collarbone. As I rolled onto my back, she straddled me. I brushed those downy white feathers away from her breasts and kissed her nipples. Running my hands down her sides, I could tell she was a lot more relaxed than she'd been before the wedding. I cupped her buttocks and lifted her up as she leaned forward to kiss me, deep and long. I lowered her slowly down, enjoying every second of the sensation. Didn't old-fashioned weddings include something about becoming one flesh? I didn't remember the vicar yesterday saying that. I'd check later. Right now, I had more important things on my mind.

We took our time making love. While Fin showered, I got everything together which needed to go back in our overnight bag. I was putting my suit in its carrier when her phone pinged with a notification. As she came out of the en-suite, drying her hair with a towel, I waved at the bedside table.

'Your phone—'

'I heard.' She picked it up and swiped the screen. 'Mum says we can go over before we head off, to leave our wedding clothes at her house if we like.'

I hesitated as I shook out the duvet. Stray feathers floated through the air to join the others sticking to Fin's damp skin.

She nodded. She could tell what I was thinking. 'By the time we've had breakfast and gone over to Saw Edge... Mum's bound to offer us coffee and want to sit and chat. It'll be lunchtime before we get away, if we're lucky.'

I was relieved to see she wasn't any keener on the idea than I was. 'I know it's Sunday and the traffic shouldn't be too bad, but we do have a long drive.'

'I'll tell her thanks, but we want to get away.' Fin was already replying to Helen. 'We'll need to stop somewhere before the supermarkets shut, for one thing. Besides, if we leave our stuff at the house, we'll have to come all the way over here to fetch it sometime. I mean, I'm not going to be wearing that dress again any time soon, but you might need your suit.'

'Right.' I reckoned the chances of that were so low they were subterranean, but I'd use the excuse. I headed for the en-suite bathroom as Fin put down her phone. I'd put underwear, jeans and a yellow top ready on the bed for her.

By the time I was dressed in comfortable combat trousers and a loose T-shirt, Fin had packed away her bridesmaid's dress, along with the shoes and the silk flower headdress. She had her damp hair tied in a ponytail today. We headed down to the hotel restaurant and found the same lady as yesterday morning waiting at the desk by the door.

'Room number? I hope you had a good night?'

'Two ten,' Fin told her, 'and yes, we did, thank you.'

'Sit anywhere you like.' The hotel lady didn't need to explain the breakfast routine.

'If we make this a proper brunch, we shouldn't need to eat on the way.' Fin chose a table by the window and pulled out a chair.

'Right.' I sat down.

Fin looked at me, amused. 'What are you thinking about?'

'I'll tell you later.' The dining room wasn't busy, but this wasn't something anyone else needed to overhear.

'Fair enough. Right, I need a cappuccino.' Fin headed for the coffee machine.

I sat and waited so no one else could think this table was vacant. When Fin came back with her coffee and a bowl of cereal, I fetched myself a mug of tea. Then I headed for the hot buffet. After we both got full value for the hotel's bed and breakfast rate, we fetched our bags, checked out and headed for the car park.

'Are you driving or am I?' I wasn't bothered either way.

'You can, to begin with. I'm still stupidly tired.' Fin took out her phone while I stowed everything in the Toyota. 'I'll check for traffic reports.'

I closed the hatchback. 'Is there a route that avoids the motorways around Brum and Bristol?'

None of the routes east to west across England are what I'd call good options. It's a case of finding the least worst choice on any given day, and avoiding places where traffic jams are most likely. Places like Birmingham and Bristol.

'Our best bet is via Northampton, then Oxford, and take the A34 south to pick up the A303,' Fin said after a moment. 'That's maybe ten miles further overall and will take about half an hour longer, assuming no hold-ups.'

'Suits me.' Our time was our own today, and I'd rather take a slower road and keep moving than get stuck crawling along a motorway. We'd have more options for stops as well.

We got into the car and I followed the satnav's directions towards Peterborough. Fin relaxed in the passenger seat, looking out of the window. I half expected her to doze off. I guessed her tiredness was a reaction to being wound so tight for the last few weeks. We drove through the countryside, where the elder blossom in the hedgerows was mirrored by the cow parsley blooming along verges thick with tall, swaying grasses. These days, wildlife trusts and local councils determined to save money are all keen on No Mow May. Where the verges were cut back for better visibility at junctions and gateways, though, I could see the exposed ground was still parched. It would take more than a handful of rainy days to change that.

We were coming up on Wellingborough when Fin turned to me. 'So what were you thinking about at breakfast?'

'Feathers,' I admitted. 'Wondering what Laurel's going to do if Jack doesn't have a clue who she really is.'

'She'll manage the same way as the rest of us. Making sure she plans ahead. It does take the spontaneity out of a romance,' Fin said wryly.

Fin and her sisters each had a box with a lock where they left their feathers on days when there was a chance someone who didn't know their secret would see them in their underwear. They didn't particularly like doing that. It put them on edge. I'd learned to recognise the signs. School had been hard, Fin had told me, since they had to leave their feathers at home every day. Though, as she said, people expect teenage girls to be unpredictably moody. Maybe that was why none of Blanche's boyfriends or girlfriends before Zan had lasted more than six months. Though even with her feathers on, I found her personality could be as spiky as her hair usually was.

Since we were on the subject, I had other questions. 'Have you any idea how many feathers you need to have with you to still be able to change?'

Fairy tales about swan maidens mostly involved them being forced into 'marriage' by men stealing their feathers. I didn't think some bastard out to catch a sex slave would collect every single one though. Besides, Fin and Blanche had both given up a couple of their own wing feathers when we had needed them. The small, downy ones went astray without Fin feeling any ill effects. Occasionally I found a fluffy white speck inside my sweatshirt or in a load of laundry. I'd assume it had escaped from a pillow or a cushion if I didn't know the ones in the cottage were stuffed with foam.

'I suppose we could try an experiment.' Fin didn't sound keen on the idea though. She turned on the radio, which ended that conversation.

I focused on the road. I wanted to know more about a swan maid's feathers all the same. Working for the Green Man, I'd learned how much useful knowledge was still to be found in old myths and legends. I'd also realised that was a fraction of the lore which had faded away, lost forever, once people stopped believing in boggarts and shucks and stopped telling their stories.

While I was doing my joinery apprenticeship, Vince, who had trained me, said a practical skill that wasn't used could be lost inside a generation and a half. He'd asked if I had any idea how a slide rule worked. Before pocket calculators came along in the 1970s, everyone doing maths or engineering used them. Had I ever even seen one? No, because slide rules had been forgotten. I realised the same thing happened with stories.

A bit later on, Fin turned the radio off. 'Do you remember me telling you about that woman who won an award for finding a way to extract phosphates from rivers? To deal with the run-off from agricultural fertilisers? Her company's based near Wells. That's not far from where we're staying. Maybe I could give them a call tomorrow.'

'I thought we were getting away from work for a week? Otherwise we could have saved our money and stayed in your flat.'

The three of us had talked about this. Blanche had kicked things off, saying she needed to get away for a complete break. She said it was far too easy for her and Fin to forget to factor down-time into their work diary until one or other of them was on the edge of burn-out. She was going to the south of France for a week after the wedding. That was a much cheaper option for her than it would be for us. She only had to book one flight and a single hotel room. Zan would be waiting there when she arrived, and the air spirit wouldn't be eating or drinking either.

Fin and I had thought about staying in their flat, but she had admitted she was bound to end up doing a bit of work if the BFW Environmental office was only on the other side of a closed door. She and Blanche were always looking ahead to line up their next contract, and ideally the one after that. It's the reality of being your own boss.

To be fair, I wasn't much better. For a start, I was still getting used to the idea of holidays. We didn't go away to stay somewhere else when I was a kid. While he was still working, my dad used his annual leave to volunteer at the nature reserve where Mum lived. That was the last local remnant of an ancient wood. That's how they had met. By the time I was born, he had taken early retirement and bought the isolated house across the road from the reserve. Renovating that took up his spare time and money. In any case, Mum wouldn't leave her trees.

After I first left home, I spent a few years moving from place to place. When a job was on offer, I did it for as long as it lasted. When there wasn't any work, I didn't spend a penny I didn't have to. I had no way to know how long I might be waiting for someone to need a carpenter on a building development or for a shop refit. Working at Blithehurst, taking vacation days was my excuse for disappearing to deal with a threat the Green Man had shown us. Eleanor and I didn't need the other staff getting suspicious.

But Fin and I had been making an effort to get better at taking time off. I found I liked spending a week in a holiday cottage somewhere peaceful and rural, within reach of decent pubs for eating out and nice walks when the weather was fine. If it rained, we had books to read, films and telly to stream on a laptop, and sex to pass the time. Those holidays had been the first step towards deciding to move in together.

Fin was laughing. 'Okay, yes, you're right. I'll give them a ring about setting up a meeting when we're officially down at the farm.'

I smiled at her and turned the radio on again. Our journey went on smoothly. Traffic was pretty light, and a lot of this route was dual carriageway. That was one advantage of travelling on a Sunday. Friday and Saturday are peak holiday changeover days. The wedding did mean we were paying for seven nights in the holiday cottage, when we'd only be there for six. That was something I was trying to forget.

When we turned off the A34 for the A303, Fin took out her phone. 'I could do with a pee and a coffee, and if we're going to do some shopping, we should do that before everything shuts.'

'Sounds like a plan,' I agreed. 'Where do you want to stop?'

A few minutes later, she looked up from her phone. 'There's a retail park at Amesbury that's listed as a services. There are a couple of supermarkets just beyond it.'

'Sounds good.' I watched for road signs telling me when to pull off. I also enjoyed the views across Salisbury Plain. The road followed the high ground and we could see for miles. I also noted the road signs with red borders pointing to assorted military bases. I'd met a dryad in some MOD woodland once. I wondered if any naiads or dryads, sylphs or hobs, still lived around here.

Or maybe memories of something a lot more scary lingered in local legends. Giants, for instance. Taking the slip road to the retail park, I was startled to see an enormous statue of a man kneeling beside the roundabout. The huge figure looked up into the sky with raised hands. As far as I could tell, he was holding a spray of blossom.

'Dan? We want that turn.' Fin pointed.

'Right.' I took the exit just in time. I also realised this wasn't a service station with everything under one roof. Each fast-food place was in a separate building with its own car park as well as a drive-thru window. Whoever had laid out the parking had seriously underestimated demand on a summer weekend though. I didn't see many electrical charging points either, which was something I'd been noticing since I'd started thinking about buying a new car.

I managed to grab a parking space outside the Costa Coffee shop. We got two coffees and a couple of muffins, found a table and took turns using the loo. When I came back, Fin was looking up something else on her phone.

'Just checking the directions to Bishop's Warren.' She put the handset down and drank some coffee. 'We want to turn off for Warminster, then Frome and Shepton Mallet, then we follow what I've got here. The email says absolutely not to trust the satnav when it insists there's a more direct route.'

'Fine by me.' We'd had a couple of memorable journeys where hand-painted signs tied to signposts warned passing drivers the route they were following wouldn't get them to their destination. Once, we'd trusted the satnav instead and ended up at a locked farm gate.

We finished our coffee and muffins, seeing people with trays looking for free tables. We also didn't waste time getting to the supermarket before it closed. We bought bread, milk, tea and coffee, eggs and bacon for breakfasts, a couple of bottles of wine and other stuff. The curry meal deal for two would be a fall-back option if we fancied an evening in.

'You're not going to want to do any more driving today.' Fin paused by the fish aisle. 'How about salmon and oven chips tonight? I could do green beans with onions and mushrooms?'

'Sounds good to me.' I pushed the trolley towards the chiller cabinets.

With Fin scanning and me packing, we got quickly through the self-checkout. I retraced our route through the retail park's roundabouts. Back on the main road, I realised we were heading pretty much straight due west. I lowered the windscreen visor to cut the glare when the late-afternoon sun shone through gaps in the clouds.

Fin took her sunglasses out of the lightweight backpack she uses instead of a handbag. 'Where are your shades?'

'In the boot, in my hiking backpack with my water bottle and the map.' If I'd thought about that, I could have got the sunglasses out when we stopped at the superstore.

'Do you want to pull up somewhere?' Fin looked ahead for a lay-by or a parking spot.

'I'll be okay. Let's get on.' The traffic had slowed dramatically, and I wondered why. Then I spotted signs to Stonehenge, and as the road narrowed to a single carriageway, we saw the ancient monument straight ahead through the windscreen. The line of people walking up to it, looking tiny from here, was useful to give an idea of scale.

Fin stared at the massive stones. 'How many generations do you suppose have passed this way and wondered who on earth could have set those up, and why?'

'I wonder how much of this route follows their tracks.' I was already sure we'd been driving along stretches of Roman road to get this far. The line on the satnav had that dead-straight, uncompromising feel. After the Romans had left, people would have used the same route to the markets in the medieval towns we had passed. Turnpike houses here and there were reminders of coach roads built after that.

Right now though, the traffic was crawling along for no good reason that I could see. Then we passed Stonehenge and our lane speeded up, while the cars and lorries coming towards us had slowed right down. People were trying to get a good look at the stones, I realised. Wasn't that one reason for trying to put this road in a tunnel? I couldn't remember if that plan was on or off at the moment, but I did think building a solid fence too high for drivers and passengers to see over would be a lot cheaper.

Not long after that, we left the high plain. The road went up and down through hills and woods. We saw a few farm vehicles out and about, though it was still a few weeks before hay-cutting would start. The fields of standing crops were still pale green and it would be more than a month before the barley would ripen. I wouldn't want to be driving these roads once the harvest proper kicked off after that. Tractors and trailers and combines would be coming and going from dawn till dusk.

With Fin navigating, we passed Longleat Safari Park. I was snatching glances at what I was sure had to be an ancient hill-fort on a high point of land when she laughed.

'We haven't looked for dryads or naiads in any wildlife parks. What do you suppose lions would make of Frai or Asca? Or monkeys, or giraffes, come to that?'

'What would the dryads make of them?' I grinned at the thought of Blithehurst's tree spirits meeting a curious tiger. Though Frai could probably stare anything down, given the creatures she had encountered in her long life.

As we followed the signs to Shepton Mallet, I was surprised by the number of HGVs using this route. They clearly used it a lot, even though the road was mostly single carriageway with intermittent overtaking lanes added in when the landscape allowed. Where trees grew right next to the road, reaching over the tarmac, passing lorries had snapped off their twigs and branches to leave a right-angled void. Every time we came out from under some shade into sudden bright sun, I wished we had stopped to find my sunglasses. Between that and staying alert for HGVs swinging out wide as they came around a tight corner, I was starting to get a headache. There were a lot of corners. Maybe sitting in traffic on the M5 wouldn't have been so bad. I thought about pulling up, but any time I saw a suitable place, we were already going past it.

As we reached the Mendip Hills, signs offered us campsites, glamping and farm experiences. I wondered if those included a cockerel waking you up at first light, and having to get up to do the milking. We left the arable land behind. This was grazing country. The cows on these steep pastures presumably supplied local cheesemakers. Villages were strung along narrow roads twisting through the valleys. Solid limestone farmhouses and the occasional pub had claimed the best of the flat land on offer. Labourers' cottages had been built wherever they could be fitted in.

'Here we are. Bishop's Warren.' As we passed the village's welcoming sign, Fin sat up straight and pointed. 'There. Next left. No, not this one. By the telegraph pole. Go right down to the end.'

She gave me just enough warning. I turned into a narrow lane. Four small two-storey cottages on the right faced three identical ones on the other side of the crumbling tarmac. All but one had a gravelled parking space at the front. Only the last cottage at the far end still had a tiny front garden with flowerbeds on either side of the short path to the front door. The gravelled space that belonged to the cottage next to the one we had rented was empty, but cars were parked close to the bins in the others. I saw more cars further down the lane on the wide verges of rough, rutted turf. Beyond that, the tarmac gave way to a bare earth track and hedgerows marked a boundary.

I pulled off the road, glad to stop driving, and glad we were in the Toyota. My Land Rover would have barely fitted in this space. Fin got out of the car and went to press the buttons on the lock box fixed beside the end cottage's front door. As she let herself in, I went around to the back, opened the boot and took out our shopping. I paused on the threshold before I went into the cottage, to check the height of the ceiling. It was high enough for me not to spend the whole week stooping. Good.

I took the shopping bags through the living room into the kitchen extension at the back and put everything on the counter above the fridge. A narrow lobby for the door to the back garden separated the kitchen from the loo and shower room. I filled the kettle and switched that on. I needed a cup of tea. Going out to the front again, I saw Fin heading up the steep stairs with our overnight bag and the two suitcases of clothes we'd brought for our week away, to cope with any-thing from non-stop rain to a sudden heatwave. She'd hung her backpack and our coats on the hooks by the front door.

I went out to the car and collected the crate with our walking boots and waterproofs and my backpack. That left my suit carrier and the zipped bag with Fin's bridesmaid's outfit. There was no point leaving them in the car. I slung the suit carrier's strap over my shoulder and draped the dress bag over my arm. As I picked up the crate, Fin came out of the cottage's front door.

'Do you want a hand with any of that?'

'I'm fine. Just close the car and lock it. The keys are in my back pocket.'

Fin came over and found them. She reached up to pull down the hatchback and the lights flashed as she hit the but-ton on the fob. As I reached the front door, I heard her call out cheerfully behind me.

'Evening!'

I turned to see her wave to a white-haired old lady in sunglasses who had come out of the end cottage on the other side of the lane. She answered Fin with a wave of her own, before dead-heading the roses in her flowerbeds.

I went into the cottage where we were staying and dumped the crate with our boots under the front window.

Fin was right behind me. 'Let me take those upstairs.'

I handed over the suit carrier and the dress bag. 'I'll make some tea.'

I was pleased to find a teapot in the kitchen cupboard above the kettle as well as decent-sized mugs. While the tea was brewing, I put the shopping away and set the digital clocks on the cooker and the microwave to the correct time. I understand why they're never right in rental cottages, but

I don't have to spend my holiday being irritated when one catches my eye. I was looking out through the small window in the back door when Fin came to join me.

Each of these cottages had a long garden where the original owners had grown as much food as they could to feed their families. Stonework and old sheds at the far end by the hedge hinted at long-vanished pigsties and chicken coops. No fences separated them, so I guessed the paved path was a right of way that ran past everyone's back doors. Now, though, this garden was a low-maintenance stretch of mown grass with a washing line strung between two posts over on one side. Two ancient apple trees beyond that had clusters of tiny green spheres clinging to their gnarled grey branches. Someone needed to thin those out, or this year's crop would be a deluge of fruit too small to be worth having. The trees shaded an old, lichen-spotted wooden bench that looked back towards the cottage. That would be a nice place to sit.

Fin went into the kitchen and opened the fridge. 'I saw some tourist leaflets in the front room. Shall we find somewhere interesting to visit tomorrow?'

She put milk in the mugs. I joined her and poured the tea. 'Fine by me.' Right now, I was simply happy to not be driving and being intermittently dazzled by the sun.

I followed Fin out of the kitchen. Once upon a time, the cottage had two downstairs rooms. Those must have been tiny. Even knocked into one, this living room was full of furniture. Towards the front door, a couple of two-seater sofas framed a low coffee table at right angles. A television was fixed to the wall above the boarded-up fireplace. In the back half of the room, a small dining table with four chairs stood against the kitchen wall. The details on the website said the cottage slept four. A couple with two kids, maybe. Four adults sharing this place for a week without getting in each other's way and on each other's nerves was optimistic.

Still, white-painted walls did their best to make the room feel airy, especially once I'd opened the curtains wide to let as much daylight in as possible. The pale flooring was real wood, not laminate, and the furniture was new and modern. The two of us would be fine here for a week.

I claimed one of the grey-upholstered sofas and sipped my tea. Fin sat on the other one and put her mug on the coffee table. As well as a folder of information about the cottage for visitors, I saw a shallow wicker basket filled with leaflets. Fin started sorting through them.

'There's a lot of ancient stuff around here. A couple of hillforts. A Roman villa. This one has a couple of circular walks we could do, if we fancied looking at standing stones.'

She tossed leaflets for Wookey Hole and the Cheddar caves back in the basket. She knew I wouldn't be interested in those. I'm too tall to be comfortable in dark, cramped spaces underground.

'Right.' I closed my eyes and wondered why it's so hard to find furniture with a back tall enough for someone like me. I shifted sideways and slid down the cushions until I could rest my head properly. That made drinking my tea awkward, but I felt my headache easing.

I listened to the soft rustle of paper and Fin making faint noises of surprise and approval as she found something interesting. Then I heard something else. I opened my eyes.

Fin was staring at me, concerned. 'Was that a cat?'

'I don't know.' I sat up and put my mug on the table. 'A bird, maybe?'

We sat and listened. We heard the noise again.

'That's not a cat.' Fin dropped the leaflet she was reading into the wicker basket and stood up. 'Whatever it is, do you think it's hurt?'

'It's out the back.' I got to my feet. Something about the noise had sent a shiver down my spine. 'Where are the keys?'

'On the mantelpiece.' Fin was already heading for the kitchen.

I grabbed them and followed her. 'Wait for me.'

Fin stepped to one side in the little lobby so I could unlock the back door. I opened up cautiously. I was ready to slam the door shut, using my whole body weight to hold it closed until I could lock it, if something unfriendly was out there.

There was no danger of that. I opened the door wider as Fin and I looked down with disbelief. The baby lying on the step waved little arms and legs and started crying again. It was a whole lot louder this time.

Chapter Four

'Where did that come from?' I stared at the baby. It lay there on the step, not in a car seat or a pushchair or anything. It was wearing a white towelling all-in-one thing, and a pink knitted blanket had been wrapped around it. That had come loose as it thrashed. The baby cried some more, screwing up its little red face. I could see its scalp through a thin fuzz of fine, dark hair. It was *tiny*.

'She can't be more than a few weeks old. If that.' Fin scooped her up, assuming that pink blanket meant this was a girl. 'Call the police.'

'Right.' I took out my phone. Wherever the baby had come from, her parents would be frantic.

Unless they were the ones who had dumped her. I stepped past Fin to look down the garden past the apple trees to the hedge. I checked to left and right. There was no sign of anyone around, but with no fences or gates at the back of these cottages, someone could have come and gone without making a sound. As long as the baby kept quiet, anyway. She was screaming now.

'There, there, sweetheart. It's all right. Everything's going to be fine.' Fin walked into the living room carrying the crying baby.

I followed, wondering what the hell was going on. Fin sat down on the sofa and laid the baby on her lap, resting its fluffy head on her knees. Making shushing noises, she ran her fingertips gently over its head and down its little arms to its tiny hands. 'She doesn't seem to be hurt. I don't think she can have been out there for long. She doesn't feel cold. Thank goodness it's a warm evening.'

The baby was still grizzling. Something about that noise was pushing buttons I hadn't known I had. The urge to do something, *anything*, was startling. I looked at my phone. 'No signal. I'll try out the front.'

Stepping outside, I looked up and down the deserted lane. Nothing was moving anywhere on this peaceful summer evening scented with honeysuckle. That would soon change. I checked my phone. Three bars. I rang 999. The efficient voice taking my call asked which service I required.

'Police, please. And maybe an ambulance, just to be on the safe side. Someone's left a baby on our doorstep. It looks fine, but it won't stop crying.' I couldn't think what else to say. This was completely surreal, even by my standards.

I might have imagined it, or maybe there was a slight pause before the 999 operator answered me. 'Can you tell me your name, please.'

'Daniel Mackmain.'

'Where are you exactly?'

'We're in a village called Bishop's Warren, in the Mendips. We're in a rental cottage.' Shit. I couldn't remember the exact address. 'We only got here today. Hang on.'

I stepped back into the cottage doorway. I didn't want to go any further inside in case I lost the phone signal. Fin looked at me. She was holding the baby against her shoulder as she gently rubbed its back. It was still crying.

'What's the name of this road? Can you remember the postcode?'

'Hang on.' Fin leaned forward towards the coffee table, trying to reach the folder with the cottage's information in it. She couldn't manage that without letting the baby slip sideways. 'This is Pigeon Lane. We're in number six.'

'Did you hear that?' I asked the 999 operator.

'That's okay. We've traced your phone.' The voice on the other end of the call sounded a lot more urgent. 'Please stay where you are. Police officers will be with you shortly. Please stay on the line.'

'Yes, sure.' I tried to sound unconcerned. 'That's fine.'

I hoped this wasn't going to turn into a problem. Me and the police have a complicated history. I got caught up in a few fights in pubs and on nights out in my teens and twenties. That's when I learned some people will always blame the biggest man in the room for starting any trouble.

To be fair, I did break a man's arm with a spade once, but that was years ago. A gang of badger baiters had been trying to dig up a sett on the nature reserve. The wildlife trust had appointed Dad as the resident warden there after he retired, so he'd seen them when he'd been out making his checks one night. The arsehole had been going to attack him. So I took his spade away and smacked him with it instead. I got a suspended sentence and a community order, and I had to plead guilty to occasioning actual bodily harm, even though the fucker deserved it.

Since then, I've crossed paths with different coppers a few times when I've been sorting out trouble for the Green Man. Those cops never have a clue about what's really going on, and I can't tell them. I've never been charged with anything, but I'm pretty sure notes of our conversations come up whenever my name gets typed into an official computer. A few online newspaper stories about me don't exactly help either. So I don't like talking to the police unless I absolutely must. Right now, though, I was going to have to.

'They're sending someone,' I told Fin.

I stood in the open door, waiting for them to arrive. I heard an engine a minute later, and a patrol car turned into the lane from the main road. They couldn't have come far. The police car pulled up beside Fin's Toyota, not bothered about blocking her in, or blocking the whole lane, come to that. Two uniformed cops got out, both men. One was about my age. The other one was a good bit older. They looked grim as they walked towards me.

'The baby's inside with my girlfriend. Her name's Fin. Finele Wicken.' I stopped talking, realising I was about to say I didn't know what the baby was called. No shit, Sherlock.

'If you could step aside, please, sir.' The older one tugged at the bottom of his stab vest as he approached.

'No problem.' I moved to stand on the gravel between Fin's car and the living room window.

The younger copper was definitely assessing whether or not he thought he could take me. This was one of those times when my height and size aren't an advantage. I couldn't see if the have-a-go constable had a taser or one of those spring-loaded batons on his Batman utility belt. I spread my hands, so he could see I was only holding my phone. 'Can I hang up this 999 call now?'

'Yes, that's fine.' The older copper stepped closer to encourage me to move further away from the front door. The other copper went inside. I could hear the baby was still crying.

I looked at my phone and saw the call had already ended. Someone must have told the operator the police had arrived. I stuck the handset in my back pocket.

'If I could take your details, sir.' The copper had a notebook ready.

I gave him my name and date of birth. 'Do you want to see my driving licence?'

'In a moment, that will be helpful. And your home address?'

'I live on the Blithehurst estate in the Peak District. It's a tied cottage. I work for Eleanor Beauchene.' Since that's pronounced 'Beechen', I spelled it out for him.

The copper wrote everything down and looked up. 'Please can you tell me exactly what happened here this afternoon?'

That was easy enough. 'We arrived a bit after five. We've rented the place for a week's holiday. We were having a cup of tea when we heard a noise out the back. When we opened the door, there was a baby on the step.' Saying that out loud, it did sound hard to believe.

'What sort of noise did you hear?' The policeman looked at me intently. 'Voices? Footsteps? A car?'

'Nothing.' I shook my head. 'Sorry. I meant we heard the baby crying.'

'Nothing else?' he persisted.

I took a moment to think through everything again. 'No. That's all there was. Sorry.'

He should hear I was telling the truth. Fin would be saying exactly the same. I could hear low voices inside, even if I couldn't make out her words. It was obvious these coppers had separated us to find out if our stories matched. I didn't have to worry about that. But why had a baby been dumped on our doorstep? Who the hell had done this, and why? Now I was over the initial shock, I was getting uneasy.

The copper had more questions. 'You say you got here around five o'clock. Where have you come from today?'

'East Anglia. My girlfriend's sister got married yesterday. We stopped at a supermarket near Avebury not long before they closed.' I remembered something else the cops could check. We had a witness. I pointed across the narrow lane. 'The lady who lives in that cottage over there, she saw us arrive.'

He didn't turn his head, busy writing something down. If he had more questions, he didn't get a chance to ask them. A red Ford pulled up behind his patrol car. The policewoman driving got out, but I didn't think that was an unmarked police vehicle. The woman passenger was taking a baby seat out of the back. She wore sandals, a denim skirt and a long loose shirt over a vest top. She had short grey hair and could have been anywhere between ten and twenty years older than me. She might be a plain clothes officer called out on her weekend off, a social worker or something else entirely. I couldn't tell and I wasn't going to ask. Both women walked straight past me and the copper, going into the cottage without a glance in our direction. The policewoman in uniform carried the car seat.

'If you want to see my driving licence, my wallet's in the living room,' I told the copper who was questioning me.

'In a moment, sir.' He didn't know what to do now, any more than I did.

We waited. A few minutes later, the woman in the denim skirt came out, carrying the baby in the car seat with the pink blanket tucked around it. Its eyes were screwed shut and it screamed, fighting against the straps. The policewoman followed her out, and the younger copper who'd questioned Fin came after them both. Fin stood in the cottage doorway. She looked tense, with a faint crease between her eyebrows.

I was going to ask if she was okay when she glanced my way. She narrowed her eyes and shook her head for a fraction of a second. She nodded just as briefly in the baby's direction. What was she warning me about?

The woman in the denim skirt waited for the policewoman to open the red car's rear door. The screaming baby arched its back in the safety seat as the social worker or whoever she was lifted it inside. The woman leaned over to check everything was secure, blocking my view. That didn't matter. I had seen enough.

Thank fuck the two coppers who had taken our statements were watching the red car reverse out of the lane. When they looked at me again, I made sure my face gave nothing away.

'What happens now?' I asked the older one.

'Let me check.' He walked off and got into their patrol car.

We saw him using his radio. A few minutes later he got out and stood by the open door.

'We'll go door to door, to see if anyone heard or saw something,' he told his partner. Then he looked at me and Fin. 'Someone will want to talk to you again. You said you're staying here for the week?'

I nodded. 'Until next Saturday.'

'We came here to do a bit of walking.' Fin came over to stand beside me, sliding her arm through mine. 'Can someone ring first, to make sure we're in? You've got our numbers?'

'I'll pass them on.' The younger policeman held up his notebook and looked at his partner.

'We'll leave you to enjoy your evening.' The older copper closed the patrol car door, still leaving it blocking the lane. His glance told the younger one to follow him as he walked over to knock on the door of the cottage with the empty parking space beside us.

'Come on.' Fin went straight inside.

I followed her and closed the front door.

'Did you see its eyes?' She stood by the coffee table, looking through the front window. She kept her voice low, as if the coppers might somehow hear her through double-glazing and stone walls. 'That was a changeling, wasn't it?'

'I can't see it could be anything else.' When the woman in the denim skirt was putting the seat into the car, I had seen the baby blink. For an instant, its vague bluish gaze had turned to solid darkness. I hadn't been close enough to see the colour, but there was no way its eyes had been natural. Fin must have seen the same thing.

I went through the kitchen to lock the back door. I came back and locked up the front. Until I had some idea what was going on, nothing and no one else was getting in here.

'Where's the real baby?' Fin demanded. 'The one that's been swapped. Who or what has taken her? And why? Dan, we have to do something about this. No one else knows what's happening.'

She was right. Stealing a human baby was the whole point of leaving a changeling. To make sure no one would go looking for her. That little girl's parents, whose worst nightmare had come true, would have no idea they hadn't been given their own child. The police would have no idea what was going on.

If I had gone missing when I was small, my parents wouldn't have called the cops. My dad would have wanted to avoid awkward questions from social services or anyone else in authority. As a dryad, my mum could call on other resources to find me. I knew someone who might have an idea how to help. I found her number on my phone. 'I'm ringing Hazel.'

She's the wise woman we know best, and the one we trust the most. Most doesn't mean we trust her completely, but right now, she was the best person to... do what, exactly? Before I could find an answer, I saw my phone still had no signal inside the cottage.

'Wait a minute.' Fin had remembered something. 'She's in Patagonia. Or Paraguay, maybe. Somewhere in South America anyway.'

'Bugger.' I'd forgotten about that. 'She's looking for a giant sloth, isn't she, or was it a giant otter?'

Hazel's a cryptozoologist. I don't recall anyone mentioning that at my school jobs fair, but it's an ideal occupation for a wise woman. Trying to find animals that everybody thinks are extinct, or never existed in the first place, gives Hazel an excuse to stick her nose into all sorts of strange goings-on.

'One or the other.' Fin shrugged. She was right. That didn't matter.

I thought for a moment. 'Shall I call Eleanor?'

Before we could do anything, we needed to know more about changelings. The library at Blithehurst House has an excellent collection of books on folklore and local mythology, thanks to Beauchenes in earlier generations who had to deal with the resident dryads. Eleanor keeps up the tradition, adding more titles whenever she finds something new to research.

'If we ring her now, she'll stay up all night reading.' Fin was already heading for the steep stairs. 'Let's see what we can find out online. That'll give us a better idea of the questions we need books to answer. I'll get my laptop.'

I went into the kitchen and put the kettle on again. I stared out of the window over the sink into the back garden. I couldn't believe a changeling turning up on our doorstep was any kind of coincidence. But who knew we were coming here, apart from Fin's family and Eleanor? Hearing Fin coming downstairs, I went into the living room.

'Find me the WiFi password.' Fin shoved the folder with the house's information along the coffee table towards me.

I found the right page and waited while she plugged in her laptop and opened it up. 'Ready?'

'Go ahead.'

'The network's Freeman1967.' I read out the long string of letters and numbers for the passcode.

Fin typed carefully. I sat on the other sofa and waited. She clicked her mouse button a few times, frowning. 'Give me that again?'

I did.

'And again.' Now Fin was scowling.

'Not third time lucky?' I got up as she glared at her laptop screen. 'Let's try resetting the router.'

I'd seen that on a shelf underneath the wall-mounted TV. All the LEDs were steady and green, but I disconnected the power lead anyway. We waited in silence. Fin put the folder beside her on the sofa, so she could read the log-in details for herself. I powered up the router again. We waited for the flashing lights to settle down.

Fin typed. She sighed. 'Still nothing.'

'Let's go to the pub,' I suggested. 'They'll have free WiFi. We can use that on our phones.'

'Okay.' Fin closed her laptop and put it on the coffee table. 'We might pick up some local gossip as well.'

I nodded. Fin might, anyway. People don't often start casual conversations with me.

She followed me to the door and took her backpack off the coat hook. Outside, the two coppers were talking to a man in front of the cottage opposite, closest to the main road. I locked up and put the keys and my phone in my pocket. Fin held out her hand and I took it. We walked to the end of the lane.

'Which way's the pub?' I looked in both directions as we reached the junction. 'Oh.'

A lot more coppers were walking along both sides of the main road, knocking on doors.

'Do you think the baby's been taken from a house in the village?' Fin shivered, even though the evening was pleasantly warm. 'The real baby, I mean. The one that's still missing.'

'And we're the only people who know that.' I felt sick at the thought of someone's tiny child in the hands of... who the hell knew?

'We have to try to find her.' Fin didn't like the idea any more than I did though.

'How are we supposed to do that?' I wondered aloud.

'We need to know more about changelings.' Fin drew a determined breath. 'Let's go to the pub. It's this way.'

We turned left. It wasn't far to the centre of the village. A side road came down from the hills and split in two before it joined the main road to frame a triangular green. Three teenage girls with long mid-brown hair sat on a bench beside the bus stop. They wore jeans so tight they had to be deliberately ripped at the knees so they could bend their legs. Their strappy white tops showed their ribs, and they had a lot of make-up on for a Sunday evening in the country. They looked up from their phones in unison. Clearly they had enough signal to get online or send messages or whatever they were doing.

The one on the closest end of the bench sat forward and called out as we crossed the road. 'Can we help you?'

What she meant was, did we know what was going on? She wasn't doing a very good job of hiding her excitement. I let Fin answer.

'Do you know if the pub does food?' She pointed across the village green. 'The George and Dragon?'

One of the other two replied, 'I don't think the dining room will be open, not this evening. The police are using it.'

'Really?' Fin managed to sound suitably startled. 'Why?'

65

The first girl looked disappointed. 'You haven't heard?'

'We're on holiday,' Fin apologised. 'We only arrived this afternoon.'

'Someone snatched a baby from a house at the other end of the village.' The second girl jerked her head, indicating the main road behind us.

'It's all right though,' the third girl said quickly. 'They've found her. She's back home with her mum and dad.'

The local social networks were impressively quick if they already had that news. How soon would word spread that Fin and I were somehow involved? Other people in Pigeon Lane must have seen the police cars arrive, and the coppers talking to us. They'd have seen the screaming baby being carried out of the cottage. How long before someone shared what we looked like or posted a photo? We'd be instantly recognisable in a place this small.

Looking across the green, I saw the tables outside the pub were full. The bar was open, even if the dining room wasn't. I reckoned it would be packed. Our chances of sitting in a quiet corner and getting online were going to be somewhere between zero and none. As soon as somebody realised who we were, we'd be the centre of attention. I didn't want to answer questions when I'd probably have to lie. That would stir up suspicion, and we were outsiders here.

I checked my phone. Still no hope of a signal. 'Let's go back,' I said quietly to Fin, looking at my screen.

'Yes, I think that's best,' she murmured. She waved at the girls. 'Thanks anyway. Have a good evening.'

They were already looking at their phones again. We turned around and saw police officers going door to door, along the main road. We walked faster and turned into the lane.

Fin stopped beside the Toyota. 'We could drive somewhere to find a pub with WiFi to use.'

She didn't sound convinced. I wasn't either.

'I think we'll get pulled over inside half a mile. The cops haven't got any reason to suspect us, but if they think we're trying to leave...?'

'Do you think something else is watching us?' Fin couldn't hold back a sudden shudder. 'Whoever stole that baby, whoever dumped that changeling, they must be around here somewhere.'

Wasn't that a horrible thought? 'Let's get inside.'

I made sure the front and back doors were locked again. Fin closed the curtains at the living room window so nothing could see inside. She went into the kitchen to lower the roller blind there.

She turned to me. 'What now?'

'Salmon fillets and chips, with green beans and mushrooms.' I opened the fridge. 'There's nothing else we can do tonight. We'll drive somewhere in the morning to get online. Somewhere touristy. The cops think we're here on holiday.'

'Which we are.' Fin didn't look happy. I knew exactly how she felt.

We cooked our dinner and ate it. We didn't open a bottle of wine. We didn't need to discuss that. I wanted a clear head in case whatever was fucking with us turned up in the middle of the night. I assumed Fin thought the same.

Before we went to bed, I did go out into the back garden. Small hard green lumps crunched under my feet as I walked down to the trees. They were trying to shed some of those immature apples. June drop, gardeners call it. I pinched out a good few more of the tiny fruit. If someone didn't, the weight of so many of them growing bigger could snap these old, lichen-covered branches. I couldn't thin the crop properly on both trees right now, but I could make a start.

I paused before I took hold of a thicker branch. If only I had realised the baby was a changeling right away. I could have done this earlier. I might have got a sense of who had done it. Now all I could do was see if anything malicious was lurking out there in the shadows.

Thanks to my greenwood blood, I could feel the old tree was grateful to me for relieving some of its burden. The talent which Fin and I call dryad radar spread out like ripples on a pond. I sensed the trees and flowers in the other gardens. I could tell where roosting birds drowsed in the trees that had grown tall in the untended hedgerows. Bright spots at ground level showed me hedgehogs foraging, voles scurrying and a couple of hunting weasels. Further off, a fox loped across an empty pasture. Rabbits clustered high on a slope beyond. The village was called Bishop's Warren, so that made sense.

'Anything?' Fin stood on the back doorstep, framed against the light from the kitchen.

'Thank you,' I said to the apple tree before I answered her. 'No, nothing to worry about.'

'That's something.' Fin tried to sound positive as I came inside and locked the back door.

But it wasn't enough. I knew we were both thinking that.

I'm not sure what the time was when I realised Fin was lying wide awake beside me. We both stared at the ceiling, listening to the rain. I slid my hand towards her under the duvet. She laced her fingers through mine. We didn't say anything. We didn't have to.

The changeling was tucked up safe and warm. The new parents who'd had such a horrendous day would have changed and fed and bathed the creature, never thinking they had a cuckoo in their nest. We knew what it was, but we didn't have the faintest idea who could have stolen their daughter, or why. Never mind the changeling. Where was the real baby? Had she been left somewhere out there alone in the darkness, hungry, wet and cold? How long could such a tiny child survive?

Chapter Five

Sunrise proper happened around five a.m. We were both awake before that. The sky had been growing paler for a while and the front bedroom had thin pale blue curtains. I decided I'd listened to cheerful birdsong outside the window for long enough. I also needed a pee. 'Shall I put the kettle on?'

Fin rolled over to smile at me. 'And make some toast?'

'I can do that.' I gave her a quick kiss and threw back the duvet.

I got clear of the loo and the shower while the kettle was boiling. While I waited for the toast to pop up, I found a tray, plates, knives and everything else we needed. Taking our breakfast upstairs, I found Fin sitting up in the bed, doing something on her phone.

'No phone signal, and I still can't connect to the router.' She put the handset on the bedside table. 'So what do we know about changelings? Real changelings, I mean. Besides the theory that legends about them were trying to explain away autism or Down Syndrome and other such things.'

'That's all I can think of.' I put down the tray, making sure it was level so tea didn't spill from the pot's spout. 'We need to get a message to someone who can find out more.'

Fin buttered a slice of toast. 'So we go out for a drive and stop when we get a phone signal.'

'Eleanor can definitely help us by doing a bit of research.' I poured two mugs of tea. 'It would be good if she could ask the Blithehurst dryads if they've got any ideas. See what they might know.'

The subject of changelings had never come up, and dryads tend to wait until they can get something they want in return before they share information.

'It can't hurt,' Fin agreed. 'Come to that, where's the nearest dryad you know to here?'

'Sineya, at Brightwell.'

She was the youngest of the three dryads who had been living at Blithehurst when I'd first arrived there. For whatever reason, she had moved to the Cotswolds when I'd been working on a project converting an old manor house into a boutique country hotel in a remnant of the ancient Wychwood Forest. I'd had nothing to do with her decision. That didn't stop the older dryads blaming me.

I'd been thinking about making a detour to see Sineya on my way back to Blithehurst at the end of the week. We were trying to find ways to persuade the younger dryads who were turning up to move into their own domains. Too many dryads with forceful personalities sharing a smallish wood isn't a good idea. We didn't want them too widely scattered though. Then they'd be too far from help. Dryads on their own can be vulnerable, especially when another uncanny creature is trying to get away from the modern world. Nothing good happens if they cross paths and argue.

I grimaced as I took a bite of toast. 'I don't think we can spare the time to drive over there today. We need to find that baby – the real baby – as soon as we possibly can.'

'We need to know what we're dealing with before we can make any plans.' Fin drank her tea. 'How about asking Aled what he knows about changelings? Or the cunning men?'

'We should definitely ring Aled,' I agreed.

He lives in North Wales. He can see the same things as me and Fin, because one of his great-great-whatever-grandfathers had been a coblyn. Those earth spirits sometimes made friends with the men working in the mines. Among other things, they knocked on rocks in the black depths to warn the miners of collapses and explosions that were about to happen.

'I'm not so sure about the cunning men.'

Like the wise women, cunning men have various arcane skills and know useful things about uncanny creatures. That lore had been collected by travelling healers in days gone by. As well as setting bones and treating illnesses inside and out with herbal cures, some of them could work enchantments to help people find strayed animals and lost valuables. Sometimes the cunning men stole those things in the first place, to guarantee they'd get paid one way or the other. The ones who were paying attention went into hiding as soon as accusations of witchcraft started getting their colleagues burned. The survivors had passed their secrets down.

'We can trust Peter, can't we? He should be able to pick up a scent.' Fin helped herself to more toast. 'He might be able to track whoever dumped the changeling on the doorstep. That could lead us to the house where they stole the baby, or to wherever they went next. Finding either place would be useful.'

'That's true.'

Fin was talking about another talent the modern cunning men shared. We didn't know exactly how they did it, but centuries ago, some of their forefathers had done a deal to get the ability to turn into big black cats. Newspapers getting excited about Beasts of Bodmin have no idea what's really out there.

'It'll take him the rest of the day to get here. We're a hell of a long way from Scotland,' I pointed out.

That's where the cunning men were based these days. As far as we knew anyway. There was a hell of a lot we didn't know about them. One thing we could be sure of was any help they gave us would cost us. Though so would any assistance the wise women offered.

'He'd get here a whole lot quicker if a sylph fetched him,' Fin countered.

'Also true,' I conceded. Riding the fastest air currents, a sylph can get from Land's End to John O'Groats in under an hour. If they want to.

'Where's Zan when you need them?' Fin's smile came and went. 'I can go for a quick fly around before we leave, to see if there's one around here.'

If there was, the local sylph would know at once that she was a swan maid, whatever form Fin was in. They'd be intrigued. That's how Zan and Blanche had got together. Persuading a strange sylph to cooperate, though, that would be a whole other challenge. But we needed to do something.

'It's worth a try,' I agreed. 'If they're willing to help out, we can ring Peter and see what he has to say.'

Mind you, I wouldn't envy Peter that journey. Being swept along by a sylph feels like vertigo and travel sickness rolled into one.

'When we find this baby...' Fin bit her lip. 'What are we going to do then?'

'Swap them over, I suppose, though fuck knows how.' I shook my head. 'Sounds simple, doesn't it?'

'But simple's not the same as easy.' Fin was echoing my dad. He's said that to me ever since I was a kid, if I'm about to start something without thinking it through.

'And what do we do with the changeling once we've got the real baby back where it belongs? I have no idea.' I got off the bed and picked up the tray.

'One thing at a time,' Fin said firmly as she got out of bed. 'And we might as well get started.'

She showered while I washed up. As soon as Fin was dressed and ready to go, I grabbed the car keys and the house keys while she got her backpack off the coat hook. I followed her outside. The clunk as the key fob remote unlocked the Toyota was startlingly loud in the quiet lane. It looked like we were the only ones up and about this early.

No, not quite. I realised one of the cars I'd seen parked on the grass at the end of the lane had gone. Someone had an early start or a long drive to work. I checked the time. Just past half-six. It wouldn't be long until other people appeared. Half term was over, and without a school in the village, local kids would need a bus or a lift to get to wherever they went to be educated.

Fin was in the Toyota, cranking the driving seat forward. I opened the passenger door and reached down to lower the seat and slide it backwards. Once I could get in without braining myself on the door frame, I plugged in the satnav. It started looking for satellites. 'Where to?'

'What's the nearest town?' Fin turned the key in the ignition. Nothing happened. Not a sound. The engine wasn't even trying to start.

Fin glanced at me. 'Whoever dumped that changeling is screwing with us, aren't they?'

'Looks like it,' I agreed. We knew hobs and dryads and sylphs can scramble a car's electronics easily and undetectably. What we didn't know was who else could do that.

'So what do we do now?' Fin was frustrated.

'We get indoors before someone heading to work or to school sees us and comes over to offer some help.' I unclipped my seatbelt.

Fin didn't move. 'If they do, maybe we can borrow a phone that works.'

'To do what?' I reached for the door handle. 'We can hardly tell Eleanor or anyone else what's going on if we've got an audience. If we call out the AA, either the car will work fine when they get here and we'll look like complete idiots or you'll pay a small fortune for a new battery, or whatever has been fucked with, and I guarantee that will stop working as soon as we're on our own again. Or when we're out in the middle of nowhere.'

The satnav was still looking for satellites. I had a nasty feeling that it would do that all day if we let it.

'Time for plan B.' Fin got out of the car.

I followed her into the cottage. She dropped onto the closest sofa. 'Who do you think is doing this?'

'I wish I sodding knew.' I was getting annoyed. 'I say we get our boots on and head for high ground. We'll have a better chance of finding a phone signal, for one thing. For another, if whoever is fucking about with us thinks we're going to walk out of here, maybe they'll show themselves.'

'Maybe once we know who's doing this, we'll have some idea why.' Fin heaved a sigh and stood up again.

She went over to the crate with our hiking gear which I'd left by the front window. She found the local Ordnance Survey map we had brought with us. I joined her as she spread it out on the living room table.

'I can fly a lot further and faster than we can walk. How far do you think it is to Brightwell? I'd check on my phone, but obviously I can't do that.' Fin scowled. 'When I get there, I can find Sineya and tell her what's going on. She might know something useful. Then I can find a phone and call Eleanor.'

'I'd reckon that'll take you a couple of hours.' I'd looked at the routes I might use to get there after I'd taken Fin back to her flat and picked up my old Land Rover. I could check with the old map book she kept in the Toyota, but I didn't think I was far off. Fin would be in a hurry, and a swan flies a lot faster than most people realise.

'Make sure you've got a credit card with you.' A swan maid can't carry much metal and still transform into a bird. Thankfully, plastic's not a problem. 'Go to the pub, the Whittle and Dub.'

Fin knew where I meant. We'd met at Brightwell when the manor house's owner had needed professional advice on poor drainage, and I'd found something a whole lot more dangerous, so Sineya had asked for Fin's help.

'Let's see if we can find a local sylph first. If there are any around, they'll like the way the wind from the sea gets forced skyward here.' She tapped a spot on the map. 'They should certainly notice me taking off. If we follow that track from the end of this lane, we can take this public footpath to get there.'

I nodded. 'Right.'

Tight contour lines meant the climb from the valley to the top of the downs would be hard on our calf muscles. That didn't matter. Once we were up there, Fin could use the winds to get airborne, and it was the sort of place that sylphs like.

I tapped the symbol for a trig point marking an ancient beacon site. 'Let's make for that.'

Fin filled our water bottles while I put our sunglasses and lightweight waterproofs into my hiking backpack. I went upstairs and fetched us each a sweatshirt as well. I couldn't check the forecast on my phone, so we'd better cover our options. This year might have had the driest, warmest spring since whenever, but the weather was so unpredictable at the moment, we could easily get soaked to the skin or chilled to the bone. I took my hiking boots out and unlaced my trainers. Fin put her own boots on.

A knock at the door startled us both. I looked at Fin. She looked at me. Whoever was outside knocked again.

'Mr Mackmain? Miss Wicken?'

I went to open the door. I did my best to look discouraging. 'Yes?'

'Good morning. I hope I'm not interrupting your breakfast. I just wanted to check you hadn't been disturbed in the night?'

It was the woman who'd worn the loose shirt, denim skirt and sandals yesterday. She looked a lot more business-like in smart brown trousers and a beige jacket today. She carried a zipped leather bag on one shoulder, held close to her side with her elbow.

'We're fine, thanks.' I didn't move out of the doorway.

She showed me her police warrant card with a pleasant smile. 'May I come in?'

I wanted to say no, but that wouldn't be very sensible. I stepped back and opened the door wider. I wondered if one of our temporary neighbours had seen us get into the Toyota and rung the cops to tell them we were trying to leave.

She walked past me and introduced herself to Fin. 'Miss Wicken, we didn't get a chance to talk yesterday. I'm Detective Inspector Nicola Rickfield. How are you this morning?'

'Fine.' Fin smiled briefly.

'You're making an early start.' DI Rickfield was perfectly friendly, but I saw her taking in every detail as she looked around the living room.

'We were deciding where to go walking.' Fin waved her hand at the map on the table. 'For a bit of early morning birdwatching.'

'I'm glad I caught you.' The inspector slipped the bag off her shoulder and took out a cardboard folder. 'I have copies of your statements from yesterday. If you could read them through and sign them, that would be great.'

That wasn't the only reason she'd come. I could hear that in her voice. What else did she want? I guessed we'd find out soon enough. I took the printed A4 sheet she offered me and sat down on the closest sofa. It didn't take long to check it was an accurate record. I hadn't had a lot to say.

'There's nothing you'd like to add?' The detective looked intently at us both. 'Something you've remembered, that you didn't mention yesterday?'

'No.' I glanced up. 'Can I borrow a pen?'

'Of course.' She found a Biro in her bag and handed it over. 'Miss Wicken?'

'Just a minute.' Fin was still reading, sitting at the dining table.

I leaned forward to rest the statement on the coffee table and signed where I was supposed to. I got up and took the pen to Fin.

'Thanks.' She signed the bottom of her page.

I offered both sheets and the Biro to Inspector Rickfield. 'All done.'

'Thanks.' She put everything in her bag. 'I know you were asked this yesterday, but are you absolutely certain you didn't hear anything before you found the baby on the back step?

You didn't see anyone loitering in the area when you arrived? You haven't seen or heard anything out of the ordinary since then?'

'No.' I shook my head. 'Sorry.'

'You can't think why someone would leave a baby with you?' the inspector persisted.

'Maybe whoever took her saw us when we arrived,' Fin said thoughtfully. 'If they were regretting what they had done, maybe they thought she'd be safe with a couple. How is she? The little girl.'

Inspector Rickfield smiled in a way that made me uneasy. 'She's fine, safe at home with her parents. Do you have children?'

'No.' I answered first, and I wasn't smiling. I wanted Fin to stop talking, but I could hardly say that in front of the inspector.

Fin looked steadily at her. 'No, we don't have any children, and I've never been pregnant. We haven't had a recent miscarriage or anything like that. That's usually a factor, isn't it? When women snatch babies on an impulse and panic when they realise what they've done.'

The inspector raised her eyebrows. 'You take an interest in these cases, do you?'

'Not beyond what I see on the news or in the papers. You can check my medical records, if you like.' Fin was going to make sure this idea was completely off the board. 'Do I need to sign something to give you permission?'

Inspector Rickfield shook her head. 'That won't be necessary.'

This time, I could hear she was telling the whole truth and nothing but the truth. That was a relief.

'Don't let us keep you.' I tried to sound more friendly. 'I mean, you are still looking for whoever did this, aren't you?'

'Enquiries are ongoing,' Inspector Rickfield assured us.

Good luck with that, I didn't say. After what had happened with the car this morning, I was certain the police weren't going to find any witnesses who'd seen whoever left the change-ling on the back step. That was the inspector's problem. Our problem, mine and Fin's, would be steering clear of the cops while we were finding out who had really done this.

We also needed to find that missing baby. The cops didn't even know the real child was still out there. Every hour that went past... We had to get a sodding move on. I crossed the room to open the front door and stood there, holding it.

Inspector Rickfield took the hint. 'Enjoy your birdwatch-ing. And please, if you do remember anything else, anything at all, even if it seems completely trivial, do call me.'

'We will,' Fin assured her.

I watched the inspector walk to a dark blue Ford parked in next door's empty space. There was still no sign of life in that cottage. I remembered seeing it on the website we'd used to find this one. I'd thought it wasn't available this week, but maybe I'd got that wrong. We'd had plenty of choice, looking for somewhere to stay. School summer holidays wouldn't start until the end of next month.

I noticed several of the other cars parked along the lane had left while the detective was talking to us. I wondered what those people thought we were up to now. I closed the cottage door.

Fin was folding up the OS map. 'You don't think the police seriously think we're involved? I mean, they've got absolutely no good reason.'

'No, but they're desperate, and they can't have any other leads to follow. Not if something they can't even see is be-hind this. Until they find another suspect, they'll be looking hard at us.' That was what worried me.

'They'll be checking up on us today, I suppose.' Fin thought for a moment. 'They won't get an answer at the flat with Blanche away in France, but a phone call from the po-lice will tell Eleanor that something's up. What do you think she will do?'

'The cops might settle for verifying we are who we say and leave it at that.' I hoped so, anyway. 'If they do contact Blithehurst, the first thing Eleanor will do is try ringing me. When she can't get through, she'll leave a message and wait for me to call her back. I don't think she'll start thinking something might be wrong until at least this time tomorrow.'

Even then, I didn't think she'd drop everything and rush down here. She'd contact Blanche first. Eleanor knew Fin and I could take care of ourselves, and she had a business to run.

'Let's see if we can find a phone signal and let her know what's going on first.' Fin handed me the map and leaned forward to lace up her boots. 'Or maybe we'll get lucky and find a sylph.'

'I'll settle for a phone signal.' I put the map in my back-pack.

Once I'd locked the door behind us, Fin turned left to head down the lane. We passed the cottage with the front garden, but there was no sign of the old lady. Where the tarmac petered out, a sign told us this route was a bridleway. I kept my eyes open for horseshit.

The track soon started climbing a steeper slope, and I stopped worrying about that. This landscape was more suited to mountain goats than ponies. On either side of the path, deep gullies cut by rain rushing off these hills sheltered thickets of taller trees. We walked past twisted clumps of thorn scrub, low and stubborn, defying the wind and rain that came sweeping in from the coast. The sea wasn't far away. For the moment, the sky was overcast, and I wondered if we'd get caught in a shower.

Ahead of us, the ridge line rose and fell between stretch-es of lower ground and grass-covered high spots where the thorn scrub had given up. I was right about the climb being demanding. We didn't waste our breath on conversation. I walked beside Fin and waited for her to decide on the best place to turn into a swan. I know trees. She knows winds and air currents.

She stopped when we reached a shallow dip sheltered by a shoulder of rocky ground. 'Water, please?'

I slipped off my backpack, unzipped it and handed over her bottle. Hanging the straps on one elbow, I took a drink myself.

'Right.' Fin handed the bottle back. She gave me her phone. Finding her debit card, she slipped that into a pocket and gave me her wallet as well. I closed my eyes to avoid being dazzled by the light people like me see when someone like her transforms.

Hearing her wings flap, I opened my eyes. Fin was already airborne with her long flight feathers spread wide to catch the updraught. I took out my binoculars and settled the backpack on my shoulders. It took me a moment to find Fin as she flew along the ridge line. Thankfully, a bright white swan is fairly noticeable against a green landscape. I couldn't see a sylph, of course. I wouldn't until they decided to show themself.

Shit. Something was wrong. Very wrong. Fin was slipping and tumbling through the air. I gripped the binoculars so tight my fingers hurt, fighting to keep her in view. I saw her long white wings beating strongly. She recovered, but whatever was attacking hit her again. She regained some height. I could see that was a struggle. Was a sylph being stupidly territorial?

Fin was fighting to stay airborne, heading away from me. I started running, holding the binoculars hanging around my neck with one hand. Fin was a distant white speck. I kept my eyes on her as best I could, but I had to look down every few steps to avoid going arse over tit on this uneven ground. If I tore a knee joint, we'd be fucked.

Where was Fin? I saw her double back and head towards me, her long neck outstretched. My relief lasted barely a minute. She wheeled left and disappeared behind higher ground. My boot snagged a loop of bramble tangled in the grass. I staggered, barely keeping my balance. As soon as I could tear myself free, I searched the sky. I couldn't see Fin anywhere. Fuck.

Chapter Six

Where was Fin? What the hell had happened? My mouth was dry with adrenaline as I scrambled up the slope. I stopped at the top of the ridge, and realised what I'd seen ahead was deceptive. The high ground opened out into a broad, grassy expanse.

Get a grip, I told myself. Head for the last place you saw her. Or, you fucking idiot, find a tree and use your sodding dryad radar. The tallest tree within easy reach was an elder, laden with blossom. My hand was clammy and shaking as I took hold of the closest branch. 'Please.'

I could barely force a whisper, but I'd learned the hard way not to presume a strange tree would be willing to help me. The shock when I got rejected was like licking a battery. To my relief, this elder seemed happy enough. Sweet, familiar fragrance embraced me. My greenwood sense swept outwards as I closed my eyes. I ignored the vibrant sparks of animals and birds doing their own thing, unconcerned. An unfamiliar sensation was heading west a fair distance away, but that vanished a second later. I ignored it. I had to find Fin.

As I gripped the elder branch tighter, relief made me dizzy. There she was, not too far away. I didn't get any sense she was hurt. That was even better. Even so, she wasn't moving. Something was – maybe not wrong, but definitely not right.

I opened my eyes. That was a stupid move. Trying to map what I sensed through the trees onto the landscape I could see ahead of me was so disorienting I nearly threw up. I took a deep breath and shut my eyes. Dryad radar showed me Fin was still where I had found her. I let go of the elder tree's branch. 'Thank you.'

I got my bearings, put my binoculars away in my backpack and started walking. As I passed a blackthorn, I saw Fin sitting down about twenty metres away. Her feet were flat on the ground and her elbows rested on her bent knees. Her hands were linked and her chin was on her chest. I couldn't see her face.

I ran to her as fast as I could. 'Are you okay? Are you hurt? What happened?'

'Give me a minute.' Her voice was steady enough to reassure me.

'That looked...' I tried to find the right word. 'Bad.'

'It was.' She lifted her head and sat up straight.

I sat down beside her. 'Was it a sylph?'

'No.' Fin stretched her arms wide, arching her spine. 'I think – I think I was mazed.'

I couldn't tell if she was more startled or more outraged. 'By a dryad? Or something else?'

I'd seen the tree spirits at Blithehurst overwhelm a person's senses. When a nosy woman had been sneaking around, out to make trouble for Eleanor, they had sent her walking in random circles, with no clue where she was or which way to go. The elder tree hadn't shown me a dryad anywhere near here, but they're not the only ones who can send an ordinary person's perceptions haywire.

'I have no idea.' Fin stared straight ahead. 'I've never felt anything like it. But mazing is the only explanation I can come up with.'

I remembered the unfamiliar presence the dryad radar had shown me. Fuck. 'When I was trying to find you, I sensed something strange, but it was there one minute and gone the next.'

Fin glanced at me. 'Whatever it was, whoever did this, I'm not trying to fly out of here again until I know. Not and risk that happening again.'

'No,' I agreed. That wasn't even a question.

'Then what are we going to do?' Fin demanded. 'Our phones don't work. The car won't start. There isn't even a shop in the village when we need to buy more milk. As for getting help to sort out this changeling mess—' She broke off, shaking her head.

I tried to find a solution. 'Let's go back to the cottage. When the pub opens, we can use their payphone to ring for a taxi.'

'And keep our fingers crossed that its engine doesn't die as soon as we get in?' Fin wasn't convinced. 'Do pubs even have payphones these days?'

I had no idea. I couldn't remember when I'd last used one. We sat in silence for a few minutes.

Fin looked up at the sky. 'How do we get a message to someone who can help us find that stolen baby?'

'A message in a bottle?' I started to unzip my backpack to find the OS map. 'Literally. Could we get a local naiad to notice us dropping something in a river?'

Fin wasn't convinced. 'Anyone could pick up whatever we threw in and just bin it. Besides, naiads are spread fairly thin, and there's no guarantee any local one would be friendly.'

She was right, of course. I tried not to let that annoy me. I got to my feet and offered her a hand.

'Back to plan A. Let's see if we can find a phone signal if we walk a bit further. Or until something turns up to stop us.' I really hoped whoever was doing this did show their face. I was ready to punch their teeth out through the back of their neck.

Fin accepted my help and got to her feet. 'Doesn't look like we've got much choice.'

We carried on walking along the ridge. The tough grass fell away ahead of us, down a shallow slope, before rising again some way off. That was as far as we could see.

'Let's take a look at the map.' I had it in my hand. I turned my back to the breeze to stop the edges fluttering as I unfolded it.

Fin studied our options. She traced a route with a finger. 'If we go along here, we can pick up that footpath. See, that'll take us to Bishop's Warren. Unless you're planning on carrying on walking in a straight line until it gets dark.'

'No.' If I'd been on my own, I would have done exactly that, out of sheer bloody-mindedness if nothing else. But I wasn't on my own, and Fin's car and the rest of our things were at the holiday cottage. I'd thought of another reason to go back too.

'Whoever's screwing with us must be down there. Those girls at the bus stop said the baby had been snatched from a house in the village. Whoever did that is making sure we can't phone anyone or go online or drive away, so we can't find out how to deal with their changeling. That means they have to be somewhere close. If we can find them, we can put a stop to this, don't you think?'

'Let's hope so. How close is close?' Fin wondered. 'How far away can a dryad or sylph be and still mess up someone's phone?'

I folded the map and stuck it in a side pocket of my combat trousers. 'That's another experiment we can do when we're both at Blithehurst.'

'Or we ask Zan, if we can get hold of Blanche,' Fin said, exasperated.

'True.' I would never have thought I'd be so keen to see the sylph turn up without warning.

We hadn't seen any local sylphs either, I realised. I wondered if whoever was doing this had scared them off somehow. Who or what were we dealing with anyway? Not knowing was starting to piss me off.

We carried on walking. The clouds were lifting and it was turning into a nice day for a hike. When we reached the next high point, the views were spectacular. Then I saw something further along the ridge that wasn't grass, brambles or a thorn thicket.

I shaded my eyes with my hand. 'What's that?'

Fin pulled the map out of my trouser pocket and worked out where we were. 'According to this, it's a tumulus.'

For a moment, all I could think of was flute-playing fauns. 'Doesn't that mean a burial mound or a barrow? Those look like big stones.'

'Tumulus is what it says here.' Fin shrugged. 'Let's take a look.'

As we got closer, we saw this was no Stonehenge, but it was still impressive. Two massive grey slabs of limestone had been set into the ground at roughly forty-five-degree angles, to make a hollow wedge. They didn't quite meet. We were approaching from the pointy end, and I could see a gap big enough to get a hand through. There was no way to tell how much of the stones was hidden below the ground. Above the grass, the slab to my right was roughly two metres long and a metre and a half tall. The left-hand one was a bit longer and a bit shorter. They were both about a metre thick. I couldn't see anything that looked like tool marks on their weathered surfaces. Had whoever set them up simply kept looking until they found rocks the size and shape they needed?

A third stone on the far side closed up the open end of the wedge. That slab was more than two metres long and easily a metre and a half wide, though it wasn't anywhere as thick as the other two. It rested against them, tilted at a shallow angle, casting a shadow over the ground they enclosed.

I wondered what sort of tonnage the three stones added up to. I had no idea. I'm a carpenter, not a mason. Regardless, getting them up here would have been an enormous job. The Stone Age work crew must have known exactly what they were doing.

'I think this would have been a burial mound original-ly.' Fin stopped beside me. 'The stones would be set up and covered with earth.'

'That rings a vague bell.' I nodded. 'You can see how the wind and rain up here would have scoured a mound away. Eventually.'

'If my phone was working, I could look it up.' Fin walked around to the far end and turned towards me. 'Wow. This is some hagstone.'

A shiver went down my spine as I joined her and saw what she meant. A sizeable hole went right through the tilted slab, just off-centre to the left. It was too irregular to be called a circle, and this was far too big to be called a hagstone. Those are pebbles small enough to carry around in a pocket, naturally pierced by running water or tumbling waves, found in riverbeds or seashores. If you look through the hole, you see the true nature of whatever's there, no matter what something uncanny is pretending to be.

Having one sounded useful. Getting one wouldn't be easy. Forget buying the ones offered by occult suppliers online. Eleanor's sources in Blithehurst's library insisted a hagstone only worked for someone who found it by chance, or who received it as a gift, freely given. As soon as the stones were bought or sold, or even found by someone searching deliberately, they were useless.

I wanted to test that. What if Fin and I went to a shingle beach and searched until we each found one. If we gave them to each other as gifts, would that get around the small print?

Fin looked at me, concerned. 'Are you okay? You look like you saw a ghost.'

I shook my head. Something else was bothering me now. 'Can you hear that?'

Fin frowned. 'Is it the wind? Passing over that hole like someone blowing over the neck of a bottle.'

'No, that's not it.' I circled the stones, going clockwise.

That noise was getting louder. Shit. It sounded like a baby crying, somewhere a long way off. What was going on? I knelt down to peer through the narrow gap between the uprights wedged in the ground. All I saw was bare earth and rabbit crap. Then Fin looked through the tilted slab and her shadow blocked the daylight spilling through the hole.

'Dan,' she said uncertainly. 'You need to look at this.'

I stood up and walked to the wide end of the wedge.

Fin stretched out a hand. 'Stand next to me. Don't look through the hole directly, but try to keep it in the corner of your eye. Do you hear that? Can you see it?'

The teasing wind blew her ponytail into my face. I ignored it. 'Shit. That's the baby. The real baby. It has to be her.'

The urge to look straight through the hole was almost impossible to resist. When I did, I saw the triangular patch of earth dappled with daylight falling through the gaps between the tilted slab and the stones on both sides. When I shifted my eyes sideways though, on the edge of my peripheral vision, I could see a tiny figure wearing white, lying on a stretch of rough grass. Its feeble kicking slowed and the desolate grizzling faded away.

'She is still alive, don't you think?' Fin was looking for reassurance.

'For now.' I wished I could say something more hopeful. 'How do we get to her? How do we get her back?'

I walked backwards far enough to assess the tilted slab as a whole, wondering what the fuck to do now. On the far side of the stone, wherever the hell that was, the stolen baby was crying again. Okay, so it wasn't dead yet. That was good to know. But I couldn't think how we were going to get it back. That desolate wailing shredded my concentration like a knife scraping across a plate, over and over again.

Fin was right by the hole. She braced her hands on either side and took her right foot off the ground.

'What the hell are you doing?' I hurried forward and tried to grab her shoulder.

Too late. Fin slipped her right leg through the hole and twisted around. She bent double, pressing her chest to her thighs. 'It's okay. Thank goodness for yoga—'

She yelped as she lost her balance and fell backwards. The rough stone sides of the hole scraped her T-shirt sleeves and the skin on her elbows. I missed catching hold of her trailing boot by millimetres.

'It's all right. I'm okay.' She sounded surprised.

Now I didn't need to squint sideways to look through the stone. The hole was a window into somewhere else entirely. A place where Fin had landed on her backside on thick, coarse grass.

She stood up and brushed off her jeans as she looked around. 'This is very weird.'

That was the understatement of the fucking century. I planted my hands flat on either side of the hole and saw the thorn thickets and brambles behind her. They looked exactly like the ones we had passed walking along the ridge. I couldn't see the sky, but from the brightness, it was sunny there, just like here.

'Wait there.' I assessed the hole to work out how I could get through the stone.

Fin looked at me, wide-eyed. 'Don't be stupid. You'll get wedged like Winnie the Pooh.'

Fuck it. She was right. Well, not about me getting stuck. I wouldn't even get my shoulders through there.

'Maybe I can make the hole a bit bigger.' I looked around for a lump of stone to use as a hammer. Bashing rocks together had worked for cavemen for thousands of years. It's not as if I had any other options. We were here on sodding holiday, so I hadn't brought any tools. Though even if we'd come here in the Land Rover, there was no way I'd leave Fin on the other side of this hole while I went to fetch something I could use.

'Don't you dare!' She clapped her hands to get my attention. 'Dan! You have no idea what damaging the stone might do. It's okay. There's nothing else here. No birdsong, no anything. Just wait and I'll get the baby.'

There was nothing I could do and nothing I could say as she turned and ran towards that little figure dressed in white. Was that the stolen baby or was this a trap? Or both? The baby could be bait. We still had no idea who the hell was doing this. All I could do was wait and see what happened next.

Fin looked warily from side to side as she reached the child. I couldn't see movement anywhere. Nothing that might be a threat. Not that I could do a sodding thing if something attacked her. My heart pounded.

Fin scooped up the baby, still looking in all directions. She headed towards me, walking, not running now. She had to take more care carrying the child. Even so, she wasn't hanging about. I breathed a bit easier when she reached the other side of the tilted slab.

'Can you reach her?' With the stone looming over her head, Fin had to crouch to get close enough to offer me the baby through the hole. We could be pretty sure we'd found who we were looking for. This tiny girl was wearing a white towelling onesie, exactly the same as the changeling.

'Careful,' Fin warned. 'Make sure you support her head.'

I wiped my sweating palms on the sides of my trousers. 'Let me find somewhere to put her down. Then I can give you a hand.' Fin wasn't going to find getting out of there nearly so easy as going through in the first place.

I cupped my hands to take the baby. Like the changeling, she was so *tiny*. She couldn't weigh more than three kilos, maybe three and a half. I brought the stolen child slowly and carefully through the uneven hole. Fin leaned forward, keeping her own hands on the baby, ready to catch her if she slipped.

When I stepped back, everything went wrong. As soon as Fin let go of the baby, everything on the other side of the slab vanished completely. All I could see was bare earth in the shadowed hollow between the ancient stones.

Where was Fin? More importantly, how did I get her back?

The baby wriggled in my hands. I was so startled, I nearly dropped her. The tiny girl stared up in my general direction. I wasn't convinced she could see me. She blinked, and I saw her wandering pale blue gaze was wholly and undoubtedly human. Thank fuck for that, at least. She'd stopped crying as well, for the moment.

I backed away slowly from the stones, trying to get my brain in gear. Trying not to panic. I found a place where I could sit down, slowly and carefully, making sure I could still see the stone with the hole.

First things first. Cross-legged on the dry grass, I remembered how Fin had checked over the changeling. I laid the stolen baby down in front of me and did the same. Thankfully the tiny girl was dry and warm. That was good. A moment later, I realised it was also very odd. If she had been lying on the grass all night, out there on the other side of the stone – wherever the fuck *there* might be – her towelling onesie should be sodden. I wasn't complaining, but why wasn't this little scrap already dead from exposure as well as from hunger and thirst?

I looked at the tilted slab. Dryads and naiads and sylphs don't have to experience time at the same steady pace of hours, days and weeks as ordinary people. Blithehurst's library was full of stories about people who thought they'd been away with fairies for a day and a night of dancing and feasting, but when they got home, they were told they'd been given up for dead a hundred years ago. Some found their grandchildren living in their house, grey-haired and grandparents themselves.

Did that mean we were dealing with fairies? Were there fair folk or kindly ones, or whatever they called themselves, living around here? Folklore says they live in hollow hills. With Cheddar Gorge and Wookey Hole within easy reach, the Mendips definitely ticked that box. I really hoped it wasn't fairies. I'd encountered the Tylwyth Teg causing trouble in North Wales, and they'd been seriously scary. If this was fairies, I'd ring Aled and ask for help, even if I had to walk ten miles to find a phone signal.

I'd have to take the baby with me, just to make my life that bit more sodding difficult. I looked down to see her trying to suck her own fist. I ran a cautious hand over her belly. As far as I could tell, her stomach was pretty full. Was that the last meal her parents had given her, or had she been fed by whoever had stolen her? Fairy stories are full of warnings not to accept food or drink from fairies, but a tiny baby would only know it was hungry. Did that mean she wouldn't be affected by whatever bound people who'd enjoyed their hospitality to the fairy realm?

I had no way to know, one way or the other, and there was nothing I could do about it anyway. The important thing was I couldn't see any significant difference between this baby and the changeling. Hopefully, losing a day or so at this age wouldn't affect her in the long run. I looked at the stone again, and wondered how fast was time passing for Fin on the other side.

No. I couldn't think about that. Wherever Fin was, I had to believe she was safe. I had to believe she would stay alert and use her wits to search for a way back to me. She hadn't seen anything else on the other side of that hole. Neither had I. However long this stolen baby had been lying on the grass there, nothing had heard her crying and found a tasty snack.

I wished I hadn't thought that. The idea of something eating the baby was horrifying. I don't watch horror movies. I don't see the point. I know that monsters are real. Though those films do get one thing right. Everything's a whole lot more terrifying when you don't know what's after you. What the fuck was doing this?

I drew a deep breath. Losing my shit wouldn't help anyone, least of all Fin. I locked my emotions down hard and fast. It was time to compartmentalise. Fin said I was good at that.

Okay, what now? Well, I couldn't sit here on my arse all day. What was the most important thing to do? Get this baby back to her parents. That's what Fin would say. Once I'd done that, I could think about the next thing.

Besides, when whoever was behind this realised I had found the stolen baby, or maybe when I had got hold of the changeling again, wouldn't they come looking for me? I couldn't believe they'd gone to this much trouble, just to give up on... whatever they were trying to do. I was also convinced they'd used this little girl as bait to lure Fin through that stone, so I was happy to return that favour.

I'd be ready for them, whoever they were. Then we'd have a conversation about what had happened to Fin. The sort of conversation that involved my hands getting tighter around their neck until I got her back.

But first, I had to get back to the holiday cottage.

Chapter Seven

I had to get off this hill and down to the village without dropping the baby on her head. I slipped my backpack off my shoulders. Would she fit inside? I could leave the zip open at the top. But I'd have to carry the water bottles, my binoculars, the map, my wallet and Fin's, our waterproofs, both of our phones... I wear combat trousers because I like having plenty of pockets, but there's a limit to what they can hold.

Besides, I didn't think being carried along scrunched up in a bag could be good for a tiny baby. She was so small and fragile, it was honestly terrifying. I'd never even held a baby before, never mind had to look after one on my own. I knew what Fin would say to that. Tough. Deal with it.

Right. Plenty of visitors brought children to Blithehurst. Bigger babies were strapped into rucksack-like backpacks or push chairs. As far as I could recall, parents carried the small-est babies in carriers strapped to their chests, face to face, with their arms and legs splayed out.

What could I use to do the same job long enough to get us to Bishop's Warren? I took my lightweight waterproof coat out of its drawstring bag. After thinking for a few minutes, I zipped up the front and tucked the hood inside. Spreading the arms out wide and starting from the top, I rolled the rip-stop cloth up tight, until I reached the armpits.

Let's see how well this would work. I tucked the bottom of the coat well down inside the front of my trousers, with the zip towards me. Making sure the coat didn't unroll, I care-fully lifted the baby up and held her against my chest. Good. The extra material at the top would support the back of her head. But now I needed one free hand, ideally two, if I was going to tie the sleeves behind my neck...

I put the baby down on the ground again. She grizzled. I had to guess how much slack to leave as I knotted the sleeves tight. I eased her inside the coat. She fit, just about. It felt a bit tight, but that would have to do. I eased my arms through my backpack straps, one at a time, taking the baby's weight with my other hand. If the waterproof came untucked from my trousers, she'd slide straight down my thighs.

I checked her little legs weren't bent or twisted and slowly stood up. This was just about going to work, as long as I kept one hand on the baby, pressing her close to my chest. I started walking, watching where I put my feet before every single step. Someone my size tripping and falling on top of an infant didn't bear thinking about.

I followed the route Fin had pointed out earlier. Thankfully, as far as I could tell, no one else was hiking these hills today. As soon as I could see houses, I walked even more slowly and warily. I had to get to the holiday cottage without being seen. The police didn't know anything about the changeling, but they'd still be hunting for whoever had stolen this little girl yesterday.

How could I possibly explain what I was doing now to Inspector Rickfield? It was easy enough to imagine what she would say.

'You've found another baby, Mr Mackmain? Two of them in two days. And this one was abandoned on a hillside? Can Miss Wicken confirm this? Where is Miss Wicken? I see her car is still here. Let me call her number. Why is her phone ringing in your backpack?'

I could sodding guarantee Fin's phone would start working then. Whoever was doing this had to be watching us, to cut off our phones as soon as I'd called the cops yesterday, and to kill the Toyota's electronics this morning. Unless that sort of interference was something a dryad or a naiad only needed to do once and the effect would last until they decided to switch it off. That was another question I should have asked before now.

Never mind that. I needed to focus. If I was caught with this baby, I'd be in handcuffs and off to an interview room so fast my feet wouldn't touch the ground. The cops would want answers I couldn't give them. Why had I changed my mind and given the first baby back? Where had I stolen this second baby? How much of this was Fin's idea? Was she my willing accomplice or acting under duress? Had she run away as soon as she saw her chance, or had I left her dead in a ditch? I'd be in court charged with child abduction, Fin's suspected murder, or most likely both.

That wasn't all. Whatever happened to me, this little girl wouldn't be given to her real parents. As far as anyone else was concerned, they'd got their stolen child back yesterday. They'd be stuck with the changeling for good. I guessed their real daughter would be handed over to social services. Fostered, most likely, and adopted? It's not as if anyone else was going to claim her. She would never know who she really was. Even if she did one of those DNA tests years from now, no one would be able to explain what had happened to her.

So I had to give this little girl back to her parents and I had to take the changeling away. I had to hope that would give me some clue to whoever the fuck was behind this. First and most importantly, I had to avoid being seen. Fortunately, my greenwood blood could help with that. A few years ago, I found out I can blend into the background when I want to, when I'm somewhere with trees and greenery.

I concentrated very hard on going unnoticed as I approached the ribbon of houses straggling along the road at this end of the village. I checked the OS map in my hand for the footpath which circled the village. I saw the waymarked post ahead. This would take me to the bridleway at the bottom of Pigeon Lane. I wouldn't have to walk along the main road, past the village green and the bus stop. This wasn't the day to discover everyone could still see me when I had tarmac under my boots even if I was trying to hide.

This wasn't the first time I'd wondered about that. I'd better add it to our list of experiments for when we were both at Blithehurst. Because I was going to find Fin somehow. As soon as I got this baby back where she belonged.

I followed the path past a playing field. Thankfully no one was out walking their dog. People with jobs would be at work and kids would be in school. That was good, because by the time I saw our holiday cottage ahead, the baby was wriggling and grizzling inside the improvised sling. One thing I did know about going unseen was it didn't mean I went unheard.

The old lady who lived opposite wouldn't have gone to work. I had to get indoors before she came out to see what the noise was about. The other cars parked in the lane this morning had gone. There was nothing for me to hide behind.

I needed to get the house keys out without dropping the baby. I held her against my chest and shrugged the straps off my shoulders. My backpack dropped onto the path. I had to crouch down and pin it with my knee to pull the zip open one-handed. The baby was crying a whole lot louder now.

I found the keys and left the backpack where it was. I got the front door open. Stepping inside, I leaned back and closed the door with my shoulders. I pulled the baby out from under the rolled-up waterproof. She was red-faced and sweaty and seriously upset. I pulled the knotted sleeves over my head and left the coat where it fell.

Sitting on the sofa, I rested the baby on my chest, lying on her front. I tried gently patting her back, the same as Fin. The baby screamed louder, trying to lift up her little head. Her tiny arms and legs moved as if she was trying to get away. I was starting to think she really didn't like me.

I felt her backside through the towelling onesie. I'm no expert, but that nappy felt soggy. Bugger. I couldn't do anything about that. Was she hungry? Was semi-skimmed milk okay for babies in an emergency? I had no clue, and no way to check online. In any case, I didn't have a feeding bottle to get her to drink milk or anything else.

Fuck. I'd left my backpack outside, with our wallets and phones inside. I laid the baby down on the sofa on her back since she didn't seem to like being on her front. She wasn't any happier about that. Seriously, could she scream any louder?

I stood up and watched for a moment, to see how far she could move. It didn't look like she was going anywhere. Crossing my fingers she wouldn't fall onto the floor, I quickly went out to get the backpack. I picked up the OS map as well. I'd completely forgotten about that.

As soon as I was inside, I locked the door. I went into the kitchen to wash my hands. The baby was still crying, but I needed time to think. I drank a glass of water in one. If the baby had been peeing and sweating, I had to get liquid into her. The water in the kettle had boiled this morning and that would be cool by now. That should be safe enough for the time being. But I really had to get her to someone who knew what the fuck they were doing.

I remembered my dad getting water into a dehydrated fox cub before we took it to the local wildlife rescue centre. I filled a tumbler from the kettle and found a teaspoon. Going into the living room, I sat down and settled the baby in the crook of my left arm. With the tumbler in my left hand, I dripped half a teaspoonful of water into her open, gummy mouth. That surprised her so much she shut up. Fuck me, that was a relief.

I fed her more water. She sucked it down. So she was thirsty. I'd got that right. I guessed she was hungry too. Her lips pouted and she moved her head from side to side, searching for milk. I couldn't do anything about that. I fed her more water until she surprised me with a burp. Water welled up in her mouth and trickled down her chin to soak the front of her onesie. My T-shirt caught a fair amount too, but that was already sodden with sweat.

On the plus side, her little pink eyelids were drooping. The baby might be hungry, but she was definitely knackered. I sat, tense, waiting for her to fall asleep properly. If I moved and she woke up, I'd be right back where we'd started. I silently counted to a hundred. Then I counted to a hundred again.

After what felt like half a lifetime, the baby seemed to be sleeping soundly. At least, she was limp and relaxed against my arm. I held my breath as I got to my feet, dropping the spoon onto the sofa. Passing the dining table, I bent my knees and put the tumbler down, careful not to make a noise. I carried the sleeping baby upstairs. Doing that quietly in hiking boots was an effort.

I had no idea how long it would take me to find her parents' house, and I couldn't take her with me. If she woke up and started crying while I was out, I'd have to rely on these stone walls and the double-glazing to muffle the sound. So I wanted her as far away as possible from anyone passing the cottage. The bedroom at the back was even smaller than the one Fin and I were using. The double bed took up almost the entire floor apart from a narrow chest of drawers. Sleeps four in comfort? Yeah, right.

I laid the baby in the centre of the duvet and carefully eased the bottom drawer out of the chest of drawers. I put that on the floor and collected a stack of towels from the boiler cupboard tucked beside the chimney breast in the front bedroom. I lined the drawer with a bath towel and put a couple more smaller ones in the bottom.

Slowly and carefully, I picked the baby up. I lowered her down. As soon as her back touched the towels, she flung her little arms out wide. I held my breath. Her tiny fingers splayed, but her eyes stayed shut. I slid my hands out from under her, millimetre by millimetre. She stayed asleep.

I had no time to waste. I closed the bedroom door and went downstairs. Grabbing my backpack off the floor, I stuffed the folded map into the top. I hung my binoculars around my neck, left the cottage and headed for the main road. Just a holidaymaker out to do some birdwatching. Nothing out of the ordinary whatsoever.

I didn't see any net curtains twitch. I started to wonder how many of the houses here were holiday lets. How many were empty during the day with the people who lived there at work and any kids in school? Bishop's Warren didn't have much to offer beyond the pub to anyone who had retired. No shop, no library, no village hall or doctor's surgery, or anything else that they might need.

I forced myself to walk slowly. I wasn't sure how I was going to identify the house where the stolen baby's parents lived. It wasn't as if there'd be a notice board outside. I had nearly reached the end of the village when at long last something went my way. I saw a police car in front of a large L-shaped house with a red-tiled roof. It was set back from the road behind a gravel driveway shaded by a cluster of mature beech trees. The roof was new and the house's render had a fresh coat of cream masonry paint. That would cover the join where a modern extension had doubled the footprint of the original cottage. Another, older building had been converted into a double garage. Both buildings had shiny alarm boxes on the gable ends that faced the road.

This had to be it. There was no other reason for a cop car to be parked there. A uniformed officer in the driving seat was looking down at a phone or a book or whatever he had to pass the time. I walked past, forcing myself not to hurry, and went on further down the road. Once the houses ended and farmland began, I pretended to be looking at something through my binoculars until a passing Audi was out of sight. Then I climbed over a farm gate and made my way along that useful circular footpath. I concentrated on not being seen and moved as quietly as I could. It was close to midday, and it was a hot, sunny day. I drank what was left in my water bottle. I should have refilled that while I was at the cottage. I would have if I hadn't been so distracted.

The red roof was easy to see through the spindly trees of hedgerows left to do their own thing. This house had a sizeable back garden with a three-rail wooden fence separating it from the footpath. It was mostly lawn, with a couple of flower beds bright with peonies, delphiniums and sweet peas. A vegetable patch behind the garage had cane wigwams set up for runner beans. The first scarlet flowers were starting to show among the broad green leaves.

I looked at the house. Windows were open upstairs and down. That and the cop car out front had to mean someone was home. The alarm system would be switched off, but how did that help me? I stood there for a long moment, wondering what I was going to do now. Well, I wasn't going to find out anything useful from here.

I climbed the fence and walked quickly across the lawn, concentrating on not being seen. My skin crawled all the same. I expected an outraged shout from an open window. This was private property. What the hell did I think I was doing?

I could explain their baby had been left on our step. I'd come to see if the little girl was all right. I'd ask if there was any news about who had taken her. Was that close enough to the truth for the cops not to immediately call me a liar?

Nobody challenged me. As I got closer, I heard voices upstairs, in a bedroom above the kitchen. I dropped to the grass and sat with my back pressed against the wall of the house. I spread my hands out and dug my fingertips into the soil. I tried to believe I was invisible.

'I'm telling you. That's not my baby.' A woman's voice was ragged with frustration and exhaustion.

'You're in shock. You don't mean that.' The man answering her sounded equally shattered.

'Stop saying that. I know exactly what I mean.' The woman bit off each word. She was fighting not to lose her temper. 'What I don't understand is how you can't see it!'

101

'Spend some time with Alice,' the man pleaded. 'You'll get over this. It'll be hormones or something.'

'I don't want to get over it!' The woman burst into tears. 'I want *my* baby.'

'Why don't you give her a feed?' the man persisted. 'You need to bond. They said at the hospital—'

'No!' The woman was close to screaming. 'Get that thing away from me!'

'Okay, okay, I'm going!' Now the man sounded angry too.

I heard a door slam. Shit. Where was he going? I didn't move, listening to the woman crying in the room upstairs. A few minutes later, I heard a door open somewhere inside on the ground floor.

'All right, Alice. You have a little nap while I ring Granny. Mummy will feel better once she's had some sleep.' The poor bastard was absolutely desperate to believe that.

I heard him come into the kitchen. He opened and closed a cupboard. I heard the gush of the tap and him drinking. Bastard. I was horribly thirsty. A chair scraped on quarry tiles as he sat down.

'Hi, Mum.' His voice cracked.

I clenched my fists as I listened to his half of the conversation.

'She's still saying Alice isn't hers.' He sounded completely defeated. He listened to his mother's reply. 'No, it really isn't. Yes, I've heard about the baby blues. This isn't that.'

He listened some more. 'I've been looking online. Have you heard of post-partum psychosis? And there's a delusion where people think they're surrounded by imposters. Maybe—'

His mum interrupted. I couldn't make out her words, but her tone convinced me she wasn't having any of that.

'All right, all right. No more googling. It's all AI nonsense these days anyway.' He heaved a shuddering sigh as he listened to his mum.

'I can give her all the time she needs,' he protested a few minutes later. 'But how long will it take? What if she never gets over it? No one expects to have their baby stolen out of her cot before she's a week old.' He was crying now.

I heard his mum trying to offer some comfort. I heard another noise through the open window upstairs. Baby Alice's mother was snoring. I hoped a bit of sleep would do her some good. But the only way to make this horrible situation right would be giving her back her baby.

'Hang on a minute, Mum,' Alice's dad said hoarsely.

I heard him blow his nose. He came over to the sink and turned on the tap. Water splashed and I heard paper towels being torn off a roll. He blew his nose again.

'Sorry. It's just – I'm absolutely wrecked. We didn't get any sleep last night. Sonja was sure she could hear somebody downstairs or out in the garden.'

I wondered what had been snooping around. Whoever was responsible, or something else drawn to the changeling's presence?

'The police doctor offered her a sedative. She won't take it. I'm starting to wonder if she needs to be in hospital. Honestly, what if she hurts Alice? I'm sure she wouldn't do anything on purpose, but I've never seen her like this.'

He was genuinely scared. I had to get their real baby back to them before something awful happened and Sonja ended up on a locked ward.

'I'm keeping her with me.' He sounded a bit calmer. That was a relief. 'She's sleeping in the travel cot in the dining room. I managed to persuade Sonja to use the breast pump this morning. The family liaison officer went to the shops, to get a tin of formula just in case, and spare bottles and stuff. It's not what we wanted, but...'

I could pretty much hear him shrugging wearily.

'There's a car outside. They say it's in case any reporters turn up. We did have a couple of phone calls this morning. I don't know how the hell they got my number. The family liaison told them no comment and said we're asking for privacy. No, Mum, please, I don't want to know what's in the papers. I still don't understand why they put the story on the news. She was only missing for about an hour and we got her back safe and sound.'

Shit. It hadn't even occurred to me or Fin to switch on the TV last night. Had the baby's abduction been on the local news or had the story gone national? Thankfully I hadn't seen anyone who looked like a journalist hanging around the village.

He was getting angry now. 'They haven't turned up a single lead or found a single witness. Now they're asking if we're sure we locked the doors. What about the windows? I think they're trying to blame Sonja. The family liaison asked if I was sure I knew where they both were yesterday. Could Sonja have gone for a walk with Alice without me realising? What, and leave our baby on a random doorstep, because she decided motherhood was too much hassle? I think that police car's here to keep an eye on us. I told the liaison woman to leave.'

He was too furious to go on. That didn't last. He interrupted whatever his mum said next.

'No idea. They showed us a load of photos, but we didn't recognise anyone in them. The police haven't even told us their names. I think they're hoping we'll let something slip, to prove we do know them. What do they think we did? Made a deal to sell our baby to strangers on the Internet? How—'

His mum interrupted again. As he sat and listened, I wondered if my photo or Fin's would be on a newspaper's front page tomorrow. That would alert Eleanor and other people to the trouble we were in, but mud sticks. I tried to convince myself that wouldn't happen. The police had no good reason to think we were involved. I remembered a couple of cases where innocent people identified as suspects had sued the arse off the police force responsible after the tabloids made their lives a living hell. Eleanor had an attack lawyer on speed dial. She had put the fear of God and prosecution into the woman who'd caused trouble for the Beauchene family a while ago. Of course, I'd have to be able to ring Eleanor before she could call the solicitor...

Alice's dad was speaking again. 'The family liaison woman said she'll come back later today, but I don't want strangers in the house overnight. I'll sleep on the sofa bed downstairs. That should help convince Sonja she's safe. Oh god, I hope so, Mum. I thought I had locked up properly, but you do something on automatic when it's so routine. Someone got in and took Alice because I...'

The poor bastard was blaming himself. His mum wasn't having that.

'Yes, okay. I'll call you tomorrow. Yes, lots of love, and to Dad.' His voice cracked again. He put his phone down and started crying quietly. His grief and guilt were searing. Then I heard the changeling grizzling through a closed door.

'It's all right, Alice,' he called out. 'Daddy's coming. Just give me a minute.'

His forced cheerfulness was heartbreaking. I had to give these poor people their real baby and take that changeling away. But I still had no clue how to do it. I could guarantee Alice's dad wouldn't leave any doors unlocked today.

I heard him open the fridge. A minute or so later, the microwave pinged. A minute after that, the kitchen door closed.

I got cautiously to my feet. Crouching low, I risked looking through the kitchen window. I saw his phone on the table beside an empty pint glass. A couple of supermarket carrier bags were next to some keys.

Not a whole bunch of keys for the house and a car and maybe the garage as well. Just three keys on a red leather fob. One was small enough for window locks, which meant the other two had to be the front and back doors. The table was about two metres away and those keys were on the side closest to me.

Time to stop fucking about. I had to get hold of those keys. I looked around the garden. Spare bamboo canes were stacked behind the garage, a couple of metres long. I ran to fetch one. I saw pea sticks there too. I grabbed a couple of those.

I didn't bother crouching down as I came back to the window. If I got caught, I'd be so deep in the shit I wouldn't see daylight for years. I got my multi-tool out of my combat trousers' zip pocket. Fin had bought it for my last birthday. Top of the range, it offered eighteen options for cutting just about anything, plus tightening screws, opening bottles or tins, and a lot more besides.

I used the big blade to split the end of the bamboo cane. Cutting a forked twig off a pea stick, I wedged that into the split. Did that feel secure? Secure enough. I had a hook. I forced the kitchen window fully open and leaned inside as far as I could.

I could reach the keys. That's to say, I could get the end of the cane over to the table. I forced myself to stay calm as I edged the forked pea twig closer and closer to the keys. I'd get one chance at this. If I knocked the fob off the table, it was game over. That wasn't all. If I pushed the keys so the ring they were on fell flat, I wouldn't have a hope of hooking them with the twig.

I couldn't afford to get this wrong. This family couldn't afford me fucking up. They didn't deserve this horror show. When I found the bastard behind this, I'd make them regret every decision they had ever made.

I eased one end of the forked twig through the key ring. Was that going to hold? There was only one way to find out. I lifted the cane as far as I could. The edge of the uPVC window dug painfully into my gut. I gritted my teeth and ignored it. My shoulder and arm muscles were complaining about working at full stretch too. The keys came up from the table...

I focused on keeping the cane steady and level as I stepped back, passing the cane through my hands. I mustn't hurry. I couldn't risk losing the keys. The forked twig fell out of the split end of the cane as they came over the edge of the counter by the sink. I smacked my elbow hard on the window frame as I lunged forward to grab the fob before the keys could fall on the floor.

I knocked something over. I have no idea what it was. It fell to the floor with a deafening crash. I legged it. I reached the fence and half climbed, half fell over that. I chucked the bamboo cane away and I didn't wait to see where that went. No one was shouting at me to stop, so I had to believe I hadn't been seen. So far, so good, but this job was only half done.

Chapter Eight

I got back to the holiday cottage as fast as I could, running along the village boundary footpath. When I opened the front door, I heard Alice crying upstairs. Crap. How the hell was I going to get her home unnoticed when she was making that much row?

I hung my backpack and the binoculars on the coat hooks by the door. Should I wait and take her back later? How much later? The sun wouldn't set until well after nine. It wouldn't get dark for a couple of hours after that. It wouldn't get properly dark anyway, with midsummer's day in a couple of weeks. Plus, the moon would be high in the clear sky, waxing just past the half.

Besides, Alice's dad, whatever his name was, would make sure the house was locked up tight before he tried to go to sleep. He'd switch the alarm on too. I'd set that off even if I used a key to get in. I had no idea what code to enter.

That would wake everyone up. If the family liaison officer had persuaded Alice's dad to let her stay the night, she'd have me in handcuffs before back-up arrived. She'd be asking those impossible questions about where this second baby had come from, what on earth I was doing sneaking into the red-tiled house, and where the hell was Fin?

I had to try getting Alice home in daylight, so there was no point in waiting. In fact, waiting would make this more risky. At the moment, the other parking spaces along the lane were empty. It wouldn't be long before buses brought the school kids home to Bishop's Warren. Their parents would be getting home from work. If I passed back gardens with a crying baby, when people had the windows open on this warm summer evening, they would wonder where the noise was coming from, even if they couldn't see me sneaking past. They'd had the police knocking on doors for the last twenty-four hours, looking for witnesses to a baby's abduction. No one would ignore that.

I realised I was ravenous. That was too bad. I couldn't waste time making a sandwich. I grabbed a banana from the fruit bowl Fin had put on the coffee table and went through the cottage to unlock the back door. Out in the garden, I walked down to the apple trees. I ate the banana in big bites, my throat aching as I swallowed.

'Please, I need your help.' I took hold of the branch that I'd used before.

This time I looked for the Green Man. The cottages behind me were a solid barrier. Dryad radar can't see inside buildings. That didn't matter. I searched the fields and the hedgerows beyond the garden, as far from the village as I could reach. There was no sign of him. Not a trace. Could dryad radar even find him? I had never tried this before.

I let go of the tree and looked up into the shady green branches. I waited for the leaves to rearrange themselves into a face. When I was a kid exploring Warwickshire's woods, the Green Man had been Jack-in-the-Green, an ally who looked about the same age as the teenagers who caught the bus from the village to secondary school. As I grew older, he changed. These days, he's tall, broad-shouldered and bearded, with an aura of unmistakable power. His face is a mask made from oak leaves, with an emerald spark in the dark hollows beneath his heavy brows.

But there was no sign of him here. Fuck it. I said what I was thinking out loud. It wasn't as if anyone was around to overhear me.

'You owe me. If I'm going to get that baby back to her parents, I need your help. If I'm seen, if I'm arrested, the shit will really hit the fan. Not just for me. Eleanor, and Fin—'

No. I couldn't worry about Fin. I couldn't start wondering where she might be. Not now. Not yet. I shook my head to get rid of those thoughts. I had to get Alice home to her parents. Then I'd look for Fin.

I looked up into the apple tree again. Still nothing. 'You owe me.'

I went into the cottage and chucked the banana skin in the bin. Upstairs, Alice was still crying. How could something so small make so much noise for so long? I locked the back door. A busybody coming in to see what the problem might be was trouble I didn't need.

I carried a cupful of boiled water upstairs with a teaspoon. When I picked up the baby, her nappy really was sodden. I felt damp patches on her onesie. There was nothing I could do about that. I sat on the bed and tried to give her a drink. Water went everywhere. The baby screamed, red-faced and spitting, waving her tiny arms. It could have been funny if it wasn't so sad. This poor little girl needed to go home.

I put Alice down in the drawer so she could thrash in safety. Since my improvised baby sling had worked before, I went downstairs and got my waterproof coat. I took my phone, and Fin's, and both our wallets out of the backpack and left them on the mantelpiece. If I did get arrested, Fin would need those when she got back.

Upstairs, I settled Alice inside the improvised carrier the same way as before. She fought me, still crying, not as loudly but still miserable. Her little face was hot against my chest.

'Hush, hush, hush. It's going to be all right.' I tried to soothe her as I walked carefully down the stairs, holding the bannister with one hand and the baby with the other. 'Let's get you to your mum.'

I didn't bother picking anything up apart from the keys to the red-tiled house and the ones to this cottage. Once I'd locked the back door, I zipped those in my pocket. Going past the apple trees to the bottom of the garden, I walked backwards through the biggest gap in the ragged hedge. My shoulders forced the springy branches apart while my body sheltered Alice. She was still grizzling, and hiccuping against my chest. Was something badly wrong? I mean, apart from her being wet and hungry and hot? I knew sod all about babies.

I hurried along the footpath following the field margins. I concentrated on not being seen harder than I ever had before. Maybe being carried calmed Alice down. Her crying grew quieter and stopped. I felt her lying limp and still against my chest. Suddenly panicked, I remembered newspaper stories about cot death. I stopped and looked down, and tilted Alice backwards until I could see her little face. Her eyes stayed closed. I lifted her up to feel her breath on my face, to make certain she was still alive. Yes, she was okay. Thank fuck for that. How did new parents do this?

When I got closer to the red-tiled house, I had a whole lot of new problems. I couldn't simply leave Alice outside the back door. I had to take that changeling away. Alice's dad had said he had put it in the dining room. Which room was that? Where was he?

I walked across the lawn. It felt like every hair on my forearms and on the back of my neck was standing on end. My stomach was hollow. As I got closer, I looked through the kitchen windows. No one was in there. Good. Walking along the back of the house, I snatched a glance through the next window. The curtains were half drawn, but I saw enough to know this was the dining room. Jackpot.

The rigid rectangular pen made from blue nylon fabric and white mesh must be the travel cot Alice's dad had talked about. I couldn't see the changeling inside it, but the table had tiny nappies and other stuff stacked on it. The two carrier bags I'd seen earlier in the kitchen were there as well.

I ignored every instinct telling me not to walk into more trouble than I could possibly imagine. The kitchen door was locked. I fished the house keys out of my pocket. I unlocked the door, pressed the handle and slipped inside. I was sweating like I'd run a marathon. I really wanted this to be over. I left the keys I'd stolen on the table. Either I'd get away with this or I wouldn't. Either way, I wouldn't need them again.

Movement outside the window at the front of the house caught my eye. I froze. It took me a minute to get my brain in gear to make sense of what I was seeing. The police car was there with its doors open. The copper stood with his back to me. Alice's dad sat sideways on the passenger seat with his feet on the gravel. He had a can of Coke in his hand. The copper had one as well. Bastards. I could do with a nice cold drink.

They were talking about something. Alice's dad might not like having the police in his house, but I guessed he couldn't bear to be on his own right now. Sonja and the changeling must be sleeping. That was my third piece of good luck and I had better not waste it.

I walked through the kitchen into an L-shaped hall. Opposite the oak front door, the stairs went up and around a corner. A cloakroom was tucked underneath them. The dining room door was to my right. As I stepped into the hall, I saw the door on the far side was ajar. That sizeable lounge must have been the original cottage's whole ground floor.

Sonja came down the last couple of stairs. She stared at me, bleary-eyed. 'I was dreaming about trees.'

She was completely out of it. Her flowery leggings were twisted around her knees, and her baggy yellow T-shirt had damp patches on the front. She'd be combing her long dark hair for a week to get those tangles out.

She looked vaguely at me. 'Who are you?'

'A friend. I've brought Alice back to you.' I tugged the rolled-up waterproof down to show her the baby's face. 'I'll take that other thing away. But don't tell anyone I was here.'

Sonja's bitter laugh was unexpectedly loud. 'They wouldn't believe me if I did.'

Alice stiffened with a jerk. Feet crunched on the gravel driveway.

'Sonja?' Outside, Alice's dad was alarmed.

The baby started crying, high-pitched and quavering.

'Oh, sweetheart.' Sonja reached for her daughter. Tears trickled down her face.

I handed Alice over.

'Sonja?' Her husband was right outside the front door.

I retreated into the dining room as quickly as I could. The waterproof was still hanging around my neck. I couldn't leave that here.

Sonja turned her back on me, carrying Alice towards the lounge. 'You're hungry, aren't you, poppet? Oh, and you're wet. Never mind. You're home now.'

I closed the dining room door nearly all the way. I left a crack to see where Alice's dad went. The oak door started to open, filling the hallway with daylight. I heard a tearing, shattering crash outside the front of the house. Alice's dad yelped. I saw his shadow come and go as he turned back towards the police car.

'What's happened?'

Good question. The answer could wait. I looked into the travel cot. The changeling looked up at me. The thing really was identical to Alice, and it was wearing the same white onesie. Thank fuck for multipacks. Then it blinked and I glimpsed those blank, dark eyes. I still couldn't make out their colour in the dimness, but never mind. I scooped up the changeling and tucked it into my improvised baby sling.

I saw a sizeable tin with a plastic lid inside the closest carrier bag, along with a baby bottle still in its packaging. I shoved a big handful of the little nappies into the top. Hooking the bag's handles over my wrist, I went to the door to sneak a look into the hall. The front door wasn't fully closed, but Alice's dad and the copper were outside on the gravel drive, talking loudly, startled. I had to get out of here before he remembered he'd heard his wife and baby inside.

I reached the kitchen in a few long strides. Snatching a glance through the front window, I saw half of one of the beech trees had come crashing down. A raw scar showed where the trunk had split. The cop car hadn't been hit, but nothing was going in or out of that driveway until the fallen timber was cleared. Alice's dad stood looking away from me, helplessly pressing his hands to his face. He must be wondering what else could go wrong for him this week.

I could thank the Green Man for that distraction once I got back to the holiday cottage. I was already out of the kitchen door, crossing the lawn and concentrating on not being seen. I didn't let myself think about anything else.

By the time I unlocked the cottage's back door, the changeling was starting to wriggle and whimper. I dumped the carrier bag by the kettle and took the little creature out of the improvised sling. I dropped the knotted waterproof on the floor. That felt better. Sweat was sticking my T-shirt to my ribs.

I held the changeling out in front of me, with my hands under its armpits. It squinted vaguely back. If I hadn't known what had happened, if I couldn't see what this really was, I wouldn't have believed Sonja either, however much she insisted this baby couldn't be hers. Well, she had Alice safely home now, so that nightmare was over. I hoped the cops and the doctors would write off her behaviour through the past twenty-four hours as hormones or shock or something. If everyone told her that often enough, maybe Sonja would believe it herself. It wouldn't be fair, but it might be for the best in the long run, if the family were going to put this behind them.

The changeling screwed up its tiny face and started to cry, making the same high-pitched noise as Alice. If the little monster was hungry, I could do something about that. But I was going to need both hands. I carried the changeling into the living room and put it on a sofa.

I took a can of Coke out of the fridge. As I drank that, I emptied the carrier bag to find out what I had stolen. Yes, stolen. All of a sudden, I was furious. Spitting mad. Whoever was behind this fuckery had made me a thief. It wasn't the worst thing they had done, not compared to everything else, but I decided they could sodding well pay for that too, along with all the rest.

It turned out I'd stolen a big tin of powdered baby milk, a feeding bottle, a packet of baby wipes and those disposable nappies. Ignoring the grizzling changeling in the living room, I read the instructions on the tin. It turned out that a baby shouldn't be given cow's milk in their first year. The tin didn't say why, but at least I hadn't handed baby Alice to her mum with whatever problems that would have caused. I also learned a newborn baby needed feeding every two to three hours, day and night. How did new parents get anything else done?

The rest of the information was common sense. I put down the tin and put the kettle on to boil. Then I washed my hands. The formula tin emphasised the importance of keeping things clean. Taking the bottle out of the packaging, I fitted it together. The packaging said I should sterilise it before using it for the first time, but I didn't have time if I was going to shut the screaming changeling up with a feed.

I didn't only want some silence. I knew the changeling wasn't a real baby, but on the way here, I had decided I'd better treat it like one. When whoever was behind this wanted their creature back, I needed it to be healthy. Especially if I had to trade the thing for Fin, or for whatever I needed to know to get her back from wherever she was stuck. That was my priority now Alice was safe with her parents. I'd just have to hope this little monster was as resistant to germs as I am, generally speaking.

I poured water from the kettle. Ninety mil for a newborn feed. I opened the tin of formula and added three scoops of powder. Fixing on the rubber teat, I shook the bottle to mix the powder. Considering how fast a cup of tea or coffee goes cold when you get distracted, baby milk takes bloody ages to cool down. When I couldn't take the changeling's crying any longer, I went and picked it up. I held it in the crook of my arm while I ran the sodding feeding bottle under the cold tap.

Once I reckoned the formula was a safe enough temperature, I went through to sit on the sofa and offered the changeling the bottle. The little creature fastened on to the teat at once. It had learned that much about being a baby. Finally, peace and quiet.

Not for long. When the bottle was nearly empty and the changeling's eyes had closed, it let rip with a series of loud farts. No, those weren't just farts. Okay. Changing a nappy would be another new experience.

I stood up, carefully holding the sleepy changeling against my shoulder, and took the feeding bottle into the kitchen. I put that into the sink and put the tin of milk in the cupboard over the kettle. I didn't want anyone – especially not a copper or a reporter – seeing anything suspicious if they peered in through the windows or if I had to open the front door. Everything else had better go upstairs. I put the nappies and the wet wipes in the carrier bag, and wondered if new parents got special lessons in doing everything one-handed.

Up in the back bedroom, I dropped the carrier bag onto the bed. Still working one-handed, and kneeling down, I spread out a towel on the floor. We'd paid a cleaning deposit and I didn't want the cottage's owners complaining about stains on the carpet. I put the changeling down on the towel and discovered the onesie had poppers along the inside seams of both legs. That made getting its feet out a whole lot easier. When I pushed the onesie up to its armpits, I saw it wasn't wearing a disposable nappy. This reusable one had poppers on either side too.

I hadn't expected to find a dark, wizened stump of something stuck to the changeling's belly. The plastic clip on the other end looked like something I'd use on a bread bag. After a minute's thought, I realised that must be what was left of its umbilical cord. At least, that's what it would be on the real Alice. Whoever had created this changeling had paid attention to every detail, I had to give them that.

Since I had absolutely no idea what to do with a baby's belly button stump, I left that well alone. The disposable nappy was sodden and full, but it turned out baby crap wasn't too unpleasant. I rolled the shitty nappy up tight and put it on the edge of the towel. I'd deal with that later. I cleaned the changeling's backside with wet wipes and put on a dry disposable nappy. Thankfully that had a little divot on the front edge to avoid putting pressure on the stump. Someone had thought that through.

As I eased its legs into the onesie, the little creature woke up. Bugger. It blinked, and I froze. For the first time, I got a proper look at its eyes. I already knew it wasn't human. I'd seen that dark gaze with no white or iris. I hadn't seen the colour. Now I did. When it blinked, the changeling's eyes turned muddy red-brown, like dried blood. I'd seen that before. That was a hag's gaze.

I had been feeling hot and sweaty. Now I was chilled to the bone. I stared at the changeling. It looked vaguely around, waving its little arms and legs. I really didn't want to consider what this might mean for me and for Fin, but I didn't have a choice.

We had encountered hags last year when the Green Man had sent us up against an alliance of uncanny creatures trying to break out of the shadows and slaughter any ordinary humans they could get their claws into. That situation had started off bad and rapidly got worse. The hags had been terrifying, and we'd struggled to find out how to fight them.

Eleanor had done loads of research since then and come up with sod all. I was starting to wonder if the most useful legends hadn't faded away naturally but had been deliberately killed off. None of the dryads or naiads we'd asked had any advice to offer. They simply told us hags were horribly dangerous and not to go near them, which was stating the literally bleeding obvious.

Stories about hags in local folklore rarely even give their names. Pretty much all that's persisted are remnants of warnings not to go near particular ponds or caves or bridges. The few longer tales that survive are horror stories. Evil, powerful old women lurk unseen, waiting for their chance to steal children or murder travellers. Why? To eat them. The stories are revoltingly consistent about that.

I looked at the changeling. Was this supposed baby girl going to grow into a man-eating monster, metaphorically and literally? At least Alice's parents wouldn't have to deal with that nightmare. And I realised Fin really must have saved Alice from being a hag's next meal. I couldn't be angry with her now for climbing through the hole in that tilted stone. Even if neither of us had known what was happening.

If the changeling was a baby hag, did that mean a hag was behind this? I couldn't come up with any other explanation. I could think of a whole lot of other questions. How the fuck had we got mixed up in this? Alice had been stolen before we even arrived in Bishop's Warren. The Green Man hadn't sent us here. We'd planned this holiday a couple of months ago. Never mind. That could wait. What was I going to do now?

Assuming some hag was behind this, I reckoned we had screwed up whatever she had planned. Alice was home, I had the changeling with me, and Fin was – where? Facing a hag on her own? I'd barely managed to fight off one of them. The young dryads in my mum's wood had killed it. When two hags had come after me and Eleanor, we'd needed a naiad to take them down. Fin was resourceful, but if a hag could maze her, if that's what had happened this morning, she wouldn't be able to fly out of trouble. The fears I'd locked down so tight earlier were fighting to get free. I gritted my teeth so hard my jaw ached.

The changeling looked up at me and gurgled. Right now, it had literally baby-blue eyes. Then it blinked, and for an instant, I saw that stomach-churning darkness. The little monster whimpered. Oh, fuck. Was it going to start screaming again? Please, no. I forced myself to pick the thing up.

'It's okay. You're fine. Just go to sleep.' Holding it against my shoulder, I sat on the edge of the bed and rocked gently backwards and forwards. That way I didn't have to look at its face and see those horrible eyes.

Whoever owned this cottage had hung framed photos on the back bedroom wall. Two of them showed the houses on either side of the lane when everything had been covered in snow. Those were colour photos. Below them, black-and-white archive shots showed life here in the days when the lane was a rutted track. Women standing at the cottage doors wore long skirts and shawls. The men wore flat caps and white shirts with dark trousers and waistcoats. Pigeon Lane then and now.

Higher up, an aerial shot showed the view from a helicopter or a drone. It had been taken in the summer, or at least when the fields were green. Then I noticed something a whole lot more significant. In all the photographs, from the ones in the eighteen-whenevers to the modern shots looking towards the bridleway or down from the sky, there were only three cottages on either side of the lane.

So how come Fin and I had seen four houses opposite this one when we arrived?

Chapter Nine

The changeling was fast asleep. I laid it carefully down in the drawer. It did that jazz hands thing like Alice had when its back touched the towels. It didn't open its eyes. That was a relief. I closed the bedroom door and went downstairs as quietly as I could. The first thing I did was swap my hiking boots for my trainers.

I pulled the laces tight. Seeing a house that shouldn't be there had to be connected to whatever was going on. To the changeling asleep upstairs. To that portal closing and trapping Fin. I was going to get answers out of the old woman we'd seen outside that cottage when we arrived. Was that really yesterday afternoon?

I didn't believe for a second that old woman was as ordinary as she looked. Naiads, dryads, sylphs, you name it, they can masquerade as ordinary humans, unless you can glimpse their true nature when they blink. But what exactly was she?

Not friendly. I was sure of that much. I stood up and found my multi-tool. I had left that on the mantelpiece with my wallet and Fin's car keys before taking Alice home. I slipped it into my pocket. Most uncanny things can be hurt by iron. More badly hurt than just being stabbed like ordinary people. Fairy tales are right about that. Iron with added carbon to make steel still counts.

I found the cottage keys and went out into the lane. A car was parked by the end house, but no one else seemed to be home. I crossed the tarmac to the house that shouldn't be there. The flowerbeds on either side of the short path were crowded with rose bushes in full bloom. I could even smell their scent. A climbing rose arched up and over the front door. Sprays of deep pink blooms swayed in the breeze.

Was it really there? Clearly, I couldn't trust my own eyes. I couldn't feel so much as an itch from the faded scars on my forearm. Was that good news or not? Perhaps I could get an idea of what was really going on with dryad radar. I'd never tried using that with anything besides trees, though, and the thorns on the climbing rose's thick, dark stem looked vicious. Still, I keep my tetanus shots up to date.

Before I could decide whether or not to give that a try, the white-painted front door opened. I took a step back. I couldn't help it, even though the white-haired woman in sunglasses didn't look dangerous. She wore comfy white slip-on shoes, stretchy pink trousers and a long, loose pink-and-yellow flowery shirt. She looked like every film director's ideal choice for a much-loved granny.

She smiled as she stepped back from the doorway. 'Would you like to come in?'

Something about that made me uneasy. I half remembered a line from some old story or maybe a song. 'Won't you step into my parlour?' said the spider to a fly.

Fuck it. Whatever this old woman was, I was a whole lot bigger than she was, and I was ready for trouble. Besides, her invitation saved me the trouble of kicking in her door. That still looked real enough to keep me out, and breaking it down would disturb the neighbours. I didn't want anyone ringing 999.

'Okay.' I walked up to the door.

I stopped and took a good look before I crossed the threshold. The layout was much the same as the cottage Fin and I had rented. What had been two rooms downstairs had been knocked into one, leaving the beams exposed. Those were low enough for me to have to watch my head. A door led to a kitchen extension, and the stairs were in the far corner.

A sideboard too big for the living room was cluttered with china baskets of flowers and milkmaids in frilly frocks that no woman working on a farm would ever wear. Wide-eyed shepherd boys clutched lambs with ribbons around their necks. There wasn't room for a dining table. A fat-cushioned three-piece suite took up most of the rest of the room. The fabric on the armchairs and the sofa was cream, pink and red roses. The wallpaper was swirling embossed vinyl painted pale pink. Gold-tasselled tie-backs looped curtains with more yellow and pink roses back from the lace-curtained windows. I was surprised the carpet wasn't pink too, but that was patterned with leaves in different shades of green. The overall effect was as sickly-sweet as a cheap box of strawberry fondant chocolates.

'Well? Are you going to come in?' The old woman went over to the armchair furthest from the door. She perched on the edge of the seat with her knees together and her hands folded in her lap.

I didn't see I had any choice. I needed answers. I had to find out what had happened to Fin. I stepped into the room. The gloom felt instantly oppressive. Those heavy swags of curtains shut out half the available daylight. The old woman was still wearing her sunglasses though.

'Close the door, dear.' Her smile widened, though she wasn't showing her teeth.

More and more wary, I reached behind me to push the door without looking. I wasn't going to take my eyes off this woman, whatever she might be. I was trying not to shut the door completely – I didn't want to block my closest way out. The painted wood swung away from my fingers and I heard the latch click shut. Bollocks.

The old woman gestured towards the other armchair. 'Please, do sit down. Let's introduce ourselves.'

I didn't want to do either of those things. I'd bet those cushions would be so soft I'd sink so far down my knees would be either side of my ears. Having to fight my way out of furniture like that is bad enough in everyday life. If this place was the trap I was sure it was, getting stuck for even a moment could be fatal.

I didn't want to tell her who I was either. Plenty of fairy tales are about somebody's plans coming unstuck when someone else finds out what they're called. Rumpelstiltskin, for example. As far as I knew, nothing eerie had been able to use my name against me before now. That didn't matter. Until I knew what I was dealing with here, I wasn't taking any chances. Actually, I wouldn't be taking any chances even when I found out what the hell the old woman was.

'I'm fine.' I stayed standing by the door. 'You first. Who are you?'

'That's not very friendly, dear. Would you like a cup of tea? With a biscuit, perhaps?' She braced her hands on the chair's fat arms, about to stand up.

Not a chance. I wasn't going to eat or drink anything she offered me.

'No.' I took a step forward, to see how she'd react. Any ordinary person would be intimidated by someone my size doing that.

She folded her hands in her lap. She wasn't remotely bothered. 'Dear me. Didn't your mother teach you any manners?'

'No.' I was close enough to take a quick step forward and snatch those sunglasses off her face. I chucked them away, not caring where they landed. I wanted to see her eyes.

The old woman stared up at me for a long moment. Then she blinked, slowly and deliberately, still looking straight at me. Even in this gloom, I recognised the dark, ruddy colour of her blank eyes. It reminded me of old, clotted blood. This was as bad as I'd feared. She was a hag. Fuck.

'Where's—?' Shit. I'd been about to tell her Fin's name. 'My girlfriend. What have you done with her?'

I was about to reach for my multi-tool when I had second thoughts. Most uncanny things can't handle iron, but I'd met hags who could. Eleanor had found a few remnants of old stories that hinted others could too. The hag I'd fought before had been terrifyingly strong. I didn't want to risk giving this one even a short blade she might use against me.

'Me, dear? I haven't done anything. The swan maid chose to go through the portal.' The hag shooed me away with soft, plump hands. 'Do stop looming, dear. I'll get a crick in my neck having to look up at you like this.'

'So you were watching us up on the ridge.' I did take a step backwards. I couldn't see anything she could use as a weapon within reach, but I wasn't taking any chances.

The hag smiled, and I was surprised to see she had white, even teeth. The hags I'd encountered before had mouths like a dentist's worst nightmare. Then she opened her mouth wider and reached inside with her forefinger and thumb. She took out her dentures, top and bottom, with revolting sucking noises. Putting the pink-and-ivory plastic or whatever they were made of on the lace doily on a side table, she fished a crumpled tissue out of a trouser pocket and wiped her fingers dry.

She had a single, yellowed and worn tooth left, off-centre in her upper jaw. That must make eating stray travellers and kidnapped children difficult. Unless hags used their ability to handle iron to do things like skinning and cutting up their victims into bite-sized chunks. She might have looked like a sweet little white-haired old lady, but hags were killers

'That's much more comfortable.' The hag could still speak perfectly clearly without her dentures in. 'Now, dear, why don't you sit down?'

I didn't move. I knew she was trying to distract me. That teeth thing might even have worked, somewhere else, some other time. 'Where is she? The swan maid?'

The hag just shrugged.

I tried to work out what to say to get a response. 'I've taken Alice back to her parents.'

'Well done, dear,' the hag said warmly.

I tried a different challenge. 'I've got your changeling. If you want it, I want my girlfriend.'

'Oh, no, dear.' She wasn't remotely bothered. 'It's of no use to me now. Do whatever you want with the thing.'

124

'Then what—? Why—?' I couldn't think how to ask the questions that were choking me.

She leaned forward, clasping her hands around one knee. 'Son of the greenwood, did you think there wouldn't be consequences when you killed my kinswomen? Even if they were fools to reveal themselves to you and your friends. Do you think you came here to my domain by chance? That we didn't draw you and the swan maid to this place deliberately?'

She chuckled, smug. 'Foolish boy. You have no idea what we can do. Well, you've learned better now. After today, you'll never know which thoughts are your own, and which are notions we have put in your head.'

For a horrible moment, I believed her. We didn't know what hags could do. The idea that Fin and I had somehow been manipulated when we'd decided to come here for our holiday scared me shitless. Somehow this hag had forced us to choose this particular cottage, on this particular week, when she would be lying in wait? How long had she been watching us, stalking us, unsuspected and unseen?

She kept saying 'we'. How many hags was she working with? Where were the others? Who else was in danger? Eleanor? Fin's mum, Helen? I couldn't even make a phone call to warn them to watch out. No one could reach us to tell me they had been attacked and left horribly injured or worse.

I was fighting not to panic. Then I realised I could hear the sour note of deceit mixed in with the truth in her taunts. The hag was lying, about some of those things at least. The problem was, she was saying so much, so fast, that everything got mixed up together. Somehow she was making me afraid and letting my imagination do the rest. I wasn't being mazed, exactly, but something similar was going on. Some things she'd said were definitely true. She knew what we had done to those other hags. She had come after us looking for payback. Other things were lies. She still had a use for the changeling.

I lunged forward and grabbed her by the throat. I pressed the old woman hard against her chair, bracing myself with my other hand. 'Tell me what the fuck is going on. Tell me how I get the swan maid back.'

I felt the hag shiver. She clutched the arms of her chair. So she could be frightened. Good. But I had to get answers out of her fast. Before someone looked in through the window and saw a hulking great thug choking the life out of this sweet little old lady. Had any of the neighbours seen me come in here?

'A portal closes after a living creature has crossed in each direction,' the hag managed to choke out. 'The swan maid went through and the baby came back. That has nothing to do with me.'

'You expect me to believe that?' I stared into her eyes. 'We just happened to be passing when the portal opened in that stone? To show us right where we could find the missing baby we were searching for?'

Her gaze slid away. 'When one such door closes, another will open, for as long as a living creature is in a place where they don't belong.'

Nothing she was saying about that was a lie, even if none of those were straight answers. I didn't care. I was convinced she had opened that portal as a trap somehow. She must have followed us up to the ridge. She had to be the one who had mazed Fin so she couldn't fly off and get help. But the hag wasn't lying about other portals opening up.

'Where is it?' I tightened my grip. 'The door she can use to get back here?'

She squirmed under my hand, still clutching the arms of her chair. 'I have no way to know.'

She wasn't lying about that. Shit. Now I wasn't scared, I was getting more and more angry.

'How is she supposed to find it? How's she going to even know that it's there?'

The hag seized my wrist with her soft, wrinkled hands. She couldn't break my hold on her throat, but she came close. She was scarily strong.

'That is no concern of mine,' she sneered with sudden venom. She also had no trouble talking clearly now, despite my fingers clamped around her windpipe.

'I saw my chance to test your mettle when I followed you here. I knew my kinswomen had crossed your path to their great misfortune, so I owed them that much. They were bold, but I am old and I intend to grow older still. I prefer to go unnoticed, but if I am cornered, I will fight, son of the greenwood. Before I fight, I choose to learn all I can of my foe.'

She looked me in the eye. She wasn't afraid of me now.

'Thus far? I have done you no harm, fool of a boy, nor have I hurt the swan maid. If she keeps her wits about her, she should be able to find her way home soon enough. I will not risk the guardian of the greenwood's wrath for your sake, nor make an enemy of the Master of Fords and Ferries over her. So you had better release me. If you injure me though I have done you no lasting wrong, my kinswomen will pursue you from the dark of one moon to the next. You will not see your death before it strikes from the shadows. You will not escape us.'

Furious as well as scared for Fin, I couldn't think straight. I sure as hell couldn't tell how much of what the hag said was true. I shook her like a dog with a rat. She didn't resist me, limp as a rag doll.

'Why?' I yelled, leaning so close I felt her breath on my face. 'Why are you doing this to us?'

'You need to learn to leave me and mine well alone, you fool of a boy. You must convince those who follow your lead to do the same.'

The old woman sank her fingernails deep into my forearm. I flinched. I couldn't help it. She wasn't armed with metal claws like the last hags I had fought, but that didn't matter. Infection from the wounds those filthy spikes had inflicted had made me the sickest I had ever been. My mother's blood means I'm hardly ever ill. Anyone without my greenwood heritage would most likely have died.

If I'm cut or bruised, I generally heal fast and clean. Those hags' attacks had left thick, ugly red scars on my shoulder and the back of my leg. I hated catching sight of them in a bathroom mirror after a shower. They weren't even useful, like the marks from the hamadryad's razor-sharp nails had been.

All these thoughts overwhelmed me. My hold on the hag loosened, just barely, but that was enough. She twisted free out my hand and disappeared. To be accurate, everything disappeared. The old woman, the overstuffed furniture, those heavy curtains, the floor, the walls and the roof. The house that shouldn't have been there had gone.

I stood on an uneven stretch of rough ground between the third cottage on the other side of the tarmac and the bridleway sign that marked the end of Pigeon Lane. Thickets of bramble clustered around a few lumps of limestone. Dense clumps of nettles followed the fence line. There was no paved path, no rose beds, no anything else at all.

Chapter Ten

I'm not sure how long I might have stayed standing there, as useless as a spare prick at a wedding. I was desperately trying to work out what the fuck to do. My mind was a total blank.

A car came past and parked on the verge, in ruts which fitted its wheelbase exactly. The woman who'd been driving got out and looked at me. 'Afternoon?'

Her uncertainty got me moving. The last thing I needed was her asking who I was and what I was doing. Clearly, she wasn't freaking out because she'd just seen an entire cottage vanish into thin air, complete with those roses around the door. So there was no point in me asking her when had she last not seen it.

Were Fin and I the only ones the hag had shown herself to? I was starting to think so. I remembered that copper who had taken my statement. He hadn't even seemed to hear me mention a possible witness who could confirm the time we arrived. The hag must have done that somehow. She must have been lurking close by, invisible, listening to every word.

'Afternoon.' I forced a smile and walked quickly towards our holiday cottage. Thankfully, the woman was distracted by the two kids getting out of her car's back seat. Around eight or nine years old, the boy and girl had exciting news.

'Oscar's got a hamster!'

'Can we have a hamster, Mummy? Pleeeeease.'

'We'll see what Mummy Megan says.'

I closed the front door behind me. The kids' chattering faded as the nice, ordinary woman and her nice, normal children went up the lane to their ordinary, normal house. While I had to work out how to deal with a fearsome ene-my – or enemies – who I couldn't see, when I was stuck in a village I couldn't leave, and I had no way to call for help, for Fin or myself.

Unless...? I grabbed my phone off the mantelpiece. No, still no hope of a signal, and no WiFi. The hag had vanished, but I'd be a fool to assume she was gone. All the same, I changed a few of the phone's notifications and stuck it in my pocket. If – no, when it found some reception, I wanted to know at once.

I listened for sounds upstairs. I couldn't hear anything. Was the changeling still asleep, or had it vanished when the hag disappeared? That would be one less complication to deal with. I took off my trainers and crept quietly up the stairs.

I cracked the back bedroom door and looked in. Bugger. The changeling was sound asleep in the drawer on the floor. The old woman had said she didn't want it. Of course she didn't. Leaving me lumbered with the sodding thing while I tried to work out how to find Fin would be a bonus as far as the hag was concerned.

I had to get Fin back before anything else happened. That had to be my priority. Because there was going to be a next thing. I had zero doubt about that. That hag wasn't going to give up until I gave in and promised to leave her kind alone. Until I promised to get everyone else who listened to me to give them a free pass.

I also saw, and smelled, the dirty nappy I'd left wadded up on the towel on the floor. Shit. I'd forgotten about that. I crept quietly into the bedroom and picked it up. Thankfully, the changeling didn't stir.

I went downstairs and scraped as much crap off the nappy and into the toilet with a wodge of bog roll as I could. I realised a minute too late that there was a liner inside the nappy as well. I wasn't about to fish that out of the loo, so I hoped it was biodegradable. I flushed everything away.

I chucked the nappy into the washing machine with one of the detergent pods I found under the sink. Setting the machine to a forty-degree wash cycle, I switched it on. I wished Fin was here to tell me off about adding microplastics to the water supply, as well as how much energy I was wasting by washing a single nappy on its own. As far as I was concerned, those things were the hag's fault.

I scrubbed my hands clean at the kitchen sink and washed the baby feeding bottle. I put the kettle on and made a pot of tea. Finding a saucepan, I put the bottle and the other bits in that and filled it from the kettle. Ten minutes in boiling water should sterilise everything. I put the pan on a ring and made a stack of toast. I was sodding starving.

When the water was really bubbling, I set the timer on the cooker. I took my tea and the plateful of toast into the living room and sat down on a sofa.

I forced myself to keep calm as I thought about where Fin could be. Wherever the fuck that was, there would be a way out. The hag had told the truth about that. What I didn't know was how Fin was going to find it. What could I do to help her? The first thing I needed to do, I decided as I ate my toast, was to pick apart the lies and find the scraps of truth in everything the hag had told me.

She said she wasn't going to piss off the Green Man by hurting me. That's to say, she wasn't going to do me lasting harm, which wasn't necessarily the same thing. So I'd have to be careful about that. She'd also said she wasn't going to get on the wrong side of the Master of Fords and Ferries by hurting Fin.

That was something new. I hadn't realised Wade the Ferryman took an interest in Fin and her family. I didn't think any of them knew that either. Though it made sense, when I thought about it. I had met Wade in the Fenlands, if 'met' was the right word. 'Encountered him' might be more accurate. He is another ancient power whose story has been forgotten, like the Green Man. In the Middle Ages, everyone had known who he was. Chaucer could get a quick laugh with a passing reference to Wade and his boat. No one had seen any need to write such familiar stories down. When the tales stopped being told, they had been lost.

If this hag was wary about offending Wade, that didn't necessarily mean Fin was safe. I had no idea what else might be on the other side of that portal. I was sure the hag would claim it wasn't her fault if something over there hurt Fin. The old witch would slither through any loophole she could claim to escape responsibility.

The hag could say whatever she liked. I'd make her regret every day of her unnaturally long life if Fin's feathers were so much as ruffled. If I could find her again, of course. Fear was nagging at me. A monster you can't see is definitely scarier. And how do you beat one that vanishes instead of staying to fight?

Forget the hag. I had to focus on Fin. Where could another portal have opened? I stared across the room at nothing in particular, trying to work out how to even start searching for it.

The hag had said Fin should be able to find her way back soon enough. That had been true. So the gateway was somewhere close? Maybe, maybe not, but I could start with the nearest possibilities. If I could come up with any possibilities.

Wade... What did I know about Wade? I remembered fragments of legends that said Wayland the Smith was Wade's son. One story said Wade and his brothers had forced three swan maids to 'marry' them by stealing their feathers. Those swan maids had managed to escape. Was that why Wade watched over their descendants? To make up for his sons' offences? As for Wayland, that reminded me of something—

The timer on the cooker went off, loud and insistent. I went into the kitchen and poured the boiling water from the saucepan carefully into the sink. I put the bits of the feeding bottle onto a sheet of paper towel to dry and cool down. That should be hygiene enough.

I went into the living room. What had I been thinking about before the timer beeped? A moment later, I remembered. Wayland. I'd seen an opening to somewhere unearthly one memorable night at Wayland's Smithy, high up on the Ridgeway a few years ago. I'd found out a place could be an ancient monument, an archaeological site and something a whole lot more eerie at the same time. Just like those three stones on the hill.

I spread the Ordnance Survey map out on the dining table. I found a lot more places in the area that were marked as a tumulus than I had expected. Several local hillsides had whole clusters of the five-pointed star on the OS map's key. I could spend the rest of this week checking out each one, with no guarantee I'd find anything useful. I remembered the time we'd found a burial mound in the Fens. That had been barely visible, worn down by aeons of weather and centuries of ploughing.

Something like that couldn't be a portal, surely? A gateway had to be more substantial. I finished eating my toast and drank the rest of my cold mug of tea. I remembered Fin saying something about circular walks between local ancient monuments. I found the basket on the coffee table with the tourist leaflets she'd been reading.

One simple sheet of A4 paper had been printed by a local enthusiast. Folded into three, it had a sketch of the stones where Fin had vanished on the front. I started reading. Apparently, the titled slab with the hole was called Batt's Quoit. Local legend said Batt had been a giant who challenged a giant from Gloucestershire to a stone-throwing competition in the hills above Bishop's Warren.

I really hoped there were no giants still lurking around here. I didn't need that complication right now. Not when I'd have to face it on my own. Fin and I had dealt with one before, but we'd needed a trio of wise women's help. The hag would love that, wouldn't she? The Green Man couldn't blame her if I ended up squashed like a bug. As long as she didn't deliberately send the monster after me.

The hag would also love to know I was wasting time worrying about things that might never happen. If a giant did turn up, I'd decide what to do then. I had to concentrate. Compartmentalise. I unfolded the leaflet. A hand-drawn map offered four different hikes between six different scheduled monuments and a couple of pubs. The ancient sites were listed on the other side of the sheet with more sketches. Whoever had done this was a decent artist.

After reading the leaflet, I decided to leave Callow's Cairn until last. That sketch showed a pile of stones which apparently marked a beacon site. A portal there didn't seem very likely to me. The Pylestone was a hefty triangular lump standing on its own. Could that be a gateway? I had no idea, so I had better take a look.

I'd check Batt's Quoit as well, just in case. In fact, I'd check that first. The hag had said another portal would open. She hadn't said how soon that would happen. She hadn't said it wouldn't open in the same place as before. Hags are sly. There were endless ways she could deceive me without telling outright lies.

Assuming the Batt's Quoit gateway stayed shut, three other places looked like possibilities. Fieldfare Long Barrow was a sizeable mound with trees on top. Tall stones framed a burial chamber's entrance on one side. Sometime in the 1760s, the landowner had excavated that and found human bones.

Old Shute Gate was two standing stones close to the edge of a small wood. If this sketch was accurate, I reckoned they might be close enough to make a doorway. Regardless, there had to be a remote chance I could find a dryad or hamadryads in those trees. Right now, I'd promise them whatever they wanted if they could help me find Fin.

Stanton's Tumps was a collection of smaller barrows in the middle of a field. I couldn't tell from the sketch if there were any visible standing stones, and the brief description didn't say so. I'd have to go and take a look myself.

Now I had a plan. I matched the hand-drawn map to the Ordnance Survey's hills and footpaths. While I was going from one of the leaflet's sites to the next, I'd pass a few of those marked tumuli. So I could rule them out or take a closer look. I went to find a pen in Fin's backpack, still hung on the coat hooks by the door. I marked those five-pointed stars on the circular walk routes as best I could.

So far, so good, but I wished I could do some proper research. Local legends or more recent stories of strange goings-on in any of these places might give me useful clues. I hated going into this search blind. I hated everything about this. I wanted to take Fin to one of those pubs on the circular walks. We were supposed to be here on holiday, not fighting to find a way back to each other so we could work out how to escape this sodding hag.

Tough shit. I couldn't get online to check anything, so that was just too bad. If this idea turned out to be a waste of time, I'd think again. Yes, checking these places would take a good few hours, but there was plenty of daylight left. If I was still out on the hills when it got dark, my greenwood blood gives me excellent night vision. If anything, the long summer twilight and the waxing moon would work in my favour. It was about damn time something did.

I fetched my backpack and took out my water bottle to refill it. I checked my compass was in the side pocket. Aled volunteers for his local mountain rescue in North Wales. Every year he has more hair-raising stories about tourists who've learned the hard way not to rely on an app on their phones. What food could I take with me? I wasn't going to waste time cooking and eating before I headed out.

Going into the kitchen, I saw the baby bottle on the draining board. I heard the changeling making noise upstairs. It wasn't crying, exactly, more letting anyone around know it was awake. I had completely forgotten about the bloody thing. Bollocks.

I couldn't leave the little monster to scream its head off while I went into the hills. I wouldn't put it past the hag to do her little old lady act and ring on a few doorbells. If she could convince the neighbours to break down the door, someone would call the police when they found an abandoned baby. Did getting me arrested and locked up count as doing lasting harm? I'd bet the hag would say it didn't.

The changeling was getting louder. I went up the stairs. Was the thing hungry again? When had I last fed it? I honestly wasn't sure. Probably more than two to three hours ago. I needed to feed it again if I wanted the thing to shut up. If I wanted to avoid ending up with what looked like a dead infant. Probably the only thing worse than the police finding me with a baby I couldn't explain would be them finding me with a dead one, whether that happened in this cottage or somewhere out on the hills when I was digging a tiny, shallow grave.

I pushed open the bedroom door and stood over the towel-lined drawer. The changeling squinted up at me. It was identical to Alice. It looked like a helpless, harmless baby. Then it blinked, and that momentary glimpse of its red-brown eyes made me shiver. What the fuck were we going to do if the hag who had made the thing didn't want it back?

The changeling started to cry. Well, not cry exactly, because I didn't see any tears. It shut up when I lifted it out of the drawer. That was something. I carried it carefully downstairs. It squawked when I put it on the sofa, so I picked it up and took it into the kitchen. Working one-handed again, I put the kettle on.

I looked at the changeling in the crook of my arm. 'You're an utter pain in the arse, do you know that?'

It didn't say anything. That was just as well. I'd have dropped it if it answered me. It simply looked up, vaguely expectant. The same as Alice had. I made up a bottle of formula as quickly as I could with one hand. Leaving the baby milk to cool, I sat at the dining table with the changeling on my knee, resting against my forearm. I studied the OS map.

How far could I expect to walk and get back inside a three-hour window, if that was as long as I was going to get between having to feed the changeling? I'd have to factor in boiling the baby bottle every time, and making up the next feed. Was there a way to sterilise the bottle faster? Probably, if I could get online and look that up. For now, I'd have to settle for boiling it.

The prospect of being out as dusk turned to darkness didn't bother me. I was hardly going to get a decent night's sleep if I had to get up every three hours. Even if I was able to sleep while Fin was still missing, which I doubted. Even so, I'd have to make at least two trips, most likely three, to check those possible portal sites. That wasn't allowing time for finding something unexpected at one of the other places with a tumulus marked on the map.

Unless there was a quicker way to find Fin. I went out into the back garden and walked down to the old apple tree. I laid my free hand on the closest branch. 'I'm looking for the swan maid.'

The dryad radar reached further and faster than it ever had before. My hopes rose. The hag had said Fin could find her own way home as long as she kept her wits about her. I was sure she would have been doing everything she could think of once she realised the hole in the tilted slab was no more use to her. If she was already on her way here, I didn't need to head for those hills.

I couldn't sense Fin anywhere though. My throat closed up. Crushing disappointment didn't begin to cover it. I forced myself to take a deep breath. Concentrate. Compartmentalise.

I hadn't found Fin, but there was no trace of the hag either. I'd have recognised that after my encounters with her kinswomen last year. That was something. I still had a plan. I still had—

I was still carrying the changeling. That did show up on the dryad radar. Barely. The spark right here beside me was faint and flickering. It wasn't the same as the hag, not exactly. Before I could work out what was different, the changeling started to wriggle and grizzle.

'Thank you.' I let go of the tree and hurried back inside.

I picked up the baby bottle and walked through to the living room. The changeling sucked down the formula as eagerly as it had before. Then it coughed and sicked up everything it had swallowed. Milk covered the front of its onesie. Shit. What was wrong?

I suddenly had a horrible feeling that some changelings in fairy stories sickened and died, no matter how well they were cared for. Did the hag know that was going to happen to this one? Was this the next step in her plan to torment us?

I sat the changeling up. It belched like someone who'd just necked a pint of lager. Was that the problem? Babies needed to be burped, didn't they? I thought they did, but I was so far out of my depth it wasn't funny. I needed Fin. She had to know more about babies than me, because I knew fuck all.

I waited to see if any more milk came up. It didn't, but the changeling started wriggling and grizzling again. I offered it the bottle. That seemed to do the trick. By the time it had finished the milk, the changeling was drowsy. Drowsy or sickening for something? Shit, I didn't know.

I carried the little monster upstairs. I cautiously felt its backside. I didn't think I needed to change its nappy, and I didn't want to wake the thing without a good reason. That onesie definitely needed a wash, but I didn't have any other clothes it could wear. Would it be okay left wrapped in a towel? That probably wasn't a good idea. I'd felt colder than I'd expected, out in the garden just now.

Should I leave it on its front or its back. If it sicked up more milk, would it choke lying on its back? I was still trying to decide as I laid it down in the drawer. The changeling's head lolled to one side as it shifted its little hands and feet.

Okay, any milk it brought up while it was asleep should dribble onto the towel. Eyes still closed, it seemed to be settling down. That was good enough for me.

I went downstairs and forced myself to wash out and boil the baby bottle. I made up a feed while the plastic was still hot, which was probably against the proper advice. Right now, that was too bad. I put the bottle in the fridge.

I swapped my trainers for my hiking boots. I put on a sweatshirt. Grabbing my backpack, the OS map and the circular walks leaflet, I locked up and headed out. As I left the tarmac to follow the bridleway, I set the alarm on my phone to go off in an hour and a half. I stuck that in the zip pocket of my combats along with the cottage keys and walked faster. I had to cover as much ground as possible before I was forced to turn back.

Chapter Eleven

The hike to Batt's Quoit felt a lot shorter now I knew where I was going. It didn't make the hillside any less steep. I was ready for a breather when I reached the stones.

There was nothing to see from the pointy end of the wedge. I walked around to the tilted portal stone. I looked at it, keeping the hole in the corner of my eye. Nothing. That was still only a hole in a slab of rock. I realised I was clenching my fists. No. I couldn't let this get to me. I hadn't seriously expected anything else.

The next place to check was the Pylestone. If I'd been out for a holiday ramble, I'd have been unimpressed. The sketches on the circular walks leaflet had nothing to give me any scale. When I finally found it, half covered in brambles, the solitary stone was barely tall enough to reach my elbow. I circled it anyway, trying not to look directly at it, in case I caught a glimpse of something in my peripheral vision. Nothing. I went up close and examined it from all sides. I couldn't see any way this grey, triangular lump of solid rock could possibly be a portal.

I checked the time on my phone. I still had no trace of a signal. Was the hag somewhere around, watching me? I found an elder tree and searched the area with dryad radar. No hag, no Fin, no anyone else who might be able to help me. No late afternoon ramblers either. That was probably a plus if Fin was going to step out of thin air.

I carried on walking. How close did the hag need to be to block phone signals? I should talk to my mum about this stuff. She would explain without demanding something in return. I wondered if the hag had somehow wrecked our SIM cards. If she had, she could be anywhere and our phones still wouldn't work. That would cut both ways though. SIM cards could be replaced without the hag necessarily knowing that had happened. But I'd have to get to a shop that sold new ones to do that.

The next stretch of this hike took me past some of the tumuli I had marked on the leaflet. I could have easily walked right past the shallow, grassy bumps if I hadn't known they were there. I had no idea what they had once been, and I didn't care. What mattered was they couldn't be portals.

Next? Fieldfare Long Barrow. I tried not to get my hopes up. I checked the time again. If the long barrow was a write-off as well, if I really got a move on, I might be able to check out Stanton's Tumps before I had to head to the cottage to feed the changeling again. Though I didn't want to think about what I was going to do after that. The more I thought about Callow's Cairn, the more I was convinced it was going to be a non-starter.

I arrived at the long barrow. Whoever had drawn these sketches seriously needed introducing to the concept of using a consistent scale. The barrow was a hell of a lot bigger than it looked in the picture. Mounded earth stretched for maybe forty metres, end to end, and it had to be over three metres tall. Its highest point wasn't easy to find. The top was covered in grass, shrubs and trees that must have grown from windblown seed.

When I'd been thinking the barrow was a whole lot smaller, I had assumed the sketch showed saplings. Now I saw those were mature rowans and flourishing hazels. I couldn't be sure until I got closer, but I thought a couple of whitebeams were up there as well. Nice trees, but no dryads or hamadryads would have any particular interest in them. It didn't look like I was going to find allies here. Bollocks.

I was standing on the public footpath where a gap in the hedge offered a decent view. The barrow was easily thirty metres away. I looked at the leaflet and grudgingly allowed the sketch was accurate enough if you were looking from this far away. The uprights and lintel framing the entrance to the ancient burial chamber were immediately obvious, facing the footpath. With the sun sinking to my left, the pale grey limestone framed a dark hollow.

I shoved the leaflet into my pocket. I'd have to get closer to see if that entrance was any sort of portal. If I was going to do that, I wanted both my hands free.

There wasn't a stile and I couldn't see any trace of a path leading towards the barrow. The top strand of barbed wire along the wire-mesh fence half a metre inside the hedge was a solid hint there was no public access. I carefully eased through the hedge, silently apologising to the hawthorns and dogwoods. I pushed down the barbed wire and managed to get over the fence without tearing my trousers or worse. Technically I was trespassing, but that's not a criminal offence as long as you don't do any criminal damage. Besides, there was no one around to see me.

I approached the barrow cautiously. It would be useful to get some warning from the faded scars on my forearm if anything nasty was lurking in there. I couldn't rely on that now though, so I had better be wary. The burial chamber's lintel jutted out of the turf-covered mound slightly higher than my waist. When I was still a couple of metres away, I crouched down. No good. The shadows hid whatever might be inside there.

Sod it. I stood up and got out my phone to use the torch setting. Before I did that, I scanned for any sign of movement among the trees and shrubs on top of the mound. None of those were close enough to reach, even for someone my height, so using dryad radar was out. All I saw were leaves shifting in the evening breeze.

I crouched down and looked into the burial chamber. The light from my phone showed me three solid slabs of limestone a metre or so wide and maybe a metre and a half tall. They had been set upright in the ground to make a rough rectangle, though they weren't right next to each other or to the door uprights. The space between the big slabs had been filled with courses of skilfully laid smaller stones.

Leaning forward, braced with on one hand on the lintel and twisting awkwardly, I checked the chamber's roof. The biggest stone slabs I'd seen so far had been laid across those uprights. I wondered how heavy they were. The earth floor was covered with gravel. Dark drifts in the corners showed me where leaves had blown in and couldn't get out again. There was no sign that anything had disturbed them since last autumn and probably the autumn before that.

I gritted my teeth, trying to swallow my disappointment. I stood up. What now? I decided I might as well go right around the mound since I was here. I stepped back a few paces, wondering whether to go widdershins or deasil.

Movement snagged my eye. A rabbit darted across the pasture. It disappeared into the darkening shadows along the hedgerow. No, not a rabbit. I realised that was a hare. Was it the hag tracking me to see where I went and what I did? We knew they could change shape like that.

I tried to see where the long-eared shadow had gone. Bollocks. Whatever it was, I couldn't see it anywhere now. I looked for a place to climb up the side of the barrow. Dryad radar should be able to find it, if I could get hold of a tree. Then I'd know what it really was.

That wasn't going to be easy. The mound's grassy sides were pretty much vertical for about the first metre and a half. From the construction I'd seen inside the burial chamber's entrance, it was a fair bet a retaining drystone wall ran right the way around.

I went left. That was the quickest way to get to the other side. I had to find out if that hare was more than it seemed before it got too far away. Hopefully I'd find a way to reach a tree. I also wouldn't be seen from the footpath, which could be a plus. I'd probably get away with being caught peering into the entrance. I could say I'd been passing and was curious. No harm, no foul. Climbing on top of an ancient monument would be a lot harder to explain.

I walked fast. When I reached the end of the barrow and looked along the length of the mound, I realised it wasn't nearly as solid as it had seemed from the side. The slope was shallower here, and I could probably scramble up, but I could see the biggest trees had taken root in deep hollows. Had more burial chambers inside the barrow collapsed? Regardless, I couldn't risk an unsuspected void giving way under my weight. I would be royally screwed if I got stuck here with a broken leg, and Fin would have no idea where to find me when she got back.

I still wanted to find that sodding hare. I broke into a run along the far side of the barrow. This was even worse. A long stretch of the retaining wall had been quarried out a long time ago. Stones scattered among the tall grasses were weathered and thick with moss. The rest must have been carted away, to be slaked to make lime mortar, or for marl to improve the soil. Gentleman landowners with too much time on their hands might have invented archaeology in days gone by, but this heap of stones would have been a valuable resource for whoever farmed his land.

I still couldn't reach any sodding trees. They were too high up and far away, beyond tangles of betony, foxgloves and yarrow. Trying to climb on the mound anywhere here would be even more dangerous. The trees cast long, dark shadows, hiding unseen holes and loose stones.

How far away had that hare got by now? Maybe it was a normal animal. Even if dryad radar showed me it was the hag, what was I going to do? Chasing after her would be pointless, as long as I was on my own. That might even be what she wanted. She could have come here to delay and distract me.

I used my phone's torch to take another look at the leaflet. It was getting badly crumpled and grime from my hands had smudged the map. I needed to be more careful. Did I still have time to get to Stanton Tumps before I had to head to the cottage and feed that bloody changeling?

I suddenly smelled something that wasn't sun-warmed grass or leafy scents from branches waving over my head. This was darker and damper. I shone my phone's torch along the side of the mound. The light picked out newly split stone, pale against the black of freshly turned soil. A sizeable chunk of the barrow had collapsed, spilling uprooted bushes across the turf.

The evening breeze rustled through the leaves above me. Closer and lower, I heard a different sound, low and resonant. Very faint, it was like someone blowing over the neck of an empty bottle. I shoved my phone and the leaflet into my pockets. I definitely wanted my hands free now.

My eyes were adjusting to the dusk. As I walked slowly forward, that resonant sound grew louder. I skirted the edge of the loose soil, looking closely at the barrow. I could make out the top half of a tunnel lined with slabs of limestone reaching deep into the mound. It was choked with churned earth, and a couple of slabs lay half buried at awkward angles, showing where this end had fallen apart. If there had been an entrance on this side of the barrow, that must have been buried when the retaining wall gave way. I bent down and scooped up a handful of soil. Watching the tunnel intently, I rubbed my fingers and thumb together, feeling the moisture. The earth had barely started to dry out. This had happened today.

I noticed something else. Taller grass which the cascade of stones and soil hadn't covered up were bending towards the tunnel. The evening breeze wasn't doing that. I licked a finger and held it out. Air was definitely being drawn into that darkness. So where was it going?

I reached down, still not taking my eyes off the tunnel. My fingers found a smallish loose stone. I weighed it in my hand and took a few sidesteps to get a better angle. I hurled the stone at the tunnel mouth as hard as I could. I missed. The stone thudded into loose earth. Sod it. I tried again, not throwing the stone as hard. This time it disappeared into the darkness. I stood absolutely still and listened for any sound of stone hitting stone. All I could hear was the soft, steady movement of air through the portal.

Great. I'd found the gateway the hag had promised. Now what? Should I get as close as I could and shout for Fin, hoping she could hear me? Should I crawl into that darkness and hope I could find her on the other side? If I had seriously thought I'd have even half a chance of success doing that, I would have tried. Never mind how much I hate going under-ground and how much that looked like a tight squeeze. But I knew Fin would be the first to tell me it was a bloody stupid idea. What if this new gateway closed behind me? We'd both be trapped fuck knows where.

The alarm on my phone went off. I nearly pissed myself. I fumbled the handset out of my pocket and shut off the deaf-ening noise. That was another good reason for me to stay out of that tunnel. If Fin and I both disappeared, I hated to think what Eleanor, Blanche or Zan might find in the cottage's back bedroom when they realised we were missing and came to try and find us. That wouldn't happen for at least a week. Neither of us was expected at work before Monday. They'd probably spend the day ringing each other, trying to find out where we might be. Come to that, did any of them even have the holiday cottage's address? I didn't think I'd told Eleanor more than the name of the village.

Actually, no, I realised. Fin and I were supposed to be leaving on Saturday morning. Whoever came in to clean the cottage for the owners would find the Toyota still parked out-side. Our clothes would be there, along with Fin's laptop, and the food in the fridge. As well as whatever was lying in that towel-lined drawer. The police would be the ones raising the alarm and explaining to whoever turned up next that their holiday was ruined. If Fin and I could find our way back – when we found our way back – I couldn't begin to think how we'd explain our way out of that mess.

So I wasn't going into the tunnel. But how the fuck was I going to let Fin know there was a gateway for her here? I clenched my fists, fighting my frustration. Getting pissed off wouldn't help. I had to make some decisions, and I had to do that fast. I had to get to the cottage to feed the changeling before one of the neighbours heard it screaming the place down.

My phone alarm went off again. I'd put the bloody thing on snooze without realising. Still, the noise put the brakes on my useless thoughts. I made sure the alarm was properly turned off this time. Then I took the circular walks leaflet out of my pocket and wrapped it around a fist-sized rock. Moving cautiously on the loose, damp earth, testing my footing before every step, I got as close to the portal as I dared. I tossed the paper-wrapped stone into the darkness. I half expected to hear it hit an unseen wall with a dull clunk. It didn't, and the stealthy flow of air carried on brushing past me. That gate was staying open.

For how long? I headed for the footpath. Once I'd dealt with the changeling, I'd come straight back. While I was on my way to the cottage, I'd work out what to do next.

By the time I put the key in the front door lock, I hadn't come up with any better plan than sitting beside the tunnel through the long barrow and waiting to see if Fin appeared. On the plus side, the changeling wasn't making much noise upstairs. Well, it wasn't until it heard me come in. I dumped my backpack and took off my hiking boots.

As soon as I opened the bedroom door and looked in, the changeling started screaming. I picked it up and realised its nappy was soaking wet. I put it down on the floor to change it. Almost as fast, I had second thoughts. Carrying the little monster downstairs, I fetched the bottle of formula. This time it didn't seem keen to feed. Was I doing something wrong, or was it feeling ill? I had no idea.

I managed to get the changeling to take about half the milk. I remembered to sit it up to burp. It started farting.

That nappy was too wet to absorb anything, and shit leaked out, staining the onesie and my trousers. The changeling started grizzling, and I honestly couldn't blame it.

Right. I'd better deal with this. For a start, that onesie really had to go in the wash now. I sat the changeling up and started undoing the poppers that ran down the front. As I eased its little arms out of the sleeves, I realised that shit had oozed up its back as well as out through the nappy's legs.

Crap, literally. The changeling needed a bath. How the hell was I going to manage that when this place only had a shower room? I needed a shower myself after everything I had done today, but I sure as shit wasn't going to take this wriggling, squalling thing in there and try to hold on and wash it when it was slippery with water and soap.

Had I seen a bucket under the sink? I went to look, carrying the changeling still wearing its stinking nappy and holding the filthy onesie in my other hand. I managed to open the cupboard under the sink with one foot. I had remembered right. A newish-looking bucket in there was full of assorted spray bottles of cleaners.

'I'm sorry,' I said to the changeling as I put it down on the floor.

It looked startled. The vinyl probably felt cold against its bare skin. What mattered to me was that would wipe clean. I dropped the onesie on the floor by the washing machine and turned on the taps at the sink. Once I'd washed my hands, I emptied my pockets onto the countertop. Stripping down to my underpants, I put everything else I had been wearing into the washing machine with another laundry pod and the filthy onesie. I switched the machine on before I remembered the reusable nappy was still in there. Sod it. Giving that a second wash couldn't hurt.

The changeling was crying. I ran upstairs and grabbed towels and a dry nappy. Coming into the kitchen, I put the bucket into the sink, turned the hot tap on full and rinsed it out as thoroughly as I could. Fetching Fin's unperfumed shower gel for sensitive skin, I adjusted the mixer tap to fill the bucket with tepid water. I knelt down and took off the changeling's reeking nappy. I saw the little creature had a sore red backside. That was probably one reason why it had been crying. What the hell could I do about that?

First things first. I picked up the changeling and added a squirt of shower gel to the warm water. I swirled that around to make a few bubbles and lowered the changeling carefully into the bucket. Having hands as big as mine made that easier, but I was still scared it would slip out of my grip, or I would hurt it by holding on too hard. I washed its little backside as thoroughly as I could. The changeling didn't look happy, but I think it was too confused to start crying again.

I took it out of the bucket and left it lying on a clean towel on the floor. I went upstairs to look through Fin's things. She doesn't usually wear make-up, but she had packed what she needed to clean everything off her face after the wedding. I found some moisturiser. I decided that couldn't do the changeling's bum any harm, and I couldn't see anything better.

Downstairs, the changeling had peed on the towel. More laundry, and there were only a handful of those detergent pods left under the sink. I dried the changeling with a clean corner of the towel and smeared moisturiser over the red bits. Thankfully, its belly button stump looked okay. As I put a clean nappy on the little monster, it was shivering. I wrapped it in a towel and carried it through to the living room, to see if it was hungry now. To my relief, it drank the rest of the bottle, propped in the crook of my arm as I rested against the sofa cushions.

I woke up, startled. I'd heard a noise. What the fuck was that? It took me a second to realise the feeding bottle had fallen onto the wooden floor. Bollocks. I hadn't meant to go to sleep. A glance at the clock reassured me. I had only dozed off for ten minutes or so. The changeling was still asleep, bundled up snug and dry in a towel. But what if I had moved in my sleep and shoved it off the sofa onto the hard wooden floor? What if I had rolled over and crushed it under me? That thought made my blood run cold.

Moving slowly and carefully, I got to my feet and carried the sleeping changeling upstairs. I laid it in the drawer and put a hand towel over its legs and belly to keep it warm. I yawned as I sat on the edge of the bed. I wanted to lie down too. If I did, I'd be asleep in seconds. I was absolutely knackered. I couldn't go to bed though. Not while Fin was still somewhere out there.

I went downstairs and emptied the bucket down the plughole in the shower. I had a shower myself, hoping that would wake me up. It didn't. If anything, once I was clean and wrapped in a couple of towels, I felt even more sleepy. I was forced to admit I'd been kidding myself. There was no way I was going up to Fieldfare Long Barrow again tonight.

I was also absolutely starving. I took a microwave curry out of the fridge. Before I nuked that, I fetched the feeding bottle and washed it out. Once that was bubbling in a pan of hot water, I cooked the curry and a packet of rice and sat down to eat. That would keep me awake while I sterilised the bottle. I wouldn't wake up to the smoke alarm going off and the stink of melted plastic.

I was still hungry when I finished eating. There was another curry in the fridge. I was tempted, but that was Fin's dinner. She'd be hungry when she got back. She was going to get back. I had to believe that. I couldn't help wondering how long I would be waiting though. Long enough to run out of food, for myself and the changeling? We were getting through that tin of formula and I'd need more nappies soon.

I checked how long the pan on the stove had been boiling, and went to look at the OS map out on the dining table. Where was the nearest village big enough to have a shop? As long as Fin's car wouldn't start, I'd have to walk there. I could hike cross-country, straight as the crow – or the swan – might fly…

I looked up and stared at nothing. An idea was floating just out of reach. A moment later, it hit me like a smack in the face. I ran up the stairs, taking them two and three at a time. In the front bedroom, I emptied Fin's suitcase onto the bed. I turned over her clothes, raking them apart with my hands. Nothing.

I realised anyone outside would be able to see what I was doing. They'd also see I'd lost the towels I'd been wearing on the stairs. I quickly drew the curtains. Fin had hung the dress bag for her bridesmaid's frock on the front of the wardrobe. I pulled the zip down so hard it jammed. I forced myself to go more slowly. Taking the frock out of the bag, I shook it. The shoes and the headdress of silk flowers fell onto the floor. I didn't care about them. I carefully turned the dress inside out. I saw a fleck of white caught in a seam. A tiny, downy feather.

My hands were shaking as I pulled it free. I pressed my finger and thumb together as hard as I could. Could this fluffy scrap go through that portal? Could it find its way to Fin? Would that tell her she had a way to get here, if only she could find it?

The cooker timer went off. I grabbed my book from the table by my side of the bed. I was reading a decent thriller about an engineer whose flight home had been delayed after he had already gone through airport security. He got stuck on the wrong side of very bad guys with no way to escape or find help. I knew how the poor sod felt. I put the little feather between the pages. I'd been lucky to find that one and I didn't dare risk losing it.

I pulled on clean clothes and went downstairs. I emptied the hot water out of the pan and put the baby bottle bits on the kitchen counter to cool down. Going out into the back garden, I walked down to the apple trees in the lingering twilight. I laid my hand on the closest gnarled grey trunk.

'Thank you for passing my message on to the Green Man. I need your help again. I have to get word to the Master of Fords and Ferries.'

Begging now, desperate, I summoned up the memory of meeting Wade in the Fens. Poling a boat made from a hollowed-out log, he had been tall and lean, wearing a long, hooded cloak. Grey-haired and bearded, his eyes shining like stars in his weathered face. I'd seen him smiling from time to time, as if he found mortal people amusing.

'Fin needs his help,' I told the apple tree. 'I have one of her feathers. I'm going to let it go. I think it will find her, to show her there's a way to get back here. I don't know how to help her find the portal though. Please, if there's any way you can let Wade know what's going on, if there's any way he can help her...'

I couldn't think what else to say. I was exhausted. The old apple tree's leaves rattled overhead, Was that some sort of answer or a gust of wind? I couldn't tell.

I took the paperback out of my pocket. I ran my thumb over the edge of the pages to fan them out. The tiny white feather flew free and darted off. It moved so fast, I lost sight of it inside a second. Surely it moved too quickly for the night breeze to be carrying it off.

What now? I couldn't see any point in trying dryad radar. If the hag was lurking somewhere close, there was fuck all I could do about it. The only thing I could do now was hope. That and make up another bottle of sodding baby formula before I locked the doors and went to bed.

I did that and went upstairs. I stripped off and stood looking at the bed I'd shared with Fin on our first night here. The duvet was covered with her clothes. I couldn't face tidying up. I dropped my book on top of the heap and fell into the unused bed in the back bedroom, to get whatever sleep I could before the bloody changeling woke me up.

Chapter Twelve

The changeling wanted a feed a bit after three in the morning. I fed the thing and changed its nappy, but it wouldn't settle down. Thankfully, it wasn't crying. It just stayed awake. We sat on the sofa while the feeding bottle boiled on the stove. I might as well get that done if I had to be up.

I waved a finger in front of the changeling's eyes, wondering how well it could see. No further than around thirty centimetres, as far as I could tell. Its grip was stronger than I expected. It grabbed hold when I brushed a fingertip on its tiny palms. Its little toes scrunched up as well, when I stroked the soles of its feet. Did all babies react like this? I had no idea.

Thankfully, it finally dozed off. I left it on the sofa while I sorted out the feeding bottle. Then I remembered I'd put some laundry on, so I emptied the machine. I could hang my clothes on the washing line out in the back garden when it got light, but the changeling's onesie had better stay out of sight. I draped that over the heated towel rail in the shower room, along with the reusable nappy. Then I remembered to go back and switch the rail on so the things would actually dry.

The changeling was still asleep on the sofa. I took it upstairs and put it in its drawer. Lying down on the bed, I hoped I could doze for a couple more hours before Tuesday officially arrived.

The changeling woke up at a quarter to six, making little muttering noises. I was already stirring. I reached for my phone on the bedside table and saw how early it was. Bollocks. I also realised I'd better put the damn phone on charge. Even if I couldn't make calls or go online, I needed to know how much time I had left once I got to the long barrow this morning.

I rolled over onto my front and reached down into the drawer. I lay there, letting the changeling swipe at my hand with its tiny fists. It found my little finger and grabbed hold. As long as I didn't have to get up. My eyes were already closing again. 'How about five more minutes?'

I opened my eyes when the changeling somehow got my finger in its mouth and sucked surprisingly hard. I was awake now. I might as well get up. The changeling looked a bit annoyed when I took my hand away, then it started chewing its own fist. Hungry? Probably.

I got dressed. Picking up my phone reminded me... I'd meant to do something with that? I was so knackered I couldn't hold on to more than one thought at a time. Oh yes. Low battery. My charger was in the socket on my side of the bed in the front room.

Plugging in my phone, I looked at the clothes I'd thrown everywhere. Fin wouldn't be impressed to find that when she got back. I started picking things off the bed. The questions and worries I'd had last night crowded my thoughts again. What else could I do to help Fin get back? How long should I stay here, waiting and hoping? Should I go up to Fieldfare Long Barrow? If so, how soon? Was there any way I could lure the hag into some sort of trap and force her to help?

I couldn't answer any of those questions, but I could tidy up. I carried on doing that until the changeling started making more noise. I took it downstairs, wrapped up warm in a towel, and fetched the bottle of formula I'd made up last thing, last night.

'I'll dress you in a bit,' I told it as we settled down on the sofa.

The changeling was more interested in its breakfast. Good. As soon as it was full, I'd feed myself. I was sodding starving. I didn't reckon much to my chances of cooking bacon, eggs and toast one-handed though.

I got most of the milk down the changeling. It burped up some wind. I waited to see if input prompted output like yesterday. Yes, it filled its nappy. I carried the little monster through to the shower room and cleaned it up in there. I put the reusable nappy on it this time. Using that would stretch out my supply of disposables. Not by much though. Nappies were definitely my biggest problem. I'd run out of those by this time tomorrow. Also, while Fin's moisturiser seemed to have done a bit of good, I was sure there had to be more effective sore-bum creams.

What else would I need, and when? I got the surprisingly wriggly changeling into its clean and dry onesie. Going into the kitchen, I read the small print on the tin of baby formula. That weighed eight hundred grams and held approximately 186 scoops. That was a weirdly specific number for an esti- mate, but never mind. Using three scoops to a feed, it would last us for a week. Longer than I had guessed.

I took the changeling into the living room. I grabbed a couple of cushions off the closest sofa with my free hand and carried them into the kitchen. Making the changeling a sort of nest on the floor by the back door where it could see me solved the problem of how to make a pot of tea and cook my breakfast without getting the little monster too close to hot water or spitting fat. I washed out the feeding bottle first though, and started it sterilising in boiling water for what felt like the hundredth time.

I thought things through aloud as I cooked. My voice seemed to help keep the changeling quiet. It also stopped me thinking how silent the cottage was without Fin here.

'Can I leave you here alone while I walk to somewhere with a shop? Where's that going to be? Should I take a bus? Do you think there's a timetable at that bus stop on the green, or do they rely on everybody having a working phone these days?'

If there wasn't a timetable, I'd just have to wait. For how long? Buses weren't going to be very frequent. I'd grown up in the countryside. I knew that without having to go online.

'What do I need to buy? Another feeding bottle and sterilising fluid. A couple more onesies and laundry liquid. I'd better make a list.'

I wasn't going to trust my memory after the pitiful amount of sleep I'd had over the past forty-eight hours.

'A proper baby carrier? Are you big enough to go in one of those? If you are, I could take you with me up to the long barrow.' I had no idea if a newborn could go in one of those slings I'd seen visitors to Blithehurst using. Well, I was sure they would come with idiot-proof instructions for the sleep-deprived, given the detailed safety warnings on that tin of formula.

'Right. Breakfast. We put the bacon on the slice of toast that's got the mustard. We put the egg on top of that. Then we put ketchup on the other slice of toast, like this, and we're ready to go.'

The feeding bottle had boiled for long enough. I put the bits on the draining board to dry. I carried my plate into the living room. As I ate, I studied the map, careful not to drip tomato sauce onto the paper. Cheddar looked to be the closest place sizeable enough to have a decent range of shops. Hopefully the town would be busy enough that no one would look twice at me buying nappies and other baby stuff. Even though the story about a newborn going missing for a couple of hours had made the TV news, strangers outside Bishop's Warren shouldn't have any reason to think I'd had anything to do with it.

But that was definitely a bus ride away. If I got out on the village green here, with a carrier bag loaded with baby stuff, anyone who lived in Bishop's Warren would look at me and wonder. They'd have heard about a baby going missing. The people who lived on Pigeon Lane most likely knew Fin and

I had arrived without a child. They had to know baby Alice had been left outside this cottage.

If the neighbours were slow to get suspicious, I reckoned there was every chance the hag would give them a nudge. She had to be around here somewhere. My phone still couldn't find any signal.

'Could she follow me onto the bus?' I asked the squawking changeling as I went into the kitchen and picked it up.

Hags using iron claws to attack people was one thing, but could they get inside a vehicle made of metal? Could a hag travel unseen, fast enough to follow a bus? What if she followed in the form of a hare? Those could move fast, though I wasn't sure how long they could sustain whatever their top speed might be. Hares didn't run marathons. They sprinted to get out of trouble.

'Maybe I could take a bus there and walk back?' I sat at the dining table with the changeling on my lap. I studied the OS map, using my finger to follow what looked like the most useful long-distance footpaths. Those went over serious hills. It took me a moment to remember how to calculate walking time over distance allowing for terrain. Five kilometres an hour plus five minutes for every fifty-metre contour line. There were a lot of contours. Following the road would be quicker, but more dangerous. Drivers not paying attention can flatten unexpected pedestrians on country roads.

'That'll be a hell of a hike,' I commented to the changeling. 'And there's definitely no way I can take you with me, so can I possibly get there and back in under three hours? Is there anywhere closer?'

Being lumbered with the changeling was making getting anything done near impossibly difficult. Without doing me any actual bodily harm that would piss off the Green Man. Had the hag done this deliberately, or was it an added bonus? What did she expect me to do with the little monster? Should I dump it on someone else's doorstep a couple of villages away? No. If I did anything like that, I was certain the hag would use that against us.

My tea was cold. I went into the kitchen, made up yet another bottle of baby milk, refilled the kettle and put it on. I checked the digital clock on the microwave. I was startled to see it a fair bit later than I thought. Where had the morning gone? I certainly didn't have time to get into Cheddar and back before the changeling needed its next feed.

Could I get up to Fieldfare Long Barrow though? I wondered if Wade had got my message. If he had, what had he done? Where was Fin and what had happened to her? Was I ever going to find out? What the hell was I going to tell her family if I couldn't get her back? My throat closed up and my eyes stung.

I heard vehicles outside the front of the cottage, pulling up in the lane. Doors slammed and I heard two men talking, though I couldn't catch what they said. Shit. Had the police taken Sonja seriously when she insisted a big man with short hair had brought her real baby safely home? How was I going to explain that?

I walked cautiously to the front window. I didn't want whoever was outside to see me. Fin's Toyota was parked there, but I didn't have to answer the door. I didn't think the coppers would break it down. I held the changeling against my shoulder and rubbed its back. Did I have time to get it upstairs and out of sight before a knock or the doorbell startled it into crying?

It wasn't the police. A white Transit had parked on the gravelled space in front of the cottage next door. It was from Dolebury Electricals, according to the writing on the side. A smaller, plain white van had pulled up beside it. Both drivers were roughly my age, give or take a few years. They wore cargo shorts and grey T-shirts with the same yellow logo as the Transit's. One of them gestured and the other one got into the smaller van. He drove down the lane to park on the rutted turf.

The Transit driver had keys to the neighbouring cottage. He went in through the front door. A few minutes later, I heard him open up the back. I stayed where I was and watched the two men take big boxes out of the Transit and carry them carefully inside. They were here to fit a new hob and oven.

'That explains why there's no one staying there this week,' I remarked to the changeling.

This was also fucking inconvenient for me. There was no way I could leave the changeling here alone while I went to the barrow, or to the shops, or anywhere else. The electrician or his mate was sure to hear if it started crying. When it started crying.

Hearing their voices in the back garden, I went into the kitchen. I heard them talking about football and having a brew before they started work. How long would fitting the new oven and hob take? I had no sodding clue. I'm a chippy, not a sparks.

The changeling was dozing. I decided to put it down to sleep in its drawer upstairs. While it slept, I could wash up and sort things out down here. As soon as those inconvenient workmen were gone, I'd be ready to do... something.

I took the changeling upstairs. I went into the front bedroom to get my phone. Seeing the mess there, I remembered I still had to tidy up. I got to work. By the time I had finished putting Fin's clothes in her suitcase, my hands were shaking. My throat was tight, and my gut was hollow. How the hell was I going to find her? What the fuck was I going to do if I couldn't?

I closed my eyes. I had to keep my shit together. I had to get some help. As soon as those workmen busy next door drove away, I'd walk out of this sodding village and carry on until I found a payphone or a signal. I had plenty of numbers in my phone's contacts. Eleanor. Blanche. Aled. Peter. Will and Witta. Hazel. I'd ring everyone I could think of.

Someone knocked on the back door. Fuck. I found my hanky, wiped my eyes and blew my nose. Racing down the stairs, I nearly fell head first. Grabbing the bannister just in time to save myself, I wrenched my shoulder. I ignored it, desperate to answer the door before whoever was out there knocked harder and woke the changeling up. I'd left the sofa cushions in the way of the door. I kicked them aside and grabbed the handle. Then I realised the door was still locked.

'Hang on!' I fetched the keys as fast as I could, fumbling for the right one. 'What do you want?'

If those electricians had come round to borrow some milk—

I opened the door. Fin stepped inside.

'Good. You're already here. Now—' She used a foot to close the door behind her. Her hand on my chest drove me backwards. Upstairs, the changeling grizzled. Fin looked up at the ceiling. 'We had better—'

'Wait there. Don't move.' I hurried upstairs and fetched the changeling. When I came down to the kitchen, I picked up the bottle of baby formula I'd made earlier.

'Where did you get that?' Fin asked, startled. She frowned, looking more closely at the changeling as it started sucking down milk. 'That's not—'

'Not Alice.' I was still trying to work out what the hell to say.

'You've got her back to her parents already?' Fin was relieved. 'That was quick work.'

I stared at her. 'It's Tuesday.'

Fin stared at me, confused. 'What?'

'It's Tuesday,' I said again. What part of that was unclear? 'You've been gone since yesterday.'

'Shit.' Fin pressed her hands to her face. 'Really? Sorry. Of course. You wouldn't say that unless...' She stared at me some more.

I remembered how little Alice, the real Alice, hadn't been hungry when we'd found her. How she hadn't been cold and wet like a baby who'd been left outside all night. 'How long do you think you've been gone?'

'A couple of hours maybe.' Fin was still trying to get her head around this. 'Bloody hell. You must have been—'

'Yes.' I didn't want to talk about that. I wanted to forget these past twenty-four hellish hours as soon as I possibly could. 'How did you get back?'

Fin raised her hands to stop me talking. 'I need a coffee. Do you want a cup of tea?'

I thought a double scotch would be better for this sort of shock, but it was a bit early in the day. Beside, we hadn't bought any whisky when we'd stopped at the supermarket on Sunday.

'Yes, please.' I pulled a dining chair out from the table with one foot and sat in the kitchen doorway while Fin found two mugs. I finished feeding Not-Alice and propped the change-ling up against my shoulder to burp. I felt the warm wetness of regurgitated formula soaking through my T-shirt. Great.

Fin was still busy with the kettle. She had her back towards me. I saw her wipe her eyes a couple of times.

'Could you pick up those cushions and bring them through here?' I asked. 'Then I can put this down on the sofa.'

'Of course.' Fin blew her nose on a sheet of paper towel and did that. She watched me lay the drowsy changeling down. 'It really does look exactly the same as – how did you find out the real baby's name? How on earth did you swap them over?"

I went into the kitchen to pour myself a mug of tea. 'You first.'

'Okay. Well.' Fin leaned against the counter with both hands wrapped around her coffee.

'When you and the baby disappeared—' She shivered. 'That was a nasty moment. I managed to get back through the hole, which wasn't easy, let me tell you. I wasn't entirely sure where I was though. I walked around those stones a few times, not looking directly at the hole. I couldn't see anything, not like the first time. So I came here. At least, I came to where this village should be.'

She looked around as if she could see through the cottage's walls. She shook her head.

'There was nothing here – there – whatever. The hills looked the same, and the rivers and everything else, but there was no sign of houses or any trace to show that people had ever lived here. Absolutely nothing. That was another nasty moment. Well, more like a nasty quarter of an hour.'

She shuddered again, and coffee sloshed out of her mug onto the floor. Fin put the mug down on the counter and reached for the roll of paper towels. 'I was properly starting to panic until that feather turned up. You thought of that, didn't you?'

She managed a smile, but her eyes filled with tears. I crossed the kitchen and wrapped my arms around her. This way, she wouldn't see the tears running down my face. This was stupid though. She was here with me, safe and sound.

'I can't breathe,' Fin protested, muffled against my chest.

'Sorry.' I let her go, though I stayed standing close. 'It's just—'

'I know.' Fin's voice shook. She picked up her coffee and took another sip. She cleared her throat. 'So anyway, my feather turned up, and so did a heron, a few minutes later. A big grey heron. That had to mean something. Did you hear me when I said I couldn't hear any birdsong on the other side?'

I nodded. Fin went on.

'The heron was clearly there for a reason. It stood there staring at me for a bit, then it took off and flew around me in a circle. Then it landed to look at me some more. I can take a hint, so I went swan to see – well, to be honest, I'm not sure what I expected to happen. The heron flew off, so I followed it. It took me to the Fieldfare Long Barrow.'

'You remembered reading about it?'

'No.' Fin managed a proper smile. 'But when I was walking around the mound, trying to work out why the heron had taken me there, I found that leaflet wrapped around a rock lying on the grass. I saw you'd made notes on the paper. I knew you'd have more sense than to come through it yourself, but that had to mean there was a way to get back here through the barrow. I started checking the passages.'

'Passages, plural?' That was a surprise.

Fin drank more coffee. 'That barrow looks very different on the other side, or whatever we're going to call that place. There aren't any trees on top, or that wrecked stretch along one side. Anyway, I crawled into a few of the tunnels. What did I have to lose? When I found one where I thought I could see daylight at the other end, I kept on going. I came out on this side where the barrow has collapsed. It was a bit of a squeeze where those slabs had fallen down, but I managed to get through.'

She paused. 'I would never have found my way back without that heron showing me the barrow. Have you any idea where it come from?'

'I think we have Wade to thank for that.' And I'd pay whatever I owed him for saving Fin.

'Wade?' Unsurprisingly, that made no sense to her.

'The Master of Fords and Ferries. You remember when—'

'He fished you out of the fens. Yes, of course I do, but what's he doing here?'

'Well, the hag said—'

'Stop.' Fin took a deep breath. 'Right. I want some toast. Then you had better tell me everything that's happened to you. We can decide what to do next after that.'

'Okay.'

Fin sat and listened while I told her what I had done after the portal in the tilted stone closed. When I told her what I'd overheard Alice's dad saying on the phone, she looked uneasy.

'Do you think there's any way a journalist could have got hold of our names?'

'I don't know, but the only person they'll be able to contact right now is Eleanor. She'll shut them down with more than "no comment" if she has to. But I think we're okay. If she got a call suggesting we were mixed up in a child abduction and she couldn't get either of us on the phone, she'd come straight here. She'd have arrived by now. She hasn't, so...' I shrugged.

'Hopefully.' Fin didn't sound entirely convinced. 'So how did you find out a hag is behind this?'

I explained about the photos on the bedroom wall upstairs. I told her what had happened inside the vanishing cottage.

Fin walked through the cottage to the front window. I followed her. She stared across the lane to the empty field with those tangles of brambles and clumps of nettles.

She shook her head. 'It never occurred to me that house couldn't be real.'

'Nor me. We have to get hold of some hag stones, if we can't trust our own eyes when one of those evil witches is around.' The more I thought about what that could mean, the more it unnerved me.

Fin turned away from the window. 'So what did you do after that?'

By the time I'd finished telling her, Not-Alice was stirring again. I sat down and picked up the changeling, rocking it to keep it quiet.

Fin sat on the other sofa. 'So what do we do now?'

'The first thing we have to do is get beyond that sodding hag's reach, so we can call in help.' I looked down at Not-Alice. 'And we need someone to take this thing off our hands before somebody sees it and sends the cops to knock on our door. I know Hazel's away, but I've got a couple of other wise women's numbers.'

I wasn't necessarily keen on handing the changeling over to people I didn't really know, but I couldn't see we had any other choice. Fin and I could hardly come back from our holiday with a surprise baby.

Fin nodded. She still looked tense. 'There's something else. Something came through the long barrow after me. I'd got clear of the loose earth at this end of the passage, and I was really hoping I had got back here, when I heard claws on the stone floor behind me. I could smell it as well, even though I was upwind. It absolutely reeked. Whatever it was, it sounded big, and it was snarling. I went swan to get out of its way. I was in such a hurry, it didn't occur to me I might get mazed again until I was already in the air. Anyway, I didn't, so that was okay.'

She heaved a sigh. 'I didn't get much of a look before whatever it was ran off, but it was big and hairy and on all fours, and it was fast. I mean, really quick. Like a small bear or maybe a really big dog? Not a shuck though. It wasn't anything we've seen before.'

'Right.' Great. We needed a mystery monster like a hole in the head.

Fin looked at me, anxious. 'That portal, gateway, whatever we call it – it didn't close after the bear-dog thing came through. It's still open. I went to check. We have to find a way to close it before anything else comes through.'

I nodded, though I had no idea how we were going to do that. 'What did you do next?'

'Well, the bear-dog thing had gone and I wasn't being mazed, so I flew around a bit. Once I saw roads and houses, I came straight here. Well, straight to the other side of the hedge at the bottom of the garden. I made sure no one saw me land. I thought I'd only been gone for a couple of hours. You had my phone, so I couldn't check the time.'

'Fair enough.' I thought about this new threat. 'Do we think the hag whistled up this hairy bear-dog creature? To

165

give us a new problem? I mean, you're back, and Alice is home with her parents. We could be getting ready to leave.'

'Only if the car starts,' Fin pointed out. 'Have you tried it again? How about our phones?'

'They're still screwed,' I admitted. 'I haven't tried the car. I've been trying to work out how to get to Cheddar on the bus. Hopefully the hag won't be able to follow me if I do that. I was planning to find a payphone and do some shopping. But I couldn't leave the changeling on its own. Now you're here though—'

'I can babysit?' Fin raised her eyebrows. 'Yes, okay. You're right. Get hold of Blanche. Tell her to send Zan here at once. They can look for that bear-dog creature.'

I wondered what the mystery monster might be doing. Nothing good, I was sure of that. Why else would the hag have summoned it? She wouldn't accept any responsibility, of course.

I thought about what else she had said about portals. 'Do you think the tunnel's staying open because that thing, whatever it is, belongs on the other side? Can we shut that gateway by sending it back?'

'Let's hope so,' Fin said with feeling. 'If we can work out how to do that without ending up as its lunch.'

I nodded. 'And before any more of them come through.'

Or something even worse found its way here. I didn't say that out loud. If the hag was listening to us somehow, I didn't want to give the old witch ideas.

Chapter Thirteen

'Let me see if the apple trees can help us.' I stood up and handed Not-Alice to Fin. The changeling stared at her, faintly puzzled. Fin looked blankly at me.

'Dryad radar,' I reminded her.

'Oh, right. Yes.' Fin smiled uncertainly at Not-Alice. 'Hello again.'

I went out into the back garden. The electricians were busy in next door's kitchen. They had the door propped open. That was fair enough. It was the warmest day of the week so far, and they were working hard with a fair amount of heavy lifting. I strolled down the lawn, trying to look as casual as I could. I went to the furthest apple tree, to stand half hidden by the other one.

'Thank you for getting word to Wade, so he could send help to Fin,' I said quietly as I laid my hand on the lichen-spotted trunk. I hoped the tree could feel how truly grateful I was. 'Now we've got a new problem. Something came through the portal after her. We need to find it.'

Dryad radar was already showing me everything and everyone out and about in the fields and gardens around Bishop's Warren. I expanded my search to the hills beyond and found plenty of wildlife in the flourishing greenery. I couldn't sense anything out of the ordinary that could be a hairy bear-dog beast. There wasn't a hint of the sodding hag either, even though she was still fucking up our phones. She must have a hell of a reach, and that was a worrying thought.

So there was sod all I could do about either of them. I'd get on with things I could tackle now that Fin was here. I went into the cottage. Fin was sitting on a sofa with Not-Alice drowsing on her lap. She was looking through the tourist brochures from the wicker basket on the coffee table.

'No luck.' I took my backpack off the coat hook by the door and started emptying it onto the dining table. 'I'll go and do the shopping. We need more nappies, and I'd better buy more food. Your curry's in the fridge if you want to have that for lunch.'

I tried to remember what else was left from the supermarket stop we'd made on the way here.

'When does this – she – need her next feed?' Fin looked down at Not-Alice and up at me. 'We should start saying "she", instead of "it". Once we get away from here, when we give her to the wise women, it's going to be best if everyone treats her like an ordinary little girl.'

'If you say so.' I still had serious worries about what the changeling would grow into, but that was a conversation for another time. We had more immediate problems right now. I picked up my wallet from the mantelpiece.

'Your phone's here. Keep an eye out in case you get a signal. If the hag does follow me, if she has to concentrate to block my phone, maybe yours will start working when I get far enough away. If that happens, maybe we can use it against her. Heading in opposite directions so she can't keep track of us both.' I wasn't keen on the idea of us splitting up, but we might have no other option.

'If I get a signal, we'd better agree who we're going to call. After Blanche, I mean. Like we were saying this morning—' Fin caught herself. 'Like we said yesterday. Who can get here fast enough to be useful now that we've got this new problem?'

I thought about that. 'I can't see Eleanor suddenly discovering something crucial about hags or hairy monsters just because we happen to need to know it right now. Hazel might be able to tell us something about the bear-dog thing. What's the time difference between here and South America? We can leave her a message. Ask her to call me back. Once I know how far I have to go to get a phone signal without the hag interfering, I can go out later to check.'

I was starting to think I'd be doing a fair bit of solo hiking. I refolded the OS map and put that in my backpack. 'If Zan can't find the mystery monster when they get here, I'll call Peter. We can ask him to come down as soon as he can, to pick up its scent. Ideally, he'll agree to travel by sylph. Right. I'll get going. Not-Alice will want a bottle around midday. Lock the door behind me, and don't open it to anyone.'

'Not even for a kindly old woman offering me a nice apple from her basket?' Fin asked, mildly sarcastic.

'Sorry. I'll be as quick as I can.' I bent down to give her a kiss and headed out. I heard her turn the key in the lock as I walked past the Toyota. Then I went back and knocked on the cottage door.

Fin opened up, holding Not-Alice. 'That was quick.'

She grinned. I couldn't help grinning as well. Even with this new crap to deal with, having her here safe and sound was such a relief.

I held out my hand. 'I need to get a couple of shopping bags out of the car.'

Fin fetched the keys from the mantelpiece. 'Is it worth trying to see if the car starts?'

That was tempting, but I hesitated. 'Since our phones are still buggered, I don't think it will. And I don't think we want those blokes coming to see if they can help.' I nodded towards the works van parked next door. 'That'll mean questions and explanations, and we don't want them seeing that – her.'

'No.' Fin looked at the neighbouring cottage. 'What are they doing. Do you know?'

Of course. She'd come in through the back door after the electricians had arrived.

'Fitting a new oven and hob.' I pressed the button on the fob to unlock the Toyota. I got a couple of bags out of the boot and took the keys to Fin. She locked the cottage door again. Good.

I headed for the bus stop on the village green. I wished those fading scars on my arm would prickle with a hint that the hag was following me. I didn't want her trying to find a way to get to Fin while she was stuck in the cottage on her own. Though if the hag was going to attack me, I reckoned she'd most likely do that when I got off the bus on my way back, while I was walking on a remote path with no one else around. I resisted the temptation to pat my zipped trouser pocket where I had my multi-tool. If the hag did come after me, I'd do my very best to end her bullshit, once and for all.

For the first time in what felt like forever, a bit of good luck came my way. The bus stop had an old-fashioned paper timetable behind a sheet of Perspex in a frame, showing when the next bus was due. I could catch a ride to Cheddar in ten minutes. That was good, because the bus after that wouldn't turn up for another three hours.

The bus was half empty when it arrived. I was the only person who got on. The other passengers weren't interested in me. Most of them were busy with their phones, though onboard WiFi wasn't available on this bus. Sod's law. I took my phone and tapped the screen as if I was doing something. I watched for signal bars and any hint of a data connection.

About halfway to Cheddar, my phone went nuts. I had a whole load of missed calls, voicemails and messages from unknown numbers. I quickly muted the alerts, ignoring the glares from other passengers. Okay, that was good. The hag hadn't somehow damaged my SIM card or the handset. She was cutting us off from the network.

But who the hell were these calls from? Had I been wrong when I'd said to Fin I didn't think any journalists would try to get hold of us? If someone had persuaded a copper to share my name, they could read whatever was still online about the time the cops had suspected me of attacking a girl. That had been years ago, but like they say, the Internet is forever. Even if they only got a photo, a reverse image search would soon find me.

I wasn't going to listen to those voicemails without head-phones. I didn't need everyone on the bus hearing someone ask when I started stealing babies. I checked the texts instead. That was a relief. Every estate agent Fin and I had signed up with wanted to tell us about new properties on the market which we might be interested in viewing. Those voicemails had come from the same numbers.

I was also relieved to see that no one had been trying to get hold of me because something had happened to Dad. He's in his eighties, and there's always the chance of some-thing unexpected at that age. Of course, for people like us, the unexpected can be a whole lot worse than a sudden fall or needing help with some government department. That last time I'd got a phone call out of the blue, a hag was trying to kill my dad. Fortunately, my mum had whisked him away – to where exactly? The same place Fin had found herself? That was another lot of questions we should ask when we got the chance. When I could speak to Mum. I wasn't going to worry Dad at the moment.

Now I could check my location online, I saw I was roughly two and a half miles from Bishop's Warren. Was that how far the hag's spite could reach if she was still in the village watching Fin? Or had she been following me, unseen or as a hare, until the bus outpaced her?

I couldn't answer any of those questions, so I looked out of the window. I watched for a bus stop on the other side of the road. As soon as I saw one, I used my phone to get a fix on its location. That decades-old breeze-block shelter should make that easy to spot when the bus was heading towards Bishop's Warren. I'd get off there and walk the rest of the way.

I checked the bus timetable. I found out this service went all the way to Street. Then it turned around and retraced its leisurely route through a whole load of villages. I could spend about two hours in Cheddar if I was going to catch it on the return journey.

171

Now I could get online and look at a map, I found a su-permarket not far from the stop where the bus would drop me off. Finally things were going my way.

Which made having to sit on this bus while it wandered from village to village really frustrating. I could have driven to Cheddar in a third of the time. I had to allow for the walk to the supermarket, and I had phone calls to make as well as shopping to do. I was going to have to be careful I didn't miss the next bus to Bishop's Warren.

Eventually I arrived in Cheddar. I immediately realised the Ordnance Survey doesn't necessarily tell you what you need to know. This might look like a sizeable place on the map, but the centre where the shops were was much smaller than I expected. Stretches of pavement were narrower than my shoulders are wide in a lot of places.

The supermarket was nowhere near as big as I had hoped for. I bought what I could: newborn-size nappies, bum wipes and cream, sterilising fluid, another feeding bottle, and nappy sacks, which I hadn't even known were a thing. It also turned out you can buy ready-made formula in screw-top bottles, so I got a couple of those. But there were no baby clothes or carrying slings. I could order them and a whole load of other things from a digital catalogue for next-day delivery or collection, which I'm sure was great for the locals but was sod all use to me. I had no idea what might happen in the next twenty-four hours.

But we had to have some sort of baby carrier. We needed to take the changeling with us when we left Bishop's Warren, to hand it over to the wise women. Unless we found a way to get rid of the hag and the little monster evaporated. Some-how I didn't see us being that lucky.

I wondered what to do as I picked up two pizzas for this evening. I decided to buy something for dinner for tomor-row as well. With luck, once I'd phoned Blanche, Zan would be here inside a couple of hours. They could help us deal with the hag, but there was no saying how long it might take us to get that hairy bear-dog thing back through the portal in the barrow mound.

'Excuse me. Can I get through?' A lady with a trolley wanted to get past me.

'Right. Sorry.' I hadn't realised I had stopped dead in the centre of the narrow aisle. Moving got my brain working again. Fuck it. We had to get this sorted before the weekend. As soon as Zan got here, we'd deal with the hairy bear-dog thing. After that, we'd find that sodding hag and make her regret she'd ever thought she could take us on.

As well as a bottle of laundry detergent, I picked up a pack of spaghetti and a jar of tomato and garlic sauce. We could add a tin of tuna, and mushrooms and onion, to make a quick, decent meal. If we had everything settled by this time tomorrow, the tuna, pasta and sauce would keep. What else did we need today? I headed for the pre-packed sandwiches and snacks and chose a couple of meal deals for me and Fin. I could eat mine on the bus.

At the checkout, I put the nappies and everything else for Not-Alice into my backpack, out of sight. Thankfully, a pack of newborn nappies is fairly small. Splitting the rest between the two rope-handled carrier bags meant neither one was too heavy.

One plus of finding Cheddar had far fewer shops than I expected was it didn't take long for me to make certain none of them sold baby gear. I had just about given up, ready to turn around and head back to the bus stop, when at long bloody last some luck came my way. A sign at the entrance to a small cluster of business units advertised a discount outlet. Apparently, this was the shop that had everything you didn't know you needed. I decided I might as well see what it had to offer.

I found out it was one of those places where what you saw was what was for sale, at reasonable prices, take it or leave it, all sales final. The next time you visited, the range of goods on offer would most likely be completely different.

Right now, a set of shelves next to a rack of kids' dresses was stacked with baby clothes, changing mats and other assorted nursery equipment, brand new, in original packaging. I found a pack of three white towelling sleepsuits, and halle-bloody-lujah, a newborn-size baby carrier. I took them to the till and paid up. Thank fuck for that.

Now I had to get on the phone. I knew where I was going to do that. On my way to the supermarket, I'd passed an old market cross standing in a circle of cobbles where two roads met in a broad triangular space. Six buttressed limestone pillars supported a crenellated roof above six broad arches. Some sort of cross stuck up in the middle of the roof. That shaded a central plinth of tiered stone steps where traders in days gone by would have set out whatever they'd brought here to sell. I noticed the central pillar was octagonal and wondered if the original builders had used masonry left over from other projects.

I wasn't convinced the wooden posts around the outside would do much if an HGV ploughed into it, but right now, I was more interested in making my calls without being overheard. I crossed the road and sat down on the plinth. I didn't think passers-by would be inclined to cross a busy road to start a conversation with a stranger my size and height. If they did, I'd just glower silently until they went away. That wouldn't take long.

Blanche didn't answer her phone. Too busy having fun on the Riviera? I hoped so. One of us should be enjoying their holiday. I left her a message.

'Hi. We need Zan's help with a creature that doesn't belong here. It came through a passage in a burial mound that's a gateway to somewhere else. We have to send it back. Can Zan come and find us, please? You'll be able to reach me for the next hour or so, but you won't get an answer if you call me any later than that. A hag here is screwing with our phones. She says she won't piss off the Green Man by hurting us though,' I added quickly. The full story could wait. 'So far that seems to be true, but she's keeping us offline and Fin's car won't start. If Zan can help with any of that, it would be really useful too. Okay. Thanks. Bye.'

I really hoped the sylph could counter whatever the hag was doing to our phones and the car. If the Toyota still wouldn't start on Friday, I'd have to ring Eleanor and ask her to come and get us on Saturday morning. But if she came to Bishop's Warren, what would stop the hag fucking with her car too? We'd have to meet somewhere else and hope the hag didn't follow us. Clearing our stuff out of the holiday cottage would be a royal pain in the arse. Fin and I would have to walk to wherever we agreed to meet, carrying as much as we could with us, including the changeling. How much could we leave safely locked in the car? How the fuck were we going to get the Toyota to Fin's flat? Call a tow-truck? That wouldn't be cheap.

Those problems would have to wait. I found Hazel's number on my phone. I still couldn't remember where she had gone in South America, but regardless, the time difference would put her somewhere between four and six hours behind us. Trying not to wonder how much this call was going to cost me, I rang her number. Unsurprisingly, I got her voicemail. I kept my message short, watching out for dog walkers or anyone else who might come close enough to wonder what the hell I was talking about.

'Hi. Fin and I are in the Mendips. A hag has dumped a changeling on us. We need someone to take it off our hands. Let me know who to call, as soon as you can. We need help with something else as well. There's a creature that doesn't belong here. Fin says it's halfway between a really big dog and a bear. It's covered in hair and it stinks. It came through a passage in a burial mound which is a gateway to somewhere else. We have to send it back. If you call me in the next hour or so, I should be able to pick up, but this hag is screwing with our phones, so you probably won't get an answer after that. Leave me a message. I'm working out how far away

I need to get from the village where we're staying to check for voicemail. Thanks.'

We could tell the wise woman the whole story when we next saw her in person, whenever that might be. I stayed sitting there on the plinth for a moment and thought about ringing my dad. I decided that could wait. If Zan didn't turn up, if Hazel hadn't got back to me by this time tomorrow, if Peter and the cunning men couldn't or wouldn't help us, then I'd ring my dad. He could see if my mum had any ideas. I'd call Eleanor as well, and get her to ask the Blithehurst dryads for suggestions.

I hoped Zan turned up soon. Could the sylph scare off this hag? With or without help? I'd tell the sylph and whoever else they could enlist not to hold back. The hag could tell her kinswomen that they needed to leave us alone in future. She could suck on that and choke as far as I was concerned.

Checking the time, I walked to the bus stop, not hanging around. I wasn't going to risk being late.

I wished Fin was with me. I wished we weren't dealing with this sodding nonsense. If we were having the holiday we'd planned, we could be seeing if The Bath Arms was a decent place to have lunch. Who the hell did this hag think she was, screwing with us like this? The more I thought about it, the crosser I got. The old witch had miscalculated badly. If she wanted a quiet life, she should have stayed well away from me.

I ate my sandwiches and drank my Coke once I got on the bus. That would be less weight to carry when I got off. My phone was in the thigh pocket of my combat trousers. I was ready to answer it quickly if Hazel or Blanche rang me back. They didn't, which was disappointing. I kept watch for the bus stop where I planned to get off. It was at a junction with a side road rather than in a village. Presumably there were enough houses somewhere close by to justify this stop on the route.

I saw the breeze-block shelter. I stood up and pressed the bell button. The bus pulled up and I got off. As it drove away, I put the shopping bags down and got the OS map out of my backpack. I had remembered to put that on top of the nappies. I took out my phone. Good. I still had a signal. I checked my location and pinpointed where I was on the paper map. I didn't have to walk far to reach a footpath which would take me to Bishop's Warren by a more direct route than the road.

Sticking the map in my trouser pocket, I slung on my backpack and picked up the shopping bags in one hand. I kept my phone out and watched the screen as I started walking. I wanted to know the second the hag realised I was on my way back and cut off my signal. I also kept my ears open, walking on the side of the road that faced any possible oncoming traffic. The last thing I needed was to be hit by a car. I wondered if there was any way I could reverse my talent for not being seen?

I reached the fingerpost pointing to the cross-country footpath I wanted to follow. Carrying both bags of shopping in one hand was getting to be a pain, but I kept my eyes on my phone. I was well past the point where I'd got a signal on the bus on my way to Cheddar. Did that mean the hag was busy not watching me?

I was about a mile out from Bishop's Warren when I lost reception. I dropped the shopping bags and grabbed the closest tree branch, searching for the hag. I couldn't sense her anywhere. Bollocks. I offered the startled rowan tree a quick apology and put my phone away.

As I picked up the shopping and started walking, disappointment hit me harder than I expected. I was ready to fight this hag, or at least, I was ready to start making plans to fight her as soon as Zan arrived. We couldn't do anything, though, unless I could find out where she was. Sod it.

I was better balanced with a bag in each hand. I hadn't gone much further when my phone vibrated in my pocket.

I stopped and checked the screen. To my surprise, it had a signal again. I looked at the steep hillsides and deep gullies on either side of the path. There would be not-spots around here which had nothing to do with the hag.

I carried on, keeping my phone in my hand. As soon as the signal dropped out, I tried to find the hag again with the help of a nearby hawthorn. Still no luck. This time though, I didn't put my phone away. I got reception inside fifty metres, and lost it again ten metres after that. By now I was within half a mile of Bishop's Warren.

The next time my phone signal came and went, I picked up the briefest sense of foulness with a crab apple's help. Even though it vanished in an instant, I recognised that nauseating sting. The first time I'd sensed that was when a hag had been hunting for my dad. Right now, this particular hag was high on the hills that overlooked the village.

I realised something else I'd never asked a dryad or a sylph. Could they sense when I was looking for them? For this hag to vanish so fast, I reckoned she must have felt the brush of the dryad radar. If I was right about that, was there any way we could use that against her?

Right now, she had disappeared, and my phone still wasn't working. So she must be hiding from me and the trees somehow, but she was still close enough to cut me off from the network.

Another question occurred to me. If the hag had only just noticed I was nearly back, what had she been doing while I was away? I shoved my phone in a pocket, dropped the map into a shopping bag and started running. I had to get to Pigeon Lane as fast as I could.

Chapter Fourteen

This footpath took me to the other end of Bishop's Warren. I had to walk pretty much the whole way though the village to reach Pigeon Lane. I forced myself to go slowly. I didn't want to attract any attention. I was already sweaty from running. That might make people wonder what I'd been doing. At least this gave me a chance to cool off.

I made sure I didn't look too interested in the red-tiled house as I went past. I stopped for a moment though. Not even taking a glance at the tree surgeon's van parked on the gravel drive would have been suspicious. A grey-haired woman and a younger man were looking up into the split beech, gesturing as they talked. They didn't notice me. I couldn't see a police car or any coppers around, but they could be inside the house. Someone had been busy with a chainsaw. The fallen timber had been cut up and neatly stacked beside the garage. That would come in useful, once it had seasoned, if they had an open fire or a wood burner.

Walking along the pavement towards Pigeon Lane, I wondered how long the police would carry on with their enquiries, trying to find out who had taken Alice. Suspicion hanging over the village would make life very unpleasant. Though I guessed plenty of people would be able to prove they couldn't have been involved. How long would the cops be looking sideways at the unlucky ones who didn't have witnesses to whatever they'd been doing? The police had no chance of finding out who was really responsible to put an end to the tension.

Would the hag savour that pain? Fin and I had met monsters who thrived on misery. Though as far as I knew, a hag was a predator in the most literal sense. What was this business with the changeling about? Had she stolen a baby to set up a longer-term plan by leaving a cuckoo in some poor bastards' nest?

If somebody disappeared from Bishop's Warren right now, especially if they turned out to have something to hide, the cops would assume they'd run away. That would be as good as a confession. Case closed. If human bones were found in a ditch years later, there'd be no way to know how they had died. If they were found. If they were identified. These days hags were careful to leave no trace of their kills. The one who'd tried to murder my dad had told me that.

I'd be so glad to leave here at the end of the week. To do that, we had to deal with this hag. How long before Zan arrived? I walked faster. Turning into Pigeon Lane, I saw both electricians' vans had gone. Good. That was one less complication. There was no one else around. The half-dozen cottages looked picturesque and peaceful in the summer sunshine. Bishop's Warren should be a lovely place for a holiday.

I knocked on the cottage door. Fin checked through the window before she opened up. As I went in, I saw Not-Alice lying on the closest sofa, sound asleep. The cottage smelled faintly of microwaved curry. Fin must have had that for lunch.

I heard her relock the front door as I carried the shopping into the kitchen. Fin followed me as I was putting the pizzas in the fridge. Buying those hadn't been such a good idea. Running had shaken the toppings loose and the cheese was nearly as warm and sweaty as me.

'Tea?' Fin filled the kettle and switched it on.

'Definitely.' I filled a clean mug from the draining board with water from the tap and drank it.

'Did you get everything?' Fin kept her voice low to avoid waking Not-Alice.

'Pretty much.' I took off my backpack and took out the baby stuff. 'Did your phone get a signal while I was out?'

Fin shook her head as she put tea bags into the pot and got milk out of the fridge. 'Have you heard from Hazel or Blanche?'

'Not yet.' I saw Fin shared my disappointment.

She leaned against the counter as she let the tea brew. 'So how are we going to get your phone far enough away from the hag so you can check for messages? Or I could go and do that. It doesn't have to be you.'

'Especially if the hag's watching me. I wonder if she even knows you're back? If she doesn't, I could leave my phone here with you and hike out of the village, taking yours.'

'Lure her away.' Fin looked thoughtful. 'That might work – unless she can identify individual phones. I've just assumed dryads and naiads mess with reception generally, but I don't actually know how they do that.'

'Me neither,' I admitted. 'There are a whole load of things we need to ask Zan.'

'Let's hope they get here soon. So what are we going to do in the meantime?' She surprised me with a smile. 'Apart from play with the baby. She's quite sweet when she's awake, if you don't notice her eyes. When I—'

'She's got a hag's eyes,' I interrupted. I'd just realised Fin had no idea what she was seeing. She'd never got close to a hag before now. She wouldn't recognise that muddy red-brown colour.

Fin stared at me, appalled. 'Then she's—'

'Going to grow up to be a hag? I have no idea. Let's hope the wise women know what to do with her.' Whether or not they could, that was one more reason why I wanted Not-Alice to be someone else's problem as soon as possible.

'That's... worrying.' Fin looked uneasy as she poured tea for us both. 'But you're right. We should leave that to the wise women. Right now, we have bigger problems. What are we going to do while we wait for Zan?'

I took the mug she offered. 'Try to work out how that hag is hiding from dryad radar.'

'I might have an idea about that.' Fin heard Not-Alice waking up. 'But you're not going to like it. Pass me that bottle.'

I saw Fin had made up a feed earlier. I handed it over and followed her into the living room. Fin settled on the sofa and tucked a towel out of the airing cupboard under Not-Alice's chin. She wasn't smiling at the changeling now. A baby hag wasn't nearly so cute.

I sat down and sipped my tea. 'Go on.'

Fin nodded towards the coffee table since she had her hands full. 'You can't see what's inside buildings with dryad radar. How about what's inside caves? Take a look at that.'

I saw the leaflet on top of the pile advertised Wookey Hole. Fin was right. I didn't like the idea of hunting the hag through an underground labyrinth one bit. That didn't mean she was wrong. I picked up the brochure and started reading the local legend as recorded by Mr H.E. Balch.

In the dim and distant past, a woman had lived in the Wookey Hole caverns with her goats. H.E. Balch specifically called her a hag, though I had no way to know if that meant the same to him as it did to me and Fin. Regardless, the woman had made herself thoroughly unpopular with people living in these hills and valleys. She was so obnoxious they decided she was a witch, or an evil spirit. Either way, she was in league with the devil. The locals asked the Abbot of Glastonbury for help. He sent a monk armed with godly books and holy water. The monk chanted something at the hag and sprinkled her with holy water. That turned her to stone, and everyone heaved a sigh of relief.

Supposedly, a famous stalagmite in the first of the cavern's big caves is all that's left of the hag. I studied the photo, but I couldn't see any old woman with a beaky nose and wearing a mob cap. That didn't mean there wasn't some truth in this story. I remembered legends of hags elsewhere included ones living in caves. They could hide their murdered victims so far underground that not even a modern pot-holer would find them.

I put down the leaflet and spread the OS map on the table yet again. I sat on a dining chair and drank my tea as I studied the hills and valleys around the village. 'There are a lot of place names which include "cavern" and "hole". I don't know for certain what a swallet is, but I'm guessing that's a swallow hole?'

'It is,' Fin confirmed. 'Well, it can mean the hole itself or the stream that disappears down it, but that's a distinction without a difference.'

I thought about underground streams and the powerful spirits who might claim them. 'Do we think a hag would risk tangling with a naiad?'

Fin had met the same river spirits as I had. She knew they could go from friendly to intimidating to outright menacing in the blink of an eye.

'Only if there's one around here,' she pointed out. 'They're few and far between.'

I looked at the map again. 'I think you're right. There are plenty of places where the hag could be lurking underground where dryad radar won't find her.'

Sod it.

'If we're going to find her, we have to check these caves,' I said reluctantly. 'I need to find out how far dryad radar can reach into them. If it can't show us anything useful, I'll have to think about going in myself.'

'Or I can take a look. I can go further in than you.' Fin shifted Not-Alice and draped the towel over her own shoulder. She held the changeling upright and Not-Alice burped. 'Or we ask Zan.'

'Do sylphs go into caves?' That was yet another question I'd never needed to ask.

'I have no idea.' Fin patted Not-Alice's back. 'Right, she needs a clean nappy. I'll do that upstairs if you can bring me those baby bits from the kitchen. Then I think she might go down for a proper nap.'

'Right.' I fetched the pack of nappies, the wipes, the sleep suits and the bum cream. I took everything upstairs and left Fin to it.

In the kitchen, I ran a sinkful of hot, soapy water and washed both feeding bottles. Finding a large glass bowl in one of the cupboards, I filled that with the right mix of water and sterilising fluid. I was trying to get the parts of the feeding bottles to stay properly submerged when Fin came into the kitchen with the dirty reusable nappy rolled up in one hand.

'I wiped most of the crap off that with loo roll,' I told her. 'Then I put it through the washing machine.'

Fin turned to go through the lobby to the shower room. Before I could answer, something hit the kitchen window. We looked at each other, startled.

'Did a bird fly into the glass?' Fin went into the lobby to look through the little window in the back door.

I heard a second sharp thud.

'I can't see anyone outside. Or any thing.' Fin fished the cottage keys out of her pocket.

'Wait for me.' I hurried to join her.

Fin unlocked the door. I opened it halfway, ready to slam it shut again. Something hit me in the chest, hard enough to hurt. I looked down at the paved path. It was one of the small green apples that needed thinning to help out the old trees. Looking down the garden, I saw movement. A dark shadow crouched by the hedge.

'Is that what you saw come through the gateway in the burial mound?'

'Yes,' Fin said a moment later. 'How the hell did it find us? It can't have tracked my scent. I flew here.'

I closed the door and turned the key in the lock. 'The hag must have sent it.'

And if this thing killed us, she would insist our blood wasn't on her hands. The Green Man and Wade might disagree, but that wouldn't be much use to us if we were dead.

Moving to the kitchen window, I watched the mystery monster circle the apple trees. When it stood up on its bandy hind legs, it was easily as tall as me. That wasn't good. It was definitely hairy rather than furry. Even at this distance, I could see pale greyish skin through its coarse black pelt. For the moment it seemed more interested in the apple trees than coming any closer to the cottage.

'What are we going to do?' Standing next to me, Fin watched the monster warily.

'We have to scare it off.' Those electricians might have gone, but the nice lady with the little kids who wanted a hamster would get home from school any time now.

I pictured the black shuck who lives in Blithehurst's woods. I'd been able to call on the huge spectral black dog's help for a couple of years now, especially when I needed something big and dangerous to get between me and Fin and a threat. Like dryad radar and not being seen, it turned out that talent came with my greenwood blood. I held the image of the shuck in my mind's eye and focused on how urgently we needed it here right now.

'Dan?' Fin spoke quietly.

The back door was locked and the closed window was double-glazed. The monster still spun around as if it had heard her. Dropping onto all fours, it came past the bench on the grass. I could see its face more clearly. Its muzzle was like a dog's, though its rounded ears looked more like a bear's. Its nose was more ape-like, though, and so were its broad cheekbones and heavy brow. The hair on its pallid face was barely there. As its dark grey lips drew back in a snarl, I saw viciously sharp teeth. I couldn't see the colour of its eyes at this distance.

'Come on, shuck,' I muttered. 'Where are you?'

The bear-dog-ape thing turned to the apple trees. It reared up on its hind feet and raked claws like a handful of knives down the closest trunk. Strips of bark torn from great gouges in the sapwood fluttered in the breeze. The monster turned around to stare at the house. It raised those fearsome talons and stepped closer to the other tree. It was challenging me, no doubt about it. A moment later, it started ripping into the second tree's trunk.

'You arsehole.' I took the cottage keys out of the back door. 'Where are your car keys?'

'On the mantelshelf. What are you going to do?' Fin asked.

'The shuck's not coming and we can't wait for Zan.' I headed for the front door, swerving to grab the car keys. 'Watch that thing. Shout if it moves.'

Unlocking the front door took more time than I liked, and I hated leaving it open behind me, but I needed to hear Fin's warning if that creature came my way.

I opened the Toyota's hatchback. Pulling up the flooring in the boot, I grabbed the tyre iron and stuck that into my waistband. What I wanted was the tow rope I'd bought Fin ages ago, after her car got bogged down in a sodden field. No one who'd come to help had had one of those, so I don't know what exactly they expected to do. I bought her the same make that I keep in my Land Rover. Of course, she hadn't needed a tow since then.

I ripped off the plastic packaging as I ran into the house. Kicking the front door shut behind me, I dropped the car keys onto the coffee table. Fin stood in the kitchen doorway. I tossed her the house keys. 'Lock up the front. Be ready to open the back. Shut it and lock it as soon as I'm out there.'

While she went past me, I unzipped the pouch holding the tow rope. It came with a pair of protective gloves, which was useful. I pulled those on. Strictly speaking, this wasn't a rope but a long, wide, wire-reinforced strap with a fluorescent yellow stripe. I unrolled the red polyester before looping it loosely up again. I held the coil in my left hand

and tested the weight of the heavy-duty carbon steel towing shackle that dangled from my right. I'd bought a towing strap rated for a Land Rover. Someone might need to borrow it off Fin to tow a bigger vehicle than her Toyota.

'Let's go.'

Fin pulled the back door half-open. I dodged through the gap into the garden. Fin slammed the door and turned the key. So far, so good. I let more polyester strap slide through my hands so I was holding a long, dangling loop. The shackle nearly brushed the grass. I waited to see what the hairy bear-dog-ape thing would do. It was lurking between the apple trees again.

It stood up on its crooked hind legs. Its teeth were bared in a silent snarl. It blinked, and I saw its solid black eyes didn't change in any way. Whatever this thing was, it didn't seem to be kin to the hags. Was that good news or bad news or simply news?

'Well?' I challenged it. 'What do you want? Why are you here?'

The creature growled. I didn't see the slightest sign it understood what I'd said. I was starting to think this monster was more animal than anything else. So we wouldn't be discussing a deal to make it go away.

I took a step forward, drawing my right hand back. The shackle swung by the side of my leg. The monster came out from between the apple trees, still on its hind feet. Its gaze flickered up to the window above my head. I hadn't heard Not-Alice make a sound. The thing must have hearing like a bat's.

It was distracted. I took my chance. A couple of long strides got me close enough to swing the towing shackle at it. I missed as the bastard thing dropped to all fours. The solid steel went right over its head. I backed off fast. Swinging the shackle over my head, I hoped to hell I wasn't close enough to the cottage to smash a window.

187

The bear-dog-ape reared up onto its hind legs again. I was already stepping sideways, getting outside the arc of those murderous claws. I wanted to lure the monster away from the cottage. I lashed it with the shackle, snapping the thick towing strap like a whip.

Each time the carbon steel hit the thing, raw red welts appeared on its skin. That sparse black pelt was no protection. It retreated towards the apple trees. I followed as close as I dared, slamming it with the steel shackle as hard and as fast as I could.

It thrust out a long, ape-like arm. The broad strap hit just below its elbow. Momentum spun the shackle around its clawed hand. The monster took hold of the strap. It hauled me forward, grimacing and hissing. It was an animal, but it wasn't stupid.

Nor was I. I dropped the coiled strap. The monster stumbled backwards, barely staying upright. When it realised I wasn't coming too, it tore the towing rope off its arm. That gave me time to pull the tyre iron out of my waistband.

The monster came forward, ready to take my head off with swiping blows from those lethal claws. Now I was glad the thing was so tall. I ducked and darted forward, dodging under its arm. As I brushed past its side, I slammed the tyre iron into the back of its thigh. The creature's leg buckled and it fell forward onto all fours. I spun around, right behind it. I slammed the tyre iron down on the base of its spine. As it howled, I backed off fast. Fin was right. This thing did stink.

The monster spun around to face me, still on all fours. I could see it gather itself, like a cat ready to spring. Which way was it going to jump? No, I realised a moment later. It was waiting for me to make the first move.

Two could play at that game. I backed off a bit more. Now I was protected by the wounded apple trees on either side. The monster's mouth hung open as it crouched in the middle of the lawn. Panting, not snarling, it stared at me. What was it going to do now?

What was I going to do, come to that? The bastard thing was between me and the cottage. As I thought that, I saw the back door open. The monster heard too and turned its head. It saw Fin on the step and bounded forward, frighteningly fast. That meant it got the two-handled pot full of boiling water she was carrying full in its face. Fin slammed the door shut as the monster recoiled.

I ran forward and snatched the towing strap off the grass. Swinging it was awkward when I was still holding the tyre iron, but I landed another stinging blow on the monster's back with the steel shackle.

The bear-dog-ape thing had had enough. It ran past me, staying out of reach of the tow rope. As it crashed through the ragged hedge at the end of the garden, I couldn't see which way it went. Sod it. We had to keep track of the thing.

I grabbed the closest branch on the nearest apple tree. The ancient tree's distress was like a kick in the balls. As soon as I could catch my breath, I apologised. I'm so sorry. I didn't mean that.

I got the distinct impression I was only making things worse. I let go of the wounded tree. Thankfully I couldn't feel its pain any more. I walked backwards towards the cottage, watching the hedge for any hint of movement. As I got closer, I heard the door open.

'Can you see it anywhere?' I asked Fin.

'No, I think it's gone.'

I could tell from her voice I was close enough to get inside before the monster could reach me, even if it crashed through the hedge at top speed. Even so, the back of my neck was prickling as I hurried through the door. I dropped the towing strap and the tyre iron onto the floor and went to the window over the sink.

Fin locked up and looked at me. 'What do we do now?'

Chapter Fifteen

'I have to help those apple trees.' I took my multi-tool out of my pocket. 'Stay here and keep watch in case that thing comes back.'

'Okay.' Fin stood by the sink and looked through the kitchen window.

I took the cottage keys and went out of the front door. I didn't take the tyre iron or the tow rope, but I was still wearing the protective gloves. I crossed the lane to the waste ground where the hag's fake cottage had fooled us. Doing my best not to get my bare arms stung, I cut the longest nettles I could find, taking my multi-tool's blade right down to their roots. With gloves on, I could quickly strip off the leaves, running the long stems between my finger and thumb from top to bottom. I worked fast. As soon as I had a good thick handful of stalks, I hurried back.

'Any sign of anything moving out there?' I shouted as I stepped into the cottage.

'No,' Fin called out. 'I think it's really gone.'

I went into the kitchen. Fin had picked everything up off the floor. The thick towing strap was loosely coiled on the counter. The tyre iron was next to the kettle, in case we needed that in a hurry.

I opened the back door and paused. Nothing charged through the hedge to attack me. I sat down on the step, ready to get inside at the first hint of a threat. I started crushing the first nettle stem, flattening it against my closed multi-tool.

Fin brought a dining chair into the kitchen to sit and watch me work. 'Who or what do you think that thing was after?'

'It came through the gateway after you did. Do you think it was coming *after* you? Chasing you specifically, I mean.' I slit the nettle stem down its full length with the main blade.

'I don't know.' Fin considered this. 'I didn't notice it anywhere while I was still on the other side. When I heard something in the passage behind me, I just wanted to get out of its way.'

'Which was the obvious thing to do.' I opened up the nettle stem and bent it so the pale pith inside cracked.

'Do you think it hurt those trees to provoke you?' Fin looked down the garden.

'Absolutely.' I stripped nettle pith from the outer fibres. They were getting on for a metre long. Good. 'Maybe to stop me using dryad radar to find it, or the hag. But did it attack me because it wanted to kill me, or was it trying to get to you? Or did it want to get to Not-Alice? Did you see it look up at her window?'

'I didn't,' Fin said uneasily. 'Could it have been after her? To kill her or to carry her off?'

'No clue.' I tucked damp nettle fibres under my leg so they wouldn't blow away and reached for another stem. 'We have no idea where she came from. Like we know sweet fuck all about hags. They know about these portals though. Well, this one does. Maybe the bear-dog thing came here because it sensed Not-Alice is one of them. Maybe it's looking for her. Maybe she sent it here.'

'That's a lot of maybes.' Fin wasn't convinced.

'I'm just guessing,' I admitted. 'But we can't leave Not-Alice here on her own if there's any chance that thing will come back. It could definitely smash these windows to get to her, and it's probably strong enough to have a good chance of breaking down the door.'

Fin was silent for a moment. 'So what are we going to do?'

'First, what we can to help those trees.' I carried on crushing nettle stalks.

Fin fetched a kitchen knife and the washing-up gloves from the draining board. 'Shift and I'll do some of those.'

I shuffled to one side in the doorway so she could lift the chair out onto the path behind the cottage. After watching me for a few minutes, she started stripping fibres from the nettle stems. 'So what are we doing?'

'We'll bind those loose strips of bark in place as well as we can. Hopefully they'll stick well enough to stay put by the time the nettle fibres dry up and flake away.' I looked down the garden towards the wounded trees. 'What we could really do with is a dryad to help them.'

'We could do with a lot of things,' Fin observed. 'How long are we going to wait for Zan?'

'Good question.' I crushed the next nettle stem a bit harder than I needed to. 'We don't even know if Blanche has got my message yet.'

'Do you want to try getting out of range of the hag to find a signal again? Or to lure her away and leave your phone with me?'

Fin wasn't keen on either option. I didn't blame her.

'I don't think we should split up. Not now. Not if there's any chance that beast-thing will turn up again.' I couldn't decide which possibility worried me more: coming face to face with it on a hillside on my own or being away from the cottage when it smashed its way in and attacked Fin.

'I agree.' She sounded relieved.

We carried on stripping fibres from the nettles. We soon had enough for me to plait bundles of three or four into longer lengths. I could have made a much stronger, twisted cord, but I didn't want to tie anything around these trees that would stay there long enough to damage them.

When Fin had finished stripping the last few stalks, I fetched the bucket from the shower room and filled it from the kitchen tap. I grabbed the cleanest-looking tea towel and picked up the tyre iron from the kitchen counter. I gave the tyre iron to Fin as she handed me a last handful of damp nettle strands.

We walked down the garden. Fin watched the hedge like a hawk while I assessed the poor, flayed trees. Thankfully I soon saw the damage didn't go right the way around either trunk or any of their branches. If they had been ring-barked, there'd be no saving them. As it was, this was a long shot, but I had to try.

'I need to wash these injured areas down with clean water. After that, I'll want you to hold the strips of bark steady while I use the nettles to bind them in place.'

I looked around. I couldn't see any sign of the bear-dog-ape beast. I couldn't smell a hint of its stink on the breeze. That would probably be our first clue. I soaked the tea towel in the bucket and started work. When I was ready to start refitting the first bits of loose bark, I gestured at the tyre iron.

'Put that on that bench and give me a hand, please.'

Fin tossed it onto the wooden seat and came to join me. Tending the injured trees took a fair while. Still, I was satisfied with our work by the time we were finished. I took a few steps back to see if I could usefully do anything else.

Fin picked up the tyre iron. 'What now?'

'We hope that whoever cleans this place at the weekend doesn't come outside to check on these trees. With a bit of luck, the owner won't claim for this damage against our deposit.'

I wasn't serious, but Fin didn't think that was funny.

'Dan, don't piss about.'

'Sorry. Well, I don't think we can sit here waiting for Zan. We don't even know if they'll turn up today. I say we take a look at Fieldfare Long Barrow. Let's see if that gateway's still open, for a start.'

Fin was surprised. 'You think the beast-thing might have gone home to wherever it came from, now it's been hurt?'

'That's a possibility.' One that hadn't occurred to me, to be honest. I'd had a different idea while we were doing first aid on the apple trees. 'What if the hag is hiding from dryad radar by stepping in and out of those gateways? She clearly knows a lot about them. When I last caught a trace of her, she was up on the hillside above the village. She could be using swallow-holes and caverns as well, like you said, but they're down in the valleys. She can't have vanished from me in a cave up there.'

'You think she'll show herself at the long barrow?'

'If you're there with me, and we've got Not-Alice with us? I reckon she'll want to know what we're up to. And she might not like to fight, but she does like to talk. There's got to be a decent chance she'll turn up to try and psych us out, or just to gloat.'

'That'll be fun.' Fin grimaced.

'She said she was going to teach me to steer clear of hags,' I reminded her. 'She wants me to tell everyone who's ever helped us that they're off limits. We can't do that if we're stuck here. We can point out she needs to let us go.'

I was getting more and more frustrated with this situation. Give me an enemy to fight, and I'll take it on, with or without anyone's help. Knowing the hag was out there, and not knowing how to stop her screwing with our phones and Fin's car, was really winding me up.

'If we know her plan won't work if she keeps us here indefinitely, why don't we wait her out?' Fin countered. 'Wait for Zan to get here and put a stop to whatever she's doing. If we try to make a deal, so she'll agree to let us go, you know she'll drive a hard bargain. She's the one with the power, as long as she can stop us using the car and our phones. What conditions will we have to agree to? I think that's a bad idea.'

I didn't have an answer for that. 'Well, even if the hag doesn't show up, I want to see if that portal's closed. I don't like the idea of leaving a gateway open to who knows where, with fuck knows what coming through it. If we can't close the portal, we need to tell the wise women about it, or the cunning men. Both, probably. As soon as we can.'

Fin nodded. 'Have you got any idea how we might be able to close it?'

I hoped so. 'We know we can hurt the beast-thing with the shackles on the end of the tow rope as well as with the tyre iron. If we can drive it through the passageway, we can see if that closes the portal.'

'That sounds simple enough,' Fin observed, 'but like your dad says, simple isn't the same as easy.'

She was right, and so was he. 'I'm not planning on fighting it hand-to-hand. If we can trap it between us and the gateway, the passage is the obvious route for it to escape. If we convince it we're going to hurt it again, there's got to be a decent chance it will run.'

Fin thought about that for a moment. 'I suppose it's worth a try. When are we going up there? Tonight?'

'After Not-Alice has had her evening feed,' I agreed. 'Before it gets too dark, but when any ordinary hikers will have gone home. We don't want anyone seeing us from the footpath and calling the cops to report us trespassing on an ancient monument. Besides, if we wait for a while, the beast-thing might decide to go through on its own. We might find the portal is closed when we get there.'

'Fair enough.' Fin liked that idea. 'Let's tidy up here before we go.'

We scooped up nettle pith and bits of stalks and dumped them in the bottom of the hedge. I kept my eyes open for any hint of movement. I stayed alert for the beast-thing's stink on the breeze. I could hear thrushes and other birds singing as they enjoyed this peaceful summer's day. None of them raised so much as an alarm call to warn of a prowling cat. If Fin and I had been enjoying the holiday we'd had planned, this would have been a lovely afternoon.

We went into the cottage and locked the doors yet again. I'd thought this place was small when we first arrived. It felt more cramped every time I came inside. I really wanted to leave now. Was this the hag's doing too? Could she influence the way I saw the inside of this cottage? She'd made me believe her entire house on the other side of the lane was real.

If it was some hag-related mind-fuckery, Fin didn't seem to be affected. She put a load of towels on to wash, sorted out the baby bottles in the kitchen and tidied up. When Not-Alice started making noises, Fin brought her downstairs. She sat with her on the sofa and took the baby carrier out of its packaging. As she read the instructions aloud to Not-Alice, I tuned her voice out. I was sitting at the dining table, studying the OS map yet again. I wanted to mark every possible place the hag might be using to hide from dryad radar, from caves to tumuli. I really hoped Zan turned up soon. Checking each and every one of these would take me and Fin the rest of this month.

'Am I adjusting these straps to fit you or me?' Fin asked. 'Dan? Did you hear me?'

'What?' I looked up, wondering what she was talking about.

She waved the baby carrier. 'Are you going to be carrying Not-Alice when we're out on this night hike or am I?'

Crap. I hadn't thought about that. 'We don't want anyone noticing her with us. It had better be me. I can do my not-being-seen thing.'

Fin frowned. 'What if that beast-thing or the hag turns up? What if one of them attacks? You don't want to be fighting with a baby strapped to your chest.'

Bugger. I should have thought of that. Was the hag's influence making me thick-headed today, or simply lack of sleep? I couldn't have got more than eight hours' proper rest in these past two days. 'No, you're right. You had better take her.'

Fin nodded, but she didn't look too happy about that. 'I can't risk going swan anyway, if there's any chance that hag's around to maze me again.' She shook her head. 'Sorry. It's just – this crap is really starting to get to me.'

'I know what you mean.' Clearly, I'd been wrong to think I was the only one getting frustrated, whether or not that was the hag messing with our minds. 'Shall I put the kettle on?'

Fin managed a smile. 'Good idea. I'll have a coffee. The decent coffee, not the instant.'

While the kettle was boiling, we worked out how to adjust the baby carrier's straps. Not-Alice seemed perfectly happy when we put her into it.

'It's more comfortable than I expected.' Fin walked around the living room, testing how it felt. 'Though she's not much of a weight.'

'Will you be able to run?' That was my main concern.

Fin considered that. 'Yes, if I really have to.'

'Let's hope you won't.'

If Fin had to run, that would mean I was coming off second-best in a fight with the hag or the beast-thing. As soon as she was on her own, I'd bet good money the other one would be waiting to attack her and the changeling. I wouldn't be able to do a thing to help. I glanced at the front window and really fucking wished Zan would turn up.

The sylph hadn't arrived by the time Not-Alice had emptied her evening bottle. I cooked our pizzas while Fin fed her. I noticed she was looking dubiously at the changeling. Knowing Not-Alice's eyes were the same as a hag's wasn't something she was going to forget.

While the changeling dozed on the sofa, Fin and I ate our dinner. I took our plates into the kitchen and washed up. Fin made up a bottle of formula for when we got back, and put the bottle she'd used in sterilising fluid.

'This baby business is doing the same things non-stop on repeat.'

'Tell me about it.' I heard Not-Alice squawking on the sofa. 'I don't know how single parents cope. I don't know how any parents do more than eat, sleep and do laundry.'

To my total lack of surprise, the changeling needed a clean nappy. Wondering how long it was before a baby did more than eat, sleep and crap, I took her upstairs. When I came down into the living room, Fin was lacing up her hiking boots

'Are we sure we want to do this?' Out of nowhere, I wasn't convinced. 'Maybe we should wait the hag out.'

Strapping on the baby carrier, Fin shrugged. 'What else are we going to do? Besides, we might just have a nice evening's walk and find that the gateway has already closed.'

That would be great, but that wouldn't necessarily mean we were safe from the beast-thing, if it had got stuck on this side. And unless we saw the hag, we'd be nowhere closer to getting out of here.

'Okay.' I put Not-Alice down, kicked off my trainers and found my hiking boots. 'What are we taking with us?'

'You have the tow rope and the tyre iron.' Fin fetched the backpack she used instead of a handbag from the coat hooks by the door. 'I might as well take my phone and the keys. It's not as if I'm going to be flying anywhere.'

I hesitated. 'You should be ready to do that. If everything turns to shit, drop your backpack and get out of there. Seriously, I mean it. Drop everything, and that includes her.' I jerked my head towards the changeling.

I could see Fin wanted to argue. I went on before she could. 'One of us has to tell Eleanor and everyone else what's happened here. If I'm fighting the hag, I can keep her too busy to think about anyone else. Get beyond her reach and you can come back with help.'

Fin picked Not-Alice up off the sofa and slotted her into the baby carrier. 'Let's hope it doesn't come to that.'

We left through the hedge at the bottom of the garden. I resisted the temptation to touch the apple trees to see if I could sense them healing. That might reassure me, but from the trees' point of view, I'd be poking a bloody bandage to ask if that still hurt.

I wasn't going to try dryad radar this evening anyway. I didn't want the hag to know I was looking for her. I was also pretty sure that beast-thing had sensed my greenwood blood. That's how it knew attacking the apple trees would get me out of the cottage. Bastard. If dryad radar brushed past it, there was a good chance it would know I was coming after it. I mean, who else could be doing that around here?

As we headed for the bridleway, I concentrated hard on not being seen. That wouldn't affect Fin. She knew I was walking beside her. Right now, I was trying to hide Fin and Not-Alice as well, while we were walking close together. How far this concealment could reach was another experiment for my list once we got out of this mess.

I had the OS map in a pocket, but I'd gone over the route so often I could probably find my way to the long barrow blindfolded. Not-Alice made a few little noises to begin with but soon fell asleep in the baby carrier. We headed straight to the barrow, taking a faster route than the circular walk. We reached a fingerpost at a junction, and I slowed to be certain we were taking the right path.

'I don't think these gateways lead to somewhere else,' Fin said suddenly. 'I think it's some *when* else. It's wherever dryads and naiads go, where time moves at different speeds. Think about a river. That's a continuous stream of water, but some is flowing faster than the rest, in the middle and at the surface. Along the riverbed, and on the inside of bends, the water moves a lot more slowly.'

'Meaning what, exactly?' I'd accept whatever Fin said about rivers. She was the expert, professionally and as a swan.

'I think these portals link faster and slower bits of time, for want of a better word. They're routes for creatures, people, whatever, who can't move from a faster flow to a slower one by themselves.'

'Which helps us how?' I was asking a genuine question, not challenging her logic.

'I don't know,' Fin admitted. 'I'm simply trying to make sense of it.'

'I know what you mean.' I still had no idea if she was right or wrong about any of this.

We walked on in silence. We reached the gap in the hedge where people could stop and admire Fieldfare Long Barrow and wonder who built it. I checked both ways along the footpath in case anyone else was out and about. We were very exposed up here. I remembered reading a theory that burial mounds were often on skylines to make sure the ancestors weren't forgotten. Whether or not that was true, right now this barrow's placement was sodding inconvenient.

Since I couldn't see any hikers, monsters or hags, I turned to Fin. 'There isn't a stile. Do you need me to take her, so you can get over the fence?'

'I'll be better off going through it, if you can lift that top strand up high enough.' Fin unclipped the baby carrier and propped Not-Alice against the hedge. The changeling was still sound asleep. Fin slipped off her backpack and tossed that over the fence. 'Ready?'

I used both hands to lift the barbed-wire strand up as high as I could. Fin slid one foot over the wire mesh and leaned forward to edge sideways. She barely had enough room to get through the gap. Keeping the top wire pulled up was hard work, but if I let it sag, the vicious barbs would claw at her sweatshirt or her skin. I braced myself and looked around yet again. If something was going to attack us, this would be an ideal time.

Fin got through unscratched. As soon as she stood up, she checked the path in both directions, and searched the field and the long barrow for any signs of movement. 'All clear. Let me have Not-Alice.'

I handed the changeling to her and got carefully over the fence as she clipped the baby carrier back on. 'Stay behind me.'

'I'll let you know if anything's coming,' Fin assured me

That hadn't been what I meant, but she was right. A threat could come from any direction. Feeling better with Fin watching my back, I focused on the long barrow. I couldn't see that anything had changed. Well, it had only been a day. Coming here last night seemed an aeon ago.

I glanced over my shoulder. Fin was checking nothing was sneaking up behind us. She looked back at me and managed a quick grin. I smiled before heading for the western end of the long mound. The deep hollows claimed by trees looked exactly the same as they had last night. The long stretch where the retaining wall was robbed out hadn't been disturbed.

As we approached the fresh collapse, we saw the loose earth had been scraped away. The fallen slabs from the roof and the sides of the unsuspected passage had been heaved to one side. The portal was clear for whoever might want to use it. Though they'd have to get past the bear-dog-ape thing that was crouching in the entrance.

Chapter Sixteen

The beast saw us and got up. The roof of the tunnel kept it on all fours. That didn't reassure me. I'd seen how fast it could move.

Fin tugged at my backpack. 'I'll get the tow rope out.'

'Give me the tyre iron.' I saw the beast was watching me, wary and tense.

If it wanted to attack, it would already be halfway to us. This might be an animal, wherever it had come from, but it wasn't stupid. Dave Fulbrooke, my dad's friend and a decent copper, always said the brightest police dogs were much cleverer than the dumbest criminals.

So right now, I'd wait and see. Fin handed me the tyre iron. I held it up so the monster knew I was ready to defend myself if it came within reach. I hoped it also realised I wasn't about to use the towing rope's steel shackle on it again. Not yet anyway. I saw the dark, bruised blotches spread across the creature's grey skin through its sparse black hair. Tough luck. It had started that fight by attacking the apple trees. Hopefully it was having second thoughts about trying again.

'Dan,' Fin said quietly. 'It's looking at me.'

'At you or at Not-Alice?' I had seen its gaze slide past me. 'Let me have her for a moment.'

'What are you going to do?' Fin lifted the sleepily protesting changeling out of the baby carrier.

'Test a theory. Stay where you are.' Making sure I didn't fumble and drop the tyre iron or the changeling, I took hold of Not-Alice in both hands and walked a couple of metres away from Fin. The beast's eyes stayed fixed on me, or rather, on the changeling. I was sure about that now.

Fin was too. 'What does it want with her?' she wondered, uneasy.

'No idea. Don't move.' I held Not-Alice out at arm's length and moved her from one side to the other. The beast's gaze tracked the motion.

'Dan?' Fin stayed where she was, but she wasn't happy about this.

The beast took a step forward, still on all fours. It was looking straight at Not-Alice. I didn't take my eyes off the creature.

'Drop your backpack,' I told Fin. 'Get ready to get out of here if it attacks me.'

The bear-dog-ape thing lifted its muzzle and sniffed the warm evening air. If it did attack, could I bring myself to throw Not-Alice at it? Would a faceful of changeling distract the beast long enough for me to get away? How badly injured might she be if she hit the ground hard? What would the beast do then? Stop and eat her?

The changeling was facing me. Her wide-open eyes looked as human as mine. She wasn't crying or struggling, even though I was holding her under the arms with her little legs dangling. Did she trust me to keep her safe?

The beast moved closer, cautiously, stopping to sniff the air every few steps. I tried to get a better grip on the tyre iron as I shifted Not-Alice into the crook of my elbow, holding her close so my forearm supported her legs. The tyre iron slipped and she yelped, surprised, not hurt, as the cold metal touched her little hand.

The beast halted, startled by the noise. It reared up onto its hind legs, waving its viciously clawed forepaws.

'Dan, how about we back off?'

Fin didn't like this, and I could see why. But I had seen something else as well.

'Let's give it a minute.'

The beast wasn't snarling. Every time it opened its mouth, its long, dark tongue tasted the air. I was convinced the creature was trying to get a better look at Not-Alice, or to get her scent. I looked down as the changeling blinked. For a second,

I glimpsed that red-brown colour, so like a hag's horrible eyes.

I stuck the tyre iron in the thigh pocket of my combat trousers. If I had to, I could grab that before the beast reached me, but right now, I didn't want to look like a threat. I spread out my fingers to show it my empty hand.

The beast crept forward, sinking down. Was it trying to look less threatening? Unless it was crouching, getting ready to pounce. I watched its backside for any telltale wriggle. That would be a lot easier if the bloody thing had a tail.

It stopped about three metres away, well out of my reach. This thing wasn't stupid. It was definitely intent on Not-Alice. I tried to decide what to do if it attacked me now. Throw the changeling to Fin like a rugby ball and try cracking the bear-dog-ape's skull with the tyre iron before it got to her? Assuming Fin wasn't already flying away. I really hoped I hadn't fucked up by doing this.

The beast stayed motionless with its belly pressed to the grass. Then it slowly got up. It backed away on all fours, looking at me, then at the changeling, before looking at me again. It retreated into the mouth of the tunnel.

For one endless moment of relief, I thought it was going home to wherever – whenever – it had come from. The portal was going to close and we'd have one less problem to deal with.

No such luck. The beast settled down on the stone floor, right where it had been when we arrived. Bollocks.

'What was that about?' Fin was mystified.

'I wish we could ask it.' Not-Alice was squirming. I handed her to Fin.

'Do you think the hag knows it's here?' Fin wondered. 'Maybe she's not hiding from us. Maybe she's hiding from that.'

That was a very good question, but there was no way to know the answer. 'If she is, we've got a problem.'

Fin nodded as she eased Not-Alice into the baby sling. 'As long as that thing's not leaving, the gateway won't close.'

'Okay, two problems.' Since the beast-thing didn't look like an immediate threat any more, I focused on the hag. 'If she knows that's dangerous, she won't be coming here. So we won't be able to persuade her to let us go.'

'Then there's nothing more we can do here tonight.' Fin patted Not-Alice's back to soothe her. The changeling was starting to grizzle.

'Right,' I agreed.

Our walk to the cottage was uneventful. We didn't talk. Fin was thinking through what had happened and so was I. Before we left the hillside to walk along the last stretch of the bridleway, I stopped beside an elder tree.

'Let's see what I can find right now.' I reached for a convenient branch. 'If that's okay with you?'

Fin knew I was asking the tree's permission. She stood and waited. A moment later I let go of the branch. 'Thank you.'

'Well?'

'The beast-thing is still up at the long barrow.' Getting a sense of the creature was useful. I'd know if any more of those bear-dog-apes were roaming around the next time I checked. 'But I still can't find that sodding hag.'

We walked the rest of the way to the cottage, going through the hedge. As we passed the wounded apple trees, I tried to think of something more I could do for them. Nothing came to mind. I let them be.

Fin handed Not-Alice to me as soon as we got inside. She dumped her backpack on the sofa and unclipped the baby carrier. 'She needs a change. I'm going to try the car.'

I listened for the sound of the Toyota's engine while I was putting a fresh nappy on the changeling. I didn't hear the car start. On the plus side, Not-Alice was still drowsy when I had finished, so I put her in her towel-lined drawer. With any luck we'd get an hour or so's peace and quiet before she wanted her next feed.

As I went downstairs, Fin came in and tossed her car keys onto the mantelpiece hard enough to tell me she was on the verge of losing her temper.

'Still as dead as a bloody dodo. Still no sign of Zan. Okay. How are we going to find this bloody hag?'

'You've changed your mind about waiting her out?' I asked cautiously.

'I really thought Zan would be here by now.' Fin sighed. 'Do you think there's any way the hag could be stopping them from finding us?'

'I have no idea. We don't know enough about hags.' And now Fin had given me another possibility to worry about.

'I've been thinking,' Fin went on. 'What if she waits until the very last minute on Saturday morning, when she knows we'll be desperate to leave? If she turns up and says we have to agree to whatever she wants from us or we'll be stuck here until the cleaners arrive? Until whoever's rented this place for next week needs that parking space? Can we risk finding out that's what she's prepared to do? One thing we know about hags is they understand how the modern world works. Do we want that kind of grief when we can't even make a phone call? You're the one who's spoken to her. What do you think?'

I thought about the hag's implacable hostility, even when I'd had my hands around her throat. 'I wouldn't try calling her bluff.'

'I hate to think what she'll ask for, when she knows we're in no position to bargain.' Fin glanced up at the ceiling, to-wards the back bedroom where the changeling was sleeping. 'And how will we explain her to the cleaners or anyone else?'

'Especially if they live in this village and they already know one baby's gone astray.' I took the OS map out of my pocket. 'We start checking these caves and caverns and tu-muli first thing in the morning. There are a shitload of them, so I suggest we start with the closest and work outwards.'

'Will that help us find the hag?' Fin genuinely wanted to know.

'Hopefully she'll want to know what we're up to.' I tried to sound more certain than I felt. That hadn't worked this evening, though of course, the beast-thing had been lurking at Fieldfare Long Barrow. But I was starting to feel I was clutching at straws. I hoped I wasn't pissing in the wind.

Fin sighed again. 'I'll put the kettle on and we'll work out a route.'

'At least we shouldn't need to watch our backs for that beast-thing any more.' I tried to find something for the plus column. 'And we can take turns carrying Not-Alice.'

Fin paused in the kitchen doorway. 'We have to give her to the wise women before someone sees her with us and starts asking questions. One of us has to find a phone signal so we can contact them. If we can't find that damn hag tomorrow, maybe we should split up and walk in opposite directions, like we said earlier. We can ask if they know how to get this hag off our backs at the same time. If they say sorry, they can't help, we're no worse off. And we can try ringing Blanche again.'

'Agreed.' I still didn't like the idea of Fin encountering the hag on her own, but we were running out of time and options.

I didn't think much of our chances of getting help to foil the hag though, not unless we were asking Hazel. Centuries ago, some of today's wise women's foremothers had done an arcane deal with the hags. Whatever that bargain had been, that's how human witches had learned to turn into hares, the same as hags could. Fin and I had seen Hazel and other cunning women do it. That's how hags gained their ability to handle iron, to some extent anyway. That's what had made them such a threat to everyone else in the uncanny world, as well as to ordinary, everyday people. We had no way to know what else the wise women might have agreed.

I studied the OS map. It was getting worn where the creases met, as well as tattered along the edges. Being unfolded, refolded and carried around in my pocket was doing it no favours. Fin came in with a pot of tea and two mugs. She found a table mat to put them on.

I traced a footpath with my finger. 'How about we go this way and start at Stanton's Tumps?' That had been the next place I'd planned on going after Fieldfare Long Barrow.

'Okay.' Fin sipped her tea as she got her bearings on the map. She leaned forward, puzzled. 'There's something missing here.'

'How do you mean?'

Fin's fingertip followed a cluster of contour lines into a deep gully. 'There's a standing stone right here. I flew over it on my way here from the long barrow. Why isn't it on the map?'

We stared at each other.

'I find it hard to believe the Ordnance Survey missed that,' I said slowly.

'Especially when the damn thing's taller than you are.' Fin reached into her jeans back pocket and found the grimy circular walks leaflet. I hadn't even realised she still had that. She smoothed the creased paper out. 'Look, you'd go right past the gully if you were following this route between Old Shute Gate and Stanton's Tumps. There's no way this enthusiast could ignore that.'

'Not if they reckoned that pathetic Pylestone was worth a visit.' I drank some tea. 'There are stories about stone circles which used to be people. Like the Rollright Stones at home. They were supposedly a king and his army, and a group of knights who were plotting against him.'

Growing up in Warwickshire, the Rollright Stones had been a favourite place for school trips. I'd been in two different classes which proved the King's Men stones could in fact be counted without any difficulty, though no one I knew had got their heart's desire afterwards. There was often local gossip about idiots who'd suffered bad luck after disrespecting the stones.

'Though the legend says the witch who turned them to stone turned herself into an elder tree.' If I'd remembered that story on our first walk up to the hillside overlooking Bishop's Warren, when Fin had been mazed, I'd never have asked that elder tree for help.

'Isn't there a stone circle in the Lake District that's supposed to be dancing witches? Long Meg or something?' Fin was halfway to picking up her phone before she remembered that was pointless. She vented her frustration with a growl. 'I wish we could get online.'

'I think I've heard other stories like that, about witches and standing stones. Aren't some of them supposed to go wandering around?' I looked at the map. 'So do we think this mystery monolith can have something to do with this hag?'

'I think if we're going to find a way out of this mess, since we've got no other leads, we might as well check out anything that seems to make no sense.' Fin surprised herself with a jaw-cracking yawn. 'I have no idea why I'm so tired.'

'Fresh air and exercise and nowhere near enough sleep.' I knew that's why I was knackered. Was Fin also feeling some after-effects from missing so much time here while she was on the other side of the tilted stone portal? That was something else I should ask my mum.

'Shall we go there first tomorrow?'

'Sounds like a plan.' Fin yawned again and glanced at the clock. 'Shall we have an early night?'

'After Not-Alice has had her next bottle, sure. Do you want to do her midnight feed or three in the morning?'

'Bloody hell.' Fin shook her head. 'We really have to give her to a wise woman.'

'No argument from me.' I thought that every time I glimpsed the changeling's red-brown eyes.

Fin drank the last of her tea. 'Do you really think she could grow up to be a hag?' She couldn't help a shudder.

'If the wise women won't tell us, I'll ask my mum.' I wished I'd asked her a whole lot more about hags before now. Like my dad says, hindsight is always perfect and mostly useless.

Fin drummed her fingertips on the table. 'Should we ask them to keep us updated? The wise women, I mean. Let us know where she ends up?'

'It couldn't hurt.' That had occurred to me too.

Right on cue, we heard the changeling start squawking upstairs.

Fin rubbed her face with both hands. 'If you do midnight, I'll get up at three. Okay?'

'Fine by me. If you want to go to bed, I'll feed her now.'

'Thanks.' Fin gave me a quick kiss before we both went upstairs.

I brought Not-Alice down into the living room. She took her bottle without making too much fuss, burped and soon dozed off. Had fresh air and exercise made her sleepy too? I went through the tedious routine of washing up the used bottle and refilling the sterilised one. When I carried the changeling upstairs, Fin was fast asleep and snoring.

For a second, I thought about sleeping in the back bedroom to avoid disturbing her. Sod that. I'd spent one horrible night here on my own. I put Not-Alice in her towel-lined drawer and closed the back bedroom door. I set my phone to vibrate with a midnight alarm. I dumped my clothes on the floor at the end of the bed and put my phone under my pillow. As I slipped under the duvet, Fin didn't stir.

I definitely slept better knowing Fin was beside me. I got up and gave Not-Alice her midnight feed on what felt like autopilot and soon dozed off again. I didn't notice when Fin got up in the small hours. When I opened my eyes, early sunlight was coming through the thin curtains.

I rolled over and watched Fin sleeping. Moving must have woken her up. She opened her eyes and smiled at me. I leaned over to kiss her. She slid one hand around my ribs to pull me closer. Her feathers tickled my chest. She slid her other hand down between us, reaching down past my belly. I kissed her and cupped her breast, teasing her nipple with my thumb.

Not-Alice woke up and started screaming her head off.

Fin looked me in the eye. 'Your turn.'

Chapter Seventeen

My phone said it was ten to seven. But how in the ev-erlasting fuck was it still only Wednesday? This week already felt like it had lasted a month.

I kissed Fin and sat up. 'I'll get her if you cook breakfast. I have a feeling this could be a long day.'

'Deal.' Fin threw back the duvet. 'After I've had a shower.'

'Fair enough.' I went to deal with the changeling.

A week ago, I'd been making sure I had everything sorted at work so I could take the next ten days off. Fin had been doing the same. I was going to drive down to her flat near Bristol on Thursday so we could take her car over to the Fens on Friday. That drive through the pouring rain felt like it had happened sometime last year.

Thankfully, Not-Alice stopped screaming once I picked her up. That was a relief. I wiped the tears off her little red face and held her against my shoulder, waiting for her to calm down. When she stopped gasping and whimpering, I changed her sodden nappy and took her downstairs. Fin was coming out of the shower with wet hair.

'That's better.' She gave me a quick smile before hurrying up to the bedroom.

I fed Not-Alice. When Fin reappeared, I laid the change-ling on the sofa, wedged with a cushion. 'I'll have a shower as well.'

That helped wake me up, especially after I turned the water down to as cold as possible for the last few minutes. I dried myself in the shower room, rubbing myself hard with the towel to get my blood flowing. By the time I was dressed, Fin was putting breakfast on the dining table. Bacon for me and beans for herself to go with scrambled eggs.

'We'll be okay for food for today, but we'll need to make a plan to go shopping tomorrow.' She sat down and took some toast from the pile on a plate between us.

I buttered a slice for myself. 'What do you suggest?'

Fin pressed the plunger on the cafetière. 'If we don't make any progress today, I say you get the bus to Cheddar tomorrow and take Not-Alice with you. I'll wait here for Zan. Tell Eleanor what's going on. Get her to contact the wise women, to tell them we've got a changeling. Tell her to tell them we need someone to take her today. Then you find somewhere quiet to wait. That'll be one less thing we have to worry about.'

I reached for the ketchup. 'Or you could do that. There's a park in the middle of Cheddar where you won't be overheard on the phone. Try calling Blanche again.'

Fin looked dubious as she ate some eggs. 'What will you be doing?'

I shrugged as I swallowed a mouthful of bacon. 'Checking caves and ancient monuments for any sign of that bloody hag. You could ring Aled for me. See how soon he could get here to help.'

I hadn't seen any point in bothering him when we thought our biggest problem was finding a stolen baby. Now we needed all the help we could get, and the thought of going into caves on my own still didn't appeal.

'Aled goes pot-holing for fun,' I pointed out. 'He can bring us the proper gear for exploring underground. He's also got the experience to keep us out of trouble.'

Plus he's a foot shorter than me. If needs be, he could follow the hag into tight spaces where I couldn't go. Maybe he could call on his coblyn heritage. I'd seen that work for him before. If any of his ancestor's kin lived around here, I couldn't imagine hags were too popular with them.

'And when we've got this crap sorted out, we'll ask him to make an engagement ring.'

Fin grinned for a second. Then she nodded, serious again. 'All right, I'll go to Cheddar. If we can't find the hag today.'

There wasn't anything else to say. We finished our breakfast.

Fin gathered up the plates. 'If we're going to be out for a good long while, we had better take baby stuff with us.'

'I'll get that together.' First though, as Fin went into the kitchen and started to wash up, I got the OS map and the circular walk leaflet off the coffee table where I'd left them last night. I added the path to that narrow gully where Fin had seen the mystery standing stone to the sketch map. That would be a lot easier to handle as we were walking. Obviously, I'd stick the OS map in my backpack as well. I also decided, if we couldn't find this bloody hag, we'd go to one of the pubs the ancient monuments enthusiast recommended and have lunch. We could pretend we were having a normal holiday for a couple of hours.

Unless we were going to spend the whole day wandering in circles because the hag had mazed us. Could she do that if I was carrying the tyre iron or the tow rope with those carbon steel shackles? I had no idea. I was really sick and tired of coming up with questions and not being able to ask anyone for answers. Well, all I could do was take the tyre iron and the towing strap with me.

I put a couple of nappies, the pack of bum wipes, one of those ready-to-use bottles of formula and the empty baby bottle into Fin's backpack. I picked up the tyre iron and hesitated.

'You'd better take that.' Fin was standing in the kitchen doorway with our full water bottles in her hands. 'I'll have my credit card in a pocket, so I can get out of there as fast as possible if everything goes to shit.'

'If you think you're being mazed, if you feel anything's even slightly off, tell me at once.' I picked up the baby carrier. That was all synthetic materials, which was a shame. Even a bit of metal might have been useful against the hag. Still, the high, reinforced back and the padding should give Not-Alice some protection if Fin had to drop her on the ground in a hurry.

I put the water bottle in my backpack with the towing strap. 'I've been looking at the map. I know we said we'd go straight to the mystery monolith, but we'll go right past the Old Shute Gate. Do we want to take a look at that first?'

'It makes sense to check if there's a portal behind us, that the hag or something else might come through,' Fin agreed.

I looked around at the changeling still dozing on the sofa. 'Shall I carry her for the first stretch?'

'It'll be more hassle to have to adjust the straps whenever we swap her over.' Fin was already clipping on the baby carrier. 'It's not as if she's heavy.'

'If you're sure.' That suited me. I put the tyre iron inside my waistband. Once we were clear of the village, I'd carry it in my hand.

We left through the garden. I took a quick look at the apple trees as we passed. The nettle fibres had dried to pale, fine threads, but the plaited strands seemed to be holding the damaged bark secure. Good. All the same, I wanted to get a dryad here as soon as I could work out how to do that. The gap in the straggly hedge was getting wider, and I hoped the cottage's owner wasn't going to complain.

Fin nodded at the closest hawthorn. 'Do you want to see what's where this morning?'

'I don't think so.' I'd remembered to bring my sunglasses. I put them on. 'We don't need to know where the beast-thing is, now we know it's not a threat. I don't want to give the hag any warning that we're coming to find her.'

'You don't think she's watching?' Fin was curious. 'My phone still doesn't work.'

'We still don't know how far away she has to be to do that. Anyway, if she's watching, she can see we're going out, but she won't know why. Who knows, with luck that'll be enough to draw her out. Especially if there's something about this mystery monolith which she doesn't want us to see.' If curiosity killed the cat, I'd do my best to see it tripped up this hag.

Several cars were still parked by the start of the bridleway. Behind us, I heard traffic on the main road through the village. Bishop's Warreners with no clue what was going on were heading off to work and school. No one else was setting out on a midweek hike.

We soon left the village behind. I checked every waypoint I had marked on the sketch map. The route to the mystery monolith wasn't one either of us had walked or flown. We soon found we were following a narrow path through a deep, steep-sided valley. A stream chuckled along the bottom. I wondered if there were hag stones in there. But they didn't work if you went deliberately hunting for them. Had the hags somehow managed to arrange that?

I walked in front of Fin, gripping the tyre iron. The steep slopes and the lack of trees meant there was no useful cover for anything trying to sneak up on us. Anything visible, anyway. On the other hand, the winding path made it difficult to see very far in front of or behind us. I breathed much easier when the path led us upwards onto an open stretch of hillside.

I double-checked where we were. 'Old Shute Gate is this way.'

The path headed straight up the steep hill. We both stopped to take a breather when we reached the level ground at the top.

Fin lifted up Not-Alice to resettle the baby carrier's straps on her shoulders. 'You know I said this one wasn't too heavy? I might have been a bit optimistic.'

I was studying the landscape ahead. Short-cropped grass ended at a fence line marking the boundary of a mature wood. About halfway between us and the edge of the trees, two roughly rectangular stones stood a metre or so apart, on the edge of a shallow dip in the ground. One wasn't quite two metres tall, maybe half a metre wide and a bit less deep. The other was noticeably smaller.

'I don't think that's any sort of portal. For a start, this place is so high up and exposed.'

'We should take a closer look, but I think you're right,' Fin agreed. 'The other ones make you go through a space with stone on all sides.'

That was true, though we knew of a grand total of three examples so far, including Wayland's Smithy. 'Don't get between the stones though. Just in case.'

'I can see why someone would call this a gate,' Fin commented as we walked towards the stones. 'I mean, if you were trying to imagine why the stones are here. Whoever put them up must have had a reason.'

'Don't archaeologists say "ritual" when they find something they can't explain?' We reached the stones. Crystals in the pale grey rock sparkled in the sunshine. I looked more closely at the taller one's base. 'Hang on. That's concrete. This stone's been broken.'

Fin came to join me. 'Does the leaflet say anything about that?'

I checked the write-up. 'Apparently the stones were almost taken away sometime in the 1920s, to be used as hardcore for building roads. They must have got as far as knocking this one down. Somebody put it up again.'

'If there had been a portal here, would that have broken the – whatever makes them work?' Fin wondered.

'When we find someone who might know the answer to that, we can ask.' I turned to look in the other direction. 'Still, I'm glad we came up here. This is a great view.'

'It really is,' Fin agreed.

We could see for miles. The landscape rose and fell in shallow swells as far as the horizon and the silvery sheen of the sea. Between here and there, lush pastures, fields of crops and pockets of woodland were threaded through with hedgerows. Once upon a time, those would have been layered and staked every winter to make solid, stock-proof boundaries. Modern farming meant taller trees had taken their chance to flourish among the lower-level blackthorns and field maples. I could see oaks, ash trees and the occasional beech spaced out like beads on scattered necklaces. Fin smiled as the breeze ruffled her long blonde hair. She had left it loose to dry after her shower.

I put my arm around her shoulders. We stood for a few minutes, enjoying the summer sunshine. Not-Alice slept on.

'Right,' Fin said briskly. 'Let's get going.'

We made our way carefully down the steep path. The route I had marked took us around the hill's broad base and into another narrow valley. This path was wide enough for us to walk side by side.

Fin took off her sunglasses, shading her eyes with her hand. 'Places do look different on the ground when you've seen them from the air. We're getting close, aren't we?'

'We are.' I took the lead, alert for anything unexpected and gripping the tyre iron.

We reached a sharp bend where the main path veered off to the left. The steep-sided gully straight ahead was thick with long grass and wildflowers. At the far end, the hillside rose vertically behind a single tall pillar of dull, dark stone.

'There is no way whoever wrote that leaflet could possibly miss this,' I said aloud.

'So what do we do now?' Fin came to stand beside me.

'Have a drink. Can you get my bottle out, please?' I turned my shoulder so Fin could unzip my backpack. I didn't take my eyes off the mystery monolith. Whatever this was, that rock wasn't limestone. It had none of the rainbow sparkles we'd seen in the Old Shute stones. Something else nagged at me as well...

'Here you go.' Fin handed over my water bottle. 'Care to return the favour?'

'Thanks.' I got out her water, still looking at the monolith. 'Does Not-Alice need a bottle?'

'I think she's okay for the moment.' Fin frowned as she took a drink. 'It's very quiet here.'

'Too quiet.' That was what I'd been trying to pin down.

These dense clumps of grasses and wildflowers should have been full of insects. Buzzing bees should be foraging for pollen. We should hear grasshoppers chirping as they sprang from stalk to stalk. Butterflies should be everywhere. I should be seeing meadow browns, fritillaries, painted ladies, maybe even rare blues.

'Let's take a closer look.' Fin took the water out of my hand. We put both bottles away.

'Let me go first. I'll make a path.' Taking slow, careful steps, I trampled down the vegetation between us and the mystery monolith. Fin followed close behind me. The dark rock loomed ahead. There wasn't a breath of air moving, but that's not why the warm summer day felt so oppressive.

'Can you feel that?' I asked.

'Yes,' Fin confirmed.

I wished I could see what dryad radar would show me right now, but there were no trees anywhere close, not even spindly saplings. That was wrong as well. A sheltered spot like this should have seeds and nuts dropped by birds taking root.

The nearer we got to the stone, the more the harsh smell of crushed greenery caught in my throat. Not-Alice started grizzling. Was she hungry or uncomfortable, or could she feel a hostile presence? I was convinced I could.

'Hush, hush.' Fin tried to soothe the changeling. 'That thing really doesn't want us coming any closer, does it?'

'What's it going to do about it?' I was within arm's reach of the monolith now.

I didn't want to be here. No, that wasn't true. Those thoughts were coming from outside my head. Something or someone was desperately trying to convince me to go away. Tough shit.

Fin stopped a few paces behind me. She raised her voice. Not-Alice was wailing even louder. 'What are you going to do?'

I slammed the tyre iron into the dark grey rock. Pins and needles shot up my arm like the shock from an electric fence. A fence set up to keep elephants out. The clang was like nothing I'd ever heard. Good building stone rings with a sweet, pure note when you strike it with a trowel. The sour noise bounced around the gully. That wasn't right either. This much vegetation should absorb sound, not reject it.

Not-Alice was screaming now. Glancing over my shoulder, I saw Fin wince as she rocked the changeling. Our eyes met.

'Warn me before you do that again.'

'Do you want to go back to the main path?'

'No. Just warn me first.'

I didn't know what to do next. Despite that ear-splitting noise, the tyre iron hadn't left a mark on the dark stone. Did I need to get on a bus to Cheddar to buy a hammer and a mason's chisel? Or a sledgehammer? But if I left, would the monolith be here when I got back?

Fuck it. I lifted up the tyre iron and looked at Fin. 'Ready?'

'Give me a minute.' She had a packet of tissues in her hand. Ripping one up, she screwed white twists into her ears.

'Let me have some of that.' I'd rather have proper ear defenders, but this was better than nothing.

'Ready.' Fin cupped her hands around Not-Alice's head. The changeling tried to twist away. She was getting more and more upset. Because of the noise from the stone? Somehow, I didn't think so.

I drew my arm back, turning my body to put everything I could into my next strike.

'Dan!' Fin screamed.

The monolith was moving. It was toppling towards me. I was going to be crushed. Killed. No, I wouldn't be killed. I'd be trapped, left lying there in agony. I should run as fast as I could. But my feet were caught by the tangling grass. I had to tear myself free. I had to get away. I had to—

No. I recognised the feeling of someone trying to shove invented terrors into my head. The hag was trying the same tricks as before. Also, this was bullshit. I'd faced things a fucking sight scarier than a single stone pillar. Besides, it wasn't about to fall on my head. As soon as I looked straight at it, the stone stood there, upright and motionless. A second later, the monolith vanished.

'What the hell?' Fin exclaimed.

I snatched a glance over my shoulder. 'Are you okay?'

I saw her sliding down the side of the gully, pressing Not-Alice close to her chest. She looked at the fistful of grass she was clutching. 'I was trying to pull myself up out of the way—'

I looked back to where the monolith wasn't. 'It's the hag. Can you see her anywhere?'

I could really have used a sodding hagstone right now. I swept the tyre iron around in a wide arc, backwards and forwards. Stamping down the grass, I forced my way further into the gully.

I hit something and the hag appeared. For an instant, she flickered into an indistinct black shape. Before I could see what she really looked like, she fell backwards and vanished.

Then she reappeared. Now she was the little old lady we had seen before, wearing the same stretchy pink trousers and that pink-and-yellow shirt. She wasn't wearing sunglasses though. I could see her whiteless eyes, dull red like clotted blood. Her face was twisted with fury.

'Do you want to kill that poor, innocent child?' Her snarl showed me that solitary tooth in her gums. 'Can't you see how much you have hurt her?'

I tried to pick the truth out of the hag's lies again. Not-Alice was still crying, but she wasn't about to die. I could hear that for a fact. The changeling was in pain, but that wasn't the whole truth either. The hag was rubbing her thigh, trying not to let me see her do it. Cold iron for the win.

'You're talking crap.' I raised the tyre iron. What was that expression? Steeling myself? That seemed appropriate if I was going to have to beat the shit out of what still looked like a little old lady. I swallowed a surge of nausea. This wasn't going to be easy, even if it was what I had to do to get this evil bitch to leave us alone.

'Wait!' The hag tried to back away. Losing her footing, she scrambled backwards on her hands and her heels. She lost a slip-on shoe in the thick, tangled grass. The shoe vanished. For the blink of an eye, I saw her long, bony toes with thick yellow nails hooked like a bird of prey's talons. In the next instant her bare foot was as soft and plump as her hands. A second later, she wore two shoes again.

'Now, dear, there's no reason not to be civilised.' She stopped retreating when she couldn't get any further away. The steep ground rose up behind her. Trying to stand, she held out a hand. 'If you could help me?'

'Not a chance.' I calculated how many strides I'd need to reach her with the tyre iron. I had to be careful here. Very careful.

'You've done very well to find me.' The hag forced a smile as she managed to get to her feet. 'Both of you. Oh, forgive me, my dear. We haven't been introduced. Tell me, what is your name?' She leaned sideways to see past me, smiling at Fin.

Fin didn't answer, and she didn't smile back. She rocked Not-Alice, stroking her fluffy head. Thankfully, the changeling had stopped that nerve-shredding crying.

'That's not very friendly, I must say.' The hag tried to sound hurt.

'You want to be friends?' This close, I could hear the real emotions behind her words. Anger. Anger and fear. Good. 'Stop fucking with our phones. Let us start our car and we'll get out of here.'

'You could ask a little more politely, dear.' She flinched as I raised the tyre iron. Only for a moment. She folded her arms and narrowed her eyes. 'If you want a favour from me, you had better do me some service. You don't want to be in my debt, greenwood boy, I can assure you of that.'

'Or I could cave your head in?' I suggested. 'I bet that would solve a lot of our problems.'

'You might be rid of me, but have you forgotten my sisters?' she hissed, suddenly vicious.

Vicious and definitely scared. I reminded myself that cornered animals are most dangerous. But I wasn't going to give up this advantage. I weighed the tyre iron in my hand. 'How are they going to know what's happened to you?'

Fin followed my lead. 'I say we take that chance. This'll be, what, the fourth hag you've beaten, Dan?'

Beaten as in defeated, not killed. Fin was telling the most effective truth, not necessarily the most accurate version. I stared at this white-haired, little old lady, trying to remember how hideous those other three hags had looked before they ended up dead.

'Please, my dear—' The hag broke off her sickly-sweet appeal to Fin with a sudden shiver. She glanced at me for a second, before she tried again. 'I can give you a gift, swan maid. Something you surely desire. As long as your greenwood hero does what I say.'

Any pretence of charm and politeness had gone. The hag was ready to bargain.

'Go on.' Fin wasn't offering her any encouragement.

'You care for that infant,' the hag said flatly. 'I can tell you how to make her wholly human. You can keep her for your own.'

Fin looked into the baby carrier. She smiled and slowly shook her head. 'No thanks.'

She was telling the absolute truth. I could hear it, and so could the hag. The evil witch looked completely confused. It was almost funny. Almost. This shit we were in was no laughing matter. I chose my next words very carefully indeed.

'I'm not agreeing to anything. You can tell us what you would like me to do. Then we'll consider our answer.'

The hag narrowed her eyes at me. 'Your foolish little swan maid failed to close the gateway when she returned to you. A dangerous wight has come through it. A creature that does not belong in this land. It will wreak havoc before it is done. I cannot let your folly stand. You must kill it. As soon as the wight is dead, the gate will close. That will settle accounts between us. Once that is done, you may go on your way and I will go on mine.'

'Kill it how?' I challenged her.

'That is your problem to solve, fool boy.' The hag flickered like an eerie shadow despite the bright summer sun.

I lunged forward, trying to try to grab her, or to hit her, I wasn't honestly sure. My foot slammed into a nub of grey limestone hidden in the long grass. I went sprawling and lost hold of the tyre iron. It didn't matter. The hag was gone.

'Fucking hell!' Fin protested.

She didn't often swear like that. I was too pissed off to speak. I stood up and brushed myself down. I looked for the tyre iron and found it easily enough.

'What now?' Fin asked.

I took a deep breath and crushed down my anger so I could think straight. 'Let's go to the pub.'

Chapter Eighteen

The closest pub recommended by the local monuments enthusiast was The New Moon. An enterprising Georgian owner had given the long, low medieval building a facelift by putting in bigger windows and adding a new wing. Freshly chalked advertising boards outside promised craft ales, local cider and home cooking. Since it was nowhere near lunchtime, we settled for coffee.

Before we went inside, Fin said something to me. When I couldn't hear her clearly, I realised I still had those bits of tissue in my ears. Seeing me pull them out, Fin quickly did the same.

Once we had our tray of coffee, we sat in the pub's beer garden. There was no one else there to overhear us discuss what had happened. Fin hoisted Not-Alice out of the baby carrier while I found the ready-made formula and filled her feeding bottle. She was overdue a feed and letting us know about it. Fin handed her to me, so she could unclip the baby carrier and put it on the bench seat beside her.

Thankfully, shoving the rubber teat in her mouth shut Not-Alice up. 'Do all babies suck this strongly?' I wondered. 'You could stick this one to a pane of glass.'

'Why does this hag want the beast-thing dead? What did she call it? A wight?' Fin reached for her latte. 'There's got to be more to that than closing the gateway through the burial mound.'

'She threw that same mix of truths, half-truths and lies at me last time. It's a bitch to untangle.' Though it was a tactic I might try some day. I shifted the feeding bottle to make sure Not-Alice wasn't sucking down air. 'I'm not sure it's worth the effort though. Yesterday, I was nearly at the village before she blocked my phone. I think something distracted her. That could have been the wight. What else is there around here that could threaten her?'

'You think it's after her?' Fin considered this idea. 'That would explain why she wants it dead.'

'If she's done something to hurt it, that's got to be a possibility. Maybe their paths crossed on the other side of the portal, when she was stashing Real-Alice over there.'

'And when the wight caught my scent a bit later, it realised I'd come from the same place? It took its chance to follow me?' Fin sipped her coffee. 'It's a theory.'

It was, though we had nothing to prove it. Still, we didn't have anything else to go on.

'How about this?' I suggested. 'When that wight came through the gateway, it tried to pick up the hag's scent. Instead, it got a whiff of Not-Alice. Maybe because I'd already been up to the barrow. We know there has to be some sort of link between her and the hag. We can see that in their eyes. Maybe that scent brought the wight to the cottage. But once it got a good look at Not-Alice last night, it realised she's not the threat it's hunting down. That's why it's not interested in us any more.'

'That makes sense,' Fin agreed. 'But how do we know we're not adding two and two to make nine?'

'Give me a minute.' I stood up and passed Not-Alice to her, careful not to knock the tall coffee glasses over.

I walked to the far end of the beer garden. A notice in the bar said the apples from this small orchard were sent to the local cider maker. I wondered if that meant the factory we had seen driving through Shepton Mallet or a smaller operation. Regardless, whoever looked after these trees had done a good job thinning this year's fruit.

I rested my palm lightly on the closest branch, speaking quietly. 'I could really use your help.'

The tree let me know it was willing to cooperate. It felt sharper somehow, wary and more aloof than the ones in the

cottage garden. Imagine the difference between a placid riding school pony and one used to roaming moorland.

Regardless, the cider apple tree showed me what I needed
to know. The beast-thing, the wight, was there in the gully where the mystery monolith had been. As far as I could
tell, it was scrambling up and down the steep, grassy slopes.
It could do that a hell of a lot more easily than me or Fin.
I couldn't see exactly what it was doing. Dryad radar isn't
CCTV. Even so, this convinced me we were right. The wight
was hunting the hag. I didn't need to know why. The enemy of my enemy should at least be an ally. Making friends
wouldn't be an option when we couldn't talk to each other.

On the downside, there was no trace of the hag anywhere,
and the cider apple tree was showing me everything bigger
than a badger moving between here and Bishop's Warren.
I took my hand away and stood with my eyes closed for a
moment until the unsettling sensations of being outside my
own skin faded.

'Thank you.' I went back to Fin and Not-Alice.

'Well?' Fin used the paper napkin that came with her latte
to wipe the changeling's milky chin.

'The wight is searching that gully.' I sat down and drank
my tepid coffee. 'There's no sign of the hag though.'

'She's still around.' Fin picked up her phone and waved it.
'No signal, and I can't log on to the pub WiFi. I've tried three
times.'

'We can ask if there's a landline we can use before we go.'
Phone calls could wait, as far as I was concerned. 'How did
that wight know she was in that gully? Even if it got there too
late to catch her.'

'Maybe it heard that godawful clanging?' Fin winced at the
memory. 'That wasn't a normal noise.'

I considered that. 'She really didn't want me to do that
again. She showed herself at once, and I don't think that was
just because the tyre iron hurt her. I mean, clearly it did, but

we've seen hags take a lot more damage than that without backing down.'

'How much damage could that wight do?' Fin speculated. 'It looks like it could rip her to shreds.'

'She's a lot stronger than she looks, but I think you're right. She'd be no match for that thing in a straight fight. That's not a hag's style anyway. Wicked witches in fairy tales go in for gingerbread houses and poisoned spinning wheels. They rely on flying monkeys and huntsmen to do their dirty work.'

'What does that make you?' Fin grinned.

'Well, I can't fly, can I?' I went back to making my point. 'These days hags rely on working out what buttons to press to get under someone's skin with their supervillain speeches. They must be experts at reading body language after people-watching for hundreds of years. Picking up on micro-expressions and stuff. She won't be able to do any of that with a wight.'

'Maybe she knows more about it than we do.' Fin was serious again. 'Maybe she knows the wight won't give up until it finds her and kills her. Can't be bargained with, can't be reasoned with, and it absolutely will not stop.'

That reminded me of something I'd meant to say earlier. 'About those supervillain speeches. I don't think hags can pick up more than people's surface thoughts. They can try to make us afraid, but once you know what's going on, it's not that hard to keep their bullshit ideas out of your head.'

'Did you think they could read minds?' Fin was startled.

I realised I hadn't told her this hag had claimed to have been influencing us for months. That she was responsible for us coming to Bishop's Warren in the first place. I explained.

'Well, she was sure I'd want to keep this one, and she's a hundred per cent wrong about that. She was probably assuming every woman wants a baby and playing the odds. Ow.' Fin pulled a strand of her pale blonde hair out of Not-Alice's grasping fist.

I looked at the changeling. 'She was telling the truth about there being a way to make her wholly human.'

'I heard that,' Fin agreed. 'But she can't be the only one who knows. We can ask around.'

'I wonder how not-human she is.' Not-Alice was staring up at Fin. The changeling blinked, and I saw her red-brown gaze again. 'And if there is a link between them... Do you think there's any way the hag could be using her eyes and ears to spy on us?'

Of course, if that was something the evil witch was doing, now she knew we were wondering about it.

Fin looked startled again. 'That's a nasty thought.'

'Maybe that's why she left the changeling with me.' I'd been trying to work out the reason ever since the hag had lied about having no more use for her.

'Or she was lumbering you with the endless hassle of looking after a baby. Regardless, we need to hand her over to the wise women as soon as we can.' Fin circled back to our biggest problem. 'And we have to convince this bloody hag to leave us alone, if we're ever going to leave Bishop's Warren. If we're going to do that, we have to find her.'

'Maybe she'll find us first. We know she really wants that wight dead.' If she was listening in, maybe she'd take the hint that I was willing to pick up our conversation where we had left off. Saving her own skin had to be more important than keeping us here. I stood up. 'If you've finished your coffee, let's head back to the cottage.'

Fin heard something in my voice. She looked at me curiously.

I nodded at Not-Alice, lying content in the crook of Fin's arm. 'She'll be ready to go down for a nap by the time we get there, don't you think?'

Fin paused for a fraction of a second before she replied, 'Yes, I think she will.'

She understood me. That was a relief. 'I'll go and see if they've got a landline here.'

If the hag heard that, it might get her talking to us before help arrived.

When I went into the bar, the pub's owner was refilling the chiller cabinets behind the counter with bottles of lager and fruit juice.

'Excuse me,' I asked. 'Do you have a payphone?'

He looked a bit surprised. 'We do, as it happens. Through there.' He pointed to the door with the sign showing the way to the toilets.

'Thanks.' Since I had the chance, I had a pee. Then I used the phone. Thankfully I could pay with my debit card, because I didn't have any coins on me. I looked up Gillian Adams's number on my useless mobile. She was the one wise woman I knew, apart from Hazel, who arguably owed me a favour.

I got her voicemail. Bollocks. I rang off, thought fast, and rang back. 'Hi, Gillian, it's Dan Mackmain. Fin and I are on holiday in the Mendips. We need your help with something. You won't be able to call me, but we're staying at number six, Pigeon Lane, in Bishop's Warren. If you can get down here as soon as possible, I'd really appreciate it. Bring a car seat for a newborn with you, please.'

The wise woman would definitely have questions when she heard that message. Hopefully wanting to know what was going on would get her down here later today. She'd have around a four-hour drive, I estimated, and she'd have to get hold of a car seat first, so she wouldn't be able to set off straight away. She'd also have to come up with an excuse to leave work, but Gillian's a psychiatric nurse, so hopefully she could claim a patient was having an emergency. Crucially, the hag would have no idea she was coming. I hadn't mentioned Gillian's name around Not-Alice, and I wasn't going to, just in case.

I went out to the beer garden. Fin stood up and held Not-Alice out to me. 'Take her for a moment, while I go to the loo.'

While I was waiting, I worked out how to adjust the baby carrier's waistband and shoulder straps. I put it on and slid Not-Alice inside. Fastening the top strap that supported the changeling's back, I checked her arms and legs were where they should be. Then I put my backpack on.

Fin smiled when she came out of the pub and saw us. 'Let's go.'

We didn't say much as we walked to Bishop's Warren. Neither of us was going to risk it, after I'd raised the possibility of the hag using Not-Alice to spy on us. If she was, I hoped she realised I was carrying the changeling because I wasn't going to attack her if she turned up.

We used the village's boundary footpath to skirt around to the cottage's garden, even though I couldn't see anyone around. Not-Alice was drowsy after the long walk. I took her upstairs and put her in the towel-lined drawer without her waking up.

Downstairs, Fin had put the kettle on. 'Tea?'

I found a packet of chocolate digestive biscuits. 'Let's have that outside.'

We went down the garden to sit on the bench shaded by the apple trees, facing the back of the cottage. I opened the biscuits and put them on the seat between us.

'I'm not going to kill that wight.' I'd made up my mind on our way here. 'For a start, I'm honestly not sure I could, not on my own. Besides, it's done us no harm. I mean, yes, it attacked these apple trees—' I glanced up at their leafy branches, hoping they weren't offended '—but I'm certain it only did that to lure me out. It wanted to get past me to find Not-Alice. If it was really determined to kill these trees, it would have ring-barked them or worse.'

'Fine. So what do we do about the hag?' Fin helped herself to a biscuit.

I'd been thinking about that too. 'She's spiteful and she is evil. The other ones we've met have been stone-cold killers, and I'll bet good money so is she. I don't want to let her go

231

off to who knows where, to torment other people. I want to put a stop to her, once and for all. Who else is going to do it? She's going to stay well away from the wight.'

'I can't see Glastonbury Abbey having a magic monk on their staff now it's a ruin and a tourist attraction,' Fin observed. 'But how are you going to do that?'

'That's where I'm getting stuck,' I admitted.

I had racked my brains for everything we knew about hags, trying to find an alternative to smashing in her skull with the tyre iron. I hadn't come up with anything remotely helpful.

We sat in silence, eating biscuits and drinking our drinks.

'We know hags can't shift into hares if they're holding something made of iron,' Fin said after a while. 'If you could snare her in hare form with steel wire, wouldn't she be trapped in that shape?'

I nodded. 'That's a good idea, but I'm no hunter. I wouldn't bet on me being able to set a snare that even an ordinary hare wouldn't spot and dodge. The hag won't be fooled. She'll have her wits about her, whatever shape she's in. And I wouldn't want to catch an innocent animal.'

Even if we used wire too blunt to cut through skin, I knew fighting a snare in a panic could cause horrible injuries. I'd seen foxes caught in illegal traps when I was a kid. That was a shame. Cutting a hare's throat, or wringing its neck, would be unpleasant, but I knew I could do it. It would also be much less risky than getting caught beating a little old lady to death. Killing a hare meant a potentially crippling fine and up to six months in prison. Being convicted of murder, even if the victim couldn't be identified, would see me jailed for life.

But this hag had a third form, didn't she? Something we hadn't come across before. 'When she's pretending to be a standing stone to hide from the wight, do you suppose there's a way we could trap her inside it?'

'Possibly,' Fin said cautiously.

I started to see the first steps of a possible plan. 'Wrapping barbed wire around the stone has to be worth a try, don't you think?'

'If we can find the mystery monolith,' Fin agreed. 'Where are you going to get barbed wire?'

'From the field by the long barrow.' I fished my multi-tool out of my pocket. 'This has wire-cutters.'

I knew they worked. I'd tested all eighteen tools on my first day in my workshop at Blithehurst after the Christmas break.

Fin finished her coffee. 'Supposing that works, then what? If we leave her trapped in a stone wrapped with barbed wire, she'll get free as soon as someone takes that off. You might even say we're doing her a favour. She might not be able to get out of the stone, but the wight won't be able to get to her.'

'I'm sure we'll come up with something.' I had been thinking about that too. I hadn't found an answer I liked so far. 'The most important thing is us getting away from here. As long as wrapping her in barbed wire stops her fucking with our phones and the car, we can leave. We can do some research, find out how to kill her, come back, do that, and go home.'

'You do remember that simple and easy aren't necessarily the same things?' Fin pursed her lips. 'Okay, but we've got to trap her first. How are we going to find out where she's hiding? Me spotting that fake monolith from the air was pure luck. We can't rely on that again.'

'No,' I agreed. 'So I'm going to ask the Hunter to show me where she is.' Mentioning huntsmen earlier, and talking about hunting with snares just now, had reminded me of someone else I could ask for help.

'Seriously?' Fin looked at me, wide-eyed.

'The Green Man has helped us out, and so has Wade.' I drank my tea. 'Third time's the charm.'

'But the Hunter...' Fin shook her head, uncertain. 'I mean, I know he's turned up when we've been sorting out trouble for the Green Man, but he's had his own reasons for getting involved. Ask him directly for help and you'll owe him a favour. A big one. What do you think he'll want in return?'

'I have no idea.' I understood Fin's hesitation.

The Green Man and Wade are aeons-old, mysterious powers whose realms are the ancient greenwood and long-lost wetlands. No one knows much about them, even those of us who've seen them in person. Most people believe they're guardians of the natural world. As long as you don't piss them off, they seem to be benign.

The Hunter, though, he's different, whether you call him Herne or Cernunnos or the Horned One. Those names are tied to tales of bloody violence. Those aren't only stories. I'd seen one person who'd got on the Hunter's shit list die an agonising death.

'We know he doesn't like bullies, or anyone who enjoys being cruel to someone who can't fight back. I'd say this hag qualifies after stealing Real-Alice from her parents.' I looked up into the branches above us. 'Our friends here got word to the Green Man and to Wade. Let's see if they're willing to send him a message.'

I stood up. First, I looked closely at the damage the wight had done to the old apple trees. I kept my hands behind my back so I didn't touch anything. The nettle-fibre bindings were still secure. As far as I could tell, the loosened bark was reattaching itself. Good.

I reached for an unwounded branch, but I didn't take hold. 'May I?'

I waited for the trees to warn me off with a rattle of leaves or some other signal. Nothing happened. I touched the lichen-covered bark with my fingertips. I didn't feel a shock of rejection. So far, so good.

I focused on remembering the last time I'd seen the Hunter. Anyone catching a glimpse of him from a distance might think he was human, before they wondered what he was doing out in the countryside, barefoot and bare-chest-ed, wearing ragged leggings that could have come from any century. If they got any closer, they would realise he was over seven feet tall. When they noticed the branching antlers in his dark, tangled hair, and his piercing, vivid gold eyes, they'd run away as fast as they could, if they had any sense.

'Please let the Hunter know we need his help,' I asked the apple tree. 'This hag's a menace, and not only to us. We think we can put a stop to—'

'Dan,' Fin interrupted, warning me.

I turned and saw a Black woman walking down the garden towards us. She wore a bright blue nurse's tunic and navy trousers. A sizeable bag with lots of zips and pockets hung from a strap over her shoulder.

Who the hell was this, and where had she come from?

Chapter Nineteen

'Daniel Mackmain?' Her accent was pure Bristolian. 'Gillian Adams sent me. I'm Charity.'

I could see that from her name tag, and I guessed she was somewhere around forty. I managed a smile as I walked towards her. I supposed Gillian sending somebody else made sense, since Charity was obviously closer. But that's one of the things about the wise women that irritate me. They always think they know best.

I shook the hand the nurse offered me. 'Hi.'

Our visitor let the strap slide off her shoulder and lowered her bag to the ground. That looked heavy. 'And you're Finele Wicken?'

'Fin, please.' She shook hands as well.

Charity looked from Fin to me and back again. 'So what can I do for you?'

'How do you know Gillian?' I asked cautiously. I was assuming Charity was a wise woman. We were going to have problems if she wasn't.

She grinned. 'There was an incident with a mermaid.'

Fin had other concerns. 'Did anyone see you arrive?'

'If they did, they won't remember,' Charity assured her.

I hoped she was right about that. Things have changed since I was a kid, when people would literally have stopped and stared to see her in the village where I went to primary school. Even so, rural areas have a long way to go before they get anywhere near multicultural.She looked at me. 'So what's this about a baby? I'm a health visitor,' she added. 'That's my day job.'

'Let's go inside.' I reached for her bag. 'Can I carry this for you?'

'Absolutely,' Charity said cheerfully.

I was right. Her bag was extremely heavy. Fin gathered up our mugs and the packet of biscuits and went ahead. Charity followed her into the cottage. I followed them into the living room and put the nurse's bag on the table.

'Please, have a seat.' Fin gestured at the sofas. 'Can I get you some tea? Coffee?'

'I'm fine, thank you.' Charity sat down. 'So, whose is this baby? What's going on?'

'It's a changeling.' I corrected myself. 'She's a changeling.'

Charity's eyes widened. 'Goodness.'

That wasn't encouraging. 'That's unusual, is it?'

'These days?' She nodded. 'Nobody I know has ever had to deal with one.'

I could hear she was being honest with us.

'I'll get her while you explain.' Fin was already on her way to the stairs.

Charity looked at me expectantly. I sat on one of the dining chairs. 'We found her on the back step, on our first evening here.'

Telling the whole story took more time than Fin needed to bring Not-Alice downstairs. She sat with her on the other sofa. The changeling blinked, sleepy-eyed. Charity glanced at Fin a few times as I told her how the portal had closed once Real-Alice had passed through it. I explained how I had swapped the changeling for the baby, who was safely home with her parents. Fin looked surprised when I mentioned a few details I must have forgotten to tell her earlier.

I told Charity how I found the hag who was behind this. I explained what had happened when I had challenged her. Then I stopped talking. If there was any chance the hag could possibly see or hear through Not-Alice's eyes and ears, she wouldn't have learned anything new so far. I wasn't going to risk sharing what we planned to do next and give the hag something she could use against us.

Charity's expression made me think she realised I wasn't telling her everything. I wondered what Gillian had said to her about me, and about Fin. But she didn't ask any awkward questions.

'So you want us to take care of her? That's fine. Let me check her over. Give me a moment.' Charity raised a hand, seeing Fin was about to give Not-Alice to her.

I moved away from the dining table to give her space to put her bag on a chair. Charity unzipped a side pocket and took out a brown paper protector for the table, with a water-proof underside and a layer of tissue on top.

'Have you given her a name?'

'Not—' I coughed. 'Not so far.'

Fin shot me a grin as she brought Not-Alice over. 'We didn't think it was our place. It's not as if we're going to keep her.'

We watched Charity strip the changeling down to her sodden nappy. The nurse picked the stump of umbilical cord out of the sleep suit, still with its clip. I was glad that hadn't come loose when I had been changing her.

'She needs a dry nappy.' Charity leaned forward, taking a close look at Not-Alice's belly button.

'Of course.' Fin hurried upstairs.

I didn't say anything as Charity continued examining the changeling from head to toe. When Fin came down with a fresh nappy and a clean sleepsuit, Charity took a spring-loaded scale with a digital read-out from her bag. It wasn't much different to the scales I'd seen coarse fishermen using when they caught a particularly impressive carp.

She took off Not-Alice's sodden nappy and weighed her in a cloth sling. 'Obviously we don't know what her birth weight was, or rather, what the real baby's weight would have been, but she's doing well as far as I can see. Her navel looks fine, though she could do with a bath. That will help with the nappy rash for a start.'

'There's only a shower room here,' Fin apologised.

I decided not to say anything about the bucket.

Charity laid Not-Alice on the table and put a nappy on her. She threaded both arms and one of her legs into the clean white sleepsuit. 'You're sure you don't want to keep her? We can help sort that out.'

'No,' Fin said firmly.

'Wait,' I interrupted.

Fin looked at me, startled.

'No, we don't want to keep her,' I told Charity, 'but what are you doing?'

She had taken a plastic-mounted needle and a card covered in writing and bar codes out of another pocket in her nurse's bag.

'Newborn blood spot test.' Before I could stop her, she pricked Not-Alice's bare heel with the needle. 'Changeling or not, we should do the usual checks for rare medical conditions. Especially if we're going to say she's a foundling.'

Squeezing Not-Alice's foot, Charity caught drops of blood on the circles printed at one end of the card. The bright red soaked in and turned dull.

'Dan,' Fin said suddenly. 'Look at her eyes.'

'I see it.'

The baby was yelling more than crying. She seemed outraged at being unexpectedly stabbed in the foot. I couldn't argue with that.

'What?' Charity looked at us both. 'What is it?'

'Didn't you see her eyes change?' I had assumed the wise woman saw the same muddy red-brown colour as me and Fin whenever Not-Alice blinked.

'No.' Charity had no idea what I was talking about.

I watched the baby to be sure I had really seen it. Not-Alice blinked, and her eyes stayed the same pale, slatey blue as Real-Alice's. There wasn't a hint of the hag in her gaze.

'What's happened?' Charity demanded.

Fin looked at me. 'This is what happened to Annis Wynne?'

I nodded. 'I think so.'

'Please can one of you tell me what you are talking about?' Charity put a tiny sticking plaster on Not-Alice's foot and tucked her leg into the sleepsuit.

'There are old stories about the Tylwyth Teg who live under the mountains in Wales.' I tried to remember how much Gillian knew about Annis Wynne. 'If they're pierced just once with a steel blade, they turn mortal. But only if they suffer a single wound. A second strike restores them, and they're the same as they were before.'

'Really?' Charity stared down at Not-Alice. 'Who goes through life without cutting themselves by accident even once? Maybe this is why we don't see changelings any more. I wonder what interval—'

She broke off and stared at me. I had taken the plastic-mounted heel prick needle out of her hand before she realised what I was doing.

'You are not going to experiment on her,' I said forcefully.

'I wasn't—' Charity bit her lip.

There was no point in her trying to deny it. All three of us could see she'd been about to test what I had told her. I should have expected that. Any wise woman I'd ever met would have done the same.

'Is she going to be safe with you?' Fin was angry. 'Can we trust you, if we let you take her away?'

'Yes, of course.' Charity didn't meet my eyes as she did up the poppers on Not-Alice's sleepsuit. The nurse was embarrassed. That was okay. We could both hear she was telling the truth.

'What happens to her now?' I decided we should move on. 'If you say she's a foundling.'

'Are many babies abandoned these days?' Fin was still scowling, but she went with the change of subject.

'About one a month, sometimes two. That's across the UK.' Charity was relieved to talk about something else. She picked up Not-Alice and cuddled her. The baby's sobs subsided.

240

'It is unusual, but still common enough for us to have policies and procedures. I'll say someone rang our office with an anonymous tip-off and I went out to collect her. We won't say she came from anywhere around here, obviously. We don't want anyone wondering about a link to the abduction at the weekend. The police will have to be informed. They'll try to find the mother, in case she needs medical attention. In the meantime, this little one will be fostered. Once the police are convinced they're not going to find her mother, she'll be put up for adoption.'

'Will you – the wise women, I mean – will you keep an eye on her? After she's been adopted?' Fin wanted to know.

So did I. 'Even if she's fully human now, she'll most likely be able to see uncanny things. Ask Gillian about Annis Wynne, the old woman this happened to.'

'We'll choose the right family for her,' Charity assured us. 'People who can explain what's happening as she grows up.'

'Okay. Thanks.' I looked at Fin.

Charity looked at us both. 'If you change your minds, she'll be fostered for a while. You could apply to have her yourselves.'

'We won't.' Fin was certain.

So was I. 'We'd never be able to look at her without remembering where she came from. If she's going to have a normal life, she needs to be with people who'll treat her like any other child.'

Until she started asking about the nice ladies who lived in the rivers and trees, but the wise women would have to take care of that.

I couldn't tell if Charity had a talent for hearing the truth or if she was simply an experienced nurse. Either way, she nodded and started packing up the stuff she'd taken out of her bag. 'Let's get her things together and I'll be on my way.'

'You do the kitchen,' I said to Fin. 'I'll do upstairs.'

Up in the back bedroom, I stuffed everything I could find into the carrier bag I'd stolen from Real-Alice's parents. I'd be relieved to get that evidence out of the cottage. When I came downstairs, Fin was putting the damp reusable nappy and a sleepsuit she had washed into a plastic bag marked 'Patient Property'. That must have come out of another of the nurse's kit's zipped pockets.

Still cuddling Not-Alice, Charity turned to me. 'That's everything?'

'Yes.' I hesitated. 'I was wondering. I assume the police will test an abandoned baby's DNA? Will they test whatever she's found with as well, to see if they can trace who's handled her?'

I'd given a sample to the cops once, years ago. That was supposed to have been destroyed, but mistakes happen. Sometimes they happen deliberately.

'Nothing you give me will be handed over.' Charity raised a hand, seeing I was about to say something else. 'We'll find a family who can make good use of that nice new baby sling and these other bits and pieces. There's a lot of need out there.'

Fin wasn't satisfied. 'When they test her DNA and someone sees a match to the real Alice...?'

'We'll make sure that doesn't happen,' Charity said briskly as she carried the baby towards the front door. 'If you could bring those bags, Dan? I'm parked at the end of the lane. The green Golf.'

I glanced at Fin behind Charity's back as I picked up her nurse's bag and the plastic carriers. Fin shrugged and went to open the front door. Outside, we walked down to her car. Fin looked around. So did I. There was no sign of anyone watching us.

'I told you. No one will remember seeing me here.' As we reached the Golf, Charity looked straight at me for a long moment. I got the distinct feeling she knew exactly what I'd been thinking earlier, about her being particularly noticeable in a place like this. She knew what she was dealing with, and she knew what to do about it.

As soon as I thought that, Charity smiled briefly and offered the baby to Fin. 'Hold her for a minute.'

She found her keys and unlocked the car. I put the heavy nurse's bag and the other stuff in the boot. Charity strapped the baby securely into a rear-facing seat in the back. The baby barely made a sound.

'It was nice to meet you.' Charity offered her hand to me and to Fin. 'I'll keep Gillian updated. Call her with any questions. It'll be best if we don't talk directly.'

She didn't wait for us to answer before she got into the driver's seat. Fin and I watched the nurse make an efficient three-point turn and drive away. The green Golf turned out of Pigeon Lane and Not-Alice was gone.

Fin took a deep breath. 'That's that then.'

I heard something in her voice I wasn't sure about. 'You're not having second thoughts about keeping her?'

'Me? No.' Fin shook her head, emphatic. 'Can you imagine trying to explain where she came from to my mum or your dad, never mind anyone else? It's not like coming home with a stray kitten.'

'Right.' We walked back to the cottage. 'So what are we going to do now?'

'Have lunch?' Fin headed for the kitchen. 'What have we got left to eat anyway?'

'I have no idea.' I opened the fridge.

Fin bent down beside me to look. 'Still, I was thinking. Your baby. Our baby. Some day. That might be nice. Maybe. After we've sorted out buying a house and everything else.'

'Some day.' I couldn't help smiling as Fin handed me a packet of cheese. 'Maybe.'

She stood up and froze. She stared out of the kitchen window. 'Dan.'

'What is it?' I closed the fridge and looked down the garden.

A sizeable owl was perched on the bench under the apple trees. It looked our way with vivid orange eyes. Those mottled cream, russet and brown feathers would camouflage it very effectively when it was flying through woodland, especially at dawn or dusk. Its most striking feature were tall tufts of feathers sticking upright on its head.

'That's a long-eared owl.'

'What's it doing here?' Fin wondered. 'Out in broad daylight.'

As I looked at the owl, my vision blurred. For a few seconds, I saw something else. A silhouette with antlers instead of feathery ear tufts. The black shadow's unblinking eyes were burning gold.

'The Hunter sent it.' I wondered what he was going to want from me in return for this.

I opened the back door to see what the bird would do. Fin stood beside me on the step. The owl spread its wings wide. Their span was around a metre. It didn't fly away. Gliding noiselessly towards us, it landed on the grass in front of us. It stared up at Fin.

'I don't speak owl,' she said nervously.

The bird took off again, startling us both. It flew in a wide circle above the garden before swooping down again and landing in front of us a second time. It gazed steadily at Fin.

'That's what Wade's heron did,' she said. 'I think it wants me to go with it.'

'I think you're right.' We didn't have a choice, did we? 'What do you want me to do?'

'Be ready when I get back.' Fin took a determined breath and nodded her agreement to the bird.

The long-eared owl sprang into the air, its wings beating hard and fast. I don't know if it saw the same dazzling brightness as me when Fin shifted into her swan shape. By the time I stopped blinking and could search the sky, both birds were flying towards the hills. Fin followed the owl's lead. Any birdwatchers seeing them would be extremely confused.

I closed the door. I didn't feel like eating now. We could have lunch when Fin got back. What could I do in the meantime? The cottage felt smaller than ever, as well as unnervingly quiet and empty now I was there on my own.

I went upstairs and collected the towels from the back bedroom. I put the empty drawer where it belonged and straightened the duvet and pillows. There was nothing to show a baby had ever been there. That was good, wasn't it?

These past few days had been an experience. A stressful and knackering one. Presumably, looking after a tiny baby would be different, if Fin and I had nine months' warning to get our heads around the idea. Did I want to get my head around it? Maybe. If I could be absolutely certain there was no chance of some wicked witch turning up at the christening or whatever party we held to introduce a child to our families and friends.

I tidied up the front bedroom where Fin and I were sleeping. I went downstairs and put the towels into the washing machine. Switching on a hot wash solved the silence issue. I tidied up everything else I could find. That didn't take long. I still felt the cottage walls closing in on me. Did that mean the hag was close by, trying to mess with my thoughts?

No, I didn't think so. If she was somewhere around here, why had the owl led Fin away? Though what if I was wrong? If the hag had noticed the Hunter's owl had seen her, she could have fled from wherever it had found her. I left the doors unlocked, front and back. If the hag came in here to challenge me, she wouldn't be getting out again. Not if I had any say in it.

I checked my phone. No signal. I looked out of the cottage windows. No sign of anything unusual. Who was I kidding? The hag wouldn't outfox the Hunter or the owl he had sent.

I wondered about going out to cut some barbed wire from the Fieldfare Long Barrow fence. But if I wasn't here when she got back, Fin wouldn't know where I'd gone. I could leave a note, I supposed, but at this time of day I definitely risked being caught vandalising a farmer's property.

I made a pot of tea and ate a few biscuits. I tried to think of different ways to guarantee the hag would never get loose if we managed to trap her inside a stone. I really hoped the owl was keeping Fin safe. When I had asked for the Hunter's help, I hadn't expected she would be sent to see where the hag was hiding, running whatever risks that involved.

All I could do was wait for her to come back. For the second time in three days.

Chapter Twenty

A bit later the washing machine beeped to say its pro-gramme was finished. I hung the towels on the line outside to dry. I looked up at the cloudless blue sky. Where the hell was Zan? I should have rung Blanche again when I'd used the payphone at the pub. Hindsight. The world's most exact science.

I remembered seeing a spray bottle of shower screen cleaner under the kitchen sink. I went to find that. By the time I had finished, the shower screen was spotless. I cleaned the loo and the basin and the sink while I tried to work out a plan for getting rid of the hag. After that I walked around the cottage again. Nothing else I could usefully do had material-ised, and the place still felt far too small.

Assuming Fin would come back knowing where to find the hag, I filled our water bottles. I put the tow rope and tyre iron in my backpack with the waterproofs and sweatshirts. I put our hiking boots by the front door. On the plus side, I didn't have to pack nappies and wet wipes, or plan for the next time Not-Alice would need a bottle.

I was in the kitchen rethinking my decision to wait until Fin reappeared to have some food when she came in from the garden.

She stretched her arms over her head to ease her shoul-ders. 'Where's the map?'

'On the dining table.' I'd left that out ready.

'Right.' Fin went through to the living room. She leaned forward and studied the landscape. 'There.'

She tapped the map nowhere near any of the places we'd been to so far. I couldn't see symbols for a tumulus or any other sort of ancient monument. This spot overlooked a quarry (disused) at the broad, blunt end of a steep ridge. Above the quarry, the hillside rose to a crest before plunging down a slope so steep I couldn't pick apart the densely packed contour lines. At the bottom of the hill, a narrow road swerved and dodged between a handful of swallets, pots and holes. Each one had an obscure name which must have meant something sometime. I wondered if anyone remembered their significance. None of the names looked likely to refer to a hag.

'What did you see? The mystery monolith again?'

'No, she's hiding in a lump of weathered stone. It's about the same size as the one you tripped over in the gully.' Fin went into the kitchen. 'I wouldn't have even noticed it if the owl hadn't flown down to perch on the top.'

Bollocks. I remembered what I'd been thinking earlier. If the owl had somehow tipped off the hag, there was no guarantee we'd still find her when we got there. But I had to trust the Hunter knew what he was doing. 'How close did you get?'

'Don't worry.' Fin raised her voice as she turned the tap on and off. 'The owl made it absolutely clear I needed to stay high up, keeping a good distance. It swooped beneath me whenever I tried to go lower, blocking my way.'

She stood in the doorway, sipping from a glass of water. 'The hag is definitely there. I felt... something I recognised, even if I couldn't put a name to it. Anyway, that's where she is, and I'd say she's trying very hard to hide from the wight.'

'I wonder why.' I assessed the distance between here and there on the map.

'Let's have something to eat before we go and tackle her.' Fin turned back into the kitchen. 'If she thinks the wight's after her, she should stay put. If she doesn't, there's nothing we can do about it. We'll have to ask the Hunter for his help again.'

I wanted to argue, but Fin was right. Also, I was hungry. Hag-hunting on an empty stomach was probably a bad idea. 'How about pasta?'

'Have you come up with any ways to get rid of her for good?' Fin found a knife and a chopping board. She stripped the outer skin off an onion.

'I was assuming you'd find the same monolith as before.' I took the jar of sauce and the tin of tuna out of a cupboard. 'If we can trap her inside a stone by wrapping it in wire, I've been wondering if we could shatter the rock somehow. Ideally, we'd build up a fire around it, to get it as hot as possible. Then if Zan would bloody turn up, they could douse it with rain or hail. That should bring the temperature down to freezing in a second and do plenty of damage. Without Zan? I can't see how we could get enough cold water up there without their help. It would be a lot easier to build a fire around a smaller stone, but we'd still have to be careful not to set the whole hillside alight. We could also get arrested for vandalising an ancient monument.'

'Can it be an ancient monument if it's not on anyone's map?' Fin went over to the sink to clean the mushrooms. 'Any other ideas, now you've seen where she is?'

'Chuck the rock off the crest of that hill? If we can stop the traffic on the road down below. We don't want her going through some unlucky bastard's windscreen. It'll depend how much of the stone is buried in the ground.'

Everything I came up with would be so much easier if we had a sylph to help. Well, it wouldn't be the first time we'd ended up winging it when the Green Man had sent us to solve a problem. I'd much rather have a proper plan, but that wasn't always possible.

Fin nodded. 'Well, whatever we decide, building a fire around the stone might be a good way to get her out of it. Instead of hitting it with that tyre iron and the noise alerting who knows what else might be around that something's going on.'

'Right.' That was a very good point. I remembered the legend of Batt's Quoit. The last thing we needed was a giant turning up. Fuck it. There were too many things we didn't know about this place. And there'd be things we didn't know we needed to know. We had no way of finding out any of it.

Fin fried the onions and mushrooms and added the jar of sauce and the tuna. I boiled the kettle for hot water and cooked the pasta. Shovelling everything into shallow bowls, we sat at the table to eat.

'Charity taking the baby away went a lot more smoothly than the other evening,' Fin said suddenly. 'When that policewoman put her into a car.'

I remembered how violently the changeling had struggled and screamed. 'I've been thinking about that. Drinking baby formula must have started binding her to this world, even before Charity stuck that needle in her foot. She was still a changeling, but she was already becoming more human.'

We'd found out the 'don't accept food or drink from the fae or you'll get stuck in their realm' rule worked both ways. I wondered how many of the wise women were aware that preying on humans had downsides for monsters.

'What ties does the hag have here?' Fin wondered. 'If she's been eating people for hundreds of years? Even if she only kills a few at a time.'

'I have no idea.' Though I wondered if that was why she had stayed instead of sodding off once she knew the wight was after her. You'd think saving her own neck would be more important than staying to screw us around. I wondered if I could provoke her into explaining what had kept her here. Of course, she'd most likely lie.

We finished eating, washed up and set off. First things first. We needed barbed wire. We followed the path to the Fieldfare Long Barrow, and I wished I'd thought of using wire to trap the hag when we were still at the pub. We could have done this on our way back to Bishop's Warren. Still, I couldn't see anyone around to interfere with what we had planned this afternoon.

Was there anyone around who I couldn't see? I found a sturdy hazel sapling and reached for a branch. 'If you don't mind?'

I didn't get a shock, so I guessed the sapling didn't object. Dryad radar showed me plenty of birds and wildlife, but no hikers or farmers or any other people close by. I wondered if we had the Hunter or someone else on our side to thank for that.

Fin was watching me. 'Well?'

'No wight. No hag. Thank you.' I let go of the hazel sapling and got carefully over the fence. 'Let me know if you see anyone coming. Say I climbed over the fence for a pee.'

I didn't care if a stranger didn't believe me. They wouldn't be able to prove I hadn't needed a slash, as long as they didn't catch me with a coil of wire in my hand.

Fine looked each way along the footpath. 'How much are you going to cut?'

'How long is a piece of string?' I realised that wasn't helpful when she glared at me. 'Give me an idea how big this stone is. How tall and how far around is it, at its thickest point?'

'It's pretty much the same size as one of those old-style concrete bollards.' Fin sketched a shape in the air with her hands.

'Right.' I walked away along the hedge line, crouching to stay as hidden as well as I could. That was bloody uncomfortable, but I couldn't risk being caught.

I reached the corner of the field and took out my multi-tool. The hawthorns in the hedgerow were flourishing. That was useful in two ways. Those natural spikes should discourage any animals turned into this field to graze from trying their luck when they found the non-barbed length of fence. The leafy branches were also thrusting through the wire mesh and the fence was almost hidden. There was a good chance no one would see the top strand was missing before autumn.

I took a close look at the wire. Two steel strands were loosely wound around each other, with double twists of sharply pointed wire fixed between them every ten centimetres or so. Each barb was actually two bits of wire twisted tight into a capital H shape, so four spikes were pointing up and down. This was high-tensile fencing, and the wooden posts were roughly three metres apart. I checked the staple fixing the barbed wire to the one closest to me. With a bit of effort, I could work that loose. I stepped back and assessed my options. I reckoned I could get six metres or so of barbed wire if I was careful. That should be enough.

It would have to be. I took the work gloves and the bag for the tow rope out of my backpack. Putting on the gloves, I held the wire I was about to cut as firmly as I could. I didn't want that springing loose, thrashing about and taking half my face off. I keep my tetanus jabs up to date, but there's no need to take stupid risks.

Slowly and carefully, I cut the wire as close to the staple on the post as I could. I felt it try to fight me as the tension was released. I rolled the wire up as I walked to the next post, trying to keep the barbs lying flat against each other. I laid the first coil on the turf and followed the fence line to the next post. Cutting the wire there, I made a second coil as I walked back again. Working the middle staple out of the central post took a couple of minutes.

I folded the two coils of wire together and eased the awkward, jagged circle into the tow rope bag. It wasn't much protection, but hopefully it would save my backpack from the worst those barbs could do. Thankfully, my water bottle was metal. I walked over to the gap in the hedge.

'All clear?' I handed the backpack to Fin. 'Careful with that.'

'There's no one around.' She retreated to give me plenty of space.

Once I was on the footpath again, I took the backpack from her and slid the straps carefully onto my shoulders.

Now I had to make sure not to fall over. If I did, I'd have to land on my front. Anything else would be very bad.

'Let's go.'

We had to retrace our steps. That was a pain in the arse, but following any direct route cross-country to the disused quarry would have taken us three times as long. We didn't bother stopping at the cottage. This time we headed out of Bishop's Warren along the road that had brought us here. I found it hard to believe that was only three days ago. The road would reach a fork which offered drivers the choice of continuing towards more major routes or taking a narrow back way which cut through the high ground, winding between caves and swallow-holes.

Fin walked ahead of me on the right-hand side of the tarmac, facing any oncoming cars. That meant we couldn't talk, but we didn't have anything to say. There wasn't much traffic, but after a couple of locals came racing around blind corners, I was relieved when we found the footpath we needed.

We followed that through a couple of fields and up the hillside. The path was wide enough to walk side by side, but the climb was steep enough to stop us wasting breath talking. I kept constant watch ahead and to either side. Every so often, I looked back down the path. That was one plus of hag-hunting in daylight. We should see anything coming after us well before it was close enough to be a threat. Fin glanced upwards from time to time. There was no sign of the long-eared owl. Zan didn't turn up either.

I was ready for a breather when we reached the top of the hill. So was Fin. We had a drink of water, sharing a glance that didn't need any words. Putting my bottle away, I saw years of quarrying for stone had gouged a massive rectangular hollow out of the ground at the blunt end of this long ridge. Work had stopped long enough ago for greenery to soften the sharp edges, but the unnaturally straight lines caught my eye at once.

'Where's—?'

Fin pointed. 'Halfway between the deep end and the skyline.'

I could see why the quarry reminded Fin of a swimming pool. The hole was about the same length and width. The gradual slope of the ground meant the drop close to us was a metre or so. Not much beyond a patchwork of scrubby grass had found a foothold down on the bare rock. I looked over at the far end. Assuming the base of the quarry had stayed roughly level as the labourers worked, the uneven rim over there must be around three metres above whatever floor was hidden by thorn trees and brambles. They would have quickly taken root as windblown leaves with nowhere else to go had decayed into mulch. Beyond the quarry, the slope was a lot steeper, rising quickly to a ragged, rocky crest that cut across the sky.

I shaded my eyes with a hand. I could just make out the stone where the hag was hiding. Half hidden in a snarl of bramble, it reminded me of the limestone lumps in the rough ground at Pigeon Lane, where the hag had created her cottage illusion. Thinking that, I felt suddenly on edge and knew the hag was trying to force fears into my mind again.

'She's still here. Keep your eyes open and don't believe anything you see is real,' I warned Fin.

She nodded. 'Which way are we going to go? Do we split up and each take a side, or do we stay together?'

That was a tricky question. I wasn't sure of the best answer. 'If we stick together, I can try to keep us hidden by blending in with the vegetation. Though I don't know if she'll still be able to see us coming. I mean, I'm carrying a fair amount of metal. If she does make a break for it and we're both on the same side, she's bound to go the other way. If we split up, she'll have to decide which way to run. With luck she'll waste a few minutes wondering what we're planning. But she only has to get past one of us to escape.'

And if the hag abandoned her hiding place in the stone, I was going to have to get up close and personal to snare her with my coils of barbed wire. That was an unpleasant prospect.

'We stick together,' Fin said firmly. 'If she does try to run, I can go swan and get in her face. I should be able to hold her long enough for you to reach us.'

'Unless she mazes you. She'll be desperate to get away.' Desperate enough to do things I didn't want to think about.

'She can try that whatever shape I'm in,' Fin pointed out. 'She could try to maze you as well. If we stick together, we can shake each other out of it. Hang on though. Here's an idea. We should split up, and you can do your best to not be seen. Then she'll be watching me and wondering where you've got to. If she decides to run, she'll be heading straight for you.' Fin snapped her fingers to get my attention. 'Dan? Are you listening?'

I was looking around. 'Did you hear that?'

'No. What?'

'I don't know.' I slipped off my backpack and unzipped it. I put on the gloves and took out the vicious barbed wire. 'The longer we hang around here discussing it, the more chance the hag will try to get away. I'll go left. You go right. Do you want the tyre iron? Just in case?'

'Yes.' Fin didn't need a second to think that over.

I handed it over.

She tested the weight of the metal bar in her hand. 'Let's go.'

I waited for a moment, watching Fin walk away. Once she reached the other side of the quarry, I started walking towards the stubby stone at the far end. I concentrated as hard as I could on not being seen. That might be a waste of time, but I might as well try.

Glancing across the abandoned quarry, I made sure I kept pace with Fin. She was walking fast. She was also checking in every direction every five or ten paces. Something besides the hag's malign presence was making her tense. Had she heard whatever that strange noise had been? I strained my ears, but I didn't hear it again.

This was no time to get distracted. I focused on the stone at the far end. Fin and I reached our respective corners of the quarry at roughly the same time. The ground here was an ankle-breaking mess of holes and shallow ruts hidden in tangled grass, with lumps of broken stone to trip over for a bit of variety. How we'd get back down that steep hill if Fin or I was injured up here didn't bear thinking about. That wasn't the hag trying to put fears in my head.

It looked like rabbits had been busy in the steep slope up to the ridge, and maybe badgers as well. I shook my head. I wasn't here to survey the wildlife. Was that the hag trying to distract me?

The ragged edge of the quarry was on my right as I rounded the corner. I definitely wanted to stay well away from there. However deep it might be, the quarry bottom was invisible beneath dense brambles, thorn saplings and other wind-sown plants. If one of us fell in there, getting out would be a nightmare. Assuming the greenery broke our fall instead of skewering us.

I stopped and separated the two coils of barbed wire. Now I held a metre or so of thin steel bristling with spikes between my gloved hands. Fin had stopped a few metres past the corner on her side of the quarry. She raised the tyre iron to let me know she was ready. She was as pale as I had ever seen her.

I nodded, and we both walked towards the stone. My heart was racing and my palms were sweating inside the gloves. I forced myself to picture the hideous hags I had encountered before. I was here to wrap barbed wire around one of those horrors, not a little old lady.

I didn't take my eyes off the stone until Fin and I stood a couple of metres apart. The unremarkable lump of rock was halfway between us. Fin gripped the tyre iron, ready for whatever happened next.

JULIET E. MCKENNA

I forced my way through the thick brambles to the squat stone. Bending over to wrap the barbed wire around it wasn't going to work, I realised. The damn thing was too low to the ground. Dropping onto my knees, I ignored thorns stabbing my shins through my combat trousers. I wrapped the wire around the limestone, doing my best not to tear my skin and clothes on the barbs.

A second later, I realised I hadn't thought this through. The hag appeared, crouching inside the circle of my arms. Her face was inches from mine.

She wasn't pretending to be a sweet little old lady now. Her sparse white hair was a tangle of filthy strands barely hiding scabs and pus-filled boils on her scalp. Her whiteless eyes were the colour of dried blood. The grey skin of her cheeks looked dry enough to split and curl away from the bones underneath. As she sneered, her cracked black lips curled to show her toothless gums. She wore stinking black rags that might have once been some sort of gown from the oldest pictures in Blithehurst's gallery. Or possibly from one of the coffins in the Beauchene family crypt. Any horror movie offering up this nightmare would be told to tone it down.

Chapter Twenty-One

'Fool boy, I have you now!' The hag sprang to her feet. Now she loomed over me. Her breath was as foul as a backed-up sewer. I nearly threw up on her feet. Instead, I swallowed hard and passed the coils of wire between my hands. As I crossed the steel barbs behind the hag's thighs, she seized my shoulders. Her fingernails were thick, yellow and jagged-edged, sharp enough to rip through my T-shirt. Sharp enough to tear the skin underneath? I remembered the infection that had made me so horribly sick after my last encounter with hags. I pulled away as far as I could, leaning on my heels.

The hag stooped and tried to bite me. Good luck doing that with one tooth. It took me a moment to realise the evil bitch was sucking at my neck. Sucking hard. Hard enough to hurt, even if she couldn't break the skin. Not yet, anyway.

Fin hit her on the head with the tyre iron. That knocked her sideways, breaking her hold. I dropped the wire coils and slammed my fists into the hag's gut, just below her ribcage. Her arms flailed as she tried to keep her balance. She tee-tered for a moment. I planted one foot on the ground, forced myself up and staggered backwards. Twisting my head, I tried to wipe her spit off my neck with my shoulder.

Somehow the hag stayed on her feet. Hobbled by the barbed wire, she couldn't come after me. Hissing like a feral cat, she bent down to tug at the steel strands. The barbs snagged on her foul black rags. She couldn't get loose.

'Dan?' Fin was ready to hit her again.

'Wait.' I stepped towards the hag.

She straightened up and raised her hands, ready to claw at my face if I came within reach. Fat chance. I dodged behind her and snatched up the coils of wire. I spread my hands as wide as I could. Barbed steel dug into the hag's thighs. She

258

screamed, excruciatingly loud. I was about to pull harder, ready to rip her legs out from under her, so she'd fall flat on her face.

'Wait!' Fin stepped behind the hag and thrust the tyre iron under the evil thing's chin, across her withered neck. 'Get her hands.'

She gripped each end of the metal bar and braced her elbows against the hag's shoulder blades. The tyre iron forced the monster's head up, tight underneath her jaw. The hag crooked her filthy fingers. I saw her elbows bend. She was going to tear Fin's hands with those ragged nails.

I dropped one wire coil and grabbed the hag's wrists. Even with my wide grip, I could barely hold them both in one hand. Barely was good enough. I wound barbed wire round and around the hag's wrists and forearms. I could see she was bleeding, if you could call that slow black ooze blood. My own arms were smeared with red from scrapes and gouges where barbs and brambles had caught me.

I pinned the vile witch's arms to her sides. That wasn't easy. I had to pass the coils between her and Fin without tearing Fin's clothes to shreds. I didn't want to snag the barbs on the hag's rags either. Every time the wire got caught, freeing it took time and meant I had to get closer.

The hag spat repellent stickiness at me. Sucking in breath, she rasped vile threats.

'I will slice the tendons in your elbows and ankles, you fool of a boy. I won't kill you for months, for years, no matter how you beg me. I will enjoy leaving you limp and helpless, unable to resist as I drain your blood. You will live on to feed me in darkness and misery for as long as I choose to keep you.'

Fin was on her shit list too.

'I will pluck out your feathers one by one, bird brain, and I will savour your agony. Don't imagine I will let you die before I gut you and roast you on a spit. After I crack your bones to suck out the marrow, I will throw your carcass to the vermin and boggarts. I will—'

The hag flickered like somebody in a dark room getting caught in a strobe light. Even with the sun shining bright overhead, that's the only way I can describe it. One moment, she was there, foul and threatening. In the next instant, we stood behind an awkwardly shaped stone ringed with barbed wire. Everything flickered again. The ground seemed to shift beneath my feet. Fin retreated, dropping the tyre iron on the grass. I dropped the last loops of wire and backed off fast. Whatever was going on, we didn't want to be caught up in it. Besides, I had wrapped nearly all the wire around the hag by now.

The flickering stopped. That was a relief. The hag was still gone. That was even better. Now the stone was an uneven pillar, roughly the same height as the hag. It was maybe a metre around at its widest point, two-thirds of its length from the ground. Where the mystery monolith had been dull and dark grey, this was sickly pale, and it didn't look like limestone to me.

The barbed wire wasn't simply wrapped around it. The metal was embedded in the grainy surface. Here and there, the gleaming steel disappeared completely. Only the sharp points of spikes showed where the hidden wire ran.

'Is she trapped, do you think?' Fin looked at me. 'What should we do with her now? If another hag comes to find her, we know they can stand to handle metal. They could have a way to get her free.'

'Give me a minute.' More than anything else, I wanted to stand under a scalding-hot shower for half an hour to wash off the hag's spit and slime. No, make that an hour. Then I'd burn these clothes. I tried to decide if I felt even a little bit feverish. Had the hag's blood or worse got into my cuts and grazes? Well, I'd find out soon enough, one way or the other. Fin was right. We had to tackle the problem in front of us.

'For the moment, she's going nowhere, so let's get out of here.' I raised a hand before Fin could say anything else. 'We can ask around. Maybe the dryads or the naiads will know how to keep her trapped like this for good. Or one of the hobs.'

Thinking about it, asking an earth spirit might be the best idea. Whether that was the hobs or the coblynau or the brown men of the moors who Aled and I had met up near Berwick. He could well be the best person to find out. Maybe some of them could carry the hag deep underground. They could leave her where the flowstone that makes stalactites and stalagmites would seal her up in the darkness forever.

'The wise women might know, or the cunning men. Where's your phone?' Fin picked up the tyre iron. 'Let's see if we can make some calls.'

'I left it at the cottage with yours.' I hadn't even considered bringing either of our phones, not even to check the time. There was too much risk of them getting broken. I knew that from expensive experience. Besides, we'd be finished when we were done. Clock-watching wouldn't make anything happen any faster.

Fin chewed her lip. 'Okay.'

'Let's tidy this up.' Picking up one of the trailing lengths of wire, I walked around the stone.

Fin circled the other way. We were both wary, braced for the hag to reappear. She didn't. When we were down to the last half-metre of wire, I held out my hand. Fin passed her end to me. I twisted the steel together, over and over. This wasn't coming loose by accident. Even someone with wire-cutters would have trouble freeing it up.

'I wonder how deep this stone goes down.' I backed off a few paces. I recalled reading somewhere that half the lengths of some monoliths were below ground, to keep them stable and upright.

'How heavy do you think it is?' Fin prodded the stone with the tyre iron. 'Oh shit!'

261

The damn thing toppled over. I took a deep breath. 'That answers one question.'

'Dan,' Fin said urgently.

She was looking at the edge of the quarry. I turned my head to see the wight climbing up out of the dense greenery. It stopped on the edge of the drop. Squatting on its haunches, it brushed twigs and leaves off its coarse pelt and stared at us.

The creature must have crept the length of the old quarry floor, hiding down in the undergrowth. I wondered if it had followed us here from Fieldfare Long Barrow. Maybe it had picked up our scent there. It might even have seen me cutting the barbed wire. If it was lurking in the burial mound's tunnels, I could have missed it when I searched the place with dryad radar. Either way, what the fuck was it doing here?

The wight's gaze fixed on Fin. She put the tyre iron inside her backpack and zipped it up. The wight glanced at me. I waved a hand at the strange pale stone lying flat on the ground.

'If you want to take a look, go ahead.' Obviously the wight wouldn't understand what I said, but I hoped my tone and the gesture got my meaning across.

The wight edged forward, moving on all fours. It glowered at me, and then at Fin, before looking back to me. I couldn't really blame it. The bruises left by the steel shackle were still visible through its sparse dark hair. Though the beating didn't seem to be bothering it too much. It wasn't limping or showing signs of stiffness.

A couple of metres from the fallen stone, the wight stopped. Fin and I backed off some more. The wight moved a little bit closer and stopped again. I checked I wasn't going to put my foot down a rabbit hole and retreated another few paces. Fin did the same, coming closer to me.

The wight went up to the fallen stone, still on all fours. It showed its fearsome teeth as it sniffed warily. Its muzzle didn't touch the uneven surface. Crouching lower, it studied the barbs embedded in the stone. I realised I could see dark lines on the surface, showing where the wire was hidden.

The creature growled deep in its throat. I had no idea what that might mean.

'Do you think it knows she's in there?' Fin whispered to me.

The wight's head whipped around. It bared its teeth at us.

'Let's get out of here,' I suggested.

'Absolutely,' Fin agreed.

I took her hand, ready to go back the way she had come around the quarry. The wight sprang away from the stone. Scarily fast, it bounded right past us. It stopped, spun around and crouched on all fours. It was blocking our path. It bared its teeth again.

'Watch where you're putting your feet.' I nudged Fin sideways, to see if we could get around it.

As soon as we moved, the wight growled a warning.

'What does it want?' Fin wondered, apprehensive.

I took out my water bottle and had a drink. 'Fucked if I know.'

Fin slipped off her backpack and drank some water as well. The wight seemed satisfied we were going to stay put, for the moment anyway. That was unexpected. Not that I was complaining.

It bounded over to the edge of the quarry and looked at me, expectant. What was I supposed to do? Throw it a stick and shout 'Fetch'? I had no clue. I thought about trying to get up to the top of the ridge. No, that was a bad idea. The wight would reach us well before we got there. If it didn't try to stop us, the slope down to the road on the other side was damn near vertical. Tripping and falling up here, one of us might break a leg. Slipping and falling down that drop, we could easily snap our necks.

I spread my hands and raised my eyebrows. I tried to look as much like one of those 'What the fuck are you on about?'

emojis as I could. I wished I had brought my sodding phone now. Maybe we could have used those little pictures to communicate. That would be one use for the stupid things.

The wight made a weird chattering noise. It went over to the fallen stone. Then it loped to the edge of the quarry. It stared at us with those dark, unblinking eyes. We didn't move. The wight made a huffing sound which made me think it was getting frustrated. Either that, or it didn't like what it could smell. If the hag's scent was still clinging to me, I couldn't blame it. That said, the wight itself was still stinking like a wet dog that had rolled in sheep shit.

It slammed its hands or its forepaws or whatever on the ground. It went over to the fallen stone and circled it three times, slowly and deliberately. It walked to the edge of the quarry and fixed us both with that expectant stare. Three times is the charm. I didn't think that was a coincidence.

'Do you think it wants us to help it throw the stone down there?' Fin wondered.

I was thinking the same. 'It would be a good way to hide the thing from anyone who might come looking for the hag. The wight is the enemy of my enemy and all that. With luck, it knows a lot more about hunting them than we do.'

'Which would be helpful if we could talk to each other.' Fin put her water bottle away. 'How much do you think that stone weighs? A tonne. More than that?'

'I have no idea.' I didn't know what limestone weighed, never mind whatever sort of rock this was. My best estimate was sodding lots. 'But the wight looks strong. I mean, I assume it's going to help.'

I knew chimpanzees, orangutans and gorillas are massively more powerful than humans. Strictly speaking, I didn't think the wight was any sort of ape, any more than it was a bear or a dog. Even so, I still reckoned it had a damn sight more chance of moving that stone than the two of us.

The wight came towards us. I didn't move and neither did Fin. The wight stood on its hind legs and turned to wave at the stone. It made the exact same gesture that I had used, a few minutes ago. That was deliberate, no question.

'That's pretty clear,' Fin concluded. 'Okay. How are we supposed to move it? We're not trying to build Stonehenge, but there are only two – three – of us.'

I took the towing strap out of my backpack. 'I reckon we can drag it with this, using tree branches as skids. If that doesn't work, we could try rolling it over and over with poles and fulcrums.'

I took my multi-tool out of my pocket and unfolded the little saw blade. I wondered how long it would take for that to cut what we needed, whether that was skids or poles.

The wight bared its teeth and snarled a warning. Wherever it had come from, and even if it was closer to ordinary animals than uncanny creatures, it definitely had a problem with steel.

I put the multi-tool away. 'All right, genius. Let's try this.'

I took a step towards the fallen stone. I stopped and waited for the wight to react. It walked over to stand opposite me on the other side. Fin stayed where she was. Good. I hoped she was ready to fly away if what I was going to try went pear-shaped.

I knelt down by the stone at the narrower end. I couldn't work out if this had been the hag's head or her feet, but there was a gap between the underside and the ground. I looped the heavy-duty woven polyester around the stone. A solid steel bar with a screw thread secured the steel shackles, to make sure the strap couldn't come loose when a vehicle was on tow. I unscrewed the bar, hooked the shackle over the strap and re-secured it. That shackle wasn't going anywhere.

I got up and walked along the stone. The wight kept pace with me on the other side. I knelt down again. Getting the towing strap around this end wasn't going to be anywhere near as easy. I decided I was going to have to dig right under the stone, to make a space to pass the strap through.

'Fin? Can you give me the tyre iron, please?' That wasn't anywhere near the right tool for the job, but it was better than nothing, and I was still wearing what passed for work gloves.

She came over. 'What's the plan?'

'I'm going to start digging a hole so we can pass the strap under the stone at this end. Hopefully our friend will get the idea. If not, we'll have to think again.'

'Okay.' She passed me the tyre iron.

'Back off, please.' I forced a smile as I watched the wight. I'd done a customer service training day at Blithehurst where the trainer said smiling was a good way to keep your voice calm and friendly, even if you didn't mean it. 'Give yourself enough distance to shift and fly off before it can reach you. Just in case.'

'Okay.' Fin didn't like that, but she did as I asked.

I took out my multi-tool and unfolded its biggest blade. Forcing the sharp steel into the coarse grass's matted roots, I cut a square as close to the stone as I could. I ripped the grass away and exposed the dark soil. I put my multi-tool in my pocket and broke up the earth with the end of the tyre iron. I scooped out a few handfuls.

The wight leaned over the stone to see what I was doing. The reek as it got close made my eyes water. I coughed as I looked up. The wight stared at me, unblinking. I held up the end of the towing strap. Then I put the shackle in the shallow hole I had made. I mimed pushing it through the earth and under the stone.

The wight did that huffing thing again. It dropped to the ground on the other side of the stone. I heard scrabbling, but I couldn't see what it was up to. 'Fin, can you—?'

'Already on my way.' She walked around in a wide circle, keeping well away from the wight. 'It's digging. Those claws are coming in useful.'

I got to work, using the tyre iron and my hands. As I heaped soil on either side of my hole, I heard a patter like falling rain on the other side of the stone. I guessed the wight was flinging earth out behind it, like a burrowing dog.

I carried on. When I was closer to lying on the rough ground than kneeling, reaching into a hole that went past my elbow, I stopped and straightened up. Sitting back on my heels, I tried to brush the worst of the dirt off my arms and chest. Who was I kidding? These gloves were caked with soil, and even if the hag hadn't torn the shoulders, this T-shirt was done for.

'Fin? How's our friend doing?'

I watched her assess the wight's progress.

'It's about halfway through, I think.'

'Do you think we're roughly in line?' If the wight had cocked this up, we were both wasting a lot of effort. In case we were on course, I pulled the tyre iron out of the hole. The wight wouldn't appreciate me ramming that into its knuckles.

'Let me take a look.' Fin moved so she could see more clearly, still keeping her distance. 'I'd say you're good.'

Her confidence reassured me. I scraped out more damp earth. The next time I reached into the hole, I felt soil at the far end crumble. My gloved finger touched the wight's hairy paw. I quickly pulled my hand away, not wanting those claws to cut me, even accidentally.

'We're through.' As I spoke to Fin, the wight made that chattering noise.

I stood up. The wight backed away from its hole. It stood upright on its hind feet – paws – whatever – watching me intently.

I bent down to pick up the shackle at the end of the towing strap and showed it to Fin. 'If I pass this to you, can you pull it through?'

I'd much rather she stayed well away from the wight, but I didn't see we had any other option.

'Go for it.' She knelt down.

I reached into the hole on my side of the stone. I felt her fingers brush mine underneath it. Fin took hold of the shackle and dragged the strap past my arm. I stood up as she got to her feet. She handed the shackle to me, and I secured the strap a second time. So far, so good.

The wight moved closer and Fin backed off fast. The creature extended a pale, hairy finger and prodded the strap. It snatched back its hand with a growl. Bollocks. I had forgotten the heavy-duty polyester was reinforced with steel wire. That was sodding inconvenient.

'Dan?' Fin had seen the problem too.

Before I could come up with any sort of answer, the wight came around to my side of the stone. It picked up the strap and passed the long loop over its head. As it leaned in with one shoulder, the strap dug into its chest and belly. The creature's chattering was edged with pain as its clawed feet dug into the ground. It didn't give up though, pressing against the strap until it was leaning forward at almost forty-five degrees. The stone shifted a few centimetres. The wight bared its teeth and snarled, but not at me or Fin. Its gaze was fixed on the edge of the quarry. The stone moved a little bit further, sliding on the crushed grass. Tears trickled from the wight's dark eyes.

There wasn't room for me to get under the strap, to try to drag the stone forward beside it. How else could I help? I stripped off my ruined T-shirt and held it out.

The wight got the idea at once. With an explosive huff, it stood upright and dropped the strap. I wound the filthy material around the polyester, covering as much as I could. The wight picked it up and leaned in again, keeping the padded length over its shoulder. The stone moved before I was ready. I got out of the way just in time. Now the wight had got the thing going, it wasn't about to stop.

'Dan!' Fin had found a stick from somewhere. She prodded the ground between the toiling wight and the quarry's edge. 'There's a rut here. If the stone hits that, it'll get stuck.'

'Wait.' I stood in front of the wight and held up a hand. 'Wait!'

'Look!' Fin dragged tangled grass aside with the stick, to show the creature the problem ahead.

The wight stood up again, letting the towing strap fall to the ground. I grabbed the biggest lumps of stone I could see and hurried over to drop them into the long hollow. No, that wasn't going to do it.

'Fin, get me as much of that dirt I dug out as you can.'

Panting, the wight stood and watched us. I found more stones. Fin carried over double handfuls of damp soil. We packed the rut as fast as we could. Fin ripped up handfuls of grass to cover it.

The wight roared and threw itself sideways, hauling on the strap. As Fin went one way and I went the other to get out of the way, the wight brought the broad end of the stone around. I held my breath as it hauled that towards the crudely filled rut. End on, the pale, stained rock skidded safely across it. Whatever the wight might be, it definitely wasn't stupid.

The creature dragged the stone right to the edge of the quarry. It planted both of its hands or forepaws on the side and braced itself. It looked at me. Its meaning was clear. It wanted my help shoving the thing into the quarry

'Okay.' I went to do that.

It wasn't easy, given my height. I had to crouch down with my feet spread wide. That wasn't my only problem. I couldn't exactly ask the wight if we were going on a count of three. I watched for the first twitch of its muscles beneath that coarse black fur. As soon as it moved, I pushed as hard as I could. The stone slid away and I fell forward onto my hands and knees.

The stone toppled into the quarry, crashing through the dense vegetation. The wight watched it go, crouched on all fours peering over the edge. As the stone disappeared, I moved to stand up. The wight sprang forward and grabbed my arms. I tried to pull free. I didn't have a hope. The wight tightened its grip, dragging me forward. Rolling onto its back, it wrapped its bandy legs around my thighs. Now it had me pinned, it let go of my arms. I didn't get a chance to fight free. The wight crushed me to its chest in a brutal hug.

Now it rolled right over me. Its weight left me breathless. The last thing I heard as we fell into the quarry together was Fin screaming my name.

Chapter Twenty-Two

The wight released me as we fell and sprang away to land fuck knows where. Thick greenery slowed me down. That was good because this end of the quarry was a lot deeper than I had guessed. When I finally stopped crashing through snapping and flailing branches, I landed flat on my back. Lying still and fighting to catch my breath, I could see the edge of the quarry. At a rough estimate, I was a bit over five metres down. Nearly twenty feet in old money. Fuck.

On the plus side, I hadn't broken any bones as far as I could tell. I forced myself slowly onto my hands and knees. Standing up, I checked myself for other damage. I felt like I'd been whipped. I looked as if I had been too. Dark red lines criss-crossed my arms and chest, as sore as hell. Some hadn't broken the skin. Plenty of others had. Feeling something crawling down my back, I reached around to try and brush it away. When I looked at my hand, it was covered in blood. Fuck.

I couldn't see the wight, but I could hear it crashing around somewhere close. I had no clue what it was doing, and I didn't care. I just wanted to get out of here. Which way should I go to find the shallow end of the quarry? I couldn't see further than the length of my arm, and there was nothing approaching a path through this dense undergrowth. Never mind that. I'd make a path if I had to. Once I knew the right direction, I could walk out of here.

'Dan!' Fin's voice was high and tense. 'Dan?'

I couldn't see her. Too many leafy branches blocked my view.

'I'm here.' Telling her I was okay would be a lie, and she would hear it. 'Where are you?'

As I moved, looking up, trying to find a clearer patch of sky, the wight charged out of the undergrowth and grabbed hold of my arm.

'Fuck you.' I tried to punch it in the face.

It smacked my fist away so hard I thought it had broken my wrist. And it wasn't even trying to hurt me. It held on tight above my elbow and dragged me through the scrub like a little kid. Barely able to stay on my feet, I tried to catch hold of something, anything. Wherever we were going, I sure as shit wasn't going willingly.

I got hold of a branch. The wight kept on going. The dogwood bent, too green to snap. The wight realised something was slowing it down. It glanced over its shoulder and snarled at me, pulling harder. I had to let go of the branch before the wight dislocated my shoulder. Either that or the dogwood's twigs slipping through my hand would slice my palm open.

'Where the fuck are we going, arsehole?' I yelled.

I didn't expect the wight to answer me. I hoped Fin could hear my voice. If she was still shouting, I hadn't got a hope of hearing her. The wight was making far too much noise as it trampled and smashed a path to wherever it was taking me.

Then I realised the wight was dragging me towards a cave. A dark void opened up ahead of us on the other side of some scrubby bushes. Was that why quarrying here had stopped? Had the workmen broken through to somewhere unexpected? Had something unimaginable broken out?

I fought as hard as I could. That was no use whatsoever. I went limp in the wight's grip, making myself dead weight. That just meant I got a whole lot more scratches from the undergrowth as the wight hauled me onwards across the quarry floor. I dug my fingertips into the creature's hand where it gripped my arm. I don't think it even noticed. I keep my nails cut short for work and I was still wearing those sodden, filthy gloves.

The wight dragged me though the last few brambles to an unexpected open space. The cavern I had glimpsed gaped

like a hungry mouth ahead of us, where a corner of the
quarry had collapsed. The roof was ragged and stained where
years of wind and rain had got to the stone. A few ferns and
other scraps of greenery clung to the rocky sides. The bottom was a dead-straight edge with obvious tool marks, barely
a metre in front of me. I tried to work out which rock face
was the end wall of the quarry and which one was the side.
That should give me an idea where Fin might be, and the
direction to go to get out.

The wight threw me over the drop. No trees broke my fall
this time. I managed to land on my feet, but the shock of the
impact sent pain knifing through my shins. I lost my balance
and fell backwards onto the bare rock. That impact wind-
ed me. Agony crushed my chest and jagged flashes blurred
my vision. I drew up my knees and tried to remember our
school rugby coach's advice.

I managed to roll onto my side. That did something helpful. I sucked in a whooping lungful of pungent air. Gritting
my teeth, I forced myself to breathe out slowly. My chest
ached like a giant had stamped on me. I was starting to think
I must have cracked a rib. I had to ignore that. Right now,
I had to concentrate. In through the nose. Out through the
mouth. In through the nose. Out through the mouth. Slow
and steady. The light-headedness faded.

Something hit the rock ledge behind me. The resounding
thud echoed away down the cavern and I rolled over to face
it. As soon as I saw what had landed, I struggled to my feet.
The wight – it could only be the wight – had thrown down
the stone where Fin and I had trapped the sodding hag. It
had landed frighteningly close.

Wet stains were spreading along the dark lines I had seen
on the pale grey rock. The grainy surface began to split.
Sharp echoes rang around the cavern. The black-streaked
cracks widened. Small pieces flaked off, followed by larger
lumps. The stone was fracturing where the barbed wire was
buried.

273

I backed away, wrapping my arms around my chest
to hold in the pain. More stone shattered. I glimpsed the
trapped hag's filthy dress. The crack expanded and I saw her
arm. A big piece fell away and I saw one hand. She made a
fist and twisted it. The hag was trapped inside the rock, but
she was fighting to get free. The barbed wire was still holding
her for the moment.

What the fuck was the wight up to? No, that could wait.
How the hell could I get out of here before the hag got loose?
Where the fuck was I, to begin with? Apart from up shit
creek without a paddle.

The wight had dumped me on a ledge not quite three
metres wide and a bit over four metres end to end. I could
see where limestone had been cut and carried away, but fuck
knows how those quarrymen had got up and down from
here. The rocky wall was sheer, and the edge the wight had
thrown me over was two metres or more above my head.
Would it have killed those long-ago workers to cut steps? Or
had they got out as fast as they could when whatever they
had done caused the corner of the quarry to collapse?

All I could see beyond the ledge was emptiness. I forced
myself to go closer. I had to know what was down there. I saw
a steep slope thick with chips of stone that was quickly swallowed up by the darkness. I sure as shit wasn't going that way.
Not just because I didn't have any sort of torch. If – no, when
that scree shifted under my feet, I wouldn't stop sliding until
I was buried under tonnes of rock at the bottom. The only
question was would the crush kill me first, or suffocation?

A breath of dank air brushed past my face. I realised I was
assuming the cavern had a bottom. I remembered the map
showing those potholes and swallets on either side of the
road beyond this end of the ridge. I might not be crushed. I
might fall into an underground river and drown instead.

The hag hissed. I looked back to see what was happening.
I wouldn't die falling into the depths of that cavern if she
killed me first. I stood frozen with shock. The rock that had

imprisoned her had completely broken apart. The towing strap had fallen away. Now she fought to free herself from the barbed wire. How the hell was any of this possible?

I'd thought she looked bad before. As she staggered to her feet, black lines criss-crossed her arms and legs. No, those weren't lines. They were deep, oozing cuts. Her rags barely covered her grey skin now. The wire seemed to have sliced through them. Where her thigh pressed against the twisted steel, black scraps of cloth shrivelled and fell onto the rocky ledge. With a convulsive twist, she took a step towards me, as far as the wire wrapped around her legs allowed. The gashes in her flesh gaped wider.

She didn't speak. I couldn't tell if she could see me. Her eyes were blank hollows of clotted blood webbed with grimy creases. She paused and sniffed the air. Her toothless mouth gaped wider and she ran her wizened tongue around her cracked lips. She cackled as glistening drool ran down her chin. If she couldn't see me, she could smell me. I was bleeding, and that made me her prey. That was terrifying.

Her hands were still bound together. Barbed wire held her arms tight to her sides. Swaying from side to side, she twisted her shoulders. The hag's whole body writhed as the merciless wire cut clean through her wrist. Her left hand fell onto the rocky ledge. For a moment, I couldn't believe what I was seeing. The hand lay there, palm up, with its fingers curled like a dead spider's legs.

The hag hissed, triumphant. Losing that hand gave her enough slack to fight free of the wire. She pulled at the steel with her remaining fingers. I saw her claw-like fingernails splitting down to the bones. She howled. This clearly hurt. That didn't stop her. She forced the loops of wire apart with the black-stained stub of her other wrist.

I backed away, patting my pockets to find my multi-tool. That would have been easier if I dumped these gloves, but I wasn't going to give up the slightest bit of protection against the hag. I wasn't sure how much use this little blade would

be, but it was all I had. Could I possibly kill her? She looked
like a dead thing already. Should I stab her in the eyes, or cut
her throat? Knock her over and stamp on her face or try for a
kick that would rip off her head?

The hag stepped free of the barbed-wire coils. I braced
myself. She crouched down, sweeping the ledge with her
outspread fingers. Her talons brushed the hand she had
discarded. Those severed fingers twitched. She picked up
the hand and pressed it against her stump. A moment later,
she spread her arms wide and flexed both hands. Her fingers
moved as if she'd never been injured.

She cackled, triumphant, and charged at me. I stepped
aside at the last second, spinning around so I didn't lose sight
of her. The hag struggled to stop, skidding almost to the edge
of the drop into the darkness. Bugger. Seeing her feet leaving
slimy prints on the limestone, I'd hoped she might slide onto
the scree and disappear into the void. I backed off quickly
again, keeping as much space between us as I could.

The hag hissed and spat as she spun around. She sprang
at me again. I dodged a second time. As I backed off, I wondered how long I could keep this up. Every time I moved,
hot pain stabbed me in the side.

Since her first tactic wasn't working, the hag moved to the
centre of the ledge and spread her foul hands wide. Whether
or not she could see me, she could smell me and hear my
boots on the stone. Now she waited for me to move. She'd be
ready, whichever way I went. She'd trap me against the rocky
wall, or we'd both fall off the ledge into that bone-breaking
darkness. Okay, so I wouldn't move. That wasn't a long-term
strategy though. Where was Fin? I wished I knew but didn't
call out to her. That might provoke the hag to attack.

Stones cascaded down the slope beyond the ledge, crashing into the depths of the cavern. The wight shot up from
the darkness. With her attention fixed on me, the hag had
barely turned her head before the wight seized her from behind. It wrapped its arms around her, pinning her elbows to

her sides. The hag threw back her head and screamed as the wight drove its claws deep into her chest.

Rocks fell from the cavern roof as the wight heaved the hag off her feet. The creature staggered backwards towards the slope. The hag's feet thrashed as she shrieked with fury, throwing her head from side to side. It was no use. She couldn't get free. The wight threw itself off the ledge, disappearing into the darkness with the hag in its merciless embrace. A minute or so later, the hag's screams were cut short, as if someone had flicked a switch.

Thank fuck for that. My ears were ringing. I leaned against the rocky wall to catch my breath and watched pale dust rise out of the cavern's shadows like smoke. The rattle and growl of broken stone tumbling down the slope gradually slowed and faded. I forced myself to breathe slowly and carefully. Doing anything else sodding hurt.

'Dan?' Fin looked cautiously over the edge of the drop. She froze when she saw the remains of the broken stone that had held the hag. 'Are you—? Where's the wight? Where's—?'

'Gone. Both of them.' I shoved my multi-tool in my pocket.

'For good?' Fin asked, tense.

'I sodding well hope so.' After waiting a moment for the pain in my ribs to ease off, I went to pick up the towing strap. I held a shackle in each hand, ready to smash solid steel into the face of anything that came near me as I moved slowly to the edge of the slope. As I looked down, the cavern looked very different. Even through the swirling dust, I could see a shallow pit filled with quarrying debris. You'd never guess this had been a route into the depths inside the hill. Wherever it might have led, the path was blocked now, once and for all.

'Dan?' Fin was still anxious. 'I'm coming down.'

Taking a breath to shout to her was a bad mistake. A lungful of dust started me coughing. I sank to my knees and hugged my ribs.

'No.' I forced myself to my feet. I spat to clear my throat and turned to see where she was. 'We can't risk us both getting stuck here.'

Swans need a long run-up to get airborne. Fin would get down here easily enough, but I wasn't convinced she'd have enough room on this ledge to get out again. There are good reasons why people in myths and legends turn into eagles and hawks. Those are a lot more manoeuvrable.

'How are you going to get out then?' Fin didn't sound happy, kneeling on the edge of the drop.

I coiled up the heavy-duty polyester strap and secured it by linking the shackles. 'If I throw this up to you, can you find a tree that will take my weight? One close enough to leave me enough of this to climb up?'

'Let me see.' Fin stood up and retreated out of sight.

I tried not to think how much climbing out of here was going to hurt. While I waited, I kicked the tangle of barbed wire into the pit of broken stones. No point in leaving that in plain sight, where some idiot might be tempted to try climbing down to get it.

A few minutes later, Fin looked over the edge of the drop. 'I think I've got one.'

I weighed the towing strap in my hands. 'Get well away from there. I can't tell where this is going to land, and I don't want to hit you.'

'Right.' Fin vanished again.

I hurled the coiled strap upwards. At the last moment, a spasm of pain in my chest took the power out of my throw. The strap hit the rocky wall and bounced back. For one horrible moment I thought it was going to disappear into the pit. That cavern might have a bottom now, but the heap of loose stone would still be treacherous to walk on. Thankfully, the strap landed just short. I walked over to pick it up.

'Dan?' Fin wanted to know what was going on.

'Second try coming up,' I called to her, hoarse.

I forced myself to concentrate. More haste, less speed, and other such clichés. Third time's the charm and all that. As I tried a more measured throw, the heavy coil spun up and over the edge of the drop.

'Got it!' Fin sounded relieved.

'Okay.' I waited.

Sooner than I expected, Fin reappeared and dropped the end of the strap down the rock face. It hung straight, thanks to the weight of the shackle, though the end dangled by my shoulders. Could I climb high enough using my arms to be able to use my legs before I fell off?

Since my choices were try it or stay here for the rest of my life, I grabbed the strap. Hand over hand, I hauled myself up. My side was sheer agony. When the steel shackle bumped against my knees, I managed to catch it between my thighs. Another burst of effort got me far enough up to trap the strap between my boots. That took the punishing weight off my hands and arms. I hung there for a moment, and the burning in my shoulders faded a bit. The hot ache in my ribs didn't.

I managed to get to the top, but I couldn't have climbed any further. When Fin saw I was close to the edge, she hauled on the strap, leaning back to use her full weight. That bit of help probably made the difference. I got to my feet, panting like a dog.

'I would hug you, but...' Fin looked dubiously at me.

'Please don't.' I managed a crooked grin. 'I think I've cracked a rib.'

'I suppose it could be worse.' Fin had brought both of our backpacks with her. She unzipped mine and pulled out my sweatshirt.

'Thanks.' I threaded my arms through the sleeves before easing the neck over my head. I pulled the hem carefully down over my cuts and bruises. 'Which way do we go to get out of here? Come to that, how did you get in?'

'I ran down to the shallow end and looked for the wight's trail. Follow me.' Fin slung both backpacks over one shoulder and turned to leave.

'Hang on a minute.' I went over to the sturdy dogwood Fin had found and unfastened the towing strap. 'Let's not leave this behind.'

She raised her eyebrows as I coiled it up. 'Are you planning on posting an online review?'

I managed not to laugh as I handed it over. I wanted to, but I knew it would hurt. 'Five stars. Ideal as a supernatural threat restraint.'

Fin put the heavy roll away. 'Let's get to the cottage and see if the WiFi's working.'

To my intense relief, she knew exactly where she was heading. Barely a minute later, we reached a freshly trampled path, wide enough for one. Fin went ahead of me. That was fine. Any more explanations could wait until we were out of here and I'd had tea and painkillers.

The undergrowth gradually thinned until we reached the patchy grass and weeds at the shallow end of the quarry. Fin climbed out first. She watched me follow her slowly and carefully.

'Do you want to check on Fieldfare Long Barrow before we go to Pigeon Lane? I could fly over there and see?'

I shook my head. 'We can take a look tomorrow. But I reckon the portal will have closed. The wight got its hands on the hag, and I don't see her coming back from wherever it's taken her. That's what it wanted all along.'

Fin smiled briefly. 'The enemy of my enemy is my friend.'

'This enemy of my enemy didn't give a toss who I was until it realised it could use me as bait.' As I started walking, I remembered something else from that customer service training day. Assume makes an ass out of you and me, according to the nice lady doing the talking.

'I think we got in the wight's way,' I told Fin. 'Once we'd wound so much barbed wire around the hag, we had her trapped in that stone, but the wight couldn't take that through a portal. It had to break her out of our trap first. So it threw the stone onto the ledge to get those cracks started, and it used me to distract her so it could sneak up and attack.'

'Attack her from where?' Fin slipped her hand into mine. This path was wide enough for two. 'And where is she now? Where's the wight?'

'I think it opened another gateway somewhere down in the cave. I think it's taken her away to wherever it came from.' I really hoped that wasn't another assumption that would bite us in the arse.

We walked back to Pigeon Lane. To my relief, the pain in my chest shrank to a specific spot on my right side, about halfway down my ribcage. It still hurt like buggery, but I was breathing easier.

As soon as we were inside, I stripped off in the living room and headed straight for the shower. I don't know how long I stayed in there, but I only switched off the water when it started to run cold. I used an entire bottle of shower gel. If there had been bleach within reach, I'd have been tempted to try that.

Wrapped in a couple of the darkest towels I could find, so any bloodstains wouldn't show, I went to see what Fin was doing. She had her laptop open on the coffee table beside an empty cafetière and mug. My phone was next to hers. They were both plugged in and charging.

Fin looked up. 'Blanche dropped her phone at the airport in France while she was waiting to pick up her suitcase. The screen broke, but she had her tablet with her, so she decided she could wait to sort that out when she got home. She sent everyone an email to let them know, in case anyone needed to get hold of her.'

'Right.' I sat down on the sofa. 'Any other news?'

'Every estate agent we've spoken to wants to sell us a house.' Fin grinned and then got down to business. 'Hazel left the name and number of a wise woman who should be able to help us with a hag. She also left a number for you to call, to talk to someone about the Beast of Brassknocker Hill. Do you want me to look that up?'

'Later.' I couldn't see any great urgency now that the wight was gone.

'Hazel's already left a couple of follow-up messages,' Fin warned. 'You know she's going to have questions.'

'She can wait a few days. We're on holiday, aren't we?' I thought about getting up and making a pot of tea. I'd do that in a minute.

Fin stood up. 'Assuming the car will start, shall I get us a takeaway for dinner? I've found a few places that look decent online.'

'Good idea.' I leaned back carefully against the sofa cushions. 'Let's have a quiet night in.'

Chapter Twenty-Three

The curry house Fin found was more than okay. We had a good dinner and went to bed. Fin put antiseptic on my cuts and scrapes while I told her everything that had happened after the wight threw me into the quarry. I went to sleep in a T-shirt to try to keep any blood off the holiday rental's sheets. Doing anything more energetic than holding Fin's hand as we both drifted off was going to take careful experimentation until my cracked rib healed.

I slept surprisingly well, everything considered. Even so, I woke up early the next morning. Fin was snoring beside me. I pulled on clean underpants and went downstairs to put the kettle on. As I sipped my first mug of tea, I looked idly through the kitchen window. Someone was sitting on the bench under the apple trees. A short, grey-haired and bearded man who wore a collarless shirt with a waistcoat and dark trousers. Apart from his bare feet, he could have strolled off one of those photos in the back bedroom, showing Pigeon Lane in days gone by. I put down my mug and went to put on some clothes.

Assessing my cuts and scrapes, I was relieved to see I was healing as fast as I usually did. My arms and shoulders still ached from the strain of the climb up from the ledge, but that would sort itself out. The sore spot on my ribs wasn't as bad as yesterday, though if I moved the wrong way without thinking, sharp pain made me catch my breath. Fin was still snoring, so I went downstairs.

The stranger waved as I unlocked the back door and stepped outside. 'Come and join me, friend,' he called. 'Fine morning, isn't it?'

'It is.' I walked down the path carrying my tea. As I got closer, I saw this unexpected visitor was no more than five feet tall. He also had eyes which shimmered between the soft blush and pale green of ripe apples. I hadn't seen anything like that before.

'Sit with me for a moment.' He patted the bench. 'I came to thank you for taking such good care of my friends.'

He glanced up into the leafy branches. The apple trees rustled though there wasn't a hint of breeze. The strands of plaited nettles had dried up and blown away. That didn't matter. I could see the gashes in their bark closing up and fading fast. A lot more than natural healing was going on. I guessed that was thanks to my visitor. I thought about apologising. The trees wouldn't have got hurt if the wight hadn't come here hunting the hag. I decided if my new friend wasn't going to mention that, neither would I.

'I believe I should thank you for passing on my messages.' I wondered what he was going to want in return. Whatever it was, I owed him, and I wouldn't try to haggle.

He grinned as if he knew what I was thinking. 'Pour cider on our friends' roots here and sing them a song before you go. We'll call it even.'

'Thank you, and yes, I'll do that.' My mind went blank as I tried to think of a suitable song, or any song come to that.

My visitor's smile faded. 'I was glad to lend a hand, seeing you go up against a hag. We haven't seen one of that foul kindred here for many a long year.'

That was good to know. But it didn't answer my two most nagging questions. Where had the hag come from? Why had she targeted me and Fin?

'She's gone for good, I hope,' I said. 'I think a wight carried her off through a portal.'

'So it did, and we will see her no more. The wights will have their revenge and rightly so.' The friendly stranger nodded, approving.

'They come here regularly?' If they did, they were good at staying out of sight. Apart from the Beast of Brassknocker Hill, which had made the local press as a cryptid a few startled people had encountered. I'd looked that up online while Fin was out getting the curry.

'We see them from time to time.' The friendly stranger shrugged. 'For now, every door they use to come and go is shut tight.'

'Have you any idea why this wight was so determined to kill the hag?' I tried to sound as casual as he did.

My visitor gazed silently up into the apple trees' branches for so long, I didn't think he was going to answer. When he did, he chose his words carefully.

'If I were to guess? Hags find hunting this world's heedless mortals becomes more of a challenge with every passing year. If they found their way to easier prey?' He left that hanging. 'I leave them well alone. Then they have no reason to plague me and mine.'

'That's good advice.' I'd follow it, as long as I could. If some hag had other ideas? All bets were off.

Fin opened the cottage door, curious to see somebody sitting with me in the garden.

My new friend chuckled. 'You're a lucky man, son of the greenwood. No wonder that hag was jealous. Please, give my compliments to your master, and to your lady mother. Oh, and I think you might find a use for this.'

He reached into his waistcoat pocket and flicked something into the air, like someone tossing a coin with a thumb to call heads or tails. Instinctively, I reached out and caught it. As my fist closed around something smooth and cool, my visitor disappeared. The apple trees rustled their leaves overhead with a sound like distant laughter.

Fin walked down the garden to join me. 'Who was that?'

'I'm not sure, but hopefully my mother will know.' I opened my fist and saw I'd caught a small flat stone pierced by a smooth hole. I held it up so Fin could see. 'He gave this to me.'

'That would have been useful a week ago.' She didn't sit down. 'I was thinking I should fly over to the long barrow and see if that gateway is closed. That's the quickest way to find out.'

That explained why she was wearing shorts and a T-shirt, and had come into the garden with bare feet. I also saw she wasn't going to relax until she knew nothing could be using the tunnel through the burial mound. That was fair enough.

'My new friend just now, he told me every local portal is shut.'

'That's good to know.' Fin sat down. 'What else did he have to say?'

'He as good as told me the hag has been going through the portals to kill wights.'

'Really?' Fin thought about that. 'I wonder if that's why she couldn't leave? Not as long as a gateway was open. Her ties to that other place were too strong, since she'd been hunting there.'

'Could be. I don't suppose we'll ever know.' I wasn't convinced we'd be able to learn what we needed to stop hags being a threat. But at least I had a hagstone.

I held it up and looked through the hole. Everything in the garden was what it seemed to be. 'We can share this until we get hold of another one.'

I offered the stone to Fin. She took a quick look and handed it back. 'Let's have breakfast. Then we really must go shopping to buy more food.'

We toasted the last of the bread. After we'd eaten, we used Fin's laptop to find interesting places to visit for the last two days of our holiday. We wouldn't be going to the local show caves though. And we agreed we'd plan a proper holiday as soon as we could. Once we'd recovered from this one.

We packed up on Saturday morning. The Toyota started on the first turn of the key,. I drove us to Fin and Blanche's flat near Bristol. Fin went to collect Blanche from the airport. I rang Eleanor at Blithehurst and brought her up to date.

'And I was thinking you were enjoying a nice, peaceful break,' she said wryly. 'Do you want me to tell the dryads what your visitor said about the hags hunting wights on the other side of those portals?'

'I think so. If that's where they go when they step outside the usual flow of time, they should know. So should the naiads and sylphs and the hobs. Hags are a menace wherever they are.'

'Agreed.' Eleanor had no doubt about that. 'And if we're ever facing them again, the more we know, which is to say, the more the dryads can be persuaded to tell us about them, the better off we will be.'

'They'll owe us something in return for that warning. I'll stop off and talk to my mum and dad on my way up tomorrow. Hopefully she'll know something useful too.'

I was sorting out our clean laundry on the dining table when Fin and Blanche arrived. I was only wearing a pair of shorts. T-shirt seams kept snagging on scabs where my deepest cuts were healing. As they came through the flat's front door, I reached for a shirt. Not fast enough.

'Bloody hell, Dan.' Blanche walked into the living room and stopped dead. She was tanned and relaxed. Clearly, she'd had a brilliant holiday. 'You look like someone attacked you with a hedge-trimmer.'

'Hello to you too.' I pulled on my shirt.

Zan knocked on the door by the window that opened onto the balcony. That saved me from having to say anything else. I let the sylph in. Zan shimmered from their ethereal form into their familiar guise of Blanche's boyfriend.

The sylph could see at once that something was up. 'What has happened?'

I looked at Fin. She shook her head.

'Your turn. I told Blanche everything on the drive here. I'll put the kettle on.'

Fin went into the kitchen. I pulled out a dining chair. Zan and Blanche sat on one of the sofas by the telly. I explained what Fin and I had done on our holiday.

When Zan realised I had finished speaking, the outraged sylph's eyes flashed lightning bright. 'This cannot stand!'

Oh shit. What were they going to do now? I saw Fin was wondering the same, sitting on the other sofa.

Blanche reached for Zan's hand. 'Let's think this through. This wight—' She broke off and looked at me. 'Wights? From a barrow mound? Seriously?'

I shrugged. 'It's an old word that means "person" or "creature"'. Eleanor had told me that when I'd asked earlier.

'Have you ever come across one of them?' Fin asked Zan.

'I have not.' The sylph was mystified.

'If they come and go through caves, we could see what the hobs and their kin know about that,' Blanche said thoughtfully. 'And we should ask any friendly naiads how to get hold of more of those hagstones.'

'I will see what I can learn.' Zan wasn't going to be left out.

'Thanks.' Turning the sylph's competitive nature to good use was fine with me.

'I'll have to tell Mum what happened, obviously.' Fin wrinkled her nose. 'If she's going to ask the local hobs what they know. We'll tell Iris, so she can see what she can get out of Conn.'

Blanche was thinking about something else. She grinned at me. 'So did you pour cider on those poor apple trees? What song did you sing to them?'

'We bought a jug of local cider from a pub that has an orchard. That seemed to go down well.' I stood up and picked up the laundry basket.

'We found a wassailing song online,' Fin told Blanche. 'Most people do that at New Year, but we thought that would be okay.'

I saw Blanche's smile widen. I left the room before she or Zan could ask us to sing for them.

I rang my dad before I set off on Sunday morning, so he knew when to expect me. He suggested I pick up dough-nuts on my way. When I arrived, he made a pot of tea and we sat outside in the back garden.

Barely a minute later, my mum arrived with the handful of young dryads who now tended the oak trees in the nature reserve on the other side of the lane. They sat on the grass while my mum perched on the arm of my dad's chair. The girls, as my dad called them, listened avidly, even though I tried not to make what had happened sound too dramatic. I didn't want to worry my dad any more than I absolutely had to.

I suppose the young dryads' keen interest was no great surprise. They might look like a lively bunch of sixth-formers when anyone else human was around, but I wouldn't want to get on their wrong side. They had hunted down and killed that first hag by forcing her under my Land Rover's wheels to be crushed into a bloody mess. Luckily for my old Landy's bodywork, the hag had been in her hare form at the time.

The girls looked puzzled when I told them about the old man with the shimmering, colour-shifting eyes. Mum laughed. She wasn't at all surprised. 'Of course the apple tree man was happy to help. Fruit trees and their guardians have always hated hags. Except for wild cherries, but you know how they are.'

Before I could say that no, actually, I hadn't got a clue what was she talking about, Mum sprang up. She clapped her hands to get the younger dryads' attention. 'We must find out where this foul creature came from, before any more of that vile sisterhood dares to pursue my son.'

They vanished. I managed not to swear.

'I'll ask her later, about cherry trees.' Dad looked at me over his mug of tea. 'I'll let you know what she says. Have you got any idea where this particular hag came from? Or why she came after you?'

'I can make a few guesses, but no more than that.' I told Dad what Fin and Blanche and I had come up with, talking things through last night over a bottle of wine. 'We know she wasn't living around Bishop's Warren. We know she wasn't anywhere near Fin's mum's place before the wedding. Zan went there yesterday to make sure. They swear they're certain about that. Bad news like hags travels fast, and no one had heard a whisper.'

The sylph had woken us up at midnight. They had spoken to hobs, to naiads and nereids who lived clear across the Fens as well as to their own kind. Zan had even asked the merfolk who occasionally had dealings with people on land.

'So?' Dad prompted.

'The only place we stopped on our way to Bishop's Warren was the services where we had a coffee and the supermarket where we did our shopping. We were talking about our plans for the week while we did that. If the hag was hanging around, she could have overheard us. We know dryads and naiads can tell Fin and I are a bit more than ordinarily human as soon as they see us, from some distance away. If she came close enough to listen to our conversation, we wouldn't have noticed. The place was heaving, and we had no reason to think there'd be anyone out of the ordinary there.'

The hag must have moved fast to get to Bishop's Warren ahead of us, by broomstick or whatever hags used to get about. We reckoned the timing would fit. Real-Alice had been stolen from her parents about an hour before we arrived.

'It's a theory.' Dad considered it.

'It is only a theory,' I agreed. 'But if hags like hanging around standing stones and ancient monuments, Salisbury Plain is covered with sites like that. And if they're looking for easy prey who won't be missed, like hitchhikers or runaways, a service station would be a good place for them to lurk.

They wouldn't have to worry about CCTV or eyewitnesses. They can turn up looking different every day.'

I tried not to let Dad see how much this disturbed me. Not only the idea of hags prowling for victims like serial killers. I hated the idea that Fin and I could cross paths with a predator and not even realise. That we could be pursued and not even notice.

Who was I kidding? Dad knows me too well.

'You think they're still a threat?' He wasn't really asking a question.

'I have no idea,' I said honestly. I reached into my pocket and showed Dad the hagstone tied to my keys with a loop of leather thong. 'But I think the apple tree man gave this to me because he reckons there's a chance I'll need it. Can you see if Mum can get hold of one for you? If a hag comes after any of us, we have to be ready. We can't risk being caught out like this again.'

'Forewarned is forearmed.' Dad nodded. 'I'll talk to your mum. About everything, not just hagstones. Have you heard anything from that nurse, about the little girl?'

I was glad to change the subject. 'I got a text from Gillian Adams this morning. She says the baby's been placed with a lovely family who have been hoping to adopt, so they've already passed their social services checks and everything. She said as far as anyone can tell, she's a happy, healthy human.'

'That's good to know.' Dad smiled.

I wondered if he was going to say something else, about grandchildren maybe. He didn't. That was a relief. And I hadn't forgotten what I'd said to Will. I would ask Dad how he and Mum had handled official questions and paperwork when I'd been born. Just not right now.

'I do have some good news.' Fin had agreed I should tell Dad when I saw him today. I'd tell Eleanor when I got to Blithehurst. Fin was going to tell Blanche this evening and ring her mum and dad. The Wicken family network would soon spread the news.

'Fin and I are going to see Aled next weekend, over in Eryri. We're going to ask him to make an engagement ring. We're not setting a date or anything yet. We've got to buy a house first.'

'Congratulations anyway.' Dad grinned. 'You had better tell your mum before you leave.'

'I'll never hear the last of it if I don't.' I stood up. 'I'll go over the road and see if the oak trees can find her for me.'

Which would be a good way of letting the Green Man know too. If he had anything to say, he knew where to find me.

JULIET E. MCKENNA

Acknowledgements

I'm pleased and relieved to say this year's writing has gone smoothly. Of course, that's only the first step. Publisher Cheryl Morgan of Wizard's Tower Press, editor Toby Selwyn, and artist Ben Baldwin, have contributed their essential skills and time to bringing this new book out. As ever, I am more grateful than mere words can convey.

A few friends may be reminded of conversations about weddings and other family events. My thanks and my apologies as appropriate. My thanks to my husband Steve for a long day's driving to check out routes and locations for accuracy, as well as for the unexpected which adds authenticity to a tale. Notably, I appreciate the manager of Cheddar's Discount Outlet taking the time to answer what must have seemed some very odd questions, and being fascinated when I explained.

I am extremely grateful to fellow author and fine writer Stewart Hotston for his informed perspective on rural England's relationship with people of colour, and for his patience with a nice, middle-class White lady trying to avoid egregious errors. Any infelicities that remain in this respect are my responsibility alone.

I am delighted to include Dave and Wendy Elrick on the guest list for Iris and Conn's wedding, following Wendy's winning bid for inclusion as a character in my story, as part of the second Genre Auction for Trans Rights organised by Lauren Beukes and Jeanette Ng. I salute everyone who contributed to both auctions, as creators and with bids.

LGBTQIA+ people and their rights are currently under appalling attack. I am proud to stand with the SF&F community that pushes back. Reading science fiction and fantasy, from my teens in the homophobic 1980s onwards, has continually improved my understanding of people with different lives to mine. Every person has the same rights to respect and personal safety as well as to equal rights and protections in law. Let's work to make that fact, not fiction, in the here and now.

In conclusion, and it always bears repeating, my thanks to everyone who shares their enthusiasm for these books in person and online. You make it possible for Dan's adventures to continue.

About the Author

Juliet E McKenna is a British fantasy author living in the Cotswolds, UK. Loving history, myth and other worlds since she first learned to read, she has written fifteen epic fantasy novels so far. Her debut, *The Thief's Gamble*, began The Tales of Einarinn in 1999, followed by The Aldabreshin Compass sequence, The Chronicles of the Lescari Revolution, and The Hadrumal Crisis trilogy. *The Green Man's Heir* was her first modern fantasy inspired by British folklore in 2018. *The Green Man's Quarry* in 2023, the sixth title to follow, won the BSFA Award for Best Novel. *The Green Man's Holiday* is the eighth book in the series.

Her 2023 novel *The Cleaving* is a female-centred retelling of the story of King Arthur, while her shorter fiction includes forays into dark fantasy, steampunk and science fiction. She promotes SF&Fantasy by reviewing, by blogging on book trade issues, attending conventions and teaching creative writing. She has served as a judge for the James White Award, the Aeon Award, the Arthur C Clarke Award and the World Fantasy Awards. In 2015 she received the British Fantasy Society's Karl Edward Wagner Award. As J M Alvey, she has written historical murder mysteries set in ancient Greece.

For more, visit www.julietemckenna.com

The Tales of Einarinn

1. The Thief's Gamble (1999)
2. The Swordsman's Oath (1999)
3. The Gambler's Fortune (2000)
4. The Warrior's Bond (2001)
5. The Assassin's Edge (2002)

The Aldabreshin Compass

1. The Southern Fire (2003)
2. Northern Storm (2004)
3. Western Shore (2005)
4. Eastern Tide (2006)

Turns & Chances (2004)

The Chronicles of the Lescari Revolution

1. Irons in the Fire (2009)
2. Blood in the Water (2010)
3. Banners in The Wind (2010)

The Wizard's Coming (2011)

The Hadrumal Crisis

1. Dangerous Waters (2011)
2. Darkening Skies (2012)
3. Defiant Peaks (2012)

A Few Further Tales of Einarinn (2012) (ebook from Wizards Tower Press)

Challoner, Murray & Balfour: Monster Hunters at Law (2014) (ebook from Wizards Tower Press)

Shadow Histories of the River Kingdom (2016)   (Wizards Tower Press)

The Green Man (Wizards Tower Press)

1. The Green Mans Heir (2018)
2. The Green Man's Foe (2019)

3. The Green Man's Silence (2020)
4. The Green Man's Challenge (2021)
5. The Green Man's Gift (2022)
6. The Green Man's Quarry (2023)
7. The Green Man's War (2024)

The Philocles series (as J M Alvey)

1. Shadows of Athens (2019)
2. Scorpions in Corinth (2019)
3. Justice for Athena (2020)
4. Silver for Silence (a dyslexia-friendly quick read, 2022)

The Cleaving (2023)